OF
FLAME
AND
FURY

OF FLAME AND FURY

MIKAYLA BRIDGE

FIRST INK

Published 2025 in the UK by First Ink
an imprint of Pan Macmillan
The Smithson, 6 Briset Street, London EC1M 5NR
EU representative: Macmillan Publishers Ireland Ltd, 1st Floor,
The Liffey Trust Centre, 117–126 Sheriff Street Upper, Dublin 1 D01 YC43
Associated companies throughout the world

ISBN 978-1-0350-5741-2

Text copyright © Mikayla Bridge 2025
Map copyright © Virginia Allyn 2025

The right of Mikayla Bridge and Virginia Allyn to be identified as the author of this work has been asserted in accordance with the Copyright, Designs and Patents Act 1988.

All rights reserved. No part of this publication may be reproduced, stored in a retrieval system, or transmitted, in any form, or by any means (including, without limitation, electronic, mechanical, photocopying, recording or otherwise) without the prior written permission of the publisher.

Pan Macmillan does not have any control over, or any responsibility for, any author or third-party websites (including, without limitation, URLs, emails and QR codes) referred to in or on this book.

1 3 5 7 9 8 6 4 2

A CIP catalogue record for this book is available from the British Library.

Printed and bound by CPI Group (UK) Ltd, Croydon, CR0 4YY

This book is sold subject to the condition that it shall not, by way of trade or otherwise, be lent, hired out, or otherwise circulated without the publisher's prior consent in any form of binding or cover other than that in which it is published and without a similar condition including this condition being imposed on the subsequent purchaser.
The publisher does not authorize the use or reproduction of any part of this book in any manner for the purpose of training artificial intelligence technologies or systems.
The publisher expressly reserves this book from the Text and Data Mining exception in accordance with Article 4(3) of the European Union Digital Single Market Directive 2019/790.

Visit **www.panmacmillan.com** to read more about all our books and buy them.

Trigger Note

Please note that this book depicts issues of depression, physical violence, death, illness, and grief.

For those who find solace in their rage.

The Republic of Salta

ASCIRA

Illyre

Prale

Acosta

EBRAIT

AN EXCERPT FROM *THE SALTAN BESTIARY*, PUBLISHED IN THE YEAR 1488 OF THE ALCHEMY REPUBLIC:

THE CENDORIAN COMPENDIUM OF PHOENIXES

Native to Cendor, phoenixes take 8–10 years to reach full maturity. Juvenile phoenixes maintain – on average – a steady temperature of 300°C. At maturity, their temperatures rise to 500–600°C. When nearing an end-of-life rebirth, phoenixes can reach temperatures of up to 1000°C. Phoenixes typically rebirth every 100 years, though this has been known to fluctuate.

Phoenixes naturally reside in humid forests. However, Cendorians often confine phoenixes to aviaries in order to compete in the Cendorian Association of Phoenix Racing (CAPR).

Phoenix subspecies

Blood Phoenix
Vibrant red or brown plumage. Average intelligence and speed. Above average size. The most common subspecies in CAPR due to their strength and relative obedience.

Cape Phoenix
Black and dark blue plumage capable of camouflage. Below average intelligence and speed. The smallest subspecies. The largest wild population. Their aggressive nature and small size make them ill-suited for CAPR.

Carnel Phoenix
Mottled red, yellow and orange plumage. Highly intelligent. The fastest subspecies on record. Average size. Though permitted to compete, their aggressive nature makes them a rarity in CAPR.

Cinder Phoenix
Orange and bronze plumage. Above average intelligence. Average speed. Below average size. The second most common subspecies found in CAPR, despite their fickle lifespan and high temperature.

Harrow Phoenix
Yellow plumage. The least intelligent subspecies. Below average speed. Above average size. Despite easy domestication, they cannot be incentivized to compete in CAPR.

Monarch Phoenix
Mottled, varying plumage. Highly intelligent. Above average speed. The largest subspecies on record. Considered a direct descendant of Deja, Salta's first phoenix. Their territorial nature makes them ill-suited for CAPR.

Spinel Phoenix
Pale red plumage. Average intelligence. Below average size and speed. The third most popular subspecies found in CAPR due to their comparatively docile natures.

Part One

Once our vast woodlands were feral and free
The Serpent King ruled, 'tween his cunning teeth
Then from far-off shores, four alchemists came
With hope and tribute, in peace so they claimed

'Neath the King's fanged reign, they spun webs of gold
Bestowing sweet gifts, they longed for control
With weapons so grand, the King had to cede
His land to the Four, though some call them thieves

Verse 1–2, 'The Gilded Lullaby'

Chapter One

❈

Flames raced past Kel's stinging eyes. Hotter and brighter than any sun, red collided with gold and amber in wild streaks across the sky. Along the obstacle-laden aerial track, Kel tried to follow the phoenixes' route. Though from her booth on the raised stands, they were little more than ribbons of blood.

Painters across Salta's four islands had tried to capture the phoenixes' brutal radiance. But to Kel, anything that didn't cause seared arm hair and painful blistering seemed a crude imitation.

An ear-splitting screech echoed down the track. The crowd below and beside Kel's booth roared, deafening her.

After a few loud seconds, the voices in her ear-comm returned.

'*Veer left!* Veer left – no, *too far!*'

'Tuck in nice and low. Yes! Like that!'

Kel bit down on her lip. She glanced at Rube to her right, rising onto his toes and craning his head.

'Ignore that last one, Oska,' Kel shouted into her comm. 'It'll get Savita boxed in.'

Oska – their team's rider – responded with a strained grunt, though she followed Kel's instructions. Kel's phoenix, Savita, was easy to spot, soaring above her competition, nearing the race's 150-metre height limit.

'Level out,' Dira barked. 'Any higher and you'll be shot down.'

Kel's gaze lifted to the dark, mechanical clouds barricading the sky. If any phoenix attempted to soar above them, acid rain would likely pour from the clouds' haze.

Rube removed his ear-comm and spluttered, 'Sorry Kel. I just wanted to—'

Dira clamped a hand on Rube's shoulder. 'What Kel *means*, is that you should let me – the *winger* – do the strategizing.'

Dira smirked. Her brown eyes flickered to Kel. 'The tamer should, too.'

Though they stood beside each other, the crowd, shouting with applause and last-minute bets, made it near-impossible to hear Dira without their thin headsets.

Kel bit back a retort. Dira was right. As the team's winger, she was in charge of track strategy. Kel was their tamer – responsible for the care and training of their phoenix. *Her* phoenix.

Though Rube meant well, his job was to engineer equipment, not offer tactical advice. They couldn't risk any well-intentioned blunders.

Kel's sweaty palms clamped around the metal railing separating the stands from the vast, circular track. Her knuckles turned bone-white. This race was too important, one of the biggest in their city's annual calendar. Kel's cut of the first-place prize money – *50,000 ceres* – would help her stave off the council's vultures hunting her overdue bills. They'd already started circling, as if she was a corpse to strip bare.

Today's track was narrower than usual, set inside an open-roofed stadium. Each team had to complete one hundred laps of the two-kilometre loop. Stands surrounded the race. The giant flatscreens above them, honing in on the race's minute details, climbed almost as high as the phoenixes themselves. An electric pillar rose at the very centre, creating a lethal ring that shocked any firebirds who flew too close. While also keeping them from flying too high, the dark, overhead clouds also dropped sporadic obstacles; man-made meteors falling from tiny, hidden aircrafts.

From the team's private booth in the stands, Kel watched Savita swerve to narrowly avoid a spiked, plummeting bludgeon, large enough to crush Oska.

'There's a rhythm to the falling objects.' Dira's voice rang through Kel's ear-comm. 'The clouds are moving, so no track loop is the same. But the darker clouds are throwing bigger weapons and the lighter ones are dropping things more frequently. Just stick to a steady path near the track's inner pillar and swerve when I tell you to.'

Kel shot Dira an incredulous look. The sky was an uneven tapestry with no two clouds the same colour or size. Dira was somehow predicting the objects' descent while monitoring Oska's position.

'Let's pray there's no delay in the comms,' Oska muttered, before guiding Savita closer to the track's inner pillar. A crackle of electricity sparked alarmingly close to the tip of Savita's left wing. Kel flinched.

With Dira's help, Oska avoided three more obstacles, forging a careful path behind another phoenix – close enough that Sav stretched forward and bit at the other creature's tail feathers.

Oska jostled in the saddle at Sav's sudden movement, but she managed to stay low, balanced. Relief weakened Kel's knees. Today was only Oska's third race with the team. Kel and Dira had spent a gruelling five months trying to convince Savita to let Oska on her back, and it was only in the last month that Savita had acquiesced. Even though they hadn't practised as much as Kel would have liked, Kel knew Savita was fast enough – *strong* enough – to win this race. She was a carnel phoenix, naturally the swiftest of Cendor's seven subspecies, and the race wove around the electric ring in tight loops that favoured Sav's agility. As long as Oska listened to Dira, Kel was sure they could place in the top three. That would at least guarantee them a small portion of the race's winnings.

A larger, darker phoenix soared in front of Kel's booth, half a lap behind Savita. Suddenly, silver burst through the clouds and a cluster of thick arrows shot down. The phoenix's cherry-red heat hit Kel's face a moment before hot blood sprayed the stands.

She sucked in a shaky breath and wiped the gore from her cheeks, relieved that was all that had struck the crowd. Though wire mesh divided the phoenixes' track from the audience, it was mostly a decorative safety measure. Plenty of races had led to hospitalized spectators, whether from misfired obstacles or from a blood-thirsty phoenix shoving another into the stands.

People watched at their own risk. But that knowledge never thinned the crowds.

The phoenix and its rider plunged to the ground in a ball of fire. They landed on the track with a deafening crash, beating dust into the air.

At the centre of the dirt storm, neither the phoenix nor rider moved.

Kel winced as the crowd crowed in mingled delight and despair. They screamed their bets into tele-comms and pounded them into glimmering tablets, gambling on everything from the first phoenix to die to the race's winner. Though her team stood apart in a private section of the stands, Kel's ears still ached from the crowd's violent excitement. She focused on that pain, keeping her mind clear of any pity for the fallen pair.

Another phoenix blazed past in a copper blur, moving at unholy speeds. Kel raised a hand to shield her face from the heat as black stars danced across her vision. When her sight returned, the blurred colours had transformed to feathers, and the wind forcing her back had dulled. She brushed damp brown hairs from her face.

Another unfamiliar phoenix and rider had collided with a falling obstacle – an enormous, leather mace – and plunged to the dirt track. The duo seemed surprisingly uninjured, the firebird stumbling and shaking its head. Stunned, the creature refused to lift back into the air.

Dira tucked an umber curl behind her ear. 'Serves that rider right for thinking they could gain that much speed on a turn like that. Tracks with falling obstacles always confuse phoenixes. They should've known to take their time.'

'*Shut up*,' Oska snapped through the comms. 'Since none of you can afford comms with a *mute* button, stay quiet unless you have something useful to say.'

Kel bit down on her tongue, forcing her own silence. She needed to trust that the past months Oska had spent training for CAPR – the Cendorian Association of Phoenix Racing – would be enough to keep her alive.

Kel shifted back, eyes raking the track. Twenty phoenixes lit up the sky like fireworks. Savita and Oska were placing fourth, though only by a hair's width. Across the opposite side of the track, she watched her newest teammate swerve around more falling metal and soar above another pair of blazing wings.

Moments later, a siren blasted through the air.

The leading phoenixes had entered the race's final lap.

Bile crept up Kel's throat. She watched Oska guide Sav, imagined the rider instructing the phoenix with clumsy fingers along her neck, tracing patterns to inform Savita's movements. Kel could almost feel Savita's soft, near-molten feathers beneath her fingers, like honeyed weapons straight from the forge.

Rising onto her toes, Kel spotted two blurred phoenixes pulling ahead, coming up on Savita's tail.

'Oska – two riders climbing up on your right,' Dira said sharply. 'Don't give them room to overtake.'

Though Oska didn't respond, Savita swerved to the right and stretched her wings, just in time to prevent the two riders from creeping ahead.

Kel rocked back on her heels as a human scream broke through the bellowing crowd. Heart in her mouth, Kel scanned the remaining phoenixes but couldn't spot who the sound belonged to. She wondered which riders' leathers were currently melting into their skin.

Though she pitied the poor soul, the pained cry didn't make her flinch. It was their own team's fault. Their technician was meant to monitor everything from temperature to saddle wear to leather durability. Everyone knew phoenixes grew hotter the faster they flew, and it needed to be accounted for during races. The Howlers' own technician, Rube Rohin, would never make such an easy blunder. Though he still had no clue how to interact with Savita, his tech designs would likely make him a millionaire one day.

Oska dipped low, barely skirting a falling mace.

'Good.' Dira's voice rang through the comms. 'The rider coming third leans too far to his left. His phoenix has a blind spot if you fly closer, just below its left wing.'

Oska grunted and spurred Sav on, *faster*, using the nearby phoenix's wing as coverage from falling weapons.

'Dip a little lower to avoid the phoenix's talons if they lash out,' Dira added, and Oska obeyed. 'Okay – swerve four feet to the right in three, two, one—'

Savita pivoted just as a giant, serrated scrap of metal fell from above. The phoenix overhead attempted the same manoeuvre a half-second later.

Too late.

The sharp metal pummelled into the phoenix's outstretched wing. Crimson splashed against Savita's neck as the other phoenix fell back, flailing.

The Howlers surged into third place.

Oska's ragged breath pounded through Kel's skull.

'You okay?' Kel whispered.

'Fine.' Oska's voice trembled. 'Anyone coming up behind me?'

'You're clear,' Dira answered, unfazed. 'Narrow Sav's wings to gain more speed. Maintain your height until I tell you to move.

There's still plenty of time left in the lap.'

Though Oska stayed silent, she held her ground. The falling obstacles grew scarce as the finish line grew closer, the track's electric centre and wire borders preventing too many phoenixes from flying beside one another.

Twin red-and-gold flags appeared in the distance, rippling through the heat.

Kel bunched her hands at her sides, clenching and unclenching her fists. Oska needed to move *faster*.

Slowly, Sav inched closer to the firebird placing second. The birds in first and second – two large blood phoenixes – were stretched out in a tight line. There was little chance of sliding past them without hitting the centre's electric pillar. But third place would still give the Howlers a small chunk of the prize money, enough to—

Wild laughter blared through Kel's comm, cutting through the noise of the crowd. A second later, maroon flames blazed past Oska and Savita. An enormous phoenix, moving faster than it should have been able to given its size. Through the distant sparks, Kel glimpsed the back of the rider; a flash of chestnut curls peeked out from their helmet.

Her nerves, already taut as bowstrings, snapped.

Kel bit her lip, hard enough to split the skin. Of all the riders to overtake Oska . . .

'Really?' she groaned, tilting back her head, as if to demand answers from the Alchemists themselves. 'Did it *have* to be Warren Coupers?'

As if he heard her, the prick – 'Coup', to most – whooped again, loud enough to be heard over the endless phoenix screeches.

Kel bit down on a new ulcer.

It was no surprise that the crowd adored the young rider. *Flames*, the entire *isle* adored him. He'd appeared on the racing scene not long after the Howlers, and had quickly become the poster-child for the fame, the recklessness, the shiny facets of CAPR that made Kel seethe. Phoenixes were godly creatures meant to be feared and protected. Not props for careless stunts by thrill-seeking boys with annoyingly symmetrical cheekbones.

Kel scowled as Coup gained more speed, closing in on the first and second phoenixes far too quickly, with too little care for the weapons dropping close enough to clip his phoenix's wings. He was pulling ahead so fast; there was no way that Oska and Savita could catch up. Kel's stomach dropped as Coup sent the Howlers firmly into fourth place.

The Howlers wouldn't see a single cere.

'How is he doing that?' Kel cursed.

She squinted. As his phoenix stretched its wings, Coup unbuckled his legs from their saddle, pulled his feet up behind him, and lowered himself to lie flush against the stiff saddle. Kel couldn't imagine how painful the strain must have been on his arms – holding still as his phoenix swerved and slashed through the sky, closing in on the riders claiming first and second.

With winds roaring against them, Coup's flaming beast dove between the two phoenixes ahead. There shouldn't have been enough room for Coup's phoenix to squeeze through – and yet, with his legs free and the phoenix's wings pinned, somehow Coup slipped into first place as easily as silk between fingers.

'How the hell did he do that?' Dira spat. 'Even if he's strong enough to hold himself up without buckles – if the other phoenixes had shifted closer, they could've squashed him like a bug!'

Kel shook her head, anger closing her throat. She watched Coup swing his legs back over the sides of the saddle and direct his phoenix to spread its wings as wide as possible.

The flames around him licked higher. With swift hand gestures along the phoenix's neck feathers, Coup instructed the firebird to move quicker, to grow even hotter. Kel couldn't believe what she was seeing.

'Maybe we'll get lucky and he'll barbecue himself,' she sighed, though she knew it was too much to wish for. Luck had unfairly blessed Coup ever since he'd first appeared in CAPR, almost two years ago.

The heat rolling off of Coup's phoenix would definitely burn through his riding leathers, though it would also deter any other riders from approaching. Kel could feel it from her booth. Coup had overtaken the leaders with an impossible move.

Somehow, it had worked. For *him*.

Coup howled as he sailed across the finish line.

Fourth place. The words scraped like talons through Kel's mind.

'How the hell did he pull that off?' Oska screamed through the comms. A second later, Kel heard a strange, frenzied *jingle*, followed by a squawk from Sav.

'What's that noise? What are you doing?' Kel shouted.

Oska didn't reply. Squinting, Kel spotted Oska fumbling with the buckles around her legs. Oska hissed as the metal blistered her gloved fingers.

'What the hell are you doing?' Kel screamed. 'Unbuckle your legs and you're dead.'

'We need to do *something* to place!' Oska shouted. The strain in her voice sent shivers down Kel's spine.

'Not this,' Dira said breathlessly. 'Do you have a death wish? It'll just mean we need to find a new rider—'

Oska made a small noise, something between a whimper and a laugh. 'You really think that arrogant shit is a better rider than me?'

'No,' Kel lied. 'But why would you want to imitate something *Warren Coupers* decided was a good idea?'

Oska's hands kept fumbling at the buckles pulled tight around her ankles and calves. Kel imagined the rider's face had turned as stark-white as her own knuckles.

'I can do this,' Oska rasped.

'Even if the move was doable – we're running out of time.' Kel's ears started ringing. Her heart became a wild, caged animal in her throat. 'Please. Oska. It's not worth it.'

Oska's fingers merely moved faster. She freed her right leg, straining to keep a grip of Sav's sides as she shifted over to her left leg.

Kel felt lightheaded. She couldn't believe Oska hadn't immediately flown off Sav with one leg free, moving at such wild speeds. All it would take was one errant breeze, a bump from another phoenix, and Oska would go flying – still tethered to Savita. She'd be a limp puppet chained to a flaming, adrenaline-drunk god.

'Stop, Oska!' Rube screamed from Kel's side.

Oska didn't respond.

'You do this, you're off the Howlers,' Kel shouted, a desperate, unconvincing threat as Oska flicked off the last buckle on her left leg.

'Don't do this, Oz,' Dira breathed.

Kel was almost too afraid to glance up at the overhead screens, magnifying every terrible, granular detail of Oska's fate.

With trembling hands, Oska gripped the pommel and tried to lift her legs up behind her, lying flat on her stomach. Her arms wobbled with the strain. Three fingers lost their grip as Savita released an ear-splitting shriek and pinned her wings, all too eager to recreate Coup's stunt.

A sob echoed down the comms. Pressed against the saddle, Kel imagined Oska's leathers burning away as easily as paper over a lighter.

'Jump, Oska! *Jump!*' Kel screamed.

The ground below Oska was packed with hard dirt, but breaking a few bones was better than what would come next.

Oska refused to loosen her grip, and Sav barrelled between the two phoenixes directly ahead. Sav tilted slightly to the right as one phoenix shifted, sending Oska tipping, too. Without a tight enough grip to keep her low against the saddle, Oska collided with the adjacent phoenix's wing.

The live feed from Oska's helmet camera turned to static. Kel could still see their rider being tossed into the air like a ragdoll. Talons glinted, and Kel heard the sound of shredding leather through her comm. Nausea roiled through her.

Oska screamed; a nightmarish sound ripped from her throat. Wind and static broke her cry as she tumbled through the sky. Falling.

A deafening *thud* echoed through the Howlers' comms.

The line went dead.

Chapter Two

---※---

Hot sweat blurred Kel's vision as she bolted from the Howlers' booth into the crowded stands and down a creaking staircase. She shoved past the spectators rising from their seats. Dira and Rube were close behind her, the three of them stumbling through a metal gate. By the time they reached the track, the race had already ended.

They flashed their CAPR passes at a blank-faced security guard and paused. Oska had fallen 200 metres from the finish line. A team of medics were rushing across the dirt track, towards Oska's distant, still figure.

Heart beating wildly, Kel turned to Dira and Rube. 'Check on Oska and—'

And what? Check if their rider still had a pulse?

Dira coughed. 'Don't worry, Kel. We'll stay with her. Go get Sav.'

Kel gave a terse nod and sprinted past the finish line. After Oska fell, Savita had continued on, paying Oska no more mind than a gnat on a rider's goggles.

The air rippled around the painted finish line where the surviving phoenixes had landed, slowly regaining their shapes. All at least twice as tall as Kel, over half of the creatures had blood smearing their burnished feathers. She blinked through thick clouds of dust and zipped up her leather jacket as protection against the heat.

Three phoenixes to her right snapped at each other, jostling their riders and refusing to calm. Still coursing with the race's excitement, it would be all too easy for the creatures to end the event with a massacre. Kel wove swiftly between them, giving each a wide berth until she spotted Savita, freckled with red, orange and yellow sparks. Sav grumbled at a nearby phoenix, free to cause as much damage as she liked without a rider to guide her.

Sav quickly spotted Kel and ducked her head, shifting away from the other phoenix like a cat caught toying with a mouse. Kel's shoulders slumped as she approached. Sav's adrenaline-fuelled, raging flames had already settled, returning to their usual soft, lighter flickers. She twisted her long neck to preen and pick at the empty saddle on her back.

'You scared me to death,' Kel mumbled, running her gloved hands across a row of burgundy feathers at Savita's side.

She winced at her own words as Oska's screams echoed through her ears. Though she'd witnessed Oska's bone-shattering fall, Kel couldn't stop the mantra rattling in the back of her skull:

She's fine. Oska's fine. She's fine. She's—

Oska was brash and entitled, but she was one of them. A Crimson Howler. She couldn't be . . .

Kel refused to even finish the thought.

Savita's black beak closed impatiently. Small sparks still ran across her feathers. One spark shot out at Kel's arm, catching her jacket. It burnt a glowing hole through her sleeve before Kel could pat it out. She bit down on the pain. Sav seemed too distracted to notice, the phoenix's dark gaze tracking the movement of a nearby crew. Kel waited until Sav's eyes fixed on her again before moving her hands higher up the phoenix's side, towards the saddle.

Phoenixes weren't pets to be coddled. They were just as brutal as the Saltan island they called home, unlike the harmless sprites on Ascira, or the serpentine companions on Dresva. If anyone tried to touch Savita without permission, they'd lose their hand before they could blink.

'You couldn't have stopped and stayed with Oska?' Kel sighed. 'You just *had* to finish the race?'

Sav lowered her head and nuzzled Kel's palm. Seeing Sav safe eased some of the tightness in her chest. The bird's feathers, rippling layers of yellow, orange and red, were mostly unruffled, free of injury. Her plumage darkened to burgundy along the tips of her wings, like sharp, blood-dipped knives, and her copper talons glistened despite the rising dust. The saddle sat just a little taller than Kel's head, covering the paler feathers along Savita's spine.

Kel glanced up at the surrounding phoenixes, squirming and clucking as their teams closed in. Though Sav had technically crossed the finish line fourth, without a rider, she was disqualified. Kel's eyes stung.

Oska's fall would leave her injured, perhaps permanently. Either way, the Howlers wouldn't have a rider to compete with any time soon. Not unless Kel stepped up to replace Oska, and though she'd raced occasionally, she didn't have the natural core strength and agility needed to stand a chance in CAPR.

We should have done better.

The thought made Kel grimace. Though her father hadn't endorsed CAPR racing, he would have scolded her for feeling anything but thrilled at placing fourth. He'd have grinned, fixed her mess, and spun her around until she laughed.

But Kel hadn't seen her father's grin in two years. All she had to remember him by were debts and dry fields. A dull, sunken feeling crept through her, which only grew as she heard Dira's approaching footsteps.

Behind her, she heard Dira say, 'Oska's . . . she's . . .'

Kel tried to steel herself, even as her dread tunnelled deeper. She turned to face her friend.

'She's dead,' Dira finally managed. Her face crumpled and her body sagged, breaking beneath the weight of her words.

The world blurred, and Kel closed her eyes.

Death was as much a part of CAPR as phoenixes were. Kel had known that since she'd first entered a race. But that didn't stop the ground from falling out from beneath her.

She'd only known Oska for a few months, but she knew *enough*. Oska had two younger sisters. Her favourite sprites were violet and indigo. She always tried to wear the most impractical, sequined shirts under her riding leathers. Her family had money, but she'd come to Cendor to prove that she didn't need it. She was as strong as any Saltan.

Kel heard Savita screech. The sound shocked her eyes open, and she hurried forward to wrap Dira in an embrace.

'I'm sorry,' Kel whispered, desperate to keep her voice steady.

Dira's response was a close-lipped whimper.

Kel tightened her grip. 'You should head home – I can pack up our equipment.'

Dira sniffled. 'Are *you* okay?'

Kel didn't answer. They stayed that way, staving off each other's pain, until Savita screeched again. Kel waited until Dira pulled back. Numbly, the pair lifted onto their toes and unbuckled the intricate girth around Savita's stomach. Kel forced herself to note Savita's heat through the thermometer embedded in her collar. Her temperature was a little higher than usual, which was normal after a race.

Kel caught the saddle as it fell off Sav's two-metre-tall back, stumbling beneath the heavy weight as nearby shouts grabbed her attention. She placed it on the ground and peered beneath Sav's stomach, towards the voices.

Four figures crowded around a large blood phoenix and its rider. Squinting, Kel could make out the neon, meteor emblem on the back of their uniforms, branding them as the Star Chasers – the team unfortunate enough to have the world's biggest ass as their rider.

Coup slouched back atop the phoenix as his teammates cursed and circled him. Through her shock, a petty satisfaction pooled in Kel's gut. Even if Coup had won the race, Kel doubted that his team would be pleased with his dangerous manoeuvre. The Star Chasers were well known for their prim and proper attitude to racing. Even if it didn't garner them much media interest, it meant their sponsors didn't have to worry as much about them destroying expensive gear. Kel doubted they were eager to share in Coup's hot-headed, reckless reputation.

Coup's older brother Bekn stood at a distance from the other Star Chasers, with a blank expression and folded arms. The pair always seemed to shift teams together; Coup as a rider, Bekn as a mitigator, the latter responsible for publicity and sponsorship. Most CAPR crews had the standard five members: tamer, rider, technician, winger and mitigator. It was a mitigator's job to encourage the parts of CAPR that made Kel want to pull out her hair: fame, publicity and meddlesome sponsorship. But Kel and Dira had never found a mitigator they'd liked enough to bother retaining, especially with the rates most of them charged. If Sav placed in the top three, that would provide enough fanfare and money to cover expenses until the next race.

Or, at least, it should have. If Oska's life hadn't brutally ended and Kel had been able to—

'How's Savita?' Dira asked quietly, glancing up at the phoenix.

Kel stared at her friend. 'She's fine. Dira, are you sure you're—'

Kel broke off as Rube approached. He stopped a few feet to Dira's left, as close as he ever drew to Sav. 'We should get off the track so I can check our equipment.' He gestured to the saddle on the ground. 'I've got an app linked to Oska's leathers, so I'll . . . I can see how they held up in the race. Even though the leathers are . . .'

'I doubt we'll be getting them back,' Dira offered gently.

Bile rose in Kel's throat.

The little colour in Rube's face drained away. Kel reached for the reins around Sav's neck and glared at the Star Chasers. Coup stood alone on the ground, dusting his legs off, seemingly abandoned by his teammates.

Anger writhed between Kel's ribs as she watched Coup. She latched onto that anger, wishing it hotter, letting it break through her numbness and tether her to the ground.

Kel held out Savita's reins to Dira. 'Can you lead Sav off the track? I'll be over in a second.'

'Sure.' Dira's gaze flickered to Coup. 'Just don't rip his head off completely,' she said in a low voice. 'CAPR already lost one rider today.'

Kel's throat thickened. Stiffly, she nodded. Dira reached into a pocket and pulled free a handful of dried insects. Though Sav's feathers rose as Kel moved away, her beady eyes latched onto Dira's hand.

'Come on, beasty,' Dira sighed heavily. 'Kel and I have the butcher's best cuts waiting for you at home.'

As Dira and Rube led Sav off the track, Kel marched over to where Coup dawdled, still preening like a phoenix in a pageant.

'Are you proud of yourself?' Kel hissed, clenching her fists. She let her anger swell, hotter, sharper. It was far more comforting than the sound of Oska's screams, still echoing in her ears like static.

Coup turned towards Kel. His glass goggles rested on his chestnut curls, and dimples creased the leather bandana covering over the lower half of his face. He yanked the fabric down and offered Kel a pearly grin, amber eyes glowing.

'Ah, Varra,' he sang. 'How did I know you'd be the first to congratulate me on today's win?'

It was far from the first time she'd heard that taunting voice, and still it made her blood heat. For two years, it had been rare for a race to end without Coup or Kel screaming at the other about careless manoeuvres or unearned victories. Something about his ease amidst CAPR's carnage always made her temper boil over. She stalked closer. 'Because of your reckless stunt, my rider's *dead*.'

Coup brushed a languid hand through his hair. 'I didn't force *anyone* to attempt my move. Maybe it was your job to stop her from trying to pull it off.'

Kel hoped he didn't notice her wince.

'You're just lucky you didn't meet the same fate, and you know it!' she seethed.

Red tinted her vision as she drank in his cold, cruel smile. Oska's fall, Kel's overdue farm payments, the unexpected memory of her father – all of it flooded to the surface, congealing into an easier, familiar anger at Warren Coupers.

Coup sighed. 'That *move* probably got the race an extra few million views. The only thing that's illegal in CAPR is boring the camera crew. But I don't need to tell you that, Varra,' he taunted. 'If CAPR listened to you, Cendor would be betting on which phoenix's feathers are cleanest, not the races.'

Kel's eye twitched. *That* was the fundamental difference between her and Warren Coupers. On paper, they had plenty in common. Though they hadn't met before they'd started competing, they both lived east of Fieror. They'd both started CAPR racing two years ago. Both had been initially attacked by media outlets for racing as teens, and both frequented the same local pub after each race.

That was where their similarities ended.

Warren Coupers stood for everything Kel hated about CAPR. While racing was a last resort for her, Coup relished the thrill of it. He lavished the media with all the care he should have placed on his phoenix. The media in turn adored him for it and, even worse, the vain, golden boy knew it.

'Your team didn't seem that impressed with your stunt,' she threw back, folding her arms. 'The Star Chasers are all glamour and no risk. I won't be surprised if they give you the boot.' Kel held up three gloved fingers. 'What's this? Your third crew in two years?'

A muscle feathered in Coup's jaw, though his grin stretched wider. 'Jealousy isn't a good look on you, tamer. Earn your place on the track, or get off it.' He dusted an invisible piece of lint from his jacket. 'Either way, you should mind your own business before you lose another teammate.'

Kel frowned. Coup pointed behind Kel with a wink, and she held his stare for a moment longer before turning around.

To the right of the track, Dira had led Savita to a green patch away from the other teams. Dira was squatting, rifling through a duffel bag, while Rube approached Savita with his arm outstretched. He cupped something dark – likely a dried treat – in one hand, with the other held up as if to pet Savita. The feathers along Sav's back raised, her long neck coiled tight.

Coup gave a wicked laugh as Kel bolted towards Savita, slowing down only to weave between grumbling phoenixes and narrow-eyed crews.

'Rube!' she screamed, though the surrounding phoenixes drowned her voice.

Sav prowled forwards, towards Rube. Her round black eyes locked onto his pale face, her beak hovering just above his raised fingers. Sav released a deep grumble, daring Rube to touch her.

Kel reached her teammates just as Rube's mouth fell into a wide O.

'Rube,' she said, an urgent whisper, trying to calm her heavy breathing. 'Back up, slowly. Don't meet her stare.'

Rube lowered his gaze and sucked in short breaths. Kel heard Dira swivel towards them.

That should have satisfied Savita. Instead, the phoenix mirrored Rube, taking a menacing step forward for each one Rube took back. Savita's unblinking gaze darted between Rube's head and the hand he'd tried to lay on her.

Kel guessed what Savita would do a split-second before the phoenix moved.

Savita's wings rustled and colourful flames stirred the air.

The firebird dove towards Rube, her knife-sharp beak aimed for his chest. Kel shoved Rube back and leapt in front of him, blocking Savita's path.

She heard Rube thud to the ground. Savita's rough beak was pressed against Kel's stained shirt. Kel felt a tapered edge prick her sternum, likely drawing blood, but move no further. As Kel caught her footing, Savita shuffled back, just a step. Eventually, she huffed, folded her wings, and turned towards a nearby tuft of grass.

Kel let out a relieved gasp. She turned to Rube, hoping her smile hid how fast her heart hammered. 'She doesn't mean anything by it, Rube. You haven't spent much time with her, and she's restless after the race.'

She was lying, and they all knew it. No matter how much time passed, Savita still refused to let almost anyone near her – let alone touch her.

'I just . . . I wanted to help make sure she's okay, after Oska . . .' Rube trailed off as Dira tried to help him to his feet, but he jerked away.

He shook his head and pointed a shaking finger at Savita. 'But . . . that *thing* just left Oska on the track to bleed out,' he yelled. 'It shouldn't even be allowed to race.'

Kel's guilt slipped away. Her jaw clenched and she stepped towards Rube. Though he was taller, she hovered over him, her shadow seeping along the ground.

'Leave it, Kel,' Dira muttered.

Kel poked at Rube. '*Her* name is Savita. She's a *phoenix*, Rube. Not a house cat. If you try to touch her when we've told you not to, it's *your* fault if you get yourself hurt.'

'Was it Oska's fault, too, then?' Rube fumed.

Kel felt as if he'd hit her. The ringing – *Oska's screaming* – in her ears returned, and her vision tilted.

Rube's eyes widened. He stepped towards Kel, and she stepped back. 'Kel, I—'

But Kel had already turned away, praying he didn't see the tear creeping down her cheek.

Chapter Three

---※---

Kel's knotted stomach had eased once she and Savita entered the aviary on their farm. Here, amidst the sprawling greenery and refracted light, it was easier to pretend everything was as it had been this morning. There was only Savita's full wingspan, the smell of moist earth and the scorching overhead lamps. Kel had changed into a set of protective riding leathers and still the aviary's heat prickled her skin.

She usually hired a transport unit to move Savita between locations, not wanting to tire her out any more than necessary, but today she'd flown Sav back home as Oska's fall played on a loop in Kel's mind.

Savita lumbered through the aviary's metal gates and pressed her beak against Kel's side. Kel waved a gloved hand and jostled Savita's monstrous saddle against her hip. Twice the size and thickness of a horse's, the saddle was a monstrous burden to carry – even with Kel's seventeen years of muscle helping her manoeuvre it. 'Yeah, yeah – hold on a sec.'

Savita bristled and ducked her head. Kel reached for Savita's collar, glowing like tarnished starlight. She felt the warm, yellow feathers beneath Sav's neck brush against her face as she leaned in, making her eyes water. Alongside other gadgets, a small temperature gauge was embedded in the collar. The tech was from Cristo Industries, like most equipment used for phoenix racing.

The collar was as much for Savita's protection as it was for Kel's. There were plenty of absurd superstitions about the brutality of phoenixes, but it was simple fact that a phoenix without a collar would burn down half of Cendor.

It might be a crude form of control, but there were no better options. The last time a phoenix had broken free of its collar had been ten years ago, when a new technician had mishandled a phoenix after a race. The phoenix, already agitated, took flight and burnt down the racetrack. Eight CAPR members had died, as well as five spectators, and another fifty were injured.

'Your vitals are completely normal. You had me worrying all night over nothing.'

Savita's temperature had fluctuated like a fever the previous night. A temperature spike wasn't uncommon before a race, as if Sav anticipated the track's ferocity, but Kel had still spent much of the night chewing on hangnails.

Savita threw Kel what seemed like a filthy look and snorted. Steam escaped her beak.

Kel retorted, 'You throw ear-splitting tantrums and tear up a dozen shrubs before every race, as if you don't *love* getting out on the tracks. But I should know better than to worry, right? You'd probably wake the other isles if you so much as got a splinter.'

Savita snorted again and turned away. The aviary's dome seemed to curve around the phoenix, welcoming her home as she spread her wings and rose in a whirlwind of dust.

'Thanks, Sav,' Kel coughed.

Kel shook her head and closed the metal gates behind them. The steel frame held together the aviary's tempered glass panels and rose high enough to house hundreds of native plants. Though panels and heat lamps had been replaced over the years – not nearly as often as they should have been – the looming trees and sprawling shrubs all bore her grandfather's touch. Kel's grandfather had bought Sav as a true newborn; fresh from the egg, not her own ashes. Harrin Varra must have paid a fortune for the young phoenix – though whatever money had allowed him to buy her was long gone.

Kel had been told she'd inherited her ash-brown hair and grey eyes from him, though she'd never met the man. He'd died of Armond's Blight – AB – before she was born. Before the disease was as common as a cold. Before it made you a statistic instead of a soul.

Kel often dreamt about her grandfather when she slept in the small office attached to the aviary. She wondered if he'd laid his head on the same thin mattress. If he'd watched Savita swerve and glide through the air and heard each of her cries as a ballad.

She never dreamt about her father.

She hoped she wouldn't dream about Oska, either.

Kel flinched from the thought. Oska hadn't been the kind of Howler that she'd envisioned welcoming aboard, coming from Ascira's glamorous isle, dressed in impractical ruffles and fighting most of Dira's instructions. But she'd had a fire to match any Cendorian's.

At some point, without even realizing, Kel had let herself forget the fate that befell most riders.

Shaking the thought loose, Kel dropped the saddle and shuffled over to the chest freezer at the far side of the aviary. Savita shrieked, trailing behind Kel as she lifted the freezer lid. A faint, metallic odour filled her nose. Savita lurched toward the freezer and tried to poke her head inside.

'Flames – wait – *two more seconds*,' Kel wheezed, shoving away Savita's insistent beak and grabbing a thick cut of meat from the freezer. She tossed it out onto the ground, towards a cluster of bushes. Savita launched for the icy slab as if it might flee. Kel watched Sav toss it into the air, the meat instantly defrosting and dripping from her heat, before she opened her beak wide and swallowed it whole.

Kel huffed, leaning back against the closed freezer. Frozen cuts satisfied Savita during racing seasons, when she could expel energy on the track. But during the colder Steeling Season she had to sate Sav with live prey: purchased and transported bulls and boars that put up as much fight as any mortal animal could.

Whether her prey was dead or alive, Sav didn't take kindly to interruptions.

Kel quickly skirted the aviary's glass edges, grabbed the saddle and hurried into the small, adjoining office. Kel dropped her tattered bag onto the cot, heaved Savita's saddle onto the wall hooks and pulled off her protective gloves. New blisters were already forming over old burn scars, running over her palms and down her wrists. Given how popular CAPR was, burns and scars were common across Cendor. Still, she'd need to buy new, thicker gloves soon. Savita seemed to grow hotter with every race.

Her phoenix screeched and the office's wooden walls vibrated. Two photo frames fell forwards onto the crammed desk. Kel hurried to straighten the first frame – a picture of her, Dira, and their old teammates after the Howlers' first win.

'What are we going to do, Sav?' she whispered. The office wall connected to the aviary offered a window, and Kel watched her phoenix soar and swoop in lazy patterns. Without today's prize money, Kel had no clue how she'd stave off the tax collectors who were sure to harass her this week. She'd tried everything to scramble together extra funds; night shifts at Fieror's scattered pubs and pleading for the council grants they'd showered her charismatic father with. The only thing she hadn't tried was letting kids ride Sav for money, which would likely end in an expensive lawsuit.

From the door, a husky voice asked, 'Where's your tablet?'

Limping beneath the weight of several bags, Dira stumbled into the office. Her dark brown skin gleamed with sweat.

Kel folded her arms. 'What are you doing here?'

Dira's eyes landed on Kel's desk, where her old tablet and keyboard sat. '*Aha* – never mind.'

Dira staggered forwards, dropping her bags to the ground with a heavy, expensive-sounding *thud*.

'Please, make yourself at home,' Kel said dryly. 'How are you feeling?'

'I'm *feeling* that we don't have time to . . .' Dira's voice thickened, cutting off her words. She cleared her throat and plucked a data chip loose from her pocket, lifting Kel's tablet and propping up the screen.

A moment later, Dira coughed. '*Flames*, Kelyn – I think a ghost just flew out of your keyboard. Have you even used this since the last time I was here?'

'I use the tablet in the aviary to track Savita's vitals. I haven't used that thing in months. You might as well take it.'

'You live way closer to Fieror's races. It's easier to keep the data here with our girl.'

Savita squalled and shook the office walls again. Kel let the sound wash over her like sunlight, burying the memory of Oska's screams.

'We're going to need to find a new rider,' Dira sighed, leaning back in the desk chair.

Kel's stomach dropped. She knew, beneath the even words, Oska's death ate at Dira as much as it did Kel – probably even more. Dira had been the one to discover Oska at their local inn. She'd been the one to push through Kel's qualms and insist she train as their new rider, only in part because of her infatuation with the beautiful Asciran at the time. Though Dira's crushes were as common and rapid as AB, they'd spent plenty of time together outside of training sessions. But neither Dira nor Kel had the time to grieve that money afforded.

Stiffly, Kel nodded. She began scrubbing at the hardened soot on Savita's saddle. Though she used a bristle brush, her nails were instantly coated with a thick layer of black.

Dira twisted back towards the tablet, and they both worked in silence. Though Kel was relieved neither of them forced conversation, she wished she had anything to distract her thoughts from Oska.

A numb part of Kel knew Oska would never have survived CAPR

for long. Oska hadn't been built for Cendor. She'd been too nervous to approach Savita for too long, too comfortable in the refinery and riches of Ascira, Cendor's neighbouring isle. Nothing could have truly prepared her for what CAPR would demand from her.

And Kel should have tried harder to show her.

Kel crouched on her cot, brushing her sketchpad and carving kit off the small bed. Both were gifts from her father. Drawing – and then carving her designs into leather – were perhaps the only things she could lose herself in that didn't involve Savita.

Noise from the tablet made Kel glance up. A document filled half the tablet screen, while the other half was divided into five video feeds. Each video showed today's race from a different angle.

It was Dira's job to map out what she could of racetracks, to learn about their opponents' histories and weaknesses. It helped to know which phoenixes had been born in free Vohre Forest, not captivity, and which were prone to violence. But research could only prepare CAPR teams so much. Dira had an uncanny ability to predict how different terrains would affect different phoenix subspecies, from the revered monarch phoenixes to the smallest, camouflaging cape phoenixes. Dira called it pattern recognition. Kel called it a miracle. Both were probably true.

'*Oh*,' Dira said, turning to rifle through another duffel bag. 'I forgot – you have a new postcard.'

Kel snatched the postcard from Dira's fingers. 'You went through my mail?'

'There were letters in there from months ago. You could've missed a bill or something.'

Kel raised a brow. She never missed a bill, even if she couldn't pay them. But she *did* choose to leave postcards inside her mailbox.

Dated *Day 20 of the Molten Season, Year 1509 of the Alchemy Age*, the postcard's dainty handwriting read:

> My darling Kelyn,
>
> Ascira's beautiful this time of year. The sprites are blossoming with the flowers. In the Steeling Season, the creatures mingle with the falling snow, all silvery and soft. But in the Molten Season, they blossom and light up the sky like a crumbled rainbow, blues and yellows and reds that remind me of phoenixes and your father. And the people here - you'd love them! So many visitors from across the world. You'd never think Cendor was just a few hours away.
>
> There's a few of those religious cultists leaking into Ascira from Ebrait. Most of the Fume I've seen are harmless, throwing pamphlets into the streets and getting drunk off sprite magic. Some claim to be prophets of the Serpent King, here to free Salta's creatures from us. Such garbage. Don't worry about me, though - they wouldn't dare try anything too extreme in Ascira, especially now that the island's ramping up for tourism season.
>
> I'm doing fine. Funds are a little low, but there's plenty of jobs now that more tourists are scurrying about.
>
> Hope to hear from you,
> Love,
> Mum

Kel threw the postcard onto the desk. 'Funny how she always asks me to write back, but never leaves a return address.'

The letter landed writing side down, a picturesque view of Ascira's bustling coastline facing her. Blue sprites – hazy little creatures the size of a thumb – speckled the air like sunlight catching on rain. As Salta's north-west island, closest to the larger continent, Ascira's coast was always crowded with tourists eager to witness Salta's vibrant, lesser magic. Visitors rarely ventured further. The magic of Salta's other islands wasn't quite as benign as the colourful creatures that littered Ascira's skies.

Kel wasn't worried for her mother's safety. All Saltans had heard tales of the Fume, the extremist offshoot of Ebrait's religion that worshipped Salta's serpents, sprites, phoenixes and sea monsters. They'd grown out of AB, which they saw as nature's way of fighting back against humans domesticating Salta. Her mother was right. They'd never try anything extreme on Ascira, of all the isles.

The office's rubbish bin was full of similar postcards. Photographs of Ascira's glittering sprites and romantic architecture. Watercolours of Ebrait's revered sea-dragons and gilled critters, weaving around the four isles. Paintings of Dresva's serpents and emerald forests. All sights that Kel had never seen, and never cared to. She had everything she needed in Cendor.

'When was the last time you saw your mum?' Dira pried.

'When was the last time you saw yours?' Kel retaliated.

Dira turned back to the tablet. 'Well played.'

An apology danced around Kel's tongue. Dira rarely talked about her mother, or her father, who she'd left behind on Dresva when she'd snuck into Cendor as a child. But Kel saw the hard lines around her friend's eyes, creases that grew deeper every day. Though for different reasons, they both needed racing to survive.

They'd met when they were both twelve, sneaking into a CAPR race as underage kids without guardians. They'd both burnt their hands on a lower booth's metal railings, giggling and clapping as phoenixes blazed past, and wailing when CAPR officials had escorted them both out of the stands. The shared tantrum had been enough to glue them together, and when Kel had invited Dira to her farm, her father had soon made sure Dira rarely left.

Dira had snuck into Cendor on an airship. The Dresvan girl claimed to have always dreamt of Cendor's wild, fiery magic. She'd written to her parents in Dresva over the years, trying to convince them to visit Cendor and the Varra Farm, with no luck. Kel knew there was more to Dira's story, more to why she'd fled from Dresva's quiet forestry to Cendor's deadly blazes. But Dira had never shared, and so Kel had stopped asking.

After Kel's father died, they'd grieved together, and had searched for a new orbit, side by side, until they had formed the Crimson Howlers.

Dira's tele-comm buzzed, forcing Kel from her mind. The winger glanced at the device and lowered the tablet to the desk.

'Let's go commiserate at The Ferret. Rube will meet us there,' Dira said. She stood from the creaking desk chair and cracked her back.

Kel's stomach knotted at the thought, so different from the usual warmth she reserved for The Ferret, her and Dira's usual post-race hideout. She *knew* she should apologize to Rube for Savita's outburst, and her post-race ritual at The Ferret Inn with Dira was too familiar, too cosy, to turn down.

'That sounds perfect.' She forced a smile. 'We'll toast to her.'

Dira mirrored Kel's pitiful expression. 'Good. There's something else I need to talk to you about, and it requires alcohol.' Dira paused, sucking her lower lip. 'Lots of it.'

Kel raised a brow. 'Sounds ominous. You're buying.'

Dira merely waved a hand and sauntered to the office entrance. She stopped at the door frame and leaned back over the desk, spotting what Kel had crammed against the wall. Her fingers glided over the first row of crumpled envelopes, covered in bold red letters and 'overdue' stamps, and she plucked one free.

For a heavy minute, the only sound echoing through the building was Savita's wild shrieking, rattling the thin walls.

Dira's eyebrows knitted in a tight line. 'Kelyn—'

'Let's go,' Kel said softly, turning to leave the office.

Chapter Four

※

Dira thumped her hand against their disturbingly sticky table. She yelled up at the screens broadcasting today's race. Dozens of voices joined hers.

The Ferret was overcrowded and smelt like a public aviary. Its mob stirred a small headache, but the food was hot and the drinks were sweet. Pressed beside her best friend, perched on a bar stool, she tried to focus on her surroundings – not what might come after tonight.

Finn – the pub's owner – brought over their first round of drinks, and they raised the tall glasses to Oska. The *clink* of the cups sent shivers down Kel's spine, the sound far too similar to Oska's own sharp screams.

They'd barely lowered their glasses when Rube appeared through The Ferret's front doors.

Kel and Dira shouted a welcome, though Rube remained purse-lipped. Dira clapped him on the back. 'You're late! Here – we saved you a seat.'

Rube shook his head. He remained standing. Smothering her pride, Kel leaned across the clammy table. 'Rube, about earlier today, I'm—'

'There's no need, Kelyn.' Rube's gaze lowered to the table. 'I can't stay. I just came to—'

The pub exploded as an old race began to play across the screens. Rube's words were lost to the crowd.

Dira, to Rube's left, let out a high laugh. 'It almost sounded like you said—'

'I'm leaving,' Rube said, still staring at the table.

Kel frowned. 'What?'

'Not just the team, I'm leaving Fieror, too.'

The crowd roared and the Howlers fell silent. 'If this is about—'

'It's not about Savita, or . . . Oska.' Rube shuffled back. 'I'm moving to Vohre. I sent off an application months ago for Cendor University's early-entry boarding programme. But they're offering me a partial scholarship, and my parents said they'll cover the rest.'

His features pinched, and he added, 'I know the timing is . . . I wish it wasn't so soon. I got the email this morning, but didn't check my comms before the race. After what happened . . . with Oska . . .' Rube cleared his throat. 'I don't think I'm cut out for CAPR.'

Kel opened and closed her mouth. Eventually, Dira coughed and said, '*Wow.* That's . . . really amazing, Rube.'

Rube beamed, plucking up the courage to meet Dira's eyes. His dimpled grin rounded his face, making him look even younger.

Rube was sixteen, a year younger than Kel and Dira. Kel had found him at a local market, purchasing scraps to invent and trial his own tech. Before he'd joined the Howlers, their old rider had been icing burns between races, their cheap leathers hardly up to code. But with Rube's fabrics and some inventive hardware, the Howlers had begun to hold their own against Fieror's best – and wealthiest.

It was no surprise that Cendor University had accepted Rube. Or that he intended to leave the Howlers.

But the pit in Kel's stomach, the same one she'd felt when her mother left, yawned awake.

Rube tried again, 'I never thought I'd get in. But Cendor University has the best mechatronics and software courses in Salta. *Canen Cristo* graduated from there.'

'We get it,' Kel said, voice clipped. 'When are you leaving?'

'Tomorrow morning.' Excitement glimmered in his eyes like stars, already tracing a new orbit.

Kel fumbled for Dira's hand beneath the table. She knew what it meant to lose people, and she'd tried desperately to build jagged walls that no one but Dira could cross. And yet – Rube's words suffocated her. Her mind whirred, grappling for something new, solid, to knit her back together.

Rube ran a hand through his sable-black hair. 'You're welcome to keep the suits I worked on and the software I was upgrading. Dira should be able to figure out the rest.'

'I'm sure I will,' Dira said, smiling tightly.

Kel squeezed Dira's hand. Despite their revolving door of teammates, loyalty was everything to Dira. Kel doubted her best friend would soon forgive Rube.

Kel wanted to argue, to shake Rube and make him understand all that was at stake – but she knew it would make no difference, so she offered stilted congratulations instead, and closed her eyes as he left.

She'd expected nothing less for Rube's future – just not so soon.

Dira shook her head. 'No notice in the middle of racing season, no help finding a replacement, no care that we already lost one Howler today. I'll have to ring some contacts and beg for whispers of up-and-coming talent.'

Even if they continued to survive without a mitigator, they were now without a rider *and* a technician. Kel could act as a rider if she had to, but neither Kel nor Dira had the technical knowledge to toy with their equipment.

If the Howlers couldn't compete, Kel would have no choice but to sell her farm. Her father's life insurance was running dry and the Howlers' earnings weren't enough to sustain Savita. The aviary was a black hole that sucked in money as fast as if Savita had burnt it, and the Cendorian Council had strict property expectations when it came to housing phoenixes.

I'm going to lose the farm.

I'll lose Savita.

She quickly shoved down the thought. Nothing could force her to give up Savita. She'd fight like a wild phoenix before that happened.

Dira slouched on her stool. 'Well, there goes that plan.'

'What plan?' Kel asked. She picked at the emblem she'd sewn onto her sleeve – the emblem she'd sewn onto *everything* the Howlers owned: a black, barbed infinity, overlaid by a burgundy flame.

Instead of responding, Dira glanced towards the inn's wide doors.

Kel raised a brow. 'Are you expecting more drop-byes?'

Dira merely shook her head and turned back to the nearest screen. An ad interrupted the race rerun, full of scripted smiles and vignetted montages. The camera panned to a woman in a black uniform. Her dark hair was bound in a tight bun and her olive skin was eerily flawless.

'Here at the Cendorian Defence Force, we look to the future. Join our research teams, phoenix wranglers, isle ambassadors, or even our sponsored CAPR crews, as we partner with Cendor University and Cristo Industries to fly our nation into its brightest tomorrow.'

As the ad faded to black, bile rose in Kel's throat. Her father had taught Kel to loathe the Cendorian Government before she could walk. Though she believed in the necessity of phoenix collars, she also knew that most phoenixes were removed from their natural habitat, destroying their chances of reproduction. The government would cage every phoenix in Cendor for CAPR if they could. They'd offered her father dozens of jobs over the years, but he'd never once aligned himself with the council or their allies, like Cristo Industries.

Kel's focus broke as a creak sounded at her back. Dira's gaze shifted to the front door, and Kel swivelled.

Coup and his brother, Bekn, paused inside the entrance, the soft dusk light framing their silhouettes. Bekn had changed out of his crew uniform, sporting a grey tee and black trousers. Russet-brown curls a few shades darker than Coup's fell across his forehead, and his brown eyes scanned the inn. Coup still wore his riding leathers. The gear was half-shrugged off, hanging loose around his waist, revealing a plain black shirt. A smirk pulled up Kel's lips as she spotted the purple-and-black bruise swelling Coup's right eye, presumably from one of his disgruntled teammates.

Kel's smirk vanished as Coup turned towards her and waggled his fingers. He meandered over to their table with Bekn close behind.

'Happy to see me, Varra?' Coup asked, drawing out each syllable.

It wasn't strange for the brothers to frequent The Ferret. Still, this was the *last* thing Kel needed tonight.

She looked pointedly at Coup's bruised eye. 'I hope whoever gave you that made it hurt.'

Coup waved a hand. 'Barely felt it.'

'The Star Chasers are lucky we're not seeking legal recompense for the injury,' Bekn said, inching forward, creating a slight barrier between Kel and Coup.

Dira, Kel and Coup all snorted. Cendor's council was more likely to implode than to care about punishing violence.

Bekn shook his head. The mitigator was perhaps an inch shorter than his younger brother, with a longer face and lankier build. Still, the family resemblance was strong enough that the media adored them both.

'What are you doing here?' Kel demanded.

Coup's grin widened.

Dira scrunched her nose. 'Okay, don't bite my head off . . . but after you took Sav home from the track, I started chatting with Bekn. Turns out, they're in need of a new team, and—'

Kel interrupted with a barked laugh. She swivelled to face Coup. 'The Star Chasers booted you?'

Coup merely pursed his lips. Kel turned to Bekn. 'I assume you followed suit and quit?'

Kel knew that Bekn was an ambitious mitigator who followed Coup across teams. And as much as Kel hated to admit it, Coup was a talented rider. Some sycophantic reporters had even labelled him a 'prodigy.' But he was also a spectacle, a gamble. His recklessness often attracted the wrong sort of attention, and no team would recruit him unless they were desperate. The Star Chasers were as spoilt as any sponsored team. They wouldn't want a rider who risked their reputation, and it seemed like Coup's luck had finally run out. Kel couldn't believe they'd given him a shot in the first place.

Bekn regarded Kel warily, as if sizing up a phoenix.

Dira's fingers drummed a fast rhythm against the table. '*They* need a new team, and *we* are in need of a new rider. And I know we said we don't need one, but . . .' Dira glanced up at Bekn. 'A mitigator wouldn't hurt our odds, either.'

Kel blinked. Her thoughts struggled to wade through disbelieving static, as heavy as the moisture coating the table.

Coup's smile turned angelic, and something in Kel's brain snapped.

'You're not serious,' Kel said, staring at Dira.

Dira twirled a loose curl around her finger. 'This whole conversation would've gone a lot smoother if Rube hadn't just announced his departure, but either way, we need new mem—'

'Rube left? Your technician?' Bekn interrupted.

Dira raised a hand. 'We'll find a new technician. There's plenty of scrappy inventors lurking around who'd take a shitty cut of race winnings.'

Coup inched closer to Kel's side, his mere presence grating at her nerves.

'No!' she exploded, throwing up her hands. '*No*. We're not using *Warren Coupers* as a rider.' She couldn't believe what she was hearing. 'The stunt he pulled today should make that obvious. One unlucky move and he'd hurt Savita as badly as he'd hurt himself—'

'What happened to your rider wasn't Coup's fault,' Bekn cut in. 'Besides, you need a publicist, too.' He forced a tight, practised expression.

Kel shook her head so violently that her rickety stool swayed. Had Dira forgotten that Kel *hated* Coup? Hated every thrill-seeking fibre of his being? Hated that he loved the glittery media attention? Hated everything he stood for?

'Absolutely not,' Kel barked. 'Coup and I would have to train with Sav *every day*. We'd have to . . .' She trailed off, too many objections trying to force their way up her throat.

'We'd have to spend every hour working together.' Coup's eyes drifted over Kel, heavy, unimpressed. 'I told Bekn I'd rather walk into a kraken's mouth.'

Kel's lip curled. Having to work closely with Warren Coupers would be like trying to put out fire with petrol. He would be constantly trying to creep beneath her skin, refusing to listen to her guidance and risking Sav's health. Worst of all, he'd take pleasure in knowing Kel had no choice.

Maybe Sav would bite his head off. But that was a single ray of hope amidst the nightmare her day-to-day life would become.

'Coup has already been dropped from three teams. He obviously can't be trusted,' Kel implored, turning to Dira. 'Why would this time be any different?'

'Because of *sponsorship*,' Bekn cut in. 'I've had meetings with lots of interested sponsors. But because Coup's . . . ah, methods . . . are usually different from our teammates', it's been hard to find a sponsor willing to endorse the entire team. However, if we joined the Howlers, a younger, more open-minded team, I'd have a better chance of convincing sponsors that our goals are aligned.' He gave Kel and Coup a pointed, dry look. 'All we have to do is play the part of a happy, healthy team.'

Coup sighed, resting his arms on the sticky wood. He was far too close for Kel's liking, pressing his shoulder against hers to fit around the small table.

'It might be a lost cause, Bek,' Coup said. 'Kel certainly is. The stick up her ass is wedged so deep, every time she opens her mouth you can see the other end.'

A headache twinged behind Kel's temples. Before she could bite back, Dira cursed. *'For Alchemists' sake!* What choice do we have, Kel? We all need the money. And until we can secure sponsorship, desperation is more likely to help us win than anything else.'

Kel glared at Dira. 'I just don't—'

She never finished her sentence. At that moment, a shriek sounded outside, and a storm blasted through the room.

Chapter Five

———✹———

Shockwaves surged through the inn, shaking the walls and knocking empty stools to the ground. Kel braced herself. All insults forgotten, Kel, Dira, Coup and Bekn exchanged worried frowns as another unholy scream wrenched apart the air.

Kel elbowed through the crowd to the inn's creaky porch, Dira and Coup following close behind her. Dread knotted her stomach.

At the centre of an empty construction zone across the narrow street, a flash of pale red flapped two hazy wings. Slightly smaller than Savita, its beak was sharper, longer than most phoenixes, more like a sword than a knife.

Kel stared at the phoenix batting its wings in confusion, and the dishevelled man to its right, dressed in singed sapphire clothing and holding a collar in the air like a trophy.

Shit.

Kel's breath shallowed, cold sweat trickling down her forehead.

They were all going to die.

Another man knelt on the rough ground, his shaking hands grappling for the phoenix's halter and leash, which was still tied around the creature's neck. But the phoenix – newly free – thrashed about in wild uncertainty. The creature sent rosy trails of smoke into the air and released another bone-chilling shriek that made the porch tremble.

The halter and leash would be of no use. They were flimsy things used to guide phoenixes, not overpower them. Collars were the only true means of control, and this man had removed it.

Kel glanced to the right. There was a public aviary next door, where travelling CAPR crews kept their phoenixes during racing season. The man on the ground still wore his security lanyard from today's race; he must have been the bird's tamer.

The other man waved the silver collar in the air, addressing his audience: 'Phoenixes will rise! The creatures of Salta were born to rule – and nature is fighting for their rights. You cannot tame fire, just as you cannot douse its fumes!'

Kel saw a tattoo below his wrist: two overlain double spirals; one red, one blue.

The Fume's symbol.

Nausea blurred Kel's vision.

A few other CAPR racers inched forward, as if to help the kneeling tamer. Then another, louder, primal scream escaped the phoenix, halting their steps. Despite the growing heat, goosebumps broke out across Kel's arms.

Another screech tore through the air, and a painful blaze of heat forced everyone back to the porch.

In a scarlet burst, both men crumbled to ash.

Kel's stomach roiled. Their charred bones fell to the dirt with a soft *thump*, like leaves hitting damp ground. Gasps filled the air, though no one was rash enough to cry out and risk the phoenix's attention.

She dug her nails into her palms as her knees wobbled, fighting back the memory that was trying to overlay the scene. Her father, shredded apart by an injured, wild cinder phoenix he'd tried to bandage. He was simply broken, hollow, *gone*, just like Oska—

The phoenix raised its crimson neck and released a guttural cry. Kel felt its temperature cool slightly as it folded back its wings, scraping heavy talons across the ground.

Sweat trickled down Kel's spine. Without a collar, the phoenix could destroy the entire island. It was even more dangerous than wild phoenixes – this tamed beast wasn't used to its own uninhibited power. It had clearly never felt its full strength. Though its wings stayed tucked, it began to thrash its head. The temperature around them crept up again, and the air trembled.

A few people broke free of the crowd and dashed down the street. The phoenix watched them, jerking back as if frightened.

Kel's mind replayed the last two minutes from different angles, recalling fragments of knowledge her father had taught her.

This phoenix had allowed the cultist – a stranger – close enough to remove its collar. It also looked perplexed by its own power. The bird was a foot or two shorter than Savita, with pale red colouring, and a narrow beak.

A spinel phoenix.

They were lucky it was one of the more docile subspecies; if it was a carnel or monarch phoenix, they'd all be dead already.

Kel catalogued every breath the phoenix took, every feather, every movement, and compared them against what she knew of spinel phoenixes.

They were a defensive species with an average temperature. Omnivores, like every phoenix, but with an appetite for smaller prey – insects and grains. They were scavengers, and often trained for races.

Kel knew she could help. She *knew*.

'Dira,' she whispered, 'get back inside The Ferret.'

'No way,' Dira muttered. 'I'm not leaving you.'

Kel reached for her friend's arm. 'Do *you* know anything about calming spinel phoenixes?'

Dira clenched her jaw, but said nothing. Though she could anticipate a phoenix's speed and strength on a track, it was Kel's job to react.

Kel squeezed Dira's elbow. 'Keep an eye on me through a window. Just get somewhere safe.'

Dira groaned in protest, but turned back to The Ferret's door. She tried to tug Bekn and Coup inside, too. The former followed with shuffled steps.

But Coup didn't move. His amber eyes, flaring as bright as any phoenix flame, locked on Kel's.

'Go back inside,' she repeated. 'Get as many people as you can off the street.'

'We're not in a race, tamer. You can't order me around just yet.' Coup glanced towards the growing crowd. 'They're not going anywhere, either.'

Slowly, Coup moved closer to Kel's right. 'You don't have to trust *me* – but trust that I know how to handle phoenixes and rowdy crowds. I can help.'

Kel didn't have time to argue with him, and even if she was the best tamer across Cendor, there was little chance she could pull this off alone.

'We need to get its collar back on before it realizes it can fly off,' Kel said, reluctantly. 'But it's going to be hard to get close enough with this crowd circling like vultures.'

The collar lay on the ground amidst the cultist's blackened remains. No one was close enough to reach for it.

She didn't know how she'd manage it. She'd never touched Savita – or any phoenix – without her leather gloves. But if they didn't recollar this phoenix soon, they'd all have far greater concerns than burnt hands.

Coup nodded, face taut. 'I can distract them. Are you sure you can handle the phoenix?'

Kel heard none of the usual mockery in his voice.

Slowly, she nodded.

In a few long strides, he leapt off the inn's ancient porch and moved around to the side of the building. Out of sight.

Almost a minute passed before a commotion echoed from behind the inn, drawing all attention – including the phoenix's. Seconds later, a darker trail of smoke climbed into the sky.

One by one, heads turned towards the growing smoke. The crowd was filled with enough regulars to know where it was coming from: the nearest public phoenix aviary.

Kel heard the crowd mumbling about another uncollared phoenix before they began trickling towards the smoke. Others crept back inside The Ferret whilst the phoenix was distracted. They were out of the way – but the phoenix was growing hotter, its head whipping back and its wings beginning to beat.

Kel crept forwards. Muscle memory replaced her fear, born from years at Savita's side. She pulled a handful of dehydrated insects and broken grains from her pocket. Kel felt the phoenix's gaze jerk up, but she kept hers carefully on the ground.

She heard slow, careful footsteps behind her. *Coup*. He shuffled closer, shoving something small and silver into his pocket. The sudden movement made the phoenix grumble. More smoke trailed into the air, crimson and black tangling in blistering ribbons that wove into the sky. Kel swallowed down a sharp wave of fear.

'I led everyone over to the public aviary and circled back, but they won't be fooled for long,' Coup panted, voice low. 'What's the plan?'

'Go back and keep them occupied,' she whispered, not wanting to know how he'd started the fire. 'I've got this.'

Coup moved closer. 'Get over yourself. I'm not leaving you here to become a crispy appetizer.'

She didn't have time to scold him, to tell him to *run*, as the phoenix loosed another deafening bellow. Pale flames climbed higher in the sky.

She exhaled through her nose. 'Just stay low. Try not to aggravate the phoenix more than you already have.'

Coup shuffled a few feet to her left; a safe distance from the phoenix's erratic movements. He moved slowly, squatting down so he was lower than the phoenix, keeping his gaze downturned.

Kel tossed a few treats to the ground. The phoenix didn't reach for them, but it did redirect its attention. Slowly, Kel lowered.

The collar lay amongst the ashes to her right. Her fingers ached to reach for it, but she couldn't afford any sudden movements.

Squatting lower, she shifted a little, staying in the phoenix's line of sight. She crawled to the right so she wasn't directly between the creature and the waning sun – which could be seen as a threat. She breathed out in long, hard pants, loud enough that the phoenix could hear. Shuffling closer to the collar, her breaths turned to whistles, low and even.

She managed a few more low steps before the phoenix turned towards her. It cocked its head and narrowed great, black eyes. Flames climbed even higher in the sky.

Kel's calves burnt as she crept closer. She changed the pitch of her whistle. A light, familiar flow of notes wove into the air.

It was a wordless tune she'd learnt from her father. He'd told Kel that Savita had once sung it to him, years ago. He'd been planting new seedlings in the aviary, humming to himself. Between one moment and the next, Savita had joined his chorus.

Phoenixes so often screeched and squawked. It was only when they felt truly content, free, that they dared sing, with voices said to bring even the Four Alchemists to their knees. Kel used to dream of hearing Savita's song, though it was a hope she'd buried with her father.

Kel kept whistling, crawling closer. She hoped her singing might show the creature that she was at ease. That she was no threat.

The creature watched her, snapped its beak twice. A sharper wave of heat sent sweat rolling down Kel's back. The bird stepped forward and lowered its head to the treats, scraping its talons far too close to Kel's knees. It devoured one treat, two, still watching Kel.

Kel let out a breath of relief and mingled it with her whistle.

'Coup,' she said, low and gentle, 'grab the collar.'

The creature tracked Coup as he crept to the right and, slowly, scooped up the ashy collar. Loudening her song, Kel drew its attention back. She cocked her head and paused, just a few yards away. Finally, she lifted her eyes to meet the phoenix's depthless gaze.

The beast clicked its beak a few more times, as if to communicate. All Kel could do was blink through the hot sweat dripping down her forehead and keep whistling. Keep forcing herself not to look at Coup as he crawled towards her.

She felt his rough hand press against hers. Without looking, she fumbled for the collar and curled her damp fingers around the hot metal. As Coup shifted away, she stood.

The phoenix rustled its wings and a few blush-red feathers stood around its neck, signalling its unease. She only had one shot at this.

Kel moved closer. It was hard to resist lifting a hand to block the scalding heat. Her steps were slow, steady – until she heard the scuffling of dirt. A stampede of feet.

The shouts of an approaching mob.

The phoenix reared its head. It spread its great wings and pale flames exploded into the air. Kel felt her arms singe as holes burnt into her sleeves. The phoenix lifted one of its talons – directly over her head.

Kel launched to the side just as the phoenix sank its claws into the earth where she'd been crouched. It threw its beak back, as if to strike. But Kel couldn't run – not now. Not as the creature's feathers shuddered and the air began to quake. The collar became a bar of molten soap between her sweaty fingers, blistering her skin.

Kel lurched forwards, arms outstretched.

The phoenix's feathers scalded her hands as she heaved the heavy band around its neck. Then, the collar's magnets locked together, and three green lights blinked to life, once again active.

A scream tore through Kel's throat. She struggled to pull her fingers from the metal, shock fighting her brain's commands. Her hands shook as she managed to pry them free, her breath whiny and ragged as she tumbled back, away from the phoenix.

Cradling her scorched hands, Kel looked up at the phoenix. She'd hoped the creature might calm once it felt the familiar weight of a collar.

She was wrong.

The phoenix let out a monstrous cry. Then – faster than she could follow – the bird lashed its head towards her, beak outstretched like a blade—

Something hard knocked Kel to the ground, just as a searing pain dug into her arm. Winded from the impact, Coup landed on top of her. Both of their clothes were damp with sweat, his body pressed against hers. He grimaced as the phoenix loosed another ear-piercing screech. The phoenix had missed Kel's chest but caught her right arm with a deep gash – far less lethal than it would have been if Coup hadn't knocked them both to the ground. Still, Kel winced as pain slashed across her bicep and blood streamed from the wound. The phoenix flapped its colossal wings and the force sent Coup and Kel tumbling away, grasping each other.

The phoenix screamed again, but at least it could no longer destroy Cendor. It couldn't fly more than a few metres without the collar's inhibitor stiffening its wings.

Kel and Coup struggled to untangle their limbs. Her wounded arm and blistered hands ached from the fall. Black spots danced across her vision, trying to consume her, but the feel of hands around her arms helped her focus.

Suddenly Dira was at her side, helping her stand as Bekn helped Coup. Kel bit her tongue to hide a groan of pain as they scrambled towards the inn's porch.

Now that the phoenix had its collar on, three brave souls – tamers she recognized from CAPR – were crouched low, approaching the phoenix.

The creature thrashed about, beating its wings and testing its limits. The air thickened and cooled, returning to a mundane, tepid evening. The phoenix nuzzled its beak against the sooty metal at its neck.

The three tamers managed to grab the phoenix's brown leash, hanging limply from its harness. The creature settled low to the ground, as if soothed by the familiar tug.

'How the hell did you manage to get the collar back on that thing?' an onlooker asked.

Kel slid her arm out from Dira's shoulders. 'That *thing* was just confused,' she rasped. Her throat felt stripped raw and hot needles bit into her shaking arms. 'It needed trust – not a crowd waving their arms around.'

The man coughed and stepped away as Coup approached her. His cheek was grazed, but his face glowed with his usual smile. He seemed oblivious to his torn shirt, splattered with Kel's blood.

'Not a bad first stunt for the new Howlers,' he said breathlessly. His eyes flickered down to her bleeding arm, and his grin vanished. '*Ashes!* You need a medic. How badly does it—'

'I'll survive,' she muttered, clenching her teeth around searing waves of pain. 'I've got a salve at home to treat the burns.' She winced as she tried to bend her blistered fingers. The burns would heal soon enough with her CAPR medic kit, fading into the other burns mapped across her hands. But she'd have to make sure the slash up her arm didn't get infected. 'How are you so calm? Not many people are stupid enough to dive between a phoenix and its prey.'

Coup frowned. '*Stupid* seems like a harsh word for someone who saved your life.'

Before Kel could reply, the nearby glint of something silver drew her focus. Not just a glint – but flashes.

She looked back to The Ferret's porch, expecting to see the scattered remains of the inn's crowd.

Instead, all she saw was bursts of light and video cameras, recording everything.

Recording her.

Chapter Six

※

Dawn cast Kel's six paddocks in a golden haze. Crickets whistled against the early quiet and sparrows swooped below the pink horizon, scavenging all but one paddock, bordered by honey-hued trees, where smoke rose in tendrils.

From the backsteps of her cottage, Kel lifted a bandaged hand to point. Even with the medicine she'd taken, the movement made her wince. 'I moved Sav out to our training grounds about an hour ago. She should be settled enough by now that she won't bite any newcomers' heads off.'

'She warmed up by terrorizing a burrow of bunnies under the paddock,' Dira added, arms crossed over her wine-red jacket. 'As long as she doesn't mistake you for an overgrown cottontail, your survival odds are about fifty per cent.'

Bekn fiddled with the collar of his button-up while Coup's cheery dimples merely deepened.

His eyes glimmered, metallic in the morning light. 'Let's not keep her waiting, then.'

Coup rubbed his hands together and skipped towards Savita's distant silhouette, as if eager to reunite with an old friend. Savita had her head well buried in the dirt, searching for burrows, indifferent to Coup's excitement.

Already garbed in riding leathers, Bekn had driven the pair onto Kel's lawn inside a four-wheeled auto-engine. It was an oddly heavy, protective vehicle on an island that typically preferred the smaller, more adaptable track-bikes. Engines were usually saved for Saltans who needed protection from the elements, like Ascirans or Dresvans. It made Kel wonder how comfortable Bekn truly was on Cendor.

The brothers had pulled up before the sun had risen above the farm's tree line. Kel had opened the door to Coup's incessant knocking, the sight of him shocking her awake. Apparently, last night, Dira and Bekn had organized a morning training session, while a council medic had tended to Kel and Coup. Kel had glared at her best friend, though it had helped to see Coup clearly as annoyed by their agreement as she felt. Though his annoyance had quickly shifted to something antagonistically cheery.

Kel rubbed a bandaged palm over her face and hurried to outpace Coup. He might have escaped yesterday's encounter with a phoenix uninjured – but he didn't know *Savita*. He didn't know the phoenix whose pupils dilated whenever fights broke out mid-race, whose beak clamped together, as if licking her lips, when blood was spilt.

She summoned a deep breath and forced herself to remember *why* she'd let Coup and Bekn past her doorstep: if she wanted to keep the farm – to keep *Savita* – she'd have to suffer through Coup's condescending smirks for at least a few CAPR races.

'Don't look so worried, Kel. I'm sure you two will find it *so easy* to work together after yesterday's bonding,' Dira called. 'A true match made by the Alchemists.'

Kel threw a vulgar gesture over her shoulder, and Dira laughed. Heat built in Kel's cheeks. Coup seemed unbothered by the taunt, which only made Kel's face heat even more.

It was tradition for Dira to crash at Kel's after a race. They'd raid Kel's kitchen and eyeball whatever late-night reruns the media screen offered. But last night, instead of the usual cheesy shows, every channel had blasted footage of yesterday's Fume attack. Kel and Coup recollaring the phoenix and tumbling together, blood leaking from Kel's arm, in what every channel had decided was a lover's embrace.

After she'd sweated through the infections trying to claim her wounded hands, she'd finally found sleep, but even her dreams had refused her respite. Oska's fatal screams had hammered through her skull as images of the uncollared phoenix's attack filled her night; black ash coating the ground, a beak too close to her chest, Coup clutching her as they tumbled to the ground.

At least in her dreams, she could rage at him the way she wanted to.

'Dira's right, though,' Bekn chirped, trailing at the back of their group, his voice giddy. 'Footage of the attack was replaying all night. Especially the pair of you two – er, working together.'

Kel's cheeks boiled as Coup threw his head back and laughed. The sound grated at her nerves. Savita, just a few hundred metres away, jerked her head up from a burrow in the dirt. Her beak parted, thin ribbons of smoke trailing high. A low warning rumbled through her.

Though Coup slowed, he didn't stop. Kel smirked as Savita released darker smoke into the air. If he continued at his current pace, Coup would end up trapped beneath Sav's talons as easily as a bunny.

'You don't think it's weird that they're focusing on *us* instead of the uncollared phoenix?' Kel asked Bekn, not taking her eyes off Savita.

'Of course it is,' Bekn replied. 'But what's done is done, and we might as well take advantage of the media attention.'

There was a surprising tenderness in Bekn's voice. Kel turned to the mitigator, taking in his carefully swept hair and ever-creased forehead. From CAPR gossip, she knew that Coup and Bekn's mother had passed away three years ago from AB. Bekn had quickly stepped in as Coup's legal guardian. Perhaps his lined brow shouldn't have surprised her.

Bouncing on the balls of his feet, Bekn mused about the potential sponsors that would have seen the footage. All the different ways to use yesterday's publicity for the team. *His* team.

It was an unexpected relief to have someone else fretting over their public image, to constantly be searching for ways to earn money. Dira and Kel had always maintained control of the Howlers' image and prospects. Giving that up – even to Warren Coupers' brother – made her feel lighter, as if the ground was loosening its hold on her. It was exciting – and terrifying.

Coup halted, and Kel skidded into his back, wincing as she thumped her right bicep. She lifted a bandaged hand to his arm to steady herself, then dropped it just as quickly. The rider's lips quirked.

'She's a carnel phoenix, right?' Coup murmured. 'Short fuse, aggressive, splattered colouring. High temp.'

Coup tilted his head. The movement was slow, calculated. Sav responded with her own head tilt. She stood rigid, though her neck wasn't craned to its full height. They stared evenly at each other. Both gauging a new threat.

'Yeah,' Kel grunted, 'she is.'

Though carnel phoenixes were one of the four subspecies legally allowed to enter CAPR races – along with cinder, spinel and blood phoenixes – they were easily the rarest on any track. Kel supposed his knowledge came from his fickleness, hopping teams over the past years.

'How'd your dad find her? Carnels are rare.'

Surprise flickered through her. 'He didn't. My grandfather bought her from those poachers who sneak into the forest to find CAPR fodder. He wanted to study her.'

The colourful monarchs, considered direct descendants of the *first* phoenix, were too dangerous to even attempt to capture. Yellow harrow phoenixes, with their oversized abdomens and gentle natures, weren't smart enough to train, for racing or research. Cape phoenixes, with their dark colouring and camouflaging abilities, could have been incredible racers – if they weren't too small to ride. Cinder phoenixes, blood phoenixes and spinel phoenixes were most commonly used and trained for CAPR – but of course Kel's grandfather hadn't wanted the most common. He'd wanted the most *cunning*.

Savita hadn't been purchased for racing, but for conservation. To study and monitor, so Kel's grandfather might learn – as so many tried – how to encourage phoenixes to breed outside of the forest. With phoenixes continuously captured for CAPR and killed on tracks, their population was dwindling. Kel used to dream of resurrecting his research, restoring his legacy.

'She's incredible,' Coup whispered, before throwing a pointed look at Kel. 'All your scowling, I'm surprised you haven't turned her feathers grey.'

'Do you know you're a dick?' Kel spat.

'Do you know you have the personality of sandpaper?'

Anger surged through Kel, and Sav swivelled towards her. The flickers along Savita's back turned to flames, curling overhead, as if reaching for Coup. Kel's muscles tensed.

'Stay at the paddock's edge or head back to the cottage,' Kel called to Dira and Bekn. 'We don't want her overwhelmed.'

Bekn grumbled. Coup interrupted the wordless protest with a slow, raised hand. 'I'll be fine, Bek. My new best friend isn't going to let anything happen to me.'

'Just don't trip on your own ego,' Kel muttered, keeping her face blank. She didn't want Sav to see how easily he rattled her. 'This is already dangerous enough without you falling over.'

Behind her, she heard Bekn and Dira traipsing back, towards Kel's cottage. Though Dira left without complaint, Kel knew she'd be watching from the windows.

'It'll be hard not to trip with you breathing down my neck,' Coup said.

Kel sucked in a long, deep breath and tugged on leather gloves over her bandages. She tried to breathe out the frustration tensing her muscles. If Savita sensed any reservations in her tamer, she'd grow even more anxious around Coup. And despite a near-overwhelming urge to shove Coup into Sav's fiery maw, Kel knew they both needed this to work.

Slowly, Kel shuffled towards Sav with a hand outstretched.

'Hey, Sav,' she crooned, 'try not to break *every* bone he has, okay?'

Sav leaned into Kel's hand, eyes still trained on Coup. She tilted her head and nuzzled at Kel with enough pressure to force Kel back a step. The phoenix inched forward, stepping between Kel and Coup. Her wings ruffled, stretching slightly, as if to shield Kel from the rider. A thunderous rumble echoed through Sav. Though her heart pounded, Kel fought back a laugh.

'She doesn't seem to believe we're friends.' Kel tapped a finger against her chin. 'I wonder why?'

Coup didn't respond. His features were unexpectedly taut, grave, just as they'd been last night. He lowered into a half-squat and edged closer to Savita, palms outstretched. His riding leathers hugged his broad shoulders and tense legs, far more sculpted than even a rider needed to be.

Kel cleared her throat. 'Make sure to keep your eyes on hers instead of the ground. Right – like that. Carnel phoenixes are smarter than spinels, but also more aggressive. They need to know that you're—'

'Not a threat, but also not prey,' Coup finished, under his breath. His movements were smooth, practised. 'She needs to know I'm not dinner, but that she can also trust me with her back turned. I get it, tamer. Stop micro-managing.'

Kel rolled her eyes as Coup inched closer, closer, already a hundred yards closer than Sav had let Oska – or any of the Howlers' previous riders – within their first month of meeting. Perhaps Kel should have been relieved; they could race a lot sooner than she'd anticipated. But Kel couldn't help the disappointment that snuck through her.

Couldn't Sav have injured Coup just a little?

Kel's jaw dropped as Coup approached Sav head-on, barely two feet from her beak. Still squatting, he slowly raised a single palm over his head. The sparks dancing along Sav's feathers calmed as she scrutinized Coup.

A minute passed in silence as rider and phoenix stared at each other. Kel held her breath. Palm still outstretched, held high, Coup lowered his gaze to the ground. A test.

Kel instinctively started forward. She reached towards Coup, unsure what she planned to do – intercept Coup and Sav, try to prevent the impending slaughter, despite how many times she'd yearned for it.

She looked up and saw Savita peering down at Coup's lowered head, his vulnerable posture. She blinked, slowly. Then she tucked her wings, folding red, yellow and orange feathers back on themselves, before releasing a high-pitched *squawk*.

'Your last tamer must've been thorough,' Kel said, unable to hide her disbelief. Though riders needed to understand basic phoenix nature, she hadn't expected *Coup* – who seemed to risk his phoenix's life as often as his own on the tracks – to display much competence.

Coup shrugged, still inching closer to Savita's side. 'He was rather useless, actually. I've just spent a lot of time in public aviaries.'

Curiosity hungered for Kel to ask *why* he'd been in public aviaries, but she didn't want to show unnecessary interest in Warren Coupers. Not even if her traitorous phoenix let him too close.

Sav remained focused on the rabbits burrowing beneath her. Shock – and more than a little annoyance – shot through Kel when Coup reached a hand up to Sav's neck.

The phoenix let out a low, cautioning grumble, but didn't move. Coup stayed statue-still, his gloved fingers spread against a cluster of raspberry-coloured feathers. Slowly he tilted his head towards Kel, a brow raised, as if to ask, *What were you worried about?*

Frustration hitched her breath. Somehow, he'd fooled Sav into letting him touch her on their very first encounter. It was sure to make the cocky bastard even cockier.

Kel placed her hands on her hips. 'Don't get cocky. Sav is probably just bored and eager for a new chew toy.'

Coup's lips parted into a maddening grin.

Before he could respond, a cheery voice called, 'The media was right! Looks like cosying up won't be so hard, after all.'

Kel scowled at Dira's distant, cackling figure.

At Kel's side, Sav fidgeted, raking her claws. In one swift motion, she launched at the place Coup's hand had been just a moment ago. If he hadn't moved, he likely would've lost a few fingers. Kel couldn't resist a smirk.

Coup's mouth twisted into a bitter line. 'Can you try suppressing that holier-than-thou attitude long enough to keep me alive?'

Kel's hands dug into her hips. 'Excuse me?'

Coup's head whipped towards Kel, as much movement as he'd risk beside Sav. 'You think *I* want to be spending my mornings listening to you rant about how you're too good for us? Risking my life every time Savita decides to mirror your body language?'

Hot anger filled Kel's veins, comforting in its familiarity. *Flames*, she *hated* Coup. 'You're the one who agreed to this. *You* drove to my farm and wanted *my* help approaching *my* phoenix. If we're going to work together, you need to do whatever I tell you to, whether or not you agree with it.'

As if to lend her own voice to Kel's threat, Savita let out a low growl. Thicker smoke rose from her feathers. Kel bit down on a laugh.

Coup lifted his chin. 'I'm here to win, Varra. Not be your lapdog.'

'At least a lapdog could follow basic instructions,' she retorted.

Coup rubbed his fingers over his furrowed brow. A moment later, he let out a long breath. 'Let's just try to go an hour without Sav burning me alive. *Then* I'll pledge my unwavering loyalty to you.'

Though Kel's anger burnt hotter, she relaxed her stance, wary of Sav picking up on any further body language. *Alchemists!* He knew how to push her buttons. 'If I tell you to do something mid-race, will you?'

'If it'll help us win, sure.'

If Kel had Sav's temperature, steam would've poured out of her nose. 'If *Bekn* asked you to do something, would you?'

Coup gave a surprising laugh. 'Probably not. My brother's great at a lot of things, but track strategy isn't one of them.'

She sucked in a deep breath and faced Savita. 'I doubt she'll let you on her back yet,' she said tersely. 'I'll just lead her through her usual warm-ups. We'll gauge her mood after that.'

Coup nodded silently, clearly biting back a retort. Kel tried her best to ignore him as she began coaxing Savita into her warm-ups; jumps, stretches, sprints, all before Kel guided her into the air with vocal commands and practised hand gestures.

Savita hopped in a small circle before stretching her wings wider.

Kel laughed as the phoenix loosed a joyful shriek and flapped her wings twice, three times. Kel bent her knees to brace against the instant winds as Savita launched into the air with another cry that sounded almost giddy, shooting straight into the clouds.

Savita's feathers turned to serpentine flames and her grumbles became eager, ear-splitting screams. Whether it was while she trained, raced, or simply swooped about the aviary, Savita always preferred to be airborne.

'How do you get her to follow commands while she's flying?' Coup's husky voice broke through her reverie. He was watching Savita, head tilted towards the clouds.

Kel leaned her arms to the right and Savita glided higher, at a slight angle. 'Trust. Practice. Bribery with her favourite meats. Years and years spent learning her moods and behaviour.' She shot him a look. 'Patience, which is something you probably don't know much about.'

Coup merely sighed.

Kel directed Sav higher, waving her arms about as if guiding an airship. Savita glided and pivoted through the clouds. A trail of smoke carved patterns into the sky; a figure-eight, a spiral, and then more complex movements like angled downfalls and dual talon attacks. Sav dove between tall fence posts and swooped beneath overhanging nets, weaving between the contraptions littering the paddock.

After twenty minutes, when Dira's impatience to begin training became unbearably vocal, Kel instructed Sav to land.

Dira stepped forward and lifted her hands, as if looking at the track through a camera lens. 'We should start with a simulation without anyone on her back. Let's move all the fence posts together and lower the nets. Savita was faster than the other phoenixes in yesterday's race, but she lost focus when they drifted near her. I want Sav to be comfortable the next time she has to weave through narrow tracks.'

Following Dira's instructions, they reorganized the makeshift track. By the time Dira was satisfied, Kel, Coup and Bekn were gleaming with sweat.

'You've got a pretty impressive set-up out here,' Bekn remarked.

Dira brushed dust off her hands. 'We're just missing a sancter rifle. *Then* we could really make a mark on CAPR.'

Kel threw Dira a dry look. 'In your dreams. The only mark a sancter rifle would be making is all over my farm.'

Sancter rifles were one of the few handheld weapons found on Cendor. The sleek rifles shot brilliant, electric pulses; an amplified version of what controlled phoenixes through their collars. They cost a fortune to buy. Most were used to start CAPR races or venture into Vohre Forest to capture phoenixes; they were far too dangerous to turn on people. The weapon's torrential electricity would likely tear through flesh and nerves as easily as lightning through the sky.

Kel found it amusing that – for an island that claimed to be a tech hub – it had developed little in the way of human firearms. Mostly because the council's attention was instead focused on ways to control phoenixes – the greater danger to the island.

Dira threw Kel a wry grin before stepping back with Bekn, leaving Coup and Kel to tie the saddle girth around Savita's belly. Surprisingly cooperative at Coup's nearness, Sav nuzzled her beak against Kel's cheek, staying otherwise still. Once the saddle was in place, Kel led the phoenix to the makeshift starting line and stepped back.

Savita exploded into the air upon Dira's verbal command. She launched through the sky, weaving between flag poles and swerving below the black netting.

Bekn still observed from a distance, fingers flitting about on his tele-comm at an inhuman speed. While Coup watched on from a few metres away, Dira asked, 'How long do you think it'll take Sav to let Coup on her back?'

Before Kel could reply, her small tablet blared from her pocket. She whipped it out and opened the app linked to Savita's collar, monitoring her vitals. The alarm silenced as she clicked on a notification and was greeted with great, red letters across her screen:

TEMPERATURE ABOVE NORM.
HEART RATE ABOVE NORM.
IRREGULAR BREATHING PATTERNS DETECTED.
CALM YOUR PHOENIX IMMEDIATELY, OR REMOVE
YOURSELF FROM THEIR VICINITY.

Kel's heart drummed in her ears. Though the roaring wind muffled her voice, she screamed for Sav to land.

Seconds passed before Savita glanced down at Kel. Her wings slowed until she hovered in place. She released a low grumble, and reluctantly raced towards the ground like a falling star.

Kel's eyes widened as her phoenix neared. It had been impossible to spot from such a distance, but now Kel could see that Savita's feathers weren't stirring mere colours into the air – she had become *flame*.

Soft, fiery tendrils often decorated Savita while racing, but they rarely climbed so high. Now, they shrouded Savita in a lethal dance of red and orange.

Kel hurried over to Savita. The phoenix felt surprisingly cool.

'You okay?' Kel breathed, searching her phoenix's body for any hints of distress. Savita seemed entirely at ease. Though she was still covered in flames, there was no raised temperature or rapid breathing. Kel frowned, glancing back at the tablet. The alarming notifications had already cleared and Savita's vitals were back to normal.

'What happened?' Dira panted, rushing to Kel's side.

Kel wrung her gloved hands. 'I'm not sure. Her vitals were spiking.' She ran her hands over Savita's side. 'But she seems fine, now . . . ?'

The fire wreathing Savita's body was calming into soft waves, lapping against her feathers.

'Let's keep practising,' Coup said, a few feet back. 'She's probably just a little tense from yesterday's race, and she's still getting used to Bekn and me.'

Dira nodded. Kel bit the inside of her cheek, staying silent, though she made a note to check Savita's vitals more often. Uncontrolled flames often heralded a rebirth, but Savita was barely half a century old. Immortal creatures, phoenixes usually rebirthed every century, returning to hatchlings and retaining their memories. Still – there were plenty of phoenixes that defied the norm.

Rebirths were chronically destructive. They increased a phoenix's temperature to roughly a thousand degrees, melting all but the sturdiest of metals within a hundred metres. Everything around Sav would turn to ash – and not the regenerating kind.

'Let's pause this trial-run there,' Bekn panted, appearing at Kel's back. He glanced warily at Sav, who narrowed her eyes, and he shuffled back a step. 'Coup, Kelyn – you might want to see this.'

He handed over her and Coup's tele-comms. Kel's brows shot up. 'When did you grab those?'

Bekn shrugged. 'While you two were trying to out-snark each other, I decided to be a productive member of this team.'

Kel huffed and grabbed her tele-comm. When the screen lit up, her jaw fell open.

Dozens of messages littered the screen. Missed calls from

unknown numbers, texts from other CAPR crews' mitigators, emails from local news stations.

She glanced over at Coup's screen – bombarded with similar messages.

'What the hell?' he muttered.

Distractedly, Kel lured Savita back to the aviary with dried treats and then hurried with the others back through the paddock's trampled grass. The four of them neared the side entrance to Kel's cottage, making it a few steps away before freezing mid-stride.

Kel's entire front lawn was packed with vans and cameras set up on monstrous tripods. People with voice-comms huddled at her front door.

'Alchemists help me,' she whispered.

Chapter Seven

'And what made you think you were qualified to take on an untamed phoenix?'

Kel's nails bit into her palms. 'That phoenix was just confused. If it was untamed, the town would have burnt to a crisp.'

She heard Bekn cough behind her. A warning.

Kel and Coup had quickly been ambushed by camera crews. Before either one could utter a word, Bekn had swept them into the house.

Bekn waggled three fingers. 'Three rules, and then you both need to charm the pants off those reporters.'

The mitigator spoke to both of them, but his feverish eyes never left Kel. 'Don't insult anyone. Don't boast about what happened at The Ferret. It was a tragedy and nothing more. And for the love of the Alchemists, don't let them paint you as children. If they try, end the interview.'

Kel folded her arms. 'Why would we talk to them in the first place?'

Bekn raised an incredulous brow. 'Because while yesterday *was* a tragedy, something good can come out of this media coverage. *Sponsorship.*'

'Got it,' Kel grumbled. The words tasted bitter, but if Bekn could find her money for the farm, she'd endure potential sponsors' scrutiny.

Bekn nodded. 'One more thing. You saw how well the media responded to you two working together. Lean into that angle. Pose for photos, compliment each other, do whatever you can to sell the cosy teammates story. They'll eat it up.'

'*Cosy teammates?*' Coup laughed before Kel could voice her rage. 'You want us to tell them we're hopelessly in love while we're at it?'

Kel's cheeks heated. Publicity was one thing, but she didn't have a bone in her body capable of feigning affection for Warren Coupers. She was glad to hear he felt the same.

Bekn paused – as if *actually* considering the idea – before shaking his head. 'Of course not. Just flatter each other and let the reporters fill in the gaps.'

Kel rubbed her face with her bandaged hands, the pain of last night's burns helping to clear her mind. They'd hardly merged teams twelve hours ago, and she was already tired of Bekn's demands. Dira, at least, seemed amused by them.

In a softer tone, Bekn added, 'If they see us all getting along, it'll add a bit of credibility to the Howlers. Especially after all of us have seen some . . . fluctuation in our teams' members lately.'

Ice pricked Kel's arms. Oska's face flashed through her mind, followed by Rube's. 'I can manage a couple of photos together, but that's it.'

'Five photos,' Bekn countered. 'And three compliments with at least six adjectives.'

Kel narrowed her eyes. 'Three photos. One compliment. And only if a reporter prompts it. No adjectives.'

Bekn beamed. 'Deal.'

Coup straightened his jacket and turned to Kel. 'Ready to act head-over-heels?'

'You could try loving this a little less,' she muttered.

Coup merely winked.

Bekn hurriedly led Coup and Kel back outside, where they surrendered to the cameras, pushed and pulled like waves in a rip.

As the sun idled behind hazy clouds and Kel began craving more painkillers for her hands, she found herself standing opposite a slick-haired woman – Dana from Channel Two, she'd introduced herself as – with a conspiratorial grin.

'Not many people would be brave enough – or possess the knowledge – to do what you and Warren Coupers did. But it seems like you two knew how to work together.' Dana lowered her voice. 'Sources tell me the two of you might be teaming up for future CAPR races. Is this true?'

Kel balled her fists. How had Bekn already managed to leak their new team status? Before she could reply, a warm, lean arm draped around Kel's shoulders. From Kel's right, two rows of pearly teeth flashed in the reporter's direction, amber eyes sparkling into the camera.

Coup leaned into Kel's side. It was the first time she'd been close enough to learn he smelt like riding leathers and mint aftershave.

'Absolutely,' Coup crooned. 'I can't wait to get out on a track and see what kinds of madness we can brew up.'

Kel's nails dug into her palms, focusing on anything but Coup's nearness, his camera-ready dimples, as she said, 'We've got to test the waters first with my phoenix, make sure everyone is comfortable. But unless Savita slices him in half, it seems like we'll be working together.'

Kel had meant it as a joke – mostly – but alarm flashed across the reporter's face. 'I see. And how're you feeling about working so closely with *Coup*?' Her voice softened around Coup's nickname, as if it was a secret they shared. 'He certainly has a unique racing style.'

Kel bit the inside of her cheek. 'It'll be . . . great. There's a lot *Warren* and I can teach each other.'

That counts as a compliment, right?

'Expect plenty of excitement in the Crimson Howlers' future,'

Coup added. 'You have no idea what we have in store.'

Dana let out a chime-like laugh. 'I love it. Can we take a couple of pictures of the two of you?'

Kel blinked. She stepped to move away from Coup's touch. Softly, he squeezed her shoulder.

'Three photos,' he whispered. 'Remember?'

Slowly, she smiled.

'Perfect,' the reporter crooned, as a secondary camera flashed. Ivory spots danced in Kel's vision.

'Can we grab another with you two standing a little closer?' Dana asked.

Slowly, Kel leaned into Coup's side and moved her arm around his waist, trying to touch him as little as possible. Her skin prickled, her focus acutely on every place they were pressed together. Warmth rolled off him in easy waves, and heat crept up her neck.

Once Dana had taken *three* photos – Bekn hadn't clarified if the photos had to be from different reporters – Kel fled the interview, recoiling from Coup like a snake before an open flame.

She barely made it three steps before the next reporter assaulted her with similar questions, and she hated that it became harder to answer without Coup's distracting presence.

'I suppose you could call yesterday the beginning of your relationship with Warren Coupers,' the man – Levi, from Channel Four – said, leaning closer to Kel. 'How are you feeling about what happened?'

Kel thought of Bekn's words, and recited, 'Yesterday was a tragedy. I'm sure any other tamer would have done the same.'

She wanted to scream that none of this was the phoenix's fault, and other members of the Fume should meet the same fate as yesterday's cultist.

'You're too modest, sweetheart. It was an impressive feat for a girl so young. How old are you?'

Kel grimaced – *sweetheart?* – as alarm bells rang through her head. 'Seventeen.'

The reporter faked a look of astonishment. He glanced at the camera, then back to Kel. 'Only seventeen! *Very* impressive.'

Kel didn't respond. Levi's brows raised, though he quickly pivoted. 'Last night, you and *Coup* didn't hesitate to recollar the rogue phoenix. I know your late father was quite a vocal advocate of phoenix collars with severely reduced controls. Do you agree with your father's stance?'

Kel's stomach roiled. If she'd remembered breakfast, she might have hurled it up on camera.

Her father had been a strong believer in phoenix rights, drawing just as much ire as praise, and more than a few bitter comparisons to the Fume. He'd even once revealed a naive dream of opening a sanctuary that allowed phoenixes to roam entirely uncollared. She winced at the memory. *That* statement had gotten her dad in some boiling water with the media.

Kel cleared her throat. 'I think there are experts much more qualified than I am to debate that issue.'

The words were mostly scripted, scraped together from hours spent standing beside her father for cameras. Ever since Landon Ryker, the first ever phoenix rider, collars had always existed. At first the Alchemists had created them as a way to monitor phoenix vitals, to learn from the fiery creatures. Over time, the electronic devices had shifted to a form of control.

It's in the phoenixes' best interest, her school textbooks had written, *like giving vaccines to prevent disease, or trimming animal tusks to deter poachers.*

Kel stiffened. Though she agreed that collaring phoenixes

was necessary, she did wonder if there were other, fairer ways of maintaining Cendor's safety.

Levi squinted and nodded. 'Mmhmm. Of course. Well, we're all lucky you and Coup were there to prevent any other incidents. Do you think your father is looking down, proud of your actions?'

Kel's mouth dried. She tried to never think of where exactly her father was, if he was anywhere. If his ghost watched her and bowed his head in shame for her competing in CAPR races. If he would be proud of her for doing what it took to care for Savita. If he would—

A familiar touch fell around Kel's shoulders, hitching her balance. Dira appeared to her right, tilting her head towards the reporter.

'I'm sure if Leon Varra is anywhere, he's too busy negotiating more cloud space for celestial phoenixes,' Dira quipped.

Kel wrapped her arm around Dira's waist and gave her a thankful squeeze.

Levi gave a practised chuckle. 'Of course.'

As they broke away from the reporter, Kel spotted a break in the throng and beelined for her cottage.

'Bekn will kill you for that,' Kel muttered to Dira.

Dira shrugged. 'Let him try. I'm not the one the media's trying to pick clean.'

Kel glanced over her shoulder where Coup shone at the centre of the media frenzy. He answered every question with such pitch-perfect charisma. She'd always struggled in front of cameras, never sure how to stand, how to speak. Yet Coup was like marble under the sun: warm, unyielding, effortless.

There were plenty of other, more rational reasons to want him off her team. But she couldn't help the bitter envy that slithered through her as she listened to his honeyed words.

'I don't know if I can do this,' Kel mumbled as they moved, weaving between reporters. 'Working with him long enough to earn the money we need is going to be . . .'

'A well-lit nightmare?' Dira offered. She sighed softly. 'At least the media is eating it up. You're a match made in PR heaven.'

Kel snorted. They were a *match* that would be paired together far too often. Tamers and riders worked so closely. Every training session, every moment spent familiarizing Savita and Coup would be side by side. Her patience was too fragile to tolerate that kind of constant, charming, needling presence.

Dira glanced back. 'Let's go hide in the cottage for a while. We'll figure it out.'

Kel nodded, eager for the quiet. Once inside, she'd simply convince Dira, explain that they were better off finding a new rider *now*, rather than in a few weeks, once Dira also realized that Coup was just a cocky, reckless pile of—

'Miss Varra, may I have a word?'

Kel and Dira turned towards the voice to find a tall, dark-haired man in his forties blocking the sun. Though Fieror was a bustling city, here on its outskirts, on her farm, the man's tailored suit and slicked hair were as out of place as a Dresvan serpent.

'I've had my fill of interviews. I'm trading the cameras for some lunch,' Kel said, thrusting a thumb towards her home. She was proud of herself for replying with more than a simple '*No*', and planned on telling Bekn as much.

The man laughed, the sound too crisp, controlled. 'You misunderstand. I don't wish to interview you.'

'Oh.' She was suddenly exhausted. 'What do you want?'

The man's gaze flickered between her and Dira, lips pursed.

Kel squeezed Dira's arm. 'Go save yourself. I'll meet you inside.'

Dira frowned, but moved towards the cottage's entrance. Kel turned back towards the man, folding her arms.

He reached into his jacket pocket and pulled out a card. He didn't seem bothered by her abruptness, which made Kel, hot and hungry, merely want to try harder.

'My name is Romar Harte. I work in the recruitment sector of Cristo Industries, and I have a proposition for you.'

Chapter Eight

———— ✳ ————

Romar lifted his chin. 'Mr Cristo has had you and Warren Coupers on his radar for months, but after yesterday's events he thought we should bump up our recruitment schedule before another sponsor steals you away.'

Bile filled Kel's mouth.

Cristo Industries. He worked for *Cristo Industries*.

The empire that manufactured almost all tech used by CAPR crews, built to operate alongside Salta's magic. Almost all tech used across the entire island. Across *all* of Salta's islands.

And Canen Cristo wanted to recruit *her*.

She ignored the card Romar offered. 'You want to *sponsor* my team?'

'Yes, but not in the way of traditional sponsors. We don't want to simply fund your CAPR endeavours – we want to invest in your future.' His smile grew. 'But we're looking to sponsor yourself and Mr Coupers, not the Howlers. We've seen how well the pair of you work together, and how taken the media seems to be by your . . . friendship. We'd like you two to continue your partnership under Mr Cristo's guidance, without your teammates.'

She straightened. 'I'm not interested. Not in being separated from the others in my team, or working for a corporation that plans on caging Cendor's entire phoenix population.'

The man's brow rose until it crinkled his forehead. 'Miss Varra, Cristo Industries hopes to protect and expand phoenix numbers. Not eradicate them.'

'Don't you sell your tech to the Cendorian Defence Force, who's trying to clear Vohre Forest?' Kel's voice rose, but she couldn't – didn't want to – stop. She'd attended enough rallies with Dira, seen enough Vohre protests on the news, learnt too much from her father.

Leon Varra had died because of the council's efforts to purge the forest. They'd begun cutting down outer acres they thought were vacant, and when a small dawn of phoenixes were discovered amidst the rolling machinery, and one had been injured, Kel's father had been the first they'd called for aid. It hadn't been the phoenix's fault – injured, scared, separated from its dawn – but her father's death had been the match they'd used to justify emptying more and more of the forest. To find and collar phoenixes, and then sell them to the highest bidder.

The man's brow rose to inhuman heights. 'While that may be one strategy that the Cendorian Council is considering, I can assure you Canen Cristo vehemently opposes it. Since they rarely breed in captivity, we hope to preserve wild phoenix numbers.'

'Then why ally with the council at all?'

Romar's lip twitched again. 'Because, unfortunately, even the best intentions need financing.'

Kel's anger faltered, hitting an unfair, logical wall. She didn't agree with many CAPR practices, but the races gave Savita a chance to spread her wings and burn off energy, and offered Kel the means to survive. If she argued, she'd be a hypocrite.

The kind of money that came with a Cristo job wouldn't just save her farm. It could shift her dream of opening a sanctuary into reality. Sav could retire from the dangers of racing.

Romar went on, 'The facilities we'd like you to work at also operate as our chief research centre. We want to recruit young minds who aren't simply interested in becoming famous racers

– but who are eager to learn about phoenix habitats, biology and magic. That's why, after seeing how you and Warren dealt with that phoenix yesterday, we knew you'd be perfect for this programme. Though you'll be expected to keep racing, we also want you to be directly involved in our conservation research.'

His words were too smooth – too perfect. 'The facility is in Vohre?'

Romar nodded. 'Yes, accepting our offer would require you and your phoenix to relocate, but we have on-site accommodation available and we already have replacements for your current teammates lined up.'

Maybe Kel shouldn't have hated Canen Cristo simply because her father had. She trusted her father's ghost more than this man – but her heart pounded, screaming for a way to save her farm. To save Savita.

She opened her mouth – unsure what would come out – when she heard her cottage's front door creak shut. She inched back a small step.

'I can't,' Kel managed. 'Not if you won't take my entire team.'

A soft frown creased Romar's forehead. 'Take tonight to think on my offer. I don't want you to make a decision you'd regret.'

Frustration flared through her. At him, at her own temptation, at what might happen to Savita if she didn't find money *soon*.

She lifted her chin. 'I'm not leaving my team. Not to work for a company that would rather—'

'She means to say, *no thank you*,' a familiar voice said at her back. *Coup*.

'I mean exactly what I said,' she said, to both of them.

As she turned her back to the pair and moved towards her home, she added, 'Have a pleasant evening.'

Romar cleared his throat at her back. Coup jogged to her side.

'*Ashes*, Varra,' he cursed. 'A cardboard cut-out would have better media training than you.'

'Don't speak for me,' she sneered.

'Forgive me for trying to stop you from biting that man's head off,' he retorted, equally venomous.

The idea didn't disturb her the way it probably should have. Kel leaned towards Coup and whispered, 'Did you hear what the recruiter said? He wanted you, too.'

Coup stiffened. 'I know. Another one of them pulled me from the crowd a few minutes ago.'

'What did you say?'

Coup was silent as they walked through the door. Eventually, he shook his head, chestnut locks falling over his forehead. 'I couldn't leave without Bekn.'

She glanced up at him. She'd mostly thought the brothers' closeness consisted of Bekn watching over Coup. Seeing the severity in his eyes, hearing the loyalty deepening his voice, almost made her glimpse in him what the media saw. *Almost.*

There were plenty of reasons not to work for Cristo – most of which she'd shouted in the recruiter's face – but the biggest one was currently devouring bread in her kitchen like a starving wolf. While Kel still had no clue how to stave off the bank collectors that were sure to appear on her doorstep any day now, she couldn't leave Fieror without Dira.

When Kel didn't reply, Coup added, voice sharp, 'We're no different, Varra. *You're* no different than the rest of CAPR. Just because I'm better at the parts you hate doesn't mean that I'm not just as desperate to make this damn team work as you are.'

Kel forced in short, shallow breaths as they moved through the cottage. Dira hunched over the kitchen bench, salivating at the sandwiches she had piled on a plate. Bekn was nowhere to be seen, probably still outside, prolonging the camera frenzy for as long as possible.

Coup followed Kel into the kitchen. Before shutting the door, Kel muttered, 'You wanted to accept the offer, too. Admit it.'

Even if it meant working closer with Coup – it was safety. Certainty. It was *Savita*.

Coup shook his head. 'Of course I did. But I'm not the one branding myself as some sanctimonious phoenix rights advocate until a better offer comes along.'

Shock thickened Kel's throat. Coup was silent as he perched on a bench stool opposite Dira, a lazy smile plastered across his face, with no hint of frustration. Dira grumbled as Coup plucked half a sandwich from her plate, then turned to Kel.

'What did that guy want?' Dira mumbled, around a mouthful of bread.

Kel's mind rattled for the right words. When she explained what the recruiter had offered – what she'd rejected – Dira's expression hardened.

'He just wanted you two?' Dira asked, voice sharp.

'Only because of yesterday's attention,' Kel said. Dira was the best winger Kel knew – that was clear by the amount of recruitment offers she batted away from other teams.

'You want to say yes,' Dira said softly, lowering her sandwich to the plate.

Kel shook her head. 'No. Yes? I don't know, Dira. He's not offering half-arsed sponsorship – it's a job. Maybe we could convince him to take the entire team, and—'

'And if you couldn't? Would you go?' Dira snapped, hard lines around her eyes.

Kel perched at Dira's side. 'Of course not.'

Dira didn't reply, her focus returning to the plate of food before her. Coup remained silent, and for the first time she wished he wouldn't. Though the three of them filled the cottage with chewing and hungry groans, Kel's mind filled with a different kind of noise. Not the reporters' questions or the recruiter's silky offer. Just three words that chafed against her skin like sandpaper.

We're no different.

Chapter Nine

※

That night, Kel couldn't sleep.

She picked at the mattress's tattered sheets and stared at the office's ceiling, fantasizing about convincing Dira to abandon the Coupers brothers. She tried to conjure impossible ways to pay the money she owed. She imagined what her father would have said to Cristo's recruiter.

She thought of those damn words.

We're no different.

She knew that couldn't be true. She didn't participate in CAPR for the thrill of racing or for the isle's attention. Even though she knew there were plenty of CAPR practices that, though technically legal, did nothing for the phoenixes' wellbeing, she and Dira had no choice.

Crumbling dreams and fragmented memories rattled through Kel's skull; Oska's screams and Rube's farewell. Those three words echoed in her ears the entire time.

Her whirling thoughts kept her from noticing the different timbre of Savita's squawks until it was too late. Until she felt the heat creeping under the office's door, and finally recognized the dark tint to the air.

Smoke.

Kel bolted upright and threw the blanket to the floor. The office was bathed in orange, and heat, and Savita's screams – Kel had never heard this kind of noise before.

Savita was afraid.

She couldn't see her phoenix through the window. There were only growing flames, shrouding every tree in the aviary.

Her home was burning. Not from phoenix fire or even a rebirth. This fire was entirely mundane, and far more monstrous.

Chapter Ten

---❋---

Kel stumbled out of the aviary's entrance. Smoke filled her lungs and her throat ached as she coughed. Savita swooped low over Kel's head, out the doors and into a nearby paddock. Safe. Kel didn't feel her hair singeing or the heat at her back or the glowing holes in her clothes. She only felt the fear that must have coursed through Savita when her phoenix realized she was trapped in her own home.

Phoenixes were immortal. Old age would never harm them. But in every other way that mortal creatures could be killed, they were vulnerable. Though Savita was a creature of fire and magic, impervious to phoenix fires, a mundane fire would hurt her just as it would hurt Kel.

Savita is fine, Kel told herself, hacking up more smoke and trying to slow her pulse. *She's safe.*

But her home . . .

More coughs spluttered from Kel's lungs. To the right of the gates was a panel with controls to the aviary. She might not be able to salvage everything – but maybe the sprinklers along the aviary's roof could still help.

Limbs heavy, Kel punched in the code to access the controls. A small screen above the keypad should have lit up green – but nothing changed. Kel typed in the code again.

Nothing.

She rubbed her eyes, trying to clear her vision. The heat crept up to the closed gates. She wouldn't have long before the fire consumed the entire aviary.

Kel tried the code a third time, and she let out a choked sob as her vision cleared.

The glass panel looked like a shattered mirror, pixels fracturing and scattering, a neon kaleidoscope that had needed updating a decade ago. Just like the aviary's electrical wiring. Just like *everything*.

At the top of the screen, barely legible, was a glowing word:

ERROR.

Another sob broke through her dry throat. She had nothing with her – nothing that could save the building. There were rows of enormous fire extinguishers beside her walk-in freezer, but that was across the far side of the aviary.

There was no way to call for help; she'd left her tele-comm inside the office. She couldn't ride Savita to find help without leathers – she'd burn to a crisp.

A loud *boom* echoed through the aviary, followed by an orange flash. Kel pressed her hands against the glass to see better – before jerking away in pain. The panel wouldn't shatter or melt, but it was already too hot to touch.

I don't know what to do. I don't know what to do. I don't know what—

When Kel finally saw the council's red-and-gold lights soar through the stars, for a moment, she thought everything would be all right. Help was coming. Part of her yearned for someone's – anyone's – arms to bury herself in. She couldn't remember the last time she'd let herself unravel.

That luxury had died two years ago, with her father.

When the council officers arrived and told her that the aviary was beyond help, that too many electrical faults had tripped at the same time, she shoved the ghost of that spark back inside its tomb.

A stream of vehicles pulled up beside the aviary and attempted to soothe the fire. The inferno refused to die down, but it also didn't retaliate, staying inside the aviary's glass confines. All anyone could do was ensure the blaze ran a careful course.

Kel had retreated to a hill nearby, wrapping her arms around her bare knees and watching the destruction unfold. Savita bristled and clicked her beak, sitting against Kel's back, as warm as the fire below. Her nearness was as much comfort as she could provide with the destruction wrought beneath them.

Kel let the shadows swallow her.

This was her fault.

She'd *known* how badly the aviary needed upgrades. But she didn't have the money to pay for repairs. It had simply taken one malfunction for the fire to ignite the rest, a molten domino effect.

'*Kelyn!*'

The scream echoed up from the aviary. Kel saw a clunky, grey auto-engine skid across a patch of grass beside the other vehicles. The doors flung open and two tall, familiar heads emerged.

From somewhere above her body, Kel watched the two boys take in the scene with slack jaws. An officer pointed towards her hill. Bekn remained still, waving his arms towards the aviary and speaking in unclear shouts.

Savita rustled her wings and shrieked as Coup approached, though she quietened once his face became clear. In just a few long strides, Coup stood before Kel's hunched figure.

It was the first time she'd ever seen him without his riding leathers, wearing instead tracksuit bottoms and a grey tee. From her perch, Coup's silhouette eclipsed the stars, cutting across the sky like a dark blade.

'Are you . . .' He cleared his throat. 'Are you hurt?'

Kel tried to shake her head, to tell him to leave. But she'd let the cold air sink beneath her skin. She'd refused the blanket a medic had offered her. Why should she accept comfort when Savita had none?

'We saw the fire and called the council emergency line. How – what happened?' Coup pressed.

The words bit at Kel, like little teeth gnawing on her frozen bones. 'Go home, Coup. There's nothing you can do.'

A minute passed before Coup crouched on the ground beside her.

'You should go home,' Kel repeated, her throat thick. 'We can't do anything but wait.'

More silence, as they sat and watched the flames slowly cocoon and turn to smoke. She wished he would just leave her alone, but she didn't have the energy to argue.

She wasn't sure how long had passed when Coup spoke again, his voice crackling with sleep. 'I met your dad, once. I'd seen him around Fieror before, but I'd never spoken to him. He came to a public aviary in the city centre to perform a quality check. I was just mucking out the grounds. He spotted me, ignored the fawning council attendees, and asked me if I thought the phoenixes' basic needs were being met.'

Surprise flickered through Kel's exhaustion, hot and cold.

Softly, she asked, 'What did you say?'

Coup smiled. 'I told him they treated the phoenixes like AB-infested rodents. They had no idea about different species' needs or diets or social behaviours.'

'And *you* did?'

Coup shrugged. 'The next day, *Nova Press* published his scathing review of the aviary. The day after that, the Cendorian Council issued them a warning. They had two months to up their standards, or they'd relocate the phoenixes to other aviaries and lose their very generous funding.'

Something glimmered in Kel's memory, as faint as the stars

overhead. 'I remember that. Dad came home from the inspection absolutely *fuming*.'

She'd stayed up late that night, drawing in her sketchpad while he'd typed up his livid thoughts.

Kel's tired cheeks twitched.

Bekn eventually joined them on the hill, as near as Savita would allow him. The three said nothing, and though Kel *hated* that she needed help from anyone, let alone the *Coupers brothers*, the solace of their presence draped around her like a blanket. Even if only for the next minute, the next hour, Kel wasn't alone. Savita was at her back and their nearness kept her mind from wading too deeply into static and smoke. Her chest heaved with heavy sobs and her stomach roiled with nausea. Something far deeper than tears escaped her, leaching into the night and easing her shoulders. It stole some of her fear.

As they sat upon that dark hill, watching the pyre dull to an endless grey, Kel thought she glimpsed what Savita's eternity might look like.

Chapter Eleven

———✣———

Kel pulled Savita's harness reins taut and squeezed her buckled legs. In one long, violent movement, Savita launched into the night sky. A small, flaming hurricane encircled them, sending them upwards until Sav levelled out and screeched in joy. Sharp, cold air bit into Kel's skin and the world shrank, a muted patchwork of darkening paddocks and city lights. Kel's breath caught in her throat. A familiar brew of fear and awe thumped through her and she let her mind go blank, worries drifting below them.

Her peace was short-lived, though. Sitting behind her, Coup was forced to awkwardly wrap his arms around Kel's waist for support.

'Can you move forward? I'm half off the saddle,' Coup called, voice strained against the rising winds.

Reluctantly, she inched forward. 'You're lucky I don't shove you off.'

Coup scoffed. 'If I fall, you'd have no one to complain about. You wouldn't survive.'

Kel ground her teeth as Coup fumbled for balance, legs fastened with the saddle's rarely used secondary buckles, much too close for her liking. Savita tilted to the right, curving to follow the property's borders. Her collar restrictions allowed her to soar as high as she'd like, so long as she remained within the outer fence lines of Kel's home. *Their* home. For as much longer as they could call it that.

Kel's tears had dried last night, after Bekn and Coup eventually left and Dira had appeared to swathe her in too many blankets. She'd spent the day fussing over Savita, muttering lies and reassurances about their future.

The officers had told her that outdated wiring and overloaded circuits had caused the fire. The aviary and her adjoining office had been reduced to a lifeless skeleton, dark ash and blackened rubble heaped over the ground in scorched clumps.

She wondered if Savita's rebirth would look the same. If it would leave Kel with nothing but black dust and the ghosts of her favourite memories.

Savita twisted again and Kel moved with her. Without thinking, she pulled Sav's reins back, her right elbow colliding with Coup's stomach.

'*Alchemists!* That was intentional,' he grunted, breathless.

She almost wished it had been. Against the chilling gale, she shouted, 'Can you just shut up, if you have to be here? I wanted to fly to clear my head. Not fill it with your whining.'

She hadn't lost Savita's saddle or her own riding leathers to the fire; Kel had left both in her cottage, planning to take the former into Fieror for a technician-for-hire to look at. When the stars had begun to twinkle behind the dusk, Kel had realized just how long it had been since she'd flown Savita at night. She didn't want to waste the chance – not when it might be her last.

Unfortunately, Coup had been equally keen for his *first* ride atop Sav.

'I can't believe you forced your way up here,' Kel murmured. Sav had remained traitorously nonchalant as Coup had approached. He'd made it clear that, unless Kel instructed Sav to slice through his hamstrings, nothing could stop him from joining them.

She'd been tempted to try and call his bluff; let Sav cut through a few muscles. But she needed him – and the money his riding could bring – now more than ever.

Coup huffed. 'You think I'd waste an opportunity to get comfortable on my new phoenix?'

'Your *what*?' she spat. 'You remember that Savita's home burnt down, right? There's plenty of more important things she'll have to get comfortable with soon.'

The words made her wince, her heart clanging in her throat.

'I am aware, Varra. But even if the band has to break up, it'll be a while before I can find another team.' He jostled at her back, lifting his head. 'It's such a clear night.'

The wonder in his voice made her swallow her retort. The sky darkened around them and Savita's wings lit up the muggy night. Their outline branded the air like handheld fireworks, tracing red lines around grey clouds.

Coup's whining continued, though if Kel focused hard enough on the gale in her ears, she could block most of it out. She watched the arcing patterns of Savita's glowing wings, waves cresting and falling, as clouds sifted around her wings like sea-foam. She tried to focus on the star-studded night and rhythmic grace of Sav's wings. She tried to focus on *anything* but the feel of Coup, tense behind her, seeping heat into her back, an infuriating contrast to the evening air.

Every minor shift of his weight made her squirm. She hated how aware she was of his every move – how his warm breath sent goosebumps pricking at the back of her neck, how much his body affected hers.

Both of them leaned forward as Savita rose higher through the charcoal clouds. Kel closed her eyes and tried to ignore the feel of Coup pressing closer, muscled torso tight against her back, fingers momentarily clamping on her hips.

As they finally broke above the frail clouds, Kel opened her eyes. The night stretched before them in streaks of shadow and starlight.

Savita plateaued and stretched her wings wider, glimmering with sunlit magic. Kel wondered if, from the ground, they looked like a shooting star. Maybe Cendorians would wish upon Savita. Maybe Kel could collect those wishes, like coins in a fountain, and steal them for herself.

Coup loosened his grip and leaned back in the saddle. Kel sucked in a breath as the cool air replaced his heat at her back. She relaxed her hold on Savita's reins and splayed her gloved fingers across her phoenix's neck feathers. She'd spent years wondering what Sav's feathers would feel like without gloves. Sunlit silk? Thorned fire? She ducked her gaze, memorizing the pattern of Sav's feathers, the colliding colours. Memorizing *everything*.

'If you could escape up here – just keep flying . . . would you?' Coup asked softly, breaking her reverie.

Her eyebrows arched. 'That's a very existential departure from whining.'

Coup leaned forward again, until his warm breath hit her ear and made her shiver. 'Indulge me, then I'll shut up.'

'You promise?' Kel huffed. 'Escape what, exactly?'

'Everything.'

Kel pursed her lips.

'There's nowhere else I'd rather be,' she admitted. Even if there was somewhere she could go where her debts wouldn't chase her, Cendor – in all its fiery, raging glory – was her home.

Curiosity pricked through her. 'Where would you go?'

She felt Coup shrug. 'Somewhere without sketchy public aviaries and undiagnosable diseases. Somewhere Bekn could . . . somewhere he'd be happy.' Coup chuckled, a strange, hoarse sound, so different to his usual ease.

Kel chewed on his words. She'd known his mother had died of AB years ago. Though that might not stop her from hating him, she understood a small piece of his past. They both had scars that refused to heal.

She felt Coup shake his head, as if catching himself. 'I'm not surprised you'd stay. Misery loves company.'

Clenching Sav's reins, her knuckles turned white. '*Misery* should've let Sav slash a few of your muscles,' she muttered.

Coup gave a breathless chuckle. In her peripherals, she spotted him run a gloved hand along Savita's side. 'All this power, and you're still the scariest thing in the sky.'

Good, she thought, and sent up a silent thanks to the Alchemists when Coup remained silent. She let her mind drift, as the frigid wind and high altitude built pressure in her ears. She tugged and loosened Savita's reins as they glided in endless loops around the property's parameters. Savita responded intuitively to Kel's guiding, and it loosened something inside her. No matter who raced Sav in CAPR, they would always belong to each other.

Flying on Savita had always been the only kind of escape she'd craved. But that too would soon be ripped away if she didn't find a new solution, a way to protect them both.

Despite what Dira had said, despite how much of a hypocrite it made her to admit it, there was only one place she and Savita could escape together.

Cristo Industries.

A job with Cristo would give Kel the power to ensure their future. It would give her the money to repair the aviary and the chance to earn a reputation beyond her father's legacy. One that would make sure no one ever doubted her – or Savita – again.

Despite the night's chill, warmth spread through Kel. The heat awakened her, for the first time since the aviary's destruction.

'I'm going to ring the recruiter and accept Cristo's offer,' she said, as much to Savita as to Coup. 'I'll convince him to take Dira, too.'

The hard part would be convincing Dira to come. Kel doubted her best friend had the same moral objections to working for Cristo, but she did have pride. The recruiter would need to acknowledge Dira's merits as a winger – regardless of Kel's ultimatum.

Coup rustled behind her. 'Is there a question in there, somewhere? You know they wanted us as a package deal, right?'

'I'm not exactly thrilled about it, either. But we have nothing to lose.'

If she accepted Cristo's offer, she'd be working even closer to Coup than she had in the last twenty-four hours. But what other choice did they have?

Coup bristled again. 'You're assuming I'll just follow your lead. I made it clear I won't go without my brother.'

'You can convince him to take Bekn, too,' Kel said, voice filled with iron.

When Coup was silent, she added, 'If they plan on keeping us working on the same team, we just need to make it clear that Bekn and Dira will help us to . . . *gel* more than two strangers would.'

More silence, before Coup said, 'This isn't just a gamble for me, Varra. If I agree to this, you need to be all in. I don't have the luxury of time to move on, and I don't have a family legacy to fall back on to secure me another job down the line.'

'Are you serious? I don't have—'

'No – I don't care if you agree.' His voice cut through the icy gale. 'Your surname gives you a safety net I don't have. If you fuck this up, that's it for me. I won't get any more chances. If we do this, we're all in.'

Kel seethed. What other choice did he think *she* had? Knowing her father didn't mean he knew anything else about her.

She couldn't do this. She'd have to find another way. She—

Savita released a loud screech. Kel ran her hand along her

phoenix's neck, taking a deep breath. For Sav . . . she could swallow her pride. But five minutes alone with Warren Coupers had the magic of making her forget.

If she was going to work closely with Coup at Cristo's, she knew she'd be spending plenty of time arguing with him. She didn't want to add any more headaches to her future ones.

Silently, she began guiding Savita to the ground. Coup sat up in the saddle and wrapped his hands around her waist as they descended. He didn't ask Kel to make any promises, and neither did she.

After landing and settling Savita, Kel hurried up the hill towards her cottage. With Coup just a few steps behind her, they entered through the back entrance. Kel wasn't surprised to see Dira slumped across her tatty brown couch – she'd had a key for years – but she *was* unsettled to see Bekn banging away in her small kitchen, rattling pans against the stove top and filling the joined rooms with faint smoke.

Kel coughed, inhaling the smell of burnt meat. 'I thought you'd gone home?'

Bekn half-turned. 'We'd both rather be here, for you.'

Kel stiffened at the unexpected sincerity. 'I'm glad you're both here – I . . .' She swallowed, turning to Dira. 'I think we have to accept Cristo's offer.'

Dira raised her eyebrows. 'Wow, Kel, cut right to the chase.'

Kel stepped further into the room, Coup a shadow to her left, leaning against the doorframe. 'I know what you're going to say – but Cristo will take all of us. We'll make him. We won't go to Vohre unless he does.'

Dira watched Kel, unblinking. 'You really think Savita will be safe at Cristo Industries? Just a *month* ago, you showed me an article about Cristo and said, *"He's a plague on Cendor and Savita is safer living with Ebrait's sea monsters.'"* Dira shook her head. 'The fire hasn't changed that.'

'What other choice do we have?' Kel shot back.

'There's always a choice,' Dira hissed. A muscle ticked in her jaw. 'I left Dresva to have a say in my own future. You really think working for Cristo is going to give us any more freedom?'

Frustration flared behind Kel's temples. They had no way of knowing what Cristo would ask of them in Vohre – but this was the only way Kel could protect everyone she loved without losing sight of them.

Finally, she said, 'Yes, I do.'

Dira poked a nail into the couch's tattered fabric. 'If I hadn't seen the reports, I'd think you'd set the aviary fire to get us to agree to this.'

Her stomach twisted at Dira's words. She forced herself not to bite back.

'What do you think, mitigator?' Dira asked dryly.

Slowly, Bekn wiped his hands on his trousers and turned to Dira. 'I don't think there's a mitigator alive who can solve the problems that Cendor stirs up. Money like Cristo's would go a long way. *But . . .*' he paused, raising a hand half-covered in what looked like breadcrumbs, '. . . if we do this, you two need to get along. At least when there's cameras around. Understood?'

Kel and Coup glanced at each other. Coup's golden eyes hardened to copper, a fire in them that made Kel admit that, even if they had nothing else in common, neither would abandon those they cared for.

'Understood,' Kel said.

Coup pulled his tele-comm from a pocket and dialled a number. He handed it to Kel.

'Savita is your phoenix,' Coup said. His voice was low, almost reluctant. 'Make the final call.'

Surprise rattled through her, parting her lips as Coup handed her the tele-comm. She hesitated for only a moment before grabbing the device and pressing *dial*.

It was late enough in the evening that she doubted the recruiter would answer. Yet, after just one ring, a voice asked, 'Hello?'

She cleared her throat. 'This is Kelyn Varra. You approached Warren Coupers and me about a job.'

A brief pause. Then, 'I'm very glad to hear from you, Ms Varra. Can I assume this call means you're accepting our offer?'

'Yes – on one condition,' she said, voice unwavering. 'You take my entire team.'

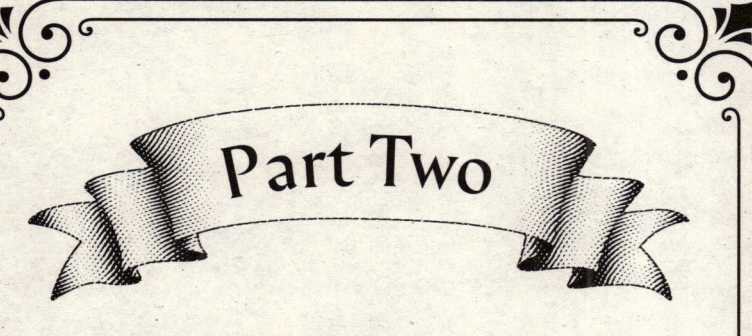

Part Two

One Alchemist loomed, named Landen Ryker
And hailed Deja, a bird of grim fire
The King's right-hand knight, she smote all with ease
But not bold Ryker, a bond they did seize

Theirs was a concord forged through baneful light
Racing 'tween the stars with such iron might
Dawn saw only them, phoenix and rider
The first pair in lore, Deja and Ryker

Verse 3–4, 'The Gilded Lullaby'

Chapter Twelve

※

By the time a blazing dawn had scared away the night's chill, the Howlers were halfway to Vohre.

Dira, Coup and Kel hadn't packed much. Dira's guitar took up the most space between the three of them, while Bekn's bulging suitcases were nearly too heavy to heave onto the overhead silver railing. Aside from the bags he'd seemingly stuffed half a house inside, the rest of the train carriage was bare; a handful of cushioned armchairs, floor-to-roof windows, three marble tables and a small cabinet with fizzy Asciran drinks. The opposing glass walls protected them from Cendor's persistent heat, and Kel rubbed her arms against goosebumps.

Bekn paced the length of the carriage, speaking into a well-abused tele-comm. Coup sat against the window opposite Kel, legs propped up on a polished table, indifferent to the glass bowl of sweets his feet knocked. His head was tilted towards the window, an open book in his lap. She watched as his eyes fluttered closed, so at ease in their carriage.

Decorated with a rich, earthy palette, Cristo's private train merely hinted at his wealth. Kel shuffled down the carriage's caramel carpet towards Dira, huddled over a table with a tablet in front of her. She didn't look up as Kel perched on the arm of her chair.

Kel wiggled a finger under Dira's ticklish chin. 'How long are you going to be mad at me?'

Dira swatted absently at Kel. 'I haven't decided.'

Kel sidled a little closer, nudging Dira with her elbow. 'Are you open to bribery? New sheet music, a new meat-free recipe book, a voucher for Vohre's best fashion boutique?'

Dira lowered her tablet. 'I'm allowed to be mad, Kel. You made this decision without even talking to me. Part of the reason I left Dresva was to stop other people making my choices for me.'

A lump formed in Kel's throat. 'I'm sorry, D. Really. I just – I didn't know what else to do. But I should've talked to you, first.'

Dira sighed. 'I care about Sav just as much as you do. I came to Cendor because phoenixes . . . *magic* . . . it's all so much more tangible here. I loved Sav before I even met her. She's the reason I don't want to do this. You don't know how Cristo will treat her.'

Guilt sagged Kel's shoulders. 'I know.'

Though she doubted Dira would ever admit it, Kel knew her pride often clouded her judgement. Wingers weren't pulled into the spotlight like tamers and riders – the positions that spent the most time with dangerous creatures. But that still shouldn't have stopped Cristo from recognizing Dira's talent.

Dira folded her arms and slouched back in her armchair. Seconds passed before she huffed, and her lips pulled up into the softest smile. 'Oska would've hated this, wouldn't she?'

Kel's chest ached. 'She'd have thought this carriage far too plain for a billionaire's tastes. And she would've told Cristo as much.'

Dira released a short, breathy laugh. 'We wouldn't have had a moment's silence this whole ride.'

They'd been informed the night after the race that Oska's family was having her body flown back to Ascira for a small, intimate funeral. It was as much closure as they'd get for their fallen rider. Still, Kel doubted the wound would ever fully heal – for her or Dira. In all their years of friendship, she'd never seen Dira cry, but hearing the news of Oska's funeral had brought Dira closer than Kel had ever seen. No one deserved to die like that, brutally raked apart above a cheering crowd.

Oska's screams still haunted Kel's dreams.

Kel placed a gentle hand on her friend's arm. 'She'd be excited to squeeze as much money out of Cristo as she could, though.'

Dira's smile grew. Her gaze flickered to Coup and Bekn. 'She'd have hated our new rider. Almost as much as you do.'

Kel rolled her eyes. 'Don't pretend you're *excited* to work with him.'

Voice low, Dira said, 'No. He's an arrogant dick. But CAPR adores him, and as long as we can channel that cockiness on the track, we can make some money.'

Dira lifted her arm and squeezed Kel's hand. A moment later, she reopened the tablet screen and waved a hand. 'Now go away. There are so many Vohre racing teams I need to pick apart before we compete.'

Kel offered a salute and rose from her perch. She moved back towards the armchair she'd claimed at the carriage's other end, opposite Coup.

Coup stretched his arms out like a sun-soaked cat. 'As Salta's tech capital, you'd think Cendor might put in a little more effort to make the rest of the island hospitable.'

Kel fell back into her chair as the train lurched around a bend. 'Cendor was built for practicality. What's the use in building beyond the cities' limits?'

There were other, smaller cities scattered across Cendor, but none nearly as large as Fieror and Vohre. The rest of the island was covered with scattered forestry. Cendor wasn't a tourist destination like Ascira. Kel was proud of their cut-throat reputation. It was a freeing, lethal thing.

'*What's the use?*' Coup repeated. 'More investments? More CAPR tracks? More land to buy for free and sell for millions? I'm sure Cristo and the council have plans to demolish this entire forest for their next big venture.'

His tone was equally dry and admiring – and it crawled beneath Kel's skin. She gestured to the trees beyond his window. 'This is the only other forest dense enough to house wild phoenixes if they completely destroy Vohre Forest. But new CAPR tracks are more important, right?'

She wasn't sure why she was picking a fight. Maybe it was because she'd promised not to once they arrived in Vohre. Maybe because Coup's bruised eye had healed far too quickly for her liking. Or maybe it was the temporary truce they'd shared last night, the feeling that she owed him something. It pricked at her constantly, like a stone in her shoe.

Coup rolled his eyes. 'Sure, Kelyn. I'd *absolutely* choose new cities over preserving the phoenix population. It's not like my career depends on the continuation of their species or anything.'

Kel stood. '*Alchemists' sake!* How selfish are you?'

Coup scoffed. '*Me?* You're the one that claims to care *so* deeply for your phoenix, while forcing her to compete in the same exact races I do.' He shook his head. 'Your virtuousness must be *such* a heavy burden. You profit off the deforestation, too, Varra. Your motives for CAPR racing are no purer than mine.'

Anger tensed Kel's muscles. 'At least I don't preen and pose for the cameras like a phoenix in heat! I don't ignore my teammates on the track, I don't pull reckless stunts that could risk *all* our lives—'

'Cut it out,' Bekn barked. He stood, blocking her view of Coup. 'We all need money, and we all have miserable little sob stories. Let's leave it at that.'

Kel narrowed her eyes, trying to burn a hole through Bekn to Coup. *Alchemists.* She couldn't *stand him.* He acted like a carefree child skipping stones across a pond, ignorant to the ripples he created.

From behind Bekn, Coup sighed. 'It's just some fun team banter, Bek.'

'Only masochists would consider your banter fun,' Bekn said, voice dry.

Coup snickered. 'You're just on edge after last night. You've had a crush on Finn Erret for a decade, and he finally bought you a drink last night.'

Kel's brows raised, watching Bekn's stubbled cheeks redden. Finn was a rugged twenty-something who had kicked Dira and Kel out of The Ferret too many times to count.

Out of mercy for Bekn's flushed face, Kel relented, sitting back on her padded chair.

Dira cackled from the back of the carriage, but said nothing. Kel raised her hands in surrender. Bekn perched on the seat next to her.

He clasped his hands together. 'Why don't we practise our bootlicking for Canen Cristo? Let's go around the room and say what we're most excited about at our new jobs. I'll go first.' Bekn cleared his throat, ignoring his teammates' eye rolls. '*I'm* going to use this job to gain the money and knowledge I'll need to open my own media company that can sponsor the Howlers. There's no better mentor than Cristo himself.'

Dira made a gagging sound, and Kel supressed a giggle. The dreams Bekn spoke of had nothing to do with phoenixes or jagged practicalities. It made Kel think Cendor's static fire and ruthless heart hadn't created the sanctuary for him that had for her or Dira, or even perhaps Coup.

It made her wonder about another Howler – *ex*-Howler – who had ambitions beyond CAPR. 'Maybe now that we've moved to Vohre, Rube can come back to the team.'

It wouldn't heal the scar that Oska's death had ripped open in

Kel. But it offered something warm, and familiar, when nothing else about their future would be.

Dira's gaze lowered. 'I've already tried reaching out to Rube. He isn't returning my calls.'

'His loss. I'm sure Cristo will have technicians five times as skilled,' Coup said, folding his arms.

'And ten times as loyal,' Bekn added.

Kel smiled tightly. 'You're right. We can do much better.'

She lay back and let her eyes unfocus. She watched the trees pass in thick clusters. Sunlight struggled to pierce the towering canopy and branches blurred together in uneven patchworks. Emerald, shamrock, brown, lime, pine—

Red.

Chapter Thirteen

✤

'*Stop!*' Kel screamed.

She jumped up and slammed her hand against the emergency button on the wall. The train lurched to a halt. Bekn fell to his knees and Coup cursed.

'*Flames*, Kel!' Dira barked.

Savita's distant screech vibrated their carriage.

Kel pressed her face to the misted window. She tried to peer to the left, where she'd seen a sharp splash of red, before hurrying to the carriage's doors. She thumped the *Exit* button over and over. The glass doors refused to budge.

'What's going on?' Bekn demanded.

Kel ignored him and tried to pry apart the heavy doors. A moment later, a pair of callused hands joined hers.

Together, she and Coup strained to part the glass. Bekn and Dira stood behind them, no longer shouting. Their curiosity fell against her back like a shadow.

Alchemists. She hoped she was wrong.

The door shuddered open.

Kel leapt to the ground and stumbled over the train tracks, stubbing her toe. The rest of the Howlers followed close behind.

A few metres back, in a small forest clearing, lay a circle of boulders. Streaks of red smudged two rocks, scarlet veins glowing against the stone.

It was so out of place in the sea of green and brown. She'd hoped it was a dead animal. A deer or a bird. But a labyrinthine pit had formed in her stomach at the amount of blood she'd seen.

So much. *Too much.*

Beneath the red smears lay two bodies. A mother and a small child, tangled together.

From the dried blood trailing down their fingernails, their nose, their every orifice, it was clear what had killed them.

AB.

'Call for help,' Kel whispered, so softly she wasn't sure anyone heard.

Dira didn't hesitate. She turned away and began shouting into her tele-comm.

Kel struggled to look away from the corpses. She couldn't see much of the mother's features. Her face was covered by dark, matted hair. But the child's face – a young boy – was perfectly clear.

Bekn stood back, eyes averted. A moment later, he marched off towards the train's steering carriage.

Coup, however, stepped closer. His focus remained on the mother's hidden face.

'They can't have died more than a day ago,' he said softly. 'We need to move their bodies before something else in the forest finds them.'

Kel nodded slowly. No matter her feelings towards him, Coup's voice – barely a croak – made her wish she hadn't stopped the train. She wished she'd just called the council to investigate. She wouldn't wish AB on anyone.

Coup and Bekn's mother had been taken by the same plague that had killed this mother and child, and from the rasp in Coup's voice, Kel knew this was an all-too-familiar sight for him.

The thick, silent pain in the air reminded her of their perch on top of the darkened hill, after her aviary had burnt to ashes.

Kel's attention drifted back to the bodies. She noticed a lump of fabric to the left of the mother.

'They both have packs,' Kel realized. The bags had fallen open, rotten food and bottled water spilling free. 'They must have been heading to Vohre.'

This far gone to the blight, they wouldn't have been permitted on a government train. No one knew how AB spread. It wasn't contagious – but fear was. Their only choices were to wait for a torturous death in Fieror, or brave the trek to Vohre's advanced medical facilities in the hopes of greeting death painlessly.

It was rare to see two AB patients in close vicinity; the symptoms of those who had it often flared up when near one another. But this mother, buried beneath a blanket of her own blood, had refused to abandon her son.

Like any Saltan, Kel knew the warning signs of AB. Confusion, memory loss, insomnia, tremors. AB struck the brain and caused rapid tissue deterioration. It killed within months of onset. The lucky few had symptoms; time to say their goodbyes.

She wondered how Coup's mother had looked. Had she passed peacefully, in her sleep? Or had her symptoms stripped her away, layer by layer?

A strange impulse itched her fingers. She wanted to reach out, to comfort Coup in some small way. But the urge itself kept her still. Her hands twitched, waging a silent war until a council van appeared beside the train tracks. She led Coup back towards the train as the mother and child were placed on stretchers and covered with white sheets.

The train driver quickly restarted their journey. Coup returned to his chair, silent.

The forest passed once more in a blur. Kel tried to count the trees, but her eyes kept focusing on the glass window. The reflection staring back at her. Not her face, but that of the mother's and son's.

Dira and Bekn nestled in chairs at the other end of the carriage. Awkwardly, with her chair's leather cushion groaning loudly, Kel leaned towards Coup. 'Are you . . . are you all right?'

Her words snapped Coup from his reverie. He whipped to face her, hands clawed into the chair arms. 'Now's not the time for you to grow a heart, Varra. I'd rather your hate than your pity.'

Kel's mouth closed. If Bekn and Dira had heard their exchange, they said nothing. Stiffly, Kel rose from her seat.

The memory of her father's body, torn apart like a ragdoll in a storm, always lingered at the edges of her thoughts. She knew what it was like to be flooded with unexpected reminders of death.

Kel moved to the next carriage. She unlocked Savita's enormous trailer, pulled on the leather gloves always stashed in her pocket, and sat cross-legged in a corner as Sav cleaned her wings. When her phoenix moved and laid beside her, Kel thought Savita might be the only creature in the world who would never truly leave her.

Chapter Fourteen

---※---

Fieror was a city of dry grass, old buildings and dust storms. With rare clouds and rarer rain, the sun scorched the ground and bathed Fieror's buildings in endlessly sharp, cinder heat. But with Cristo's help, Vohre had hurled itself a hundred years into the future.

Even from the city's outskirts, where Cristo's central compound sat, every building shone with digital screens. Sunlight beat against the tall structures, yet arching trees and plants protected the streets from the heat. It was the greenest place Kel had ever seen. Even greener than the dark forest they'd just passed on the train. In the distance, Kel could see crowds shoving past each other in an endless tide of people.

The train had tossed them out too far from Vohre's centre to make out much more. Kel turned from the cityscape at her left and jogged to catch up with the three of Cristo's employees who were struggling to lead Savita away.

'Where are you taking her?' Kel asked.

Sav ruffled her wings as a man guided her forwards, a leg of raw meat dangling between his hands. Kel had made it clear to Sav that she was safe – for now – to follow the employees, though the workers may be the ones in danger, tantalizing Sav with fresh cuts. The phoenix's head was lowered, wings pinned as she stared at the meat.

The brown-haired man to Savita's right replied, 'We're just taking her to get settled inside her new aviary. You'll be shown the way on your tour.'

Kel folded her arms. The workers had appeared beside their carriage when the train stopped outside Cristo's property. They'd asked for Kel's login details for Savita's collar, and made quick work of luring Sav away.

Kel tried again, 'She doesn't like it when you—'

'You're going to have to get used to letting others near her,' Dira said. She gave Kel's hand a squeeze.

'Two seconds after we arrive?' Kel muttered.

'If they want their hands bitten off, leave them to it. Cristo's going to want some say in who trains her.'

Kel grumbled. Dira was right. That was part of this whole arrangement; Savita would belong to Cristo just as much as she belonged to Kel. The thought grated against Kel's bones.

Dira steered Kel towards the nearest building. Bekn and Coup were having their fingerprints scanned by a tall woman in a black uniform. A moment later, the metal gates guarding the building drifted open, and the Howlers were led inside.

All four jaws dropped.

Kel had heard Cristo's estates referred to as facilities and compounds – but this was a *city*. Labyrinthine corridors weaved in every direction and sky-high ceilings were connected by delicate bridges. Every wall was pristine white, with long, tinted windows that seemed to reach the clouds. The intricately carved ceiling loomed over them like a tidal wave. The air was clinical, with the faintest taste of sweet incense wafting through the air, like a flower trying to bloom beneath cracks in cement.

The glittering grandeur filled Kel with awe and fear. Every lustrous inch of this building reminded her of the stakes now guiding the Howlers' steps. This sponsorship wasn't free of strings. Kel didn't know what those strings looked like yet, but she did know that this was her last chance – her *only* chance – to save everything she loved.

The Howlers were led through security gates and past a reception desk. When they stopped before another set of clinical, pearly doors, a figure stepped through.

Kel doubted the girl was any older than her. Her ink-black hair fell in a straight sheet down her back, over a blue coat that reached the ground. Her uptilted, hazel eyes were softer than Coup's, reminding Kel of the cooling Sheathing Season, of dry leaves bronzing and falling.

Her porcelain skin was just a shade darker than the white of her teeth, framed by rosy lips that pulled up into a grin. 'You must be the Howlers.'

Dira's eyes roamed the girl. 'We must be.'

The girl beckoned them forwards. 'Come on. I'm meant to give you a tour of the facilities.'

The Howlers exchanged another look and hurried to follow. For such a short, wispy creature, the girl certainly moved fast.

Through the doors, a large hall was partitioned into smaller offices cluttered with desks and bent heads. Dira cleared her throat. 'And you are?'

'Didn't I introduce myself?' She laughed softly. 'I'm Rahn. I'm a part of the CAPR programme. Canen asked that I show you around while he's at a conference in Dresva. He's returning soon, but he didn't want to keep you waiting.'

Silently, they each absorbed Rahn's words. She'd called the head of this entire corporation *Canen*. They all stood a little straighter.

Rahn went on, 'Cristo Industries is a bit of a maze, so I don't expect you to remember all of this. I'll just show each of you your workstations, and then your accommodation.'

She turned back to the group. 'I live here, too. It's much nicer than it seems, I promise.'

Kel raised an eyebrow. If that were the case, then it must be fit for the Alchemists themselves.

Rahn scanned her security badge, leading them down an elevator and along a corridor. Dira showered Rahn with questions as they walked, her voice an octave higher than its usual dry, gruff notes. Kel hid a smirk at Coup and Bekn's perplexed frowns. Dira had always been quick to fall for – and away from – girls who crossed their paths.

After a few more identical turns, Rahn led them into a room with no windows. At the centre sat a small rectangular desk, surrounded by leather chairs.

Rahn gestured for them to sit. 'I'll need you to sign your contracts and NDAs before we go any further. I know you must have questions, and as soon as you sign these I'll be more than happy to answer every one of them.'

A clawed hand reached inside Kel's stomach and squeezed. Bekn took a slow step towards Rahn. 'What kinds of NDAs?'

Rahn beamed. 'Oh, it's all very standard. Just a few clauses stating you won't discuss our research and projects with anyone outside the company.'

Bekn nodded, slowly, and took another step forward. They each followed, like ducklings trailing into unknown waters.

Bekn skimmed the papers once, twice. His fingers followed the text and paused halfway down the second page. 'This says that we'll be required to *"perform well"* in CAPR races. That's very vague.'

Rahn's smile wilted. 'Oh – I'm sorry. It's a standard sponsorship contract. Most sponsors ask the same. There are no set expectations when racing. Just . . . that you try your best.'

Rahn's voice fluttered as she spoke, like a balloon losing air. Kel couldn't tell if the girl's words shivered from nerves or excitement.

The former filled Kel's gut, pretzeling into a feeling she couldn't name. From Bekn's blank expression, Kel assumed Rahn's words were true.

Kel had never signed a sponsorship contract before. She didn't know what strings typically came with them. But if the Howlers didn't perform well in CAPR races, if they didn't *place*, she'd be back upon that hill, watching her aviary turn to ash, hiding from bankers, saying goodbye to Savita. To her home.

Bekn reread the contract. A few minutes later, he nodded to the Howlers, and, slowly, they each drifted around the desk. Kel picked up a pen and twirled it between her fingers, delaying the inevitable.

'Where's Savita?' she asked.

'She'll live in one of our larger aviaries with the other trained phoenixes, though she'll stay in a private space while she acclimatizes. I'll be happy to show you, but Canen will have my head if I don't get you to sign these forms, first.'

Reluctantly, they each scribbled their signatures across the papers and stood. Kel's knees felt weak as Rahn clapped her hands. 'This is perfect! Taking this job was the best decision I ever made. I was so excited when he told me the four of you would be joining us!'

Dira tilted her head. Her eyes roamed Rahn again. 'You've heard of us?'

Rahn's cheeks reddened. 'Of course I have! You might not have competed in Vohre before, but you all still have a national ranking. Everyone in CAPR knows who you are, especially now you're on the same team!'

Unease rippled through Kel. What else did this girl know about them?

'Follow me,' Rahn said with a wave. 'Now the fun can really begin.'

They followed Rahn through the Cristo Research Centre, past the medical centre, and, finally, to their workstations.

For the second time, their jaws dropped.

It was an entire racing track. *Indoors*. As large as Kel's entire farm. Adjustable netting and obstacles hung from the roof. A row of bridles, reins and collars was pinned to the far-left wall above five saddles, all bearing differently shaped pommels, seats and buckles to accommodate different tracks. The ground was covered in a thin layer of dirt, but Kel spotted grains of sand and rock scattered throughout. Remnants of different terrains to practise on.

'Is this *entire* track for us?' Kel breathed.

Rahn nodded. 'Canen doesn't develop much technology here. This compound is only used for CAPR training, phoenix research and medical studies. This is just your training track. You all have individual workstations, too.'

Coup released a disbelieving laugh. Bekn beamed, practically vibrating with excitement. Dira's own chuckle bounced around the cavernous hall. Even Kel couldn't hide her awe; the tension in her shoulders slipped away, and she grinned at Dira.

The Howlers had to prove their worth to Cristo. They had to win CAPR races in Vohre, a city with a reputation far more devastating than Fieror's. But maybe . . . this wouldn't be as terrible as she'd thought.

Chapter Fifteen

※

After Rahn showed the Howlers their lavish offices and rooms, she led them to a hall crowded with tables full of roast chicken, potatoes, steaming vegetables and chilled desserts. They scrambled to pile their plates and hurried towards the nearest table. Rahn sat with them at Dira's insistence, and Rahn in turn encouraged others to join. A dark-haired girl around their age sat to Rahn's left, and though Kel couldn't recall her name, she was struck by the way the girl interacted with Rahn; the familiar, easy warmth in every word and expression. She hadn't expected this kind of camaraderie here.

An hour later, the Howlers headed to their rooms, cradling full stomachs. Each cluster of suites shared a kitchen, dining area, and a small lounge; the four Howlers and, it seemed, Rahn, were in one such cluster.

The five separated with weary goodbyes and Kel stumbled into bed. Her room was decorated with the same earthy colours as the train and smelt faintly of lavender. A new, bow-tied tele-comm lay on her wooden desk. Two abstract paintings of phoenixes hung on opposite walls. It was simple, and homely, and exactly how Kel might have decorated her own room if she hadn't spent most nights in the aviary's office.

That fact might have unnerved Kel, if she hadn't been too tired to care.

She slumped into the dark green sheets and willed sleep to take her. She wished it, and begged it, and ordered it, for minutes and then hours. But the longer she waited, the further away it drew, taunting her.

When the clock ticked past midnight, Kel huffed and threw her clothes back on.

There was one thing that *always* helped her sleep.

She tiptoed through their small kitchen and took the elevator down to the ground floor.

Kel pulled out the map Rahn had given her. The girl had pointed out the distant building where all phoenixes lived, in an array of spectacularly green aviaries, but the facilities truly were a maze; identical rooms and endlessly spiralling white corridors. It took her a few wrong turns, but eventually she spotted Savita's smaller aviary, divided from a larger enclosure by a glass wall.

Savita still had plenty of room to roam – more than she'd had at home – and Kel was glad her phoenix hadn't been thrown in with the other birds yet. Savita wasn't prone to timidity. If she felt uncomfortable, she'd attack.

Kel scanned her new ID card and slid inside Savita's cage. Full of trees, shrubbery and buzzing insects, it was as close to Vohre Forest as Kel imagined an aviary could be.

In a thunderous *whoosh* of heat, Savita appeared before her. The phoenix towered over Kel, snapping her beak.

Kel slid off her jacket and pulled on her leather gloves. 'You know I came as soon as I could.'

Savita arched over Kel, stretching her neck. She eyed Kel, nudged her tamer's arm in reluctant affection, and turned away. She almost sent Kel flying across the room with the sway of her long, feathered tail.

Kel supposed that was as warm a welcome as she could expect. She followed Savita across the enclosure. 'Don't pretend you don't love this aviary. I saw you preening at the other phoenixes, earlier.

You can't *wait* to make them your minions.'

Savita clucked again, refusing to face Kel. Kel laughed and sat on a nearby log. She tugged off her gloves and pulled a small notebook and pen from her jacket. All notions of sleep forgotten, Kel began scribbling under the dim heat-light overhead.

She didn't know how much time had passed before the aviary's entrance beeped open.

Kel pivoted towards the door, spotting a familiar chestnut head bobbing closer.

Frustration sputtered to life inside her.

'I should have known you'd be here,' Coup said dryly, as he sat beside her.

His dark curls were flat against his head and the grey shirt beneath his jacket was half-tucked into his trousers. He must have crawled from bed. Kel hated that the thought made her cheeks heat.

'What are *you* doing here?' she threw back. *Alchemists!* She'd just wanted some peace. 'Go back to bed.'

'No.' He tilted his head back, stretching his legs. Savita had barely made a noise at his entry.

'*Yes*.'

Coup might be on her team, on her phoenix, but her nights with Savita had always been spent alone. They were sacred, and he'd already intruded on her last flight with Sav. She didn't need Coup's grating voice filling the silence *again*.

'*No*, and only because you want me to,' he sang. He rose to his feet and moved towards Savita. Kel scowled at his back. Slowly, he approached the phoenix. He placed a gloved hand on her neck before shifting away. Sav watched Coup with an indifferent curiosity, the way a lazy cat might observe a passing bird.

Splinters bit into Kel's palms and she forced her fingers to loosen around the log. Touching Sav had taken Oska *months*. Kel imagined

Coup would soon be safe to fly on his own. Despite some distant part of her knowing it would help the Howlers, the thought still sent a pang of petty jealousy through her.

'Why are you here?' she relented, leaning back.

Coup gave a small shrug, working his hands softly down Savita's side, over her wing, testing her comfort. 'The sooner Savita is comfortable around me, the sooner we can start actually training. Cristo's contract makes it sound like he has some high expectations.' He paused. 'I told you, tamer, that I can't afford to mess this up. Why are *you* here?'

'Maybe I just wanted to be somewhere *alone*,' she drawled.

'Without someone to berate?' Coup shook his head. 'Impossible.'

Kel scrunched her face. She forced a deep breath. 'I just wanted to check on Sav. I'll leave soon.'

'Liar.'

Kel huffed and drummed her fingers against the log. She wanted to keep scribbling in her notebook, talking to Sav's tired silhouette. But both felt too strange in Coup's presence, as if she'd undressed with his back half-turned.

Instead, Kel watched Coup glide beside Savita, her head lowered to the ground and her eyes closed. Watching him guide his hands along Sav's outline sparked an old curiosity.

'Why were you working in public aviaries?' The question had been biting at her ever since he'd first mentioned it. Aside from the pieces he'd offered, she had no clue how he'd spent his childhood, or what had led him to phoenix racing.

Hand still raised at Savita's side, Coup turned to face Kel. His lips quirked up. Stray moonlight caught on his crescent dimples, and Kel loathed his easy charm. 'Oh. Funny story. I was caught sneaking into a CAPR race when I was too young, so the council threw me into the grimiest place they could find to try and scare me into never going back. But that's what made me fall in love with phoenixes.' Coup paused. 'That and CAPR money.'

Kel felt that familiar, bitter frustration only Coup could stir; this time, at having something in common with him. His story was almost identical to how Dira and Kel had first met – getting caught and kicked out of a CAPR race as kids without guardians. Though they might race for different reasons now, what had led to their CAPR racing – to this moment – was almost the same.

Coup shook his head, as if freeing himself of the memory. 'What about you?' With his other hand, he gestured to Savita's sleeping figure. 'You love Savita like a firstborn. Was it always that way?'

Kel shifted her weight along the log, stalling. Coup had given her a truth. She owed him one in return. But she didn't know if she could give him the truth he'd asked for.

She took a deep breath. 'My dad used to tell me stories about phoenixes, mostly about Landon Ryker and Deja.'

It was a half-truth. Kel had adored her father's stories, tales woven as vividly as memories. Ryker had settled on Cendor, while the other three Alchemists lived across Salta's other isles. Somehow, Ryker had earnt the trust of Salta's oldest – greatest – phoenix. He'd become the first person to ever ride a firebird. Their bond had been strong enough to conquer death itself.

Kel chewed the inside of her cheek. Though she'd loved those stories, they weren't the real reason she'd latched so tightly on to Savita – at least, not in recent years. Something about Savita's immortality made Kel feel safe in a way that nothing else could. No matter what happened to her family, her friends, even Cendor, phoenixes – *Savita* – would always remain.

Sometimes it felt like death trailed after Kel, a second shadow. Savita was the only thing she couldn't get killed.

Coup laughed, oblivious to Kel's half-truth. 'My mum told me the same stories. She wasn't from Cendor, but her parents had told her stories about Ryker and Deja. That's why she came here when she fled.'

Kel frowned. 'Fled?'

Though Coup remained still, gliding his hand along Savita, his voice was sharper when he said, 'My father wasn't a good man. She escaped the continent not long after I was born. Bekn told me once she'd escaped to Cendor because of its reputation. She didn't think he'd follow her here.'

Coup shrugged, though the movement looked forced. 'It worked. She never heard from him again.'

The smallest sliver of guilt wormed through Kel, crawling between her ribs. Whatever she'd assumed of his childhood – it hadn't been that.

'I'm sorry about your mother,' she said, softly.

'I'm sorry about your father,' Coup replied, softly. 'And I'm sorry for what I said on the train. I just—'

'It's okay,' she said, crossing her legs. 'I get it.'

She hadn't realized it was true until she'd said it. Coup's words on the train had hurt, but she also knew what it was like to think you'd come to terms with something. To have that delusion yanked away with no notice.

Memories flashed behind her eyes in painful starbursts. She remembered the anger blazing through her after her father's death, the way Dira and Kel had lashed at each other night after night.

Savita ruffled her wings and lifted her head. Coup shifted towards Kel as Savita rose to her feet. Copper flames flickered along her back as she scraped her talons twice against the ground before catapulting into the air with a storm of dust.

Kel and Coup coughed. Savita's heat lingered, thickening the air into hot syrup and tangling with the strange, sudden tension of their confessions. Kel rolled up her sleeves and Coup took off his jacket, placing it on the dirt to Kel's left. Kel didn't know where Sav's heat ended and Coup's own furnace-like warmth began. His dark shirt bunched around his shoulders, tanned arms lined with lean muscles.

Kel shook her head as Coup's gaze drifted to her lap. 'What's this?'

She slammed her notebook shut. 'Nothing, it's—'

Coup wrestled the book from her lap, his heat making her flush almost as much as Savita's. She tried to stave off his attack with little success, managing to swat at his ear before he skipped out of reach, flipping through her inked pages.

A minute later, his laughter filled the enclosure. '*Twenty pages?* You wrote *twenty* pages on how Cristo has to care for Savita?'

Kel launched to her feet and snatched back the notebook. '*Eighteen* pages. I just wrote some ideas for Savita's training.'

'More like *demands*,' Coup scoffed. 'Why am I surprised that you assume you know more about phoenix care than a billionaire philanthropist who's rehoused dozens of phoenixes?'

'Leave, then, if you're just going to mock me,' she growled. She still had plenty of thoughts to pen. Most of them about the infuriating Warren Coupers.

Savita screeched overhead, her silhouette glowing amongst the trees.

Coup merely sat to Kel's left, head tilted towards Savita's glowing figure. After a few minutes she reopened the notebook and continued writing, trying to ignore his warm presence beside her.

Kel eyed him occasionally, wondering why he was still here. They sat in silence for a while. Shockingly, it wasn't as unpleasant as she'd expected.

Eventually, Kel's list of demands turned to scribbles of Savita, soaring across her hastily sketched new enclosure. Kel ran her nails over the paper and imagined her sketch coming to life, imagined feeling Savita's flames beneath her ungloved fingers for the first time.

As Kel flipped to a new page, Coup leaned over and said, 'You forgot to draw her collar.'

Kel's hand stilled. 'Oh. Right.'

Sleep finally starting to slow her fingers, she hastily added a narrow halo around Savita's neck.

Kel's father's death had made it clear to her that phoenixes needed to be collared, for theirs and others' safety. It kept people from being burnt, mauled, eaten, and it helped phoenixes to build homes, free of chronic destruction. And yet, something about the forgotten addition of the sketched collar made Kel's stomach knot.

After a few minutes of silence, Kel asked, 'Do you ever think about what it'd be like if phoenixes weren't collared?'

'We'd probably all die. But it's our own fault, isn't it?' He shrugged. 'Maybe if we'd never started collaring them in the first place, we'd have figured out a way to co-exist. But it's too late for that.'

Unease slithered through Kel, making her toes curl. She'd expected Coup to disagree, to say it was misguided to even consider that world. That his income counted on phoenixes remaining collared – controlled.

But then again, so did hers.

Behind closed, heavy lids, Kel tried to imagine Savita in the wild. If Savita was truly free, uncollared, would she be happier? Would she fly off, never to be seen again?

Kel shook her head, trying to hack the thought from her mind like a stubborn weed.

'Maybe if we'd never collared phoenixes, we could've learnt from them, like Ryker did,' Coup mused softly, as if speaking to her through his own daydream. 'Maybe they could have even taught us to grow our own wings.'

Kel shifted onto the dirt and leaned her head against the log. 'Then I suppose we wouldn't need phoenixes to race.'

Coup laughed softly. Kel turned towards him. In the dim, overhead light, his chestnut curls had turned to shadows, his amber eyes like cooling embers.

As silence drifted between them, Kel felt herself stiffening, from both the cold and the strange, unexpected truce she found between herself and Coup. She fidgeted with a corner in the notebook, biting down on her lip when a papercut sliced the tip of her middle finger.

'You all right?' Coup asked. When she didn't reply, he *tsked*. 'Careless, tamer. How do you survive seventeen years owning a phoenix and still manage something as thoughtless as a papercut?'

'Says the rider careless enough that he'd rather burn himself alive than lose a race,' Kel replied, sharper than she'd intended.

Whether it was caused by the darkness or the papercut, she felt a strange, sudden vulnerability. She needed him to *leave*.

Coup shook his head and stood. 'It's only careless if it's not intentional. At least I'm willing to do what it takes to get where I need to be. At least I don't have to lie to myself about any of it.'

Coup left the aviary before she could retort, leaving her to the quiet dark, punctured only by Savita's glowing silhouette.

Chapter Sixteen

'A new saddle isn't going to stop you from falling face-first,' Kel muttered. She pulled the buckles around Coup's ankle tight enough to bruise.

Coup shrugged. 'Savita would catch me.'

Kel huffed and stepped back. Maybe if he cracked his skull, some of the arrogance might leak out.

Part of Kel did want to wrench open his skull, to see what else lay inside. When she'd first seen Coup this morning, he'd been even snarkier than usual; biting quips and bitter comments.

There was no trace of their unexpected truce from last night, and so she quashed any hint of understanding she might have been tempted to throw his way.

Kel moved back until she stood beside Dira. To Dira's right – *very* close to her right – stood Rahn, then Bekn. Rahn had woken them at dawn, far too animated. Already dressed in a uniform consisting of a pale blue coat and white shirt, Rahn dragged them to their new training track. She offered them uniforms of their own, black and burgundy.

Coup had wriggled into his riding leathers faster than Kel could blink. Where his old gear was worn and faded, his new uniform glistened like dark metal and fresh blood. It fitted him like a tailored glove. The dense padding inside the leathers broadened his shoulders and puffed his chest. Two brown curls fell across his forehead, his hair otherwise perfectly coiffed, and the faint stubble across his cheeks only sharpened his jaw. He'd undoubtedly have a Vohre fanbase soon enough.

They all watched as Coup adjusted the buckles around his legs. Rube had been talented, but even his gear looked like junkyard scraps compared to Cristo's tech. Savita jostled beneath the new saddle, bridle and reins, stretching her wings to their full length.

Kel didn't miss Coup's slight wince as he adjusted his weight.

'Are you hurt?' she asked, thinking back to the lethal stunt he'd pulled only days ago. He'd pressed against his phoenix's saddle so tightly. Was his front covered in burns and blisters? If she asked to see him shirtless, she doubted she'd ever hear the end of it.

'Not enough to need a lecture,' he sighed, grimacing as he pulled himself further forwards.

Confusion snaked through her. 'You flew with me the other night – why didn't you say anything?'

'You'd just have used it as an excuse not to let me come.'

Kel rubbed her face, smothering her growing irritation. 'Just take it easy, okay? You shouldn't be flying if you're still injured.'

Coup brushed non-existent dust off his arm. 'I'm fine. Besides, if I die, you get to tell Dira and Bekn *"I told you so"*. I'm sure you dream about that.'

'Can you take this seriously? I actually have to care if you live or die, now.'

Coup winked before lowering his goggles into place. 'Stop brooding, Varra. You know Savita wouldn't let me up here if I was injured enough to throw her off balance.'

Kel's cheeks heated. She stepped back as Coup guided Sav away from the Howlers. Already warmed up, Sav rose from the ground with a single beat of her wings. Coup led her through a few easy flight patterns. They soared lazily around the oval track, ducking below the low netting and swerving between a few small obstacles. Envy prickled at Kel's skin as she watched Coup and Sav soar in elegant lines, already moving together seamlessly. She tried to shove the prickling down; none of them had time to waste on frustration.

Vohre was known for its inventive CAPR tracks, built for artistry and shock value over practicality. It was rare for the same track to be used twice. She'd seen broadcasted Vohre races, but until they participated in one of their own she had no clue how they'd compare to Fieror's. If they were going to place in their first CAPR race, Coup would need every advantage he could scrape together.

Coup instructed Sav to pick up speed. The phoenix seemed unfazed by the unfamiliar gravel below her, itching to move faster.

Bekn cupped his hands around his mouth and shouted, 'Show her off, Coup!'

Kel scowled at Bekn for making Sav sound like a prize auto-bike, but even she was curious to see how Rahn reacted to Savita's full speed.

Coup howled in response. Then, they were off.

Rahn yelped and grabbed Dira's arm as Savita blazed past, conjuring a storm within the hall. Winds shoved them back, knocking over loose obstacles and sending Bekn to the ground. Kel braced her knees and managed to only stumble a step.

Kel helped Bekn to his feet, grinning. *This* was familiar. Watching Savita soar, fire crackling in the air, even with a new rider on her back. *This* was safe and dangerous all at once. If Coup was thrown off at this speed, he'd be little more than a splat of red on the ground. It would be inconvenient to have to replace him so soon after arriving in Vohre.

Coup directed Savita around the track a few more times, his howls blaring through their new comms. He dove when Dira instructed, eased up when Kel demanded.

'I guess it just took million-cere gear to get you to listen,' Kel said acidly, earning chuckles from Dira and Bekn.

'I'm not opposed to following rules, Varra,' he shouted back. 'Only useless ones. My last tamer had no clue what he was doing.'

A disbelieving laugh escaped Kel. 'And you trust me, Coupers?'

'I trust you'll do what's smart for Savita. Which, by association, will be smart for me.'

Kel's mouth parted, at a loss for words. Coup's voice was matter-of-fact, with no trace of his usual teasing.

'I assume your expression means he's being unusually co-operative?' Bekn asked from Kel's side. His eyes darted to Kel's ear. As mitigator, he was the only teammate without direct comms access.

She gave a dry smile and muted her new comm. Bekn noted the action. He opened his mouth and closed it, a soft crease forming between his brows. His gaze flickered back to Coup.

'Everything okay?' she asked, searching his face.

After a pause, Bekn said, softly, 'My brother was reckless enough with cheap gear and clear limitations. Now, with the kinds of things Cristo can offer . . .' He drew in a sharp breath. 'Coup doesn't see the impossible. He only sees obstacles to crash through.'

Kel mirrored his frown. 'Coup may act the part, but he's not entirely brainless. He must know his limits.' She looked back at Coup. 'He's lucky to have someone looking out for him.'

Coup cheered again from the other end of the hall, and Bekn grimaced. 'At least with Cristo's backing, if Coup's luck ever does balance out, he has access to the best facilities in Salta.' Bekn's eyes brightened. 'This sponsorship could lead to such incredible things for your – *our* – team. We could even—'

Kel's new tele-comm beeped in her pocket, and she yanked it out to see a red notification lighting the screen. Frowning, she clicked into the app that monitored Savita's vitals.

Dread shivered down her spine.

She grappled to unmute her ear-comm. 'Coup! Are you still alive?'

Coup almost deafened Kel with his answering laughter. 'Better than ever!'

'Savita's temperature is too high. You need to land!'

Coup yelled, 'She's fine. She's just—'

'Land. *Now*.'

Coup swore and spun back towards her. Savita hit the ground seconds later with a low *thwomp*. Kel rushed over, her tele-comm beeping incessantly.

'What's happening, Kel?' Dira called.

'Is Coup okay?' Bekn asked sharply.

Kel pressed a gloved palm to Savita's feathers, not caring if more burns scarred her hands.

Savita's plumage danced with its usual tiny flames. Yet . . . her temperature was too high, higher than even mid-race. Perhaps it was caused by anxiety?

Coup yanked off his helmet, his hair still impossibly, perfectly arranged. 'What are you playing at, Varra? There's nothing wrong. Stop being paranoid.'

Kel raised her chin, refusing to let her embarrassment show. 'I'd rather be paranoid than scraping an overcooked rider off Savita's back.'

He rubbed his face. 'You need to put a cere in a jar every time you overreact.'

Kel folded her arms. 'I'm not. She's—'

'She's magnificent.'

The Howlers spun towards the new voice, deep and smooth, and Kel momentarily forgot her fears. A figure approached them in long, confident strides. A pearly smile lit his face. His eyes tracked Savita's every move with wide, glazed awe.

Canen Cristo.

He looked exactly as she'd expected. Tanned skin gleamed beneath the hall's fluorescent lights, his black hair short and gelled. A blue blazer, tailored with gold thread, fitted snugly around his strong build. If anything, he looked younger than on media screens. In his early forties, perhaps.

Rahn grinned and hurried towards Cristo. 'We thought you weren't back until tonight!'

Cristo chuckled. 'I couldn't miss my new team's first practice.'

Rahn gazed at Cristo as if he was an Alchemist reborn.

Cristo met Kel's stare. 'Rahn Xing was an easy choice as your new technician. I'm so glad she's made herself at home with you all.'

Silence.

Rahn's cheeks glowed cherry-pink. 'I wanted to give you a chance to settle in before telling you.'

Savita squawked loud enough to shake the netting overhead. She raked her talons against the hard ground, a clear demand to be airborne. Coup murmured to Savita and began unbuckling his legs from the saddle fenders. Bekn and Kel fidgeted.

Cristo seemed oblivious to the tension.

'You'll be working with us?' Dira beamed. 'Every day?'

Kel bit back an unexpected laugh. Excitement vibrated through Dira as Rahn tucked a few loose hairs behind her ear. 'If you'll let me.'

In hindsight, it was almost too obvious. Rahn was their age, she lived in their unit, and had said she worked in Cristo's CAPR department.

She was the perfect Cristo employee.

And – Kel couldn't help thinking – the ideal spy, to ensure the Howlers followed the rules.

As Dira and Rahn spoke, Coup nudged Kel's shoulder, sending

a shock of warmth down her arm. Against her ear, he whispered, 'I'm surprised, Varra. Annoyed is your default setting. You're not frustrated you don't get a say in her recruitment?'

Kel folded her arms. 'She can't possibly be more annoying than you. That's enough for me.'

Kel ignored Coup's next jab, focusing back on Cristo. Kel watched him as he watched Sav, noting the intricate hue of his irises. Near-black, speckled with varying shades of brown.

'I'm so grateful you all could come on board. I'll explain your roles soon enough, but first I'd just like you to familiarize yourself with the facilities. There's free tutoring available for anyone who'd like to continue their schooling, and plenty of fun on the floors above your rooms. This is a home.'

Dira seemed delighted at the mention of free tutoring, and Coup's eyes glowed at the word *fun*. Eagerness lanced through Kel's veins. She still believed the compound was just an oversized aviary for its workers. But . . . she was open to the *possibility* of being proven wrong.

Bekn stepped forward and shook Cristo's hand. 'Thank you for all of this. Truly.'

Cristo gave a humble nod. 'No need to thank me. This is just as much a professional partnership as it is a delight. Sponsoring CAPR teams like yours gives me a chance to show off my new-to-market tech. I expect our work to be very, very beneficial for everyone.'

'That's why you're sponsoring CAPR teams? To demonstrate new tech to a commercial audience?' Bekn asked.

'Exactly. I have my hands full with council research contracts, but I wanted a new, direct avenue to show off my team's fun creations.' Cristo toyed with his sleeves. 'It doesn't hurt that CAPR is the most profitable industry in Cendor. If all goes well, I'm open to funding entire races to show off my gifted teams.'

Cristo's voice fizzed with excitement. 'Dira and Bekn, Rahn will show you to your workstations. Coup and Kelyn – why don't we see what else Savita feels like showing us today?'

Coup's giddiness electrified the air. He climbed back onto Savita, retightened the buckles around his ankles and, after placing a steady hand on her back, spurred her into flight.

The rider and phoenix soared once more around the long track. Savita was in no mood to listen to Coup's guidance, gliding when he wanted to turn and pivoting when he wanted to soar. Kel turned to Cristo, worried that he'd judge Savita's behaviour, or that Sav would overheat again. To her surprise, his face was slack with wonder.

She had plenty of questions for the billionaire. Questions that she doubted her new mitigator would approve of. Now might be her only chance to ask them.

Kel swallowed a bubble in her throat and asked, 'Why did you recruit us?'

Cristo shifted to face her. 'Are you not aware of your own reputation, Ms Varra? You've made your own skill quite clear.'

Kel pressed on. 'Dira is just as skilled a winger. Why only ask for me and Coup?'

'If hiring Dira and Bekn is what it took to get you and Warren on board, I was willing to make the arrangements.' He paused, tilting his head. 'But that doesn't answer your question, does it?' Kel continued to stare at him, willing him on. 'I wanted to hire you because of the footage I saw. The way you worked with that uncollared phoenix... I'd never seen anything like it. My phoenixes here deserve to work with someone with that level of care.'

Kel's shoulders loosened. Most people spoke of phoenixes as creatures to be *handled* and *controlled*. Instead, Cristo had complimented how she worked *with* them.

She ticked a small box in her mental checklist. 'So, I'll be working with other phoenixes here?'

Cristo nodded. 'You'll remain Savita's primary carer, but I'd like you to help analyse the behaviour of our other phoenixes, too. We have over fifty in this facility and just a handful of CAPR teams. Some of our phoenixes need guidance, and others simply need someone they can trust.'

'What kind of guidance?'

One side of Cristo's mouth twitched up. 'Monitoring vitals, managing their socializing, exploring how we can improve conservation efforts. If we can understand their biology, perhaps we can convince phoenixes to trust us. At least, enough to reproduce in aviaries, where it's safe. I want you to split your time between CAPR training and planning for these kinds of sanctuaries.'

His words exploded through her like fireworks.

'That – I think we can make something work,' she stuttered.

Cristo beamed. 'Come with me. I have two tamers on standby to assist Warren. I'd like to show you something.'

Right on cue, three figures – presumably tamers – entered the hall across the room. A faint smell of lilies was left in their wake.

Quickly, Kel grabbed her tele-comm out of her pocket and checked Savita's vitals. Everything seemed in control. Kel had no excuse not to follow him.

Minutes later, they were near Savita's new aviary. Then Cristo turned right instead of left, and led Kel to a simple door with a sign that read, THE PRISM.

Kel pushed through the heavy door, expecting another laboratory. Instead, she was met with the most expensive, glorious array of silver light.

Never in her wildest dreams could she have imagined standing inside a room made of *diamond*.

Every facet was studded with glowing gems. A small globe hung from the roof and refracted light across the walls like a broken mirror. Kel hadn't wanted to be swept away by Cristo's wealth . . . but her resolve was melting. Just one chipped diamond could fix her farm a hundred times over.

Cristo stepped into the room behind her. 'We haven't yet used *The Prism*, but we had it built for phoenix rebirths. It's the perfect containment material.'

Kel wanted to run her fingers along the nearest wall, but she was too afraid to leave a thumbprint on the flawless stone.

'The diamond can withstand the heat,' she whispered.

She'd heard of the different materials used in attempts to contain phoenix rebirths – all of which had ended disastrously. Rebirths were catastrophic for their surroundings; there was no way to avoid the damage.

Kel had read a few recent papers on gems that might withstand a rebirth's heat. Diamond was the only stone that, theoretically, might offer results. But who had that kind of money?

Cristo chuckled. 'I shouldn't be surprised you've heard of diamond theory. But I didn't bring you here to show off. I want to prove that we've accounted for every moment of a phoenix's life. From birth to death to rebirth, we've ensured they have the best facilities in Cendor.'

He added, softly, 'Romar told me that you had some . . . reservations about joining my team. But anything that Savita needs, we can provide.'

Kel's throat dried. 'I have a list.'

She had planned it all out. She'd storm up to Cristo and *demand* that he meet her requirements, or the Howlers would leave. She would read out all eighteen pages of her instructions. She would demand that he treat her like the tamer she was – not a child.

But the speech vanished like shadows in the room's fractured light. Savita's food, gear and shelter were all far superior to anything Kel could ever afford. Her phoenix would thrive in a social environment and would receive better medical care than anywhere else.

As their sponsor, Cristo would earn a commission of their winnings. He had the power to hurtle Kel back to Fieror. But as hard as she tried, there was nothing Cristo had said that she could protest.

Cristo gave a curt nod. 'Give me your list, and I'll make sure every item is seen to.'

She fumbled for the folded papers in her pocket, feeling like a child showing a parent a pretty drawing. Cristo scanned the documents before folding them in half and placing them under his arm.

'I won't overstep, but I will care for Savita as if she were my own phoenix.' Cristo was looking at Kel seriously. 'I had a phoenix of my own when I was younger. A young monarch. I raised her from an egg. So I do understand the bond you have with Savita. I promise to respect it.'

Kel stared at him, trying to hide her shock.

Cristo's gaze was locked on hers as he went on, 'I know what . . . occurred at your farm. If you'll let me, I'll send you the names of my personal contractors. They'll give you a discounted price and will rebuild your aviary quicker than any builders across Salta.'

Kel blinked. 'I – thank you.'

Cendorians were a ruthless people. They were as fierce, crude and selfish as the phoenixes they rode. But they also protected their own. Kel supposed she'd officially entered Cristo's orbit.

'I wanted to thank you too, for what you did yesterday.' Cristo's voice softened. 'I was told you stopped the train for those two bodies. Too many of my family has suffered from AB, and I hope someone might do for them what you did.'

His words bounced around the room in splintered echoes. They were no easier to hear the second and third time.

'I'm sorry.'

Cristo lowered his head. 'Phoenix research is my passion, but curing AB is my purpose. I believe it makes sense to fulfil both my passion and purpose in the same facility. That's why I want you to know that no matter how long you stay with Cristo Industries, you'll be taken care of.'

As they shook hands and exited the diamond chamber, Kel decided that she didn't need to like or dislike Canen Cristo. She didn't need to ignore her father, who had warned her against trusting companies like Cristo's. She didn't need to fall at this man's feet with praise, taking his money and rebuilding her home. She didn't need to listen or ignore the stubborn suspicion that picked at Cristo's every word, like a crow desperate for carcass scraps.

She simply needed to protect her own, just as Cristo swore to.

Chapter Seventeen

❋

Gardens and vines burrowed into Vohre's skeleton. Kel imagined it was the same wild greenery that encompassed Vohre Forest, just beyond the city's north-east border. As much as Kel wanted to hate everything about Vohre, she was captivated by the city's green-hued lights.

'Do you think they have radar towers throughout the city?' Bekn asked. 'They've built the city centre oddly close to Vohre Forest. There must be safeguards in place, to keep any curious wild phoenixes out.'

Kel glanced up at the tall buildings. Though she wasn't as paranoid about rogue phoenixes catapulting through Vohre, it was strange that Cendor's capital bordered a forest no rational human would ever venture. She was closer than she'd ever been to where her father had died, at the forest's edge, but she desperately clung to the sights and sounds around her, refusing to let that knowledge drown her senses.

'This is nothing compared to Dresva's cities,' Dira grumbled.

Kel couldn't help a laugh. Cristo had urged them into Vohre the next morning. He'd handed them a company card and a map to the nearest CAPR office. They'd registered for an upcoming race and were meandering back to Cristo Industries, drinking in the day with giddy smiles.

Oska would have loved this.

The thought crept through Kel of its own will, and nausea stabbed at her stomach. Their Asciran rider would have adored the lights, the noise, the sleek fashion of the people passing by.

Coup rubbed his hands, and Kel let it distract her. 'If this view's any indication, I bet Vohre's tracks are fit for the Alchemists.'

Excitement glowed in Coup's eyes. He pulled up the sleeves of his green sweater, revealing tanned, muscled forearms dancing with new and faded burns similar to Kel's. She was still adjusting to seeing him in ordinary clothes, outside of his riding leathers.

'We should have waited for Rahn to show us the way,' Dira mumbled, kicking a stone.

The other Howlers laughed. Kel put a consoling hand on Dira's arm.

'Rahn was busy, right? We couldn't wait.' Though Bekn's voice was even, practical, his lips twitched up.

Dira kicked another stone. 'Yeah. She was taking a friend to an appointment. Or something.'

Kel couldn't hold back a fit of giggles. Dira's pout turned to a scowl.

'Do I have some new competition for your favourite teammate?' Kel teased, putting an arm around Dira's waist.

Dira merely stuck out her foot, trying – and failing – to trip Kel. She slipped from Kel's grip and skipped ahead, but Kel didn't miss the dark flush across her friend's cheeks.

They strolled another two blocks towards Cristo's fortress before Dira, still ahead, jolted to a stop. '*Ashes!* Look.'

Dira pointed ahead towards Cristo's entry gates. Bekn, Coup and Kel had been too busy taking in the sights to notice the three white vans obscuring the metal entrance, each crowded by cameras.

Kel grimaced. 'They're not waiting for us, are they?'

Bekn scrunched his nose. 'You and Coup are still on the news cycle. Word would've reached them about our recruitment.' He let out a long breath, then straightened his jacket. 'But this is the perfect opportunity to take advantage of their attention. Cristo and I have already started to strategize ways to keep this public interest up.'

Dira, Coup and Kel exchanged wary frowns.

Bekn pulled two strips of paper from his trouser pocket. He quickly handed one ticket to Kel and the other to Coup, who seemed equally sceptical of Bekn's sudden cheer.

Kel grimaced as she scanned the red paper – a ticket – with golden writing: *1 pass to Cendor's only Saltan Sanctuary.*

Kel had just opened her mouth to object when Bekn raised a hand. 'Oh, I know, exploring a conservation centre will be such a hardship. Cooing over animals and having a generally pleasant time sounds like utter torture. But you'll manage, because I've organized for you and Coup to attend the park and show your support for Cristo's own exhibition there.'

'When did you even have time? We've been here a *day*,' Coup huffed.

'I multitask.' Bekn shrugged. 'All you two have to do is explore the sights and wave at any cameras that coincidentally happen to be there.'

Coup and Kel cursed in unison.

'No way,' Coup barked. 'We should be training, instead.'

Kel nodded. 'We need to prepare Savita for our first race.'

Her gaze flickered to Coup, frustration clenching her fists. The *last* thing she needed was to spend an entire day *alone* with Warren Coupers.

'We can ensure race coverage, but we need a . . . *well-rounded* approach to maintaining media momentum,' Bekn said. 'This will help.'

'Why would the media care if they visit some conservation centre?' Dira chimed in.

Bekn's lips twisted to the side. 'Maybe someone extremely handsome and woefully under-appreciated has leaked Kel and

Coup's planned visit, and maybe there's a rumour that they're venturing out for their first official date.'

'Not happening,' Kel snapped. 'In what universe would I—'

'Leaning into the romance rumours will boost public ratings and encourage media attention in anticipation for our first race,' Bekn cut in. 'The more media attention we get, the happier Cristo is. All you have to do is walk around and lean into what they're starting to assume.'

'It's a waste of time!' Kel exclaimed.

'Varra and I are already going to training together,' Coup sneered. 'Now you want me glued to her side all day?'

Something about Coup's words tightened Kel's throat, but she didn't have time to dwell on it.

'The more effort we put into garnering media attention *off* the track, the fewer stunts we'll have to pull *on* the track to draw their focus,' Bekn replied.

Coup and Bekn locked eyes, long enough that Kel thought something unspoken passed between them. Eventually, Coup looked into his lap and mumbled, 'Fine.'

'But it's *not*,' Kel threw back.

Bekn leaned further forward towards her. 'Three hours at the park. Holding hands. Waving to cameras if you see them.'

'One hour,' Kel said flatly. 'And I'm *not* holding anyone's hand. Especially his.'

Coup made an offended sound.

'Two hours and you'll stand close enough to fake affection,' Bekn countered. 'Final offer.'

Kel pursed her lips. The idea of spending time alone with Coup – outside of training – made her stomach swoop in a strange way.

'Fine,' Kel muttered.

Coup sighed. Slowly, he turned to Kel. 'Ready to swoon over me at the park, Varra?'

Chapter Eighteen

---※---

Compared to Cristo's clinical, pristine compound, the conservation centre's noise made Kel's skin prickle. Other visitors skipped about and inhuman sounds filled the air. Jewelled colours shone from every direction and too many sweet smells clouded her nostrils. Kel felt as if she was walking through fireworks.

Despite the heat, she pulled her navy beanie over her ears, dampening the noise. At her side, Coup had thrown on a dark peacoat she hadn't seen before. It fit his tall build too well. She hated that she noticed. Unbuttoned with the collar unfolded, it made Coup – with his windswept curls – look like a rogue pirate.

'Have you ever been to a conservation centre?' Coup asked, as they passed through the park's brick entrance. 'Or does this much colour hurt your surly rep?'

Peeling statues of Salta's animals guarded the entrance, beckoning people inside far too menacingly. 'No to both,' she replied. 'Have you?'

Kel handed over their passes to a glazed-eyed ticket collector. The man's expression sharpened, and Kel felt his lingering stare as they passed.

Coup shrugged. 'Public aviaries are probably the closest I've been.'

'My mum's mentioned an Asciran conservation centre in a postcard. She made it sound like something out of an Alchemist fable, seeing all of Salta's magic in one place.'

So far, the centre – just west of Vohre – had yet to convince Kel of any fable-like qualities. She could only see winding stone paths and nature strips; no animals or cameras, other than the security lenses above the entrance.

Coup tilted his head back and froze. Kel frowned. 'What's wrong?'

Coup chuckled, a strange, breathy sound. He pointed up.

Kel followed his gaze. Her jaw went slack.

She'd been so preoccupied dreading the time at Coup's side, worrying about how Savita would fair without her, she hadn't even considered the creatures she might see.

Overhead, a glass tube stretched from the park's entrance to the trees ahead. She could faintly make out tiny lights dancing inside.

Sprites.

The small creatures – no bigger than her thumbpad – reflected the morning sun, stuck between the glass panels like a jewelled flurry in a snow globe. Blue, red, green, yellow – too many colours to count. She couldn't make out their little shapes; a spindly limb here and a pointed wing there, but nothing clear. Staring at them for too long stung her eyes.

Though sprites were usually fickle creatures, their magic was rumoured to affect weather and moods. Kel's passion had always lain with phoenixes, but seeing their iridescent lights flicker and swirl like trapped galaxies made her understand why Ascira was the most popular tourist isle.

Looking ahead, Kel realized the sprites' enclosure ran above the entire park, curving down in glass columns that visitors could press against.

'I wonder how they breathe inside the glass,' Coup mused as they began walking. 'It'd be difficult to make holes small enough that they couldn't escape through.'

Before she could reply, a camera flashed to their right. A few feet away, a young girl stood in front of an older man. Grinning, the girl held up a large tele-comm, one of the few capable of taking photographs.

'Sorry,' the man said feebly. 'My daughter's a huge fan.'

Coup laughed and waved at the child. As the man led her away, Coup turned to Kel. All warmth drained from his face. 'We're meant to convince people we're on a *date*, Varra. Would it kill you to look happy?'

Kel ran a hand through her hair. Embarrassment and frustration warred, tightening her throat. 'We're convincing the *cameras* we're on a date.'

Coup thrust a thumb backwards. 'She had one. You don't think her pictures will get around Cendor?'

'She's a *kid*. Not a reporter.'

Coup shrugged. 'Cameras are cameras. Don't trust any of them.'

Kel sucked on her lower teeth, biting back a response. They'd barely spent *five minutes* in the park. She refused to let him under her skin so soon.

Even worse, he was right. She needed to get over any stage-fright, even when brought on by children. But until they'd joined forces with the Coupers, the Howlers hadn't had to navigate this kind of attention.

They meandered further into the park, down a cobblestone path bordered by trees and shimmering glass columns. Certain colours swarmed together, shades of green clustering together in buzzing clouds.

She shoved her hands inside the pockets of her coat, unsure how close was too close or not close enough to stand beside Coup. It felt strange, standing beside him in the real world, beyond Cristo's confines.

They wandered deeper into the park, passing a slanted souvenir booth. Stuffed toys, wooden trinkets and framed sketches hung behind the wooden counter. The trinkets and paintings made Kel's stomach flip. She couldn't count how many nights she'd spent curled up in her aviary's office, the sketchpad and leather carving kit from her father keeping her company when Dira couldn't. Kel had once dreamt of owning a phoenix sanctuary self-sufficient enough that she could moonlight as a tattoo artist, drawing and needling her designs onto living canvases. Tattooists were popular across Cendor; living with phoenixes meant that plenty of Cendorians bore burns and scars, and the marks were often flaunted, decorated with tattoos and flourishes. Did working with Cristo – earning his money – make that dream more or less likely?

Kel felt more stares at their backs, more camera flashes. Her tongue felt too big for her mouth. She imagined slipping and stuttering around the wrong words when the reporters cornered them. What if they asked her again about her father? Or Oska? Her knees wobbled, and a sharp pang of guilt tinged with homesickness swept through her.

'Stop *looking* for reporters,' Coup hissed. 'My brother knows what he's doing. They'll be here, if they're not already. They're just waiting for something worth photographing.'

Kel fought the urge to hunch forwards, to shrink beneath her layers. 'Right.'

'We're meant to look like we're on a date. Not like we're in pain.' Coup cursed under his breath. 'I know smiling for the cameras is *beneath* a mighty Varra, but—'

'It's not that.' Kel shook her head. 'I just . . . I don't know how to do it. Not like you. I see a camera and I just . . .' Kel shuddered. 'I start overthinking every breath, every gesture. It feels like they're poking at me with needles.'

'Oh.' Coup's eyes searched her, something unnameable in his expression. 'Well, you're the expert in the aviary, tamer. Out here, let me show you how it's done.'

Kel swallowed a lump as the ground turned from cobblestone to sand. There was a question in his gaze as he awaited her answer. Eventually, she sighed. 'Okay. Let's see what you've got.'

Coup smiled wolfishly as they navigated the soft, corn-yellow sand. A few more wanderers turned their way, more cameras flashing.

He held out a crooked arm. Reluctantly, Kel looped her hand through and allowed him to guide their path. His hip bumped against hers, too warm. Too close.

Kel squeezed Coup's jacket sleeve. In response, several cameras clicked. Her head instinctively whipped around, fast enough that she felt a crick form in her neck.

Coup laughed, a loud, startlingly warm sound. He tugged her down a narrow laneway. 'Let's find a better distraction.'

The sandy laneway opened up into an emerald clearing and the air grew muggier, reminding Kel of an aviary's heated lamps. As they walked, the ground turned to glass, and beneath it Kel could see a maze of dirt tunnels.

'*Alchemists!*' Kel breathed, as the most dazzling creature slithered about. The serpent was covered in emerald-and-cinnamon scales that criss-crossed like diamonds, with two little jade horns sitting above its narrow eyes.

Dresvan serpents. Here – in Cendor. Sprites were sunny, harmless little insects, but serpents? Dira had told Kel that they were poisonous, intelligent creatures that usually kept to dense forestry. Their venom held magical properties. It was so strange to see one gliding through a glass cage in Vohre.

Though the serpents' crystalline skin was almost hypnotizing, as they shifted off the glass, Kel's attention once more stuck to her hand around Coup's solid arm. She didn't know why she couldn't relax her hand. Why couldn't she focus on anything but the feel of him pressed against her side?

Kel spotted a violently red overhead sign, signalling a nearby aviary, just as two figures carrying bulky equipment ambled towards them. The pair – a man clutching a voice-comm and a woman holding a large camera – waved at Kel.

'What a surprise, seeing a pair of rising celebrities here!' the man sang.

He gestured to the red-haired woman hovering a step behind him. 'We were just filming coverage of the sanctuary. Any chance we could steal you two for a quick interview?'

A prickling heat spread across Kel's neck. Feebly, she said, 'How can I say no?'

Coup coughed, poorly concealing a chuckle. He grinned at the suited reporter and camerawoman. 'Of course! But it can't take long – we're excited to look around.'

Coup shifted to trail his fingers along Kel's arm, down her wrist, before gently lacing their fingers together. He moved slowly, giving Kel plenty of time to shift away. After a moment, he gave her hand a soft squeeze. Her stomach flipped, though she didn't pull away.

A necessity for the cameras, she told herself.

The reporter's gaze flickered down. The camerawoman shifted back a step, likely to include a shot of their entwined hands.

'Your last race in Fieror was an incredible watch, but Vohre's tracks are known to be a little more daunting,' he goaded. 'How are you feeling leading up to your first race in our city, Coup?'

Coup's chin lifted. 'I'm hoping Vohre's tracks live up to their reputation.'

Kel clenched her teeth around a sigh. The reporter turned to Kel. 'You must be feeling some unease about watching Coup race, especially considering how inseparable you two have become.'

Kel's pulse jumped into her throat. She opened her mouth,

unsure what words would come out – when Coup squeezed her hand again. Warmth shot up her arm and thawed her muscles. Kel forced a wobbly chuckle. 'I'd probably feel less uneasy if he felt a little more.'

The reporter laughed again as Coup added, 'I don't know what I'd do without Kelyn to keep my feet on the ground.'

The reporter continued. 'On that note – we have to touch on the rumours that have surrounded your teams' recent merger. You two certainly seem to be spending a lot of time together.'

Coup flashed Kel a lopsided smile. She knew it wasn't real, but – *Alchemists help her!* – when he turned that roguish grin on her, butterflies crawled up her stomach.

Coup answered smoothly, 'I suppose our team-up is too exciting for viewers to think it's just professional.'

Kel chimed in, 'The team definitely has some explosive chemistry.' *Mostly used to scream at each other.* 'We'll leave it at that.'

'Could you imagine if we *hated* each other?' Coup made a sound of mock disbelief. 'It'd make every day unbearable.'

Kel matched his expression. 'Couldn't imagine it.'

The reporter continued to spur his own rumours, and Kel kept her eyes on Coup instead of the camera. Eventually, they waved the pair away.

Hands still twined, Kel tugged them towards the aviary ahead, past swarms of silver sprites. Growing squawks filled the air. They paused to spot a yellow-and-bronze harrow phoenix with a bandaged leg and a smaller chick tucked beneath its wing.

Excitement raced through Kel. She'd only seen one or two harrow phoenixes before and never one with such young, pale features. Until the chick reached maturity in a few years, it would remain a glowing cloud of daffodil fluff.

The chick sneezed and stumbled back into a shrub, which it

quickly turned to grumble at. Kel giggled. She imagined a young Savita acting similarly.

She felt Coup's gaze and turned towards him. 'What?'

Coup shook his head. 'I don't think I've ever seen you without a hint of a frown.'

'Don't get used to it,' she said lightly.

She soon spotted signage that claimed this aviary as Cristo's. Kel wondered whether he'd placed an aviary here to garner attention, or whether he truly cared about conservation.

She turned towards Coup. 'What do you think of Cristo so far?'

'Is *the* Kelyn Varra – self-proclaimed expert in everything – asking for my opinion?' Coup batted his lashes. 'Well, he seems benign, but anyone rich can hire a good mitigator to tell them what to say. Seeming trustworthy isn't the same as earning trust.'

His words made her think of their own mitigator, and she risked asking, 'Speaking of good mitigators . . . why is ours worried that you think Cristo's gear makes you unkillable?'

Coup stiffened. 'He said that to you?'

Kel tilted her head. 'Not in so many words. Why? Is it true?'

'Just when I thought we'd been getting along.' Coup sighed. 'It's none of your business.'

His words made her stomach flip, but she pressed on. 'If there's something that'll impact your riding ability, or the safety of my phoenix, it is.'

A muscle in Coup's jaw twitched. 'It won't.'

'That's not what Bekn seems to think.'

'Do you have a dimmer switch or something?' Coup snapped, and pulled his hand from hers. 'It's nothing. Really. Just an overprotective brother who thinks I've abandoned all self-preservation instincts.'

'Have you?'

Coup's eyes sharpened, focusing on Kel in a way that made her shift her weight. 'I owe Bekn. And I can repay that debt through CAPR. So, for now, debts overrule self-preservation.'

Kel wanted to ask what he owed Bekn, but from the hard edges in his voice, she knew he wouldn't tell her.

She didn't entirely understand why, but she wanted to draw back the version of Coup she'd seen just moments ago. The version that had kept her company atop a burning hill, had silently sat with her in Sav's aviary, had squeezed her hand when the reporter had questioned her.

'I'm terrified of losing Sav,' she quickly stuttered, like a poison to expel. 'That's my debt. I owe Sav better than having to race and bleed to pay for our home.'

She instantly regretted the brittle confession. It would only give Coup more ammunition to tease her, to call her a hypocrite. She *hated* racing, but only because she knew how lethal CAPR could be. It was just as cruel to compete and keep Sav in a gilded cage, like every animal in this park; to cling to the one creature in her life who couldn't die.

After a long silence, Coup said, 'Careful, Varra. I'd almost think we had something in common.'

Her insides lifted as if she'd been tossed from a carnival ride. Silently, they turned from the aviary – just as a new, camera-less figure approached them with delicate steps.

The girl, about Coup's age, gazed at Coup. 'You're Warren Coupers, right? Could I get your autograph?' Her lips curved up. 'I'm Alma.'

The girl – Alma – held out a pen and a photo of Coup, garbed in his riding leathers, atop the Star Chasers' flaming beast.

Coup stepped away from Kel as if bitten.

The sudden loss of warmth sent a chill down her spine.

'Sure,' he replied, flaunting his thousand-watt smile.

Coup's gaze flickered to Kel, but she was already moving away, offering them some small privacy. Alma twirled a black curl around a finger. Her long lashes were flawless and her expression sincere.

'You were so brave in that race. I'd never seen anything like it,' Alma said to Coup, her voice lilting.

Coup laughed.

Kel swallowed a metallic taste and shuffled further down the cobblestone path. Every sweet, silky word the pair traded soured her tongue. She focused on the painted fence to her right; a mural of Salta's magical attractions.

Kel shoved her sweaty hands in her trouser pockets and mentally rebuilt a familiar, jagged wall between her and Coup. Just for a moment, she'd let herself wonder what it might feel like to take a sledgehammer to that wall. Instead, she left no room for any more sharp, painful truths to slip through.

She snuck a glance back. Their heads were ducked conspiratorially.

It wasn't like Kel *hadn't* noticed Coup's looks, striking enough to turn heads wherever he went. His muscled build from years of riding, an easy grin that earnt its arrogance, sun-soaked eyes . . . But she couldn't imagine ever seeing past the smug, self-assured second skin he wore long enough to be attracted to him. *Ever.*

Kel huffed and forced her attention to the artwork before her. Ebrait's sea monsters and ash-grey temples, Ascira's glamour and sprites, Dresva's forestry and serpents, Cendor's tech and phoenixes. She shifted further from Coup, brushing a hand along the next mural of the Four Alchemists.

Before arriving on Salta, the Alchemists had been failed inventors, laughed from their homes on the continent. Salta's magic had provided the perfect ingredients for their experiments. Kel had only ever cared for her father's stories of Cendor's Alchemist, Landen Ryker, soaring on the mighty Deja, leaving fiery trails of destruction.

Before the other night, beside Coup in Sav's new aviary, she hadn't let herself think of those stories in a long, long time.

'I can't believe my date left me to fend off an admirer by myself,' a voice teased, from behind her.

Kel turned to see Coup, hands tucked into his jacket pockets, a lazy smirk across his face. His shoulder pressed against hers. She couldn't stop her spine from stiffening.

Kel swallowed down a stronger, bitter mouthful. 'Your *date* was miserable from watching that poor attempt at flirting.'

Coup's smirk vanished. 'Don't pretend you know a thing about flirting, Varra. Just stick to glaring and we'll get through this.'

Before she could reply, Coup turned back to the cobblestone path. 'Come on. We'll have to bat our eyes at each other for the cameras at least another hundred times before my brother's satisfied.'

A chill spread down Kel's arms. She flexed her hands in her pockets. She didn't know why mention of Alma made irritation bloom through her chest. She should have just kept going through the motions of their charade, counting down the minutes before she could see Sav again.

Instead, her next words escaped of their own free will, injected with as much venom as a snakebite. 'Bat your eyes another hundred times and you might actually convince them you care about people more than their praise.'

Coup slowed, half-turning towards her. 'You seem awfully concerned about who and what I care about. Just focus on your own mask and we can get back to hating each other soon enough.'

Kel didn't know whether to retort or apologize as they hurried along the path leading towards the exit. Neither slowed until they spotted a small cluster of reporters waiting inside the gates.

Coup moved to hold her hand again, but she couldn't bear it. She merely shook her head and tried to loosen the strange sinking in her stomach.

Chapter Nineteen

———— ✵ ————

'This way!' Kel shouted.

After Rahn and Dira tried – and failed – to locate their team's tent with maps, Bekn had hoisted Kel onto his shoulders. Squinting through the harsh sun, Kel scanned the grounds. Moments later, she spotted a yellow tent bearing the number *17* and their black-and-burgundy emblem.

Jumping to the ground, Kel led her crew through the dense crowd. Gold flags hung in rows overhead, and commentators with voice-comms screamed over thunderous music. From raised stands, spectators waved posters of Coup and Kel's faces inside a hand-drawn heart. The sun poured down in heavy waves. All Kel could smell was sweat and smoke.

She glanced back at her team. There was no fear on their faces. Nothing but wide grins and flushed cheeks.

Spectators and reporters were meant to remain in the raised stands, as the ground was reserved for racing teams. Still, some cameras flashed at their sides. A nearby reporter turned towards the Howlers, trying to draw her and Coup's attention, but Kel breezed past. News of their entry into today's race had spread like fire. Cristo claimed to be bombarded with requests for interviews with *Cendor's latest power couple*.

Dira had taunted her for hours after they'd seen that particular headline.

Savita raked her talons against the moist ground, feathers ruffled in agitation. Kel's arms strained against her harness.

'Not much further,' Kel crooned, trying to keep the growing tension from her voice. 'I know it's a new place. New smells, new chaos. Just . . .' Kel grunted as Sav released an agitated grumble. 'Wait until you're on the track to let out some steam.'

If Sav understood Kel's plea, she ignored her tamer, folding and unfolding her wings, forcing other scattered CAPR teams to give her a wide berth. The other Howlers meandered ahead, unaware of Sav's stubborn flailing.

Kel grunted again, trying to keep Sav's head down. Though Sav was used to CAPR tracks, the current crowd was at least twice as big as any of Fieror's, the noise like crashing waves.

Savita lashed out towards Kel as another nearby flurry of cameras flashed. Kel jumped to the right and narrowly avoided Savita's spear-like beak. Before Kel could grumble another plea, a pair of hands appeared to help tighten Sav's harness.

'Is she always like this before races?' Coup huffed, helping Kel to guide Sav forwards.

Coup was dressed in his new riding uniform, goggles on his head like a glass crown. His shoulder pressed against hers and warmth shot down her arm, making her fingers tingle. She tried to ignore his nearness, as a sudden influx of cameras flashed overhead. Her mouth went dry.

Kel didn't reply until Sav – reluctantly – shuffled towards their tent. 'She's just excited. And overwhelmed.'

She kept her focus glued to her phoenix. In the two weeks since their romantic stroll through the conservation centre, it had been a relief to sink into their new normal. Arguing with Coup over safety precautions and new manoeuvres, with no need to reignite any bitter or confusing emotions for cameras. Though memories of the park flashed through her mind more than she'd have liked, today's race had provided the perfect distraction – even if a new media parade shouted for photos of them coupled up.

As they neared their tent, Kel spotted the track's railing. Other phoenixes began to line up, hovering below the low netting overhead.

By the time Coup and Kel caught up to the others, she could see the track in its entirety.

'*Ashes!*' Dira mumbled.

'Fuck!' Bekn gaped.

Water. It was full of *water*.

'I've never seen a track like this,' Dira said, panic lacing her words. 'No phoenix will be used to this much water. It's practically a river!'

Kel swallowed a hard lump. Phoenixes *hated* water. A small fountain on a track was one thing. But a river? Phoenixes couldn't swim. Water battled against their very nature.

Rahn shuffled closer to Dira. 'How will the phoenixes react? Will they be scared or angry?'

'It'll make them destructive,' Kel said, not missing the wince on Rahn's face. She turned to the other Howlers. 'We're not racing unless we figure out how CAPR's expecting us to navigate the track.'

Kel's stomach swooped as she imagined Coup struggling to unbuckle himself fast enough to avoid any frightened phoenix attacks. Savita was fast enough, *magic* enough, to survive, but Coup . . .

The rider's mouth fell open in a mock look of surprise. 'Would you believe it – there's *four* other members of this team. We're already here, Varra. We're not backing out now.'

Any fear Kel felt for him vanished. 'You'd rather we throw Sav into a race without a strategy?'

'Let me think!' Dira exploded. 'We're missing something. There's a lot riding on our performance in our first Vohre race. Whether or not he knew what the terrain would be, Cristo wouldn't throw us into an unwinnable race.'

Suddenly, a light flared in Kel's mind.

She dashed inside their team's tent and found the nearest wooden pole. She quickly unbound the rope holding it in place and, with gritted teeth, yanked the pole from the ground. The tent tilted slightly with one fewer leg, but it didn't fall.

Kel hurried back to the track's short railing, ignoring her friends' confused frowns. On her toes, she leaned over the railing and lowered the pole down, down, until it met the water. Then she kept going.

Just when she thought she'd lose her balance and tumble forward, the pole thudded against the ground. She exhaled and, after a few seconds, pulled it out of the water.

There was a clear line across the pole, about halfway up its length. 'Does anyone have a pen?'

Wordlessly, Rahn pulled one from her pocket. Kel drew a line on the wood, marking the water's depth. 'It's only about a metre deep. There isn't enough room for anything too dangerous to be lurking.'

So this was a race about strategy – not speed.

Her team let out a collective breath.

'Nothing says high stakes like murky sewage water,' Bekn deadpanned.

Kel looked around and noticed a handful of other teams facing the same dilemma. A few were investigating the water with tent poles and measuring tapes. Two were frozen in confusion. Another three were standing in circles with their chins high, red-faced and screaming about the race's conditions at the nearest CAPR officials.

Kel ushered the Howlers inside their tent, tying Savita's harness to a nearby post and instructing her to wait. Inside, Kel turned to Rahn and Dira. 'It's like the simulation we ran a few days ago, with sand covering the ground and the low netting. Savita knew we'd buried objects in the sand, but she couldn't see what. We had to guide her around them.'

'But this isn't sand,' Coup argued. 'It's *water*. And the net isn't high enough for Sav to fly above the water if any other phoenixes block her flight pattern.'

Kel bit her lip. 'If you can distract her from the water while you guide her, we might have a chance. A lot of these phoenixes lived in the wild before they were tamed. Wild phoenixes know to fear the water, because they've flown over Salta's oceans – full of krakens, hydras, and other beasts. But Savita doesn't even know creatures like that exist. *That* is our advantage.'

The words left a bitter aftertaste in Kel's mouth. This race required them to profit off phoenixes' inherent fears. The knowledge gnawed at that seed of guilt buried deep in her gut. A seed she'd need to bury even deeper to win this race.

Coup closed his mouth. After a long, silent moment, he nodded.

Dira, Rahn and Bekn exchanged looks. If they didn't place in this race, the momentum they'd gained would evaporate, and they'd have to explain themselves to Cristo.

But Kel *knew* Savita could do this. This track was about trust. Not many phoenixes trusted their riders to navigate them over murky waters. But Savita – whether Kel liked it or not – trusted Coup.

'Okay,' Bekn whispered, after a heavy silence. 'Let's win this.'

Chapter Twenty

※

Together, Rahn and Kel strapped Coup's legs into Savita's saddle. Rahn's saddle designs had seemed strange, at first. Where Rube's designs were strong and durable, Rahn's were sleek and varied. The skirts and seats of her saddles were shaped like hourglasses, rather than the traditional rounded slope, so the leathers didn't weigh on Savita's wings. Sav would have more freedom, more speed, while Coup would have less material to secure himself to.

Kel kept a hand on Savita's side as they wove back through the crowd, feeling for any bursts of anxious heat, or hints that her temperature might flare as it had in recent training sessions. Yet Savita appeared unfazed by the commotion; if anything, she seemed invigorated. Her temperature was steady and her depthless eyes remained focused.

As Rahn shifted away from Savita's side, Kel paused. Blinding flashes – from high overhead, in the raised stands – dotted her vision. Coup smiled and waved from Sav's back, unbothered by the lights.

'You're in your element,' she said dryly.

Coup continued to wave. 'Meaning?'

Kel gestured to the media storm crowding the track's rails. 'Oh, come on, I've watched you in interviews for years. You adore the attention.'

Coup smirked. 'You've watched me for years, huh?'

Before Kel could respond, Coup shrugged, almost imperceptibly. 'It's not that hard to fake a smile, Varra. Most of us need one to earn a living.'

Kel blinked. Coup continued smiling, waving, parading.

Rahn sighed from behind Kel. Kel turned, eager for the distraction. The technician held up her tele-comm to the other Howlers. 'Canen can't make it to today's race, but he refuses to stop spamming me with fire icons until I show you this picture.'

Above a text chain littered with *far* too many fire symbols, a photo of Cristo filled half the screen. The words I'M WITH THE HOWLERS streaked his cap and T-shirt, below the Howlers' logo. Red and black paint dotted his face, pulled up in a cheesy grin, and behind him sat piles of identical shirts and caps.

'Oh no,' Dira said, grimacing.

'Who could've guessed a billionaire genius could cosplay as such a convincing dorky dad?' Coup drawled.

Rahn sighed, shaking her head and pocketing her tele-comm.

Kel forced a light laugh. Perhaps she should have been giddier, bejewelled with new gear and sponsored by Salta's leading tech-giant. But her spine was rigid and her breath kept catching. Every camera flash, every phoenix shriek – unease coiled in her chest like a spring.

The starting line – where the water began – quickly came into view. Most of the other twenty-four teams were already lined up. The track was only wide enough to fit every phoenix with their wings pinned. Once they took flight, each would have to fight for space. Kel imagined most phoenixes would try to back away from the water.

Phoenixes of all sizes and colours clawed at the asphalt ground. A honey-hued phoenix shrank back from a maroon, speckled phoenix, swiping at the former with extended talons. Blood trickled down pale feathers.

Kel's stomach dropped. She'd known Vohre races were more vicious. She'd watched plenty of reruns, had seen Dira research every team competing today. But watching Savita enter the chaos was another thing entirely.

She could see in Coup's eyes, the way he sized up the other phoenixes, that he knew it, too. But she also saw the way his jaw clenched and his hands tightened around Savita's reins.

As if noticing the same thing, Bekn murmured, 'Don't do anything *Coup*-like, okay? We just need to place.'

Coup sighed. 'Don't worry, brother. I'll give Cristo the show he wants.'

Coup, Kel, Dira and Rahn turned on the comms in their ears and the latter two whooped, sending pitchy static down the line and muffling Bekn's dry response.

Kel pressed a glove hand to Sav's side in a silent goodbye, before following Dira, Rahn and Bekn back to their tent. Usually, tents and booths were raised for sky-high views of the tracks. But this race was low enough that the ground provided the best view. It felt strange, preparing for a race without the creaking, shifting metal of raised steps.

As Kel and the other Howlers watched Coup lean forward in the saddle, Kel realized that Coup had no intention of staying safe. If his grins to the media were any indication, he was a talented deflector. Of course he told Bekn what he wanted to hear.

More importantly, Kel realized, as the starting siren wailed, Coup had never promised caution. Only spectacle.

Chapter Twenty-One

❋

A sancter rifle filled the sky with lightning, and a firestorm shrouded the track.

Almost every phoenix tried to launch upwards at once. Only half managed to navigate the slim breadth of sky between net and water. Others lost their footing and scrambled back from the water. Fearful screams polluted the air.

Five phoenixes remained at the starting line, watching the chaos unfold – including Coup. A moment later, the other riders guided their mounts into low crouches. Eventually, one by one, the other four darted through the empty patches of air and onto the track.

'Go! *Go*, Coup – hurry up!' Dira screamed through the comms.

'Shut up!' Coup grunted.

Kel could hear the strain in his words. It took every morsel of self-control not to add her own screams to the chaos.

A heartbeat later, Savita spread her great wings and darted into the sky. She wove between awkward wings and tucked talons. Her initial burst of speed wouldn't last long; every race began with a straight stretch that lasted at least a few hundred metres, allowing for phoenixes' initial take off. '*Coup* – five metres to the right, now!' Dira yelled.

Coup swerved just as a stream of water shot up like an underwater volcano, directly where he would have flown. Kel hadn't even noticed the device bubbling below them. The water's speed and pressure were enough to daze – even injure – any phoenix.

Kel's heart pounded as Savita narrowly missed the jetting water.

Instead, it collided with the phoenix to her left, jerking the creature skyward, its wings tangling with the overhead netting.

Dira let out a hard, relieved breath. 'It's hard to see the water from where you are – try to keep your focus on the track route. I'll watch for any attacks.'

Together, Dira and Coup managed to guide Sav around the rapid fountains. Below swiping talons and above murky ripples, their phoenix found a faster, steadier pace. In minutes, Savita had ducked and soared past five, ten other phoenixes.

But this wasn't a race of speed. Coup approached the tail feathers of another phoenix. Kel knew their bodies would never fit side by side. Savita gained speed and, under Dira's direction, she slowly inched below the ginger phoenix. Sav ducked her head to avoid the talons and skimmed the water's surface, lower than the other phoenixes dared to go.

But it wasn't the water jets they had to watch out for.

The phoenix above Savita finally noticed her approach. The creature released an ear-splitting crow and lowered its head. Its black beak opened and moved too fast, not towards Savita – but Coup. As if to rip him from the saddle and swallow him whole.

'Get out of there!' Dira shouted. 'Down – *now!*'

Kel clamped her fists around the rail as Savita slowed and fell back. Any slower, and Coup's head would no longer be attached to his body. She heard Bekn exhale at her back.

Kel pressed a hand to her sternum, trying to slow her breath.

As if furious at letting prey escape, the other phoenix swung its body to the right, slamming hard into Savita's side.

Savita screamed, swaying in the air. The collision wasn't enough to knock her into the water, but she tumbled and spiralled, forcing Coup to clutch the saddle pommel as he was turned upside down, dangling from Savita's back.

Kel held her breath. In the distance, softer, flickering flames seemed to stir to life along Savita's neck. By the time Savita steadied herself, six other phoenixes had swarmed past, narrowly missing her wings.

The crowd roared with delight, a violent chorus begging for carnage. Every near-collision earnt a low howl, every injury brought on a primal cheer.

The noise tinted Kel's vision red. Though Savita was unharmed, Coup had probably borne the brunt of the attack. There was nothing she could do. Nothing—

'Coup,' Dira said stiffly. She swapped a quick glance with Rahn, then placed a hand against her ear. 'Listen to me. Lie against the saddle seat and keep your arms pressed to your sides. Don't attack any phoenixes at the front of the pack – only let Savita lash out at the slower, smaller ones that the crowd doesn't care about. Even if the others attack you, stay low and stay fast. Savita isn't the biggest, but she's the fastest. Don't hold back.'

Don't hold back.

Most saddles and leathers weren't built for a phoenix's full speed. Some riders were foolish enough to accelerate near a race's end, where they could dismount before burning. Most tech couldn't handle that kind of heat.

But Rahn's designs were better than most. Dira wouldn't risk Coup's life if they weren't.

Kel watched Coup shift beside the saddle pommel and lean low, arms tucked. It was impossible to deny how well he moved with Savita, how quickly he adapted to the phoenix's moods and sudden shifts. His muscles twitched a second after Savita's, as if she guided him, rather than the other way around.

'Sav, get ready to break some records,' Coup howled.

Across the far side of the track, Savita gained speed. Her wings dipped low and the wind caused streams of water to rise into the air. Water jets attacked left and right, jets of near-black water chasing Savita a half-second too late, until one bubbling stream shot out towards her midsection.

The water collided with Savita's stomach. Sav rose as if yanked by a string. Coup jolted down against the saddle, then back up. A phoenix to Sav's left snapped its beak at her, sensing vulnerability. Though Sav swerved haphazardly to avoid a clamp around her neck, the phoenix bit into Sav's left wing and plucked a bloody cluster of feathers. Sav shrieked and managed to pull away, tilting to swipe at the attacking phoenix with a talon.

Kel felt dizzy. She watched as Savita righted herself. Coup seemed uninjured, but she could barely see through the black spots crowding her vision.

'What's going on? Is he hurt?' Bekn pleaded, eyes darting between Kel and Dira.

'Everything okay?' Dira shouted down the line.

Savita's wings still failed to correct her jilted course. Though she'd escaped the other phoenix, one wrong stroke and her feathers would catch in the thick, leather netting overhead.

'We're good!' Coup shouted back, giddiness clouding his voice.

Kel echoed his words to Bekn, and asked Coup, 'How badly is Sav hurt?'

'*Ashes!*' Coup swore, swerving around a sandy phoenix to his left. 'She's fine, Varra. The bird barely took a few feathers, and a little splash won't kill her.'

Kel ground her teeth, caging her retort. At least the black spots in her vision cleared.

Coup clung to the textured pommel as Savita flipped and spun around other phoenixes. Some tried to stop her approach with claws and beaks – but this time, Coup and Dira anticipated it. Kel watched him touch the sensitive patch of feathers at the base of Sav's neck. He stroked different feathers to warn her of attacks from behind, above, below. His movements were light, assured.

Slowly, they soared closer to the front of the pack.

The crowd crackled with energy, their shouts colliding like fireworks. Some cheered and others booed as Savita moved faster. Tiny flames began to lick at the tips of Savita's feathers. This was as fast as they'd ever dared to fly with Rube's leathers.

Coup stirred Savita faster still.

The phoenix didn't need to be told twice. Savita cried out and blasted past two more firebirds.

Others swooped and swiped, but Savita stayed close to the water. No other phoenixes were willing to fly so close to the murky depths. From the way Coup's gaze kept flickering to the phoenixes above him, Kel could tell he was itching to enter the fray, rather than stay low. Still, he listened to Dira with reluctant grumbles, anticipating her words almost before they echoed down the comms.

Though Savita was fast, nimble, even she couldn't avoid every water jet. Dira kept Sav from any direct hits, but occasional jets clipped her wings or slowed her pace. Yet there was never any fear in Savita's movements. With every drop of water that dared touch her, she seemed to grow more stubborn.

The small sparks licking at Savita's sides climbed higher. She flew faster and faster until she disappeared behind growing flames and fearless screams.

'Only two more phoenixes ahead of you,' Dira murmured to Coup. 'They've been competing against each other for years, so hopefully there's enough rivalry there to keep them distracted.'

The two competing phoenixes were side by side, swooping at each other as they raced towards the finish line, too distracted to notice Coup swooping below. The smaller creature screamed as the larger phoenix managed to drag a claw against its side. Even from a distance, Kel spotted a thin trail of blood streaming down – directly onto Coup and Sav.

Kel's nails dug into her palms. Too many emotions flurried inside her, unfamiliar and beyond her control.

The larger phoenix finally noticed Coup and Savita soaring beneath them. It swung out with sword-sharp talons; a wild, imprecise attack.

'Fall back a little,' Dira instructed. 'Third place will still make Cristo happy. It's not worth risking overhead attacks you can't defend yourself against.'

Coup grunted. Kel didn't know if it was a sound of agreement or disagreement. A moment later, Savita fell back, just a few feet, and the spring in Kel's chest eased.

Sirens wailed, signalling the last lap. Coup traced new instructions into Sav's neck feathers, drawing shapes to communicate flight patterns. Savita dashed to the left. The larger, maroon phoenix lashed out with wild talons again, catching the empty air just above Coup's head.

Coup swerved back to the right, where the smaller phoenix lashed out in turn. Savita was far enough away from the talons, but one mistimed swerve and they would slice through Coup's skull.

From Dira's right, Bekn fidgeted, shifting his weight. 'Remind my brother that he promised zero recklessness.'

Dira echoed Bekn's words down her comm. Coup answered with a breathy laugh, swerving left again. 'It's only reckless if we don't win.'

Too late, Kel realized what he was doing. Both phoenixes lashed out at him with feeble swipes. Their distracted attacks allowed Coup to sneak further ahead, which, in turn, meant that the attacks grew more erratic, causing them to slice at each other rather than Coup below.

Back and forth, Coup wove beneath the two. Between jets of water, around swiping talons, distracting the other phoenixes just enough for them to mistime the next water fountain ahead. Savita's flames grew with every swerve, high enough to blur Coup's shape.

Just a few metres from the finish line, the two phoenixes crashed together as they swooped at Coup. Their gleaming talons knotted as a water jet erupted beneath them. As Coup swerved around the bubbling jet, the phoenixes crashed into the water, sending a rush of water into the crowd.

Kel's heart thumped as Savita and Coup soared across the finish line, seizing first place. Giddy screams and disbelieving laughter echoed down their comms, overlapping and cresting like waves. Bekn stood apart from the celebrations, arms folded. Kel ignored his concern. She ignored the beeping in her pocket, notifying her of Sav's heat. She ignored everything but the euphoria coursing through her, like a fire through a dry forest, a bird from a cage, a phoenix through the sky.

Chapter Twenty-Two

The Howlers were still drowning in their own triumph when they returned to Cristo Industries. Even the swarming reporters asking about Kel and Coup's *blooming romance* hadn't soured Kel's mood.

They swaggered through the pearly facility, congratulated by familiar and unfamiliar faces. When they reached their unit, they were shocked to see a stack of wrapped gifts strewn across their kitchen table. Bekn hurriedly opened the card atop the stack, and the others crowded around him to read neat, looping handwriting:

> Congratulations, Howlers! I'm so glad this first foray was such an easy win for the team. I can't wait to see what you can achieve in Vohre's more inventive races. I'm eager to keep this momentum rolling into your next race in a few days.
>
> Regards, Canen

Dira snorted. 'That race was anything but easy.'

Kel made a sound of agreement. By Fieror's dry, looping standards, the race they'd just won had been wilder than anything they could have imagined. Her giddiness began to fade, swallowed by Cristo's latest mandate.

'Savita's never had to recover so quickly between races,' Kel said, her mouth dry.

Bekn sighed. 'We still have to prove ourselves. We're not in a position yet to refuse Cristo.'

'Especially after winning a race that he considers *easy*,' Dira snorted.

Kel grimaced, though the note didn't sour any of their moods for long. They quickly scavenged some small vials of blood gin and Asciran fizzy drinks from the kitchen and began clawing through the wrapping, each finding their allocated nametag. Kel unwrapped her gift to discover a smooth wooden box. Lifting the lid, the black kit held a variety of sharp tools for tracing, cutting and stamping leather. The tools were laid out in neat rows, far more lavish than the set from her father.

Something small and reluctant sparked to life at the sight of the tools. A startling wetness stung Kel's eyes.

On the back of the name tag, Cristo had written:

> Rahn mentioned you enjoy carving and embossing. It reminded me of the designs I used to sketch, before all of this began. Enjoy.

Kel clung to the kit for the rest of the night, spreading the tools out around her as the Howlers piled into their unit's lounge room. Dira clutched a guitar maintenance kit and a stunning ruby necklace that – from Rahn's hopeful expression – Rahn must have selected. Coup tore into an armoured jacket signed by Mott Rodeto – a long-dead CAPR legend – and a boxset of horror films, which Kel was surprised to discover he loved. Rahn held up a container of decadent pastries and a new technician toolkit. Bekn carefully unwrapped an enveloped card and a small silver box with what looked like the latest tele-comm model inside.

The Howlers refused to let Kel peel herself away until nightfall, long after their celebrations had ended and they'd huddled together on their small chaise lounge, drinking and watching Coup's horror movies. Pressed far too tightly against Coup, Kel couldn't help but notice how he laughed after every jump-scare, eyes shining with morbid delight.

Once the others had called it a night, Kel took the chance to sneak from their rooms, and eventually she found herself winding through Cristo's white labyrinth, trying to remember the damn way to Savita's enclosure. She'd walked the path dozens of times now, and still, every identical twist and turn felt like navigating Savita through clouds.

Finally, Savita's private aviary appeared around a bend to the left. Kel opened the entrance with her security pass, placed her new carving kit on the ground, pulled on her gloves, and breathed in the smoke and damp moss. *This* was her home.

A beat later, Savita descended from her overhead perch. Her copper talons glinted in the softening light and shadows pooled beneath her darker, burgundy feathers. The firebird let out a low rumble and landed in a clearing beside Kel.

Kel laughed. 'Miss me already?'

In response, Savita ducked her head. Kel lowered her own, pressing against her phoenix's beak. A moment later, Savita reared back. Her gaze searched Kel before she spread her wings to take flight again.

Something cracked inside Kel as Savita vanished, but she tried not to dwell on it. Kel moved back to the entrance and reached for the tablet bolted to the wall. If Kel couldn't be close to Savita, perhaps checking Savita's vitals from the race might ease her mind. Sav's temperature had only increased at the end of the race, but it had still flared high enough to warrant Kel's concern.

Kel typed her login details onto the touchscreen but the usual white display of tables and graphs refused to appear. Her login details were incorrect. She rubbed her eyes and tried again.

Invalid login.

Kel's fingers curled into a fist. She tried once, twice, three times, but it was no use.

Why was she locked out?

She grabbed her tele-comm and typed in her login details. The device was connected to the same account; they all linked back to Savita's collar. The tele-comm app didn't offer as many readings as Cristo's tablet did, but she could still see that Savita's vitals appeared normal. *Too* normal.

Kel glanced up at Savita's hulking silhouette. Anyone from today's race would know that these readings were a lie. By the end, Savita's flames had eclipsed her body, shrouding Coup in waves of heat. She had no idea how he'd withstood it.

Those kinds of flames weren't anxious bursts or abnormalities. Sav's vitals should have reflected that.

Kel tried to log in to the tablet again, and cursed under her breath. She heard Savita land once more and approach her.

'Why would they deny me access, Sav?' Kel whispered.

Kel slowed her breathing, ironing the wrinkles in her thoughts, trying to soothe the itchy nerves beneath her skin. If she marched into Cristo's office, would he apologize and restore her access?

Or was there more to it?

After what she'd seen – the dorky shirts and reassurances – she no longer believed that Cristo wanted to steal Savita from her. He had an entire team of specialists monitoring Savita's biology and behaviour, but she knew he still valued her insights – at least she hoped he did. Was it truly just a glitch in the system?

Whatever was going on, Kel didn't need the readings from Savita's collar. Her father had taught her to read a phoenix's vitals by hand.

Kel turned to see Savita behind her, watching her curiously. She reached out a hand.

'Please, stay still,' Kel coaxed.

Savita's head twitched, but she didn't fly away again. That was a good start.

Kel walked to Savita's side and touched the base of her left wing. The feathers were no warmer than usual.

She travelled along Savita's body and began to whistle the same lullaby she'd sung to the collarless phoenix in Fieror. Savita seemed to relax at the sound, and Kel jumped back to avoid being squashed as Savita *thwonked* to the ground in a heap.

Kel groaned. 'Just give me a few minutes.'

Savita lowered her head in response.

Kel ran both hands along Savita's back and down her tail. Sav's temperature was slightly raised, but it always was after a race. There was no hint of what had caused her to grow unruly flames on the track.

There had to be a reason.

As Kel checked the other side of Savita's body, the phoenix swivelled her head towards her. She half-opened one eye and snapped her beak, as if to say, *You're keeping me awake for this?*

'Such hardship,' Kel drawled. 'But unless you grow a vocal box and tell me why you started flaming, I don't have a choice.'

Kel moved down Savita's tucked wing, along the rows of smaller feathers. The phoenix's smoky scent wasn't any stronger than usual and each of her feathers trembled with the same temperature.

Kel sighed. 'What are you hiding from me, Sav?'

Savita was hotter than usual, but Kel could still lightly touch her feathers with thick, gloved fingers. She cursed again. It had been too long since she'd relied on her own touch, rather than tech. She was beginning to doubt her instincts.

The only reason for Savita's flames to climb so high was a rebirth. It would explain why her temperature had started soaring sporadically in their training sessions, too. But there were none of the signs she'd been taught to expect. No thicker scent of smoke, no extreme heat or taller flames.

Unless . . .

Slowly, Kel crouched down and ran her fingers along Savita's right wing. She removed her jacket and placed it along a lower, thicker row of feathers; a sturdier barrier between skin and heat.

Savita whined in protest, clicking her talons together.

'This will only take a second,' Kel promised. 'Try not to roll on top of me.'

Savita whined again and stopped fidgeting. Kel tensed her legs and gritted her teeth. With one long, excruciating grunt, Kel lifted Savita's wing.

Knees quivering, Kel ducked her head.

Her mouth went dry.

There was the proof she needed.

Deep in the skinfold where her wing met her body, a thin line of dark feathers peppered Savita. They were tucked too deeply for Kel to have noticed before. The feathers beneath Savita's wing were darker than the rest. Darker than *any* phoenix's; a mix of deep brown and ash black. A clear sign of a nearing rebirth.

Kel had suspected it, and still, she hadn't truly thought she'd find anything; yet these feathers were the first irrefutable sign. Kel guessed that Savita still had plenty of time, but even the initial stages of a rebirth promised unpredictable bursts of fire and heat, suffocating smoke and even wilder mood swings.

Kel frowned, lowering Savita's wing. Cristo and his tamers must have known this from their own tests. Why would they try to hide it from Kel?

Questions crowded her mind, begging for her attention. If Cristo knew of Savita's impending rebirth, why would he insist on another race? There was no risk yet of Savita imploding on the track, but surely he'd prefer to keep her closely monitored?

Kel slumped back against the enclosure's damp ground. In the last few hours, her bones had filled with confetti, lead and, now, hollow confusion. Exhaustion forced her eyes shut but her mind kept whirring, shattering the joy she'd felt after the race.

When sleep finally took her, Kel dreamt of her farm. Unfamiliar faces. Coup behind Kel as they soared on Savita's wings, ash raining on the ground, destroying everything it touched.

Chapter Twenty-Three

❈

As the Howlers meandered down Vohre's busy streets, Kel felt like a threadbare puppet. Though Bekn hadn't summoned the media, people still paused as they passed. Bekn would glance to the right, and Kel knew to wave. He'd shift away, and Kel and Coup knew to move closer together. Somehow, her new mitigator had rewired her muscle memory to suit his publicity schemes without her even realizing.

The crowd cleared just for a moment, and Bekn gave her a small, approving nod. 'You're getting the hang of this.'

Kel sucked in a deep breath and counted her steps, letting the glaring lights overwhelm her and empty her mind. Above her, neon greenery wove up and down skyscrapers. Vines poured over sleek balconies and wrapped around large, overhead screens flashing with advertisements.

Through a tight smile, Kel whispered, 'We should be trying to speak with Cristo. It makes no sense for Sav to be racing if she's nearing a rebirth.'

After a night spent tossing and turning, watching Sav sleep soundly, Kel hastily told her teammates what she'd discovered. She'd found Bekn, Coup and Dira huddled inside their small kitchen, the latter two eagerly awaiting Bekn's latest feast. The three had waved away Kel's concerns once they realized it usually took months for phoenixes to rebirth after initial symptoms appeared. Talking to them felt like trying to light a match in a hurricane.

'We'll figure it out after the next race,' Bekn whispered back, quiet enough that Rahn, striding ahead of them with Dira, wouldn't hear. 'There's nothing we can do until then. Besides, Cristo wouldn't let Savita compete if it would put anyone in danger.'

'Then why did he restrict my tablet access?'

'Maybe to stop you worrying like this?' Coup interjected from her left, an effortless grin across his face. The easy warmth of his expression made Kel's stomach lift, but she *knew* it wasn't for her sake.

'You said it yourself,' Coup added, still facing his adoring fans, waving from across the street. 'Savita is still ages away from a rebirth, right?'

Kel rubbed a hand over her face. On paper, their words made sense. So why wouldn't her muscles stop aching, as if always alert, waiting for danger?

'Okay – but we should at least be spending the day training.'

Coup sighed. 'I actually agree with Varra, there.'

Bekn's wicked smile grew. 'Then you're both wrong. There are only a few days between races and Savita should use the time to rest. Nothing can be gained from tiring her out, especially after her vitals were already raised in the last race.'

Kel opened and closed her mouth.

Bekn chuckled softly. 'You don't think I pay attention during races? A mitigator doesn't just scrounge up publicity, children. It's my job to consider every risk. I make sure to know everything that's going on in my team.' He crinkled his nose. 'Even when that team doesn't know what's best for them.'

Eventually, the passing crowd lost interest, and, from the front of their group, Rahn led them deeper into the crowded city.

Kel had been relieved that Rahn hadn't been present when she'd told her other teammates what she'd found. Though Dira had made it clear that she wanted to tell Rahn everything, Bekn and Coup had agreed with Kel to keep it a secret for now. They still didn't know exactly how Rahn's loyalty was divided between Cristo and the Howlers, and Bekn had made it clear that Cristo should only find out after the next race, once they'd cemented their public standing in Vohre.

To distract from Dira's grumbling and Kel's frustration, he'd wrangled them into the bustling city centre, and Rahn had been only too happy to guide them.

The deeper they wove through Vohre, the more nature and steel became indistinguishable. Green and silver fused like rough paint strokes and coloured billboards bloomed from the walls, as bright as the gardens below them.

Kel narrowed her eyes at Dira's back. Her friend's dark curls hung loose and tangled with her ruby necklace, nestled just above the thick, black collar of a jacket. 'I've been looking for that jacket for *months*.'

Dira lifted her middle finger over her back, not bothering to turn as she cooed, 'Glad I found it a better home.'

If Rahn heard their exchange, she ignored it and kept moving. The technician led them away from the city's main streets and down a darker alleyway. The narrow alley forced Kel's shoulder to bump Coup's. Though he seemed unbothered by the touch, he shifted back until there was no risk of it happening again.

Kel tried to ignore the strange tightness between her ribs. Desperate for a new distraction, she called ahead to Rahn, 'Have you always lived in Vohre?'

Rahn gave a strange, sharp laugh. The technician picked at the sleeve of her sky-blue sweater. '*Alchemists*, no! I grew up on Ebrait. I only moved to Vohre a couple of years ago.'

Bekn made a surprised sound. 'Did your parents come here with you?'

They made it halfway down the alley before Rahn replied, 'No – I didn't tell my parents I applied for a Cristo Industries internship. I never thought I'd get it. I was fascinated by Cendor's technology and CAPR mechanics, but Ebraitian schools couldn't – wouldn't – teach me much. Canen requested permission from my parents.'

Rahn laughed again, though the sound was absent of its usual warmth. Curiosity rippled through Kel, drowning her other knotted feelings.

'So he's been your acting guardian since you got here?' Bekn asked, before Kel could chime in.

If Rahn minded the questions, she hid it well. She half-turned towards them and nodded, her cheeks rosy with windburn. 'He knew what to say to get my parents on board. My dad was easy enough to convince, but my mum . . . it was harder for her to let go of what she wanted for me.'

'What would you have done on Ebrait?' Kel asked.

Rahn didn't respond. Kel assumed her question had been lost to the sudden chatter echoing down the alley. The dim lane opened into a courtyard, surrounded by smaller buildings and fewer screens. It was lit only by gas lamps, open firepits and hazy afternoon light. Kel never would have found the courtyard on her own.

Rahn tugged Dira towards a flimsy-looking booth at the space's edge, smoke rising from its roof. Heady smells filled Kel's nose, sweet and salty and familiar. At least a dozen booths fronted signs for different kinds of foods. Most were Cendorian, but a few offered other Saltan cuisines. Kel's stomach growled.

People sat around wooden picnic tables and metal firepits, fingers covered in red sauce, ignoring the Howlers' presence. Kel handed over three ceres for a plate of spicy, smoked meats. She'd half-eaten the contents by the time she found her teammates around a nearby table.

Dira and Rahn's voices overlapped, their words flowing too fast to follow. Kel glanced around at their meals, silently judging their tastes: Dira wolfed down a spiced chickpea curry, Coup dug into a mix of meats similar to Kel's, and Rahn picked at grilled crab legs dripping in creamy sauce.

Bekn glanced around the table, frowning as he picked at his own plate of crumbed tarts. 'You all have terrible taste. Everything on Cendor is cooked with enough hot peppers to turn your stomachs to iron.'

Kel grinned, burning her tongue as she swallowed a hot mouthful. 'You're one to talk. You must be single-handedly keeping Ascira's pastry exports in business.'

Bekn rolled his eyes, earning a round of laughter from the table.

'Is that what was in the card Cristo got you?' Coup asked Bekn. 'A coupon for desserts? I couldn't see what was inside.'

Bekn's cheeks flushed.

Dira folded her arms, leaning across the table. 'What was it?'

She turned to Rahn, who lifted her hands. 'I actually have no clue. Canen picked Bekn's gift out.'

They all leaned forward, staring at their mitigator.

A minute passed before Bekn sighed. 'He got me a voucher to a local health resort. He thinks I need to . . . relax.'

The table erupted with fits of laughter. Kel struggled to breathe around giggles.

'It's a compliment,' Bekn said. 'He thinks I'm a hard worker.'

Rahn chuckled. 'If *Canen*, a self-made billionaire, thinks you're overworking, you might want to take his advice.'

The other four Howlers laughed again, drowning out the other voices nearby.

Warmth raced through Kel. She hoped Bekn did use the voucher.

On an island with combusting birds and fire magic, stress didn't usually end well.

'Ha. Ha.' Bekn clapped slowly. 'Yes, let's all mock the only legal adult here.'

When that only summoned more laughter, he cleared his throat and turned to Rahn. 'You agreed with Cristo that our last race was tame by Vohre's standards. I've done some research, but it's not the same as having seen the races in person. What are they like?'

Rahn's forehead creased. 'We can't prepare any more than we have, so what's the point in worrying?'

'Come on,' Dira drawled. She looped her arm beneath Rahn's. 'What have Vohre's other tracks really been like?'

Rahn looked up at Dira. She scrunched her nose, before relenting. 'Vohre's races are all about creating danger under the guise of art. There was this one track – it was beautiful – made of sky-high mirrors, like a maze. If the phoenixes collided with any false ends, they'd break through the mirror and fly into jagged metal walls.'

Dira's eyes widened, and Coup and Bekn exchanged a look with raised eyebrows.

Oblivious, Rahn went on, 'There was another race where CAPR forced phoenixes' wings to be tied down so they couldn't fly. The ground was broken up into islands they had to jump between. If they fell . . . the drop was over two hundred feet.'

Kel's stomach hollowed as Rahn continued, 'In another race, CAPR simulated a freezing blizzard. The phoenixes were unused to the temperature drop, so most overcompensated and fried their riders.'

Bekn raised a hand. 'Okay. New team verdict. It's a terrible idea to learn specifics.' He turned towards the other Howlers. 'There's a reason three times as many riders die in Vohre's races. These are the races televised across Salta. We just have to give audiences a show, and we'll be fine.'

Bekn's voice was uneven, as if his words were to convince himself, too.

Ignoring Bekn, Dira said, 'For the mirror maze – if Sav stayed close enough to a wall, and she grew hot enough, we might be able to tell which routes were open paths. The mirrors would fog up.'

Dira's words spun cogs in Kel's mind. She glanced down at a split in the faded table, imagining the ants crawling along it had fiery wings. 'For the island track – Sav's not the strongest, but she's fast. If we waited to see what path the other phoenixes used first, Sav could jump between the islands quick enough.'

Coup nodded. 'Or we could provoke another phoenix into attacking. If we angled and timed it right, their talons could slice right through the bindings holding Savita's wings. She could fly straight to the finish line.'

Against her will, Kel was impressed.

The Howlers' voices overlapped, brainstorming ways they could best the terrains. Even Bekn tossed forward a few reluctant ideas. As an open fire warmed her back, Kel marvelled at how much had changed in just a few weeks. She couldn't deny that the five of them worked well together. Though her chest still ached when she thought of Oska and Rube, and Coup's arrogance still made her cheeks burn, these Howlers simply *fit*. Their minds attacked CAPR in different ways. Different strategies and ideas that somehow wove together into a tapestry instead of a collision.

They each dug back into their plates, returning to the table with second helpings. Kel drifted in and out of their conversation. She tried to keep her mind away from the compound, from Savita, where she couldn't do anything, and couldn't—

Rahn's laughter pulled Kel from her thoughts. Facing Dira, Rahn said, 'I love that you have no problem feeding Savita slabs of raw meat with your bare hands, but won't eat a strip of meat yourself.'

Dira licked sauce from her thumb. 'Feeding Sav keeps her from looking at *me* like a snack. I'm just outsourcing my carnivorous habits.'

Rahn giggled and nudged Dira's side. It was such an easy, familiar gesture, which Dira returned, grinning around a mouthful of food.

'Aren't Dresvan serpents carnivorous?' Bekn asked. 'They eat rodents and insects, right? Did you have to feed them, like Savita?'

'Serpents hunt their own food,' Dira replied. 'Since when do you have an interest in Dresvan serpents? Looking to move islands?'

Bekn shrugged. 'Would it be so bad to live amongst creatures that aren't big enough to eat me?'

Bekn's eyes flickered to Coup, almost too fast to notice. Quickly, he added, 'You know what I mean. That's why Cristo's work is so important. He's protecting phoenixes *and* people.'

Kel frowned, looking at Coup. The rider hung his head, unusually still.

'Canen wants to do so much more for Cendor,' Rahn chimed. 'He's willing to sacrifice so much for his research. The studies he's conducting for AB treatments seem almost magical. You wouldn't believe it.'

'He tells you everything he's doing?' Dira asked.

Rahn nodded. Her adoration was almost tangible.

Dira tilted her head. 'Really? Do you know why he'd bother trying to hide—'

Kel kicked Dira's shin under the table. A sudden, hot anger buzzed through her. Dira pursed her lips and swivelled to glare at Kel.

Rahn frowned at Dira. 'Are you okay?'

'She's talking about the gifts Cristo bought us and tried to hide,' Bekn interjected.

Slowly, Rahn nodded. Bekn kept Rahn occupied as Dira continued to glare daggers at Kel.

Ever so slightly, Dira tilted her head to the left, a silent cue for Kel to leave the table. Both rose from their seats under the guise of pilfering more food. Anger coursing through her, Kel followed Dira behind a smoking food cart, well beyond ear's reach of the Howlers' table.

'Seriously?' Dira hissed, arms folded. 'You *still* don't trust Rahn? What has she done to make you so—'

'Nothing,' Kel shot back. 'But we all agreed not to tell her. Not until we know she trusts us more than Cristo.'

Dira's nostrils flared. '*I* didn't agree to that. I trust her, Kel. Why isn't that enough for you?'

'Why do you trust *her* more than *me*?' Kel snapped. 'Why do *you* suddenly know what's best for the Howlers?'

The pain on Dira's face barely registered in Kel's mind. They'd had countless fights before – but Kel had never felt this kind of fury at her best friend.

'That's not fair. I've always put the Howlers first,' Dira spat. 'I've been fighting for the Howlers for just as long as you have. Having Leon Varra as your father doesn't mean you always know what's best.'

Dira's words hit her like a physical blow. They were too similar to what Coup had once said, claiming she had the Varra name to save her if the Howlers didn't. A painful storm brewed in Kel's skull.

'Maybe if I *knew* more about your past, I'd know if you had an opinion worth hearing. Maybe if you were half as good at strategizing as you are at keeping secrets, we wouldn't be in this mess in the first place.'

Dira's lips parted, as if Kel had slapped her. All the anger suddenly seeped from Kel's bones. She felt hollow.

Dira stepped back. She scanned Kel, as if not recognizing what she saw.

'I'm sorry,' Kel stammered, reaching for her friend. 'I didn't mean—'

Dira shoved past Kel and marched back to the Howlers.

Where had that anger come from? Slowly, Kel wrapped her arms around herself and shuffled back to their table. She tried and failed to lock eyes with Dira. If the others noticed the tension, they said nothing.

Kel sat, staring at her plate, too cowardly to join in with her teammates' laughter. She didn't know where that venom had come from. Was the stress of their upcoming race affecting her more than she'd realized? Was her concern for Sav flaring in cruel ways?

She didn't know the answer. But until she did, she suspected the venom would only keep growing.

Chapter Twenty-Four

Kel wriggled in her seat, squashed inside the oversized auto-engine carrying Sav. Dira and Rahn had taken another four-wheeled unit loaded with their racing gear. Even just a few yards ahead, Kel could barely make out their vehicle on the straight road. Dusk had already given way to heavy shadows and stars glistened overhead in clear, silvery clusters.

To her left, Coup yawned. 'I can't believe you'd rather ride with me and Bekn than your bestie.'

Kel tried to wiggle closer to the window. Coup had no qualms about stretching his arms along the back of the seats.

'You're still a pain in my arse,' Kel said. 'But I'd rather put up with you for half an hour than third-wheel Dira and Rahn's flirting.'

That, and Dira had been avoiding Kel since their fight four days ago. Kel had apologized a dozen times to her friend, yet Dira still looked at Kel with shuttered eyes.

Coup grinned. 'Sure, tamer. Tell yourself whatever you need to.'

Kel's cheeks heated. The insult she should have thrown back died in her throat. There was too little space in the auto-engine's cabin. She should've just put up with Dira's anger.

Bekn drummed his fingers against the steering wheel. 'If you're going to flirt, save it for the CAPR cameras.'

'We are *not*,' Kel growled.

Since the last race, Vohre's media had only magnified its coverage of the Howlers. Rerun commentary speculated on Coup and Kel's relationship. Magazines printed close-ups of their faces above romance headlines. It had become impossible to avoid the rumours.

Desperate for a change of subject, Kel muttered, 'I still think this race is a terrible idea given Sav's rebirth.'

'Whatever his reasons for hiding information – Cristo wouldn't let us compete if he thought Savita would implode mid-race,' Bekn countered.

Coup softly elbowed Kel. 'If you're still that worried, you and I can march into Cristo's office and demand answers. He can't say no to CAPR's latest power couple.'

Kel glared at him. Though the offer beneath the mockery was sincere, it made her lips twitch. Over the past few days, Coup had tolerated Kel's rehashed concerns more than the others. Perhaps it was because his employment was twined more closely with Savita. Still, no matter why, his willingness to listen had stemmed the paranoia from consuming her.

She ignored Coup's teasing for the rest of the journey, focusing instead on the possibilities of what lay ahead.

Kel had no clue what awaited them. It was illegal for CAPR teams to have any knowledge of a race prior to arrival. Media outlets were only permitted to release footage once every team had checked in. She shivered, trying to imagine what might lay ahead; what could be worse than using a phoenix's inherent fear of water against them?

As they unloaded the vehicles and approached the wide track, Kel's questions remained unanswered.

'Come on,' Kel said, guiding Sav from the transport unit. 'Let's find our booth.'

Their booth ended up being raised along a private stretch of stands, which they'd climb to watch the race from. Rahn and Bekn carried their gear as Dira and Kel helped Coup into Savita's saddle, along a dirt stretch not far from the starting line. Though flanked by a larger crowd than she'd ever seen, there were no obvious threats along the looping track. No mechanical clouds for weapons to drop from, no netting to tangle wings, no murky waters to spread fear. Just a clear, glittering darkness for Savita to soar through.

Tall screens towered above the stands packed with roaring fans, ready to broadcast the race. Despite the clear track, the crowd screamed their anticipation. Silver tablets glimmered through the dense crowds, fingers darting across the devices as they placed wagers.

A chill ghosted down Kel's spine. What was informing their bets? The open track didn't seem to favour agility, strength or size.

She'd much rather know what unholy dangers awaited them. The clear evening was nothing more than a prelude, but to what?

The winger and tamer moved together with their usual ease, perfected over the years. If Dira still harboured anger towards her, Kel knew she wouldn't let it affect their performance on the track.

Minutes later, when Coup was in place and Bekn and Rahn had returned, there were still no answers. Kel could see other teams similarly huddled, squinting at the track's clear sky.

When Rahn frowned down at her tele-comm, Kel almost lunged to her side. 'What is it? What's wrong?'

'It's just Canen. He's in the crowd today and wanted to wish us luck.' Rahn scanned Kel's face. 'Are you okay? You look a little . . .'

'Sleep-deprived? Wrecked? Unhinged?' Dira supplied.

'Thanks for the multiple choice,' Kel muttered. At least Dira had forgiven her enough to tease her.

Kel glanced back at the track. 'I can't remember the last time Fieror had a simple track like this. Does Vohre ever just want teams to . . . race?'

Rahn's lips twisted. 'Definitely not. There will be something waiting up there for Coup and Savita.' Rahn squinted out at the track. 'Wait – can you see that?'

Every Howler followed Rahn's gaze. Even Savita, scraping her talons in excitement, glanced up.

'I can't see anything. Just the stars,' Kel said.

'Yes!' Rahn chirped. 'No – *there*, to the right. Between those two brighter stars. See the glimmering?'

Dira scrunched her nose. 'The . . . moon?'

Rahn gave Dira a look. '*Below* that. At first, it just looks like more stars. But there are different colours to them. See?'

The technician pointed to a thicker patchwork of stars. Kel stepped closer to the track's edge, staring at the smeared fog. Tiny, glittering spots flecked the mist, like coloured gems in a grey tapestry.

The warning sirens – signalling the race's imminent start – rang before the Howlers could decipher the coloured lights, sharper and closer than starlight.

Kel guided Sav to the dim starting line, where the Howlers surrounded the phoenix in a careful constellation of their own. Fluorescent lights illuminated the stands, making it harder to spot anything amiss overhead. Kel's eyes roamed the crowd, circling the track in sky-high rows of metal seats. There, in a raised stand, not too far from their own booth, she saw Cristo. He was standing, surveying the crowd.

Kel couldn't make out much of him at this distance, just his blue blazer and pearly smile. Rahn beamed, waving both hands towards their employer. Cristo returned her enthusiasm before turning to a younger girl at his side. About Kel's age, the girl mirrored his wide grin.

'Flames, Varra.' Coup pulled her focus. 'The race hasn't even started yet, and I can tell you're looking for things to go wrong.'

Kel reached over and checked the buckles around Coup's right leg. 'Just stay low until we can figure out what CAPR's planning.'

Coup sighed. 'If brooding could make money, we wouldn't need Cristo to back the team. Stop worrying. Winging it worked for us last time.'

Kel shifted around to his left leg and tightened his ankle buckles. Unease fluttered through her, doubts buzzing through her skull, so she wasn't sure what made her lift her gaze to Coup's and mimic his usual, teasing lilt. 'Go on then, rider. Prove me wrong. Impress me for once.'

Coup blinked. 'And how would you suggest I do that?'

Kel gave a small, satisfied shrug. 'The media says you're wooing me, but so far I haven't seen many romantic declarations.'

'And phoenix racing screams romance to you?'

Kel tugged another leg buckle tight. 'More than a staged stroll through a conservation centre.'

Coup's lips twisted into a lopsided smirk, before he lowered his goggles into place. 'All right, tamer. This win is for you.'

Something coiled in Kel's gut. She lowered her head as heat crept up her neck, giving Coup's buckles one last tug before turning away.

Kel had barely climbed up to the Howlers' booth when the sancter rifle flared across the sky like lightning. She whirled around just as a roaring gale reached her, sending her staggering back into Bekn.

Powerful winds swept across the crowd as thirty phoenixes launched into the sky. The thin, metal railing dividing the track and the stands shook. Hats and scarves flew into the sky and the force of the fiery winds made it hard to suck in air, though the crowd still managed plenty of cheers as the phoenixes began their race.

Coup and Savita shot forward as if launched from a slingshot, painting a trail of fire through the stars. In a handful of seconds, he'd shot into fourth place.

'Keep an eye out for any obstacles,' Dira cautioned.

Rahn and Bekn stayed a few paces back, while Dira and Kel stood with their faces almost pressed against the sky-high metal dividers surrounding the track. Could things really be so simple?

As if reading Kel's mind, Dira added, 'If there's really no danger, the bigger phoenixes will make some to get ahead. Watch out for any overhead attacks.'

Coup muttered an agreement, voice muffled by a nearby phoenix's shriek. The sound reached Kel's ears a moment before crackling through the comms.

Coup stayed low in the saddle, helping Savita's speed. The track would eventually loop back to the crowds, but Kel didn't know how much she'd be able to see through the darkness, even with the help of the crowd's overhead screens.

'There's a cinder phoenix coming up beneath you,' Dira said. 'Let him pass. He's moving too fast and growing too hot for it to be sustainable.'

Moments later, a blazing phoenix shot past. Smaller and perfect for a race of speed, the cinder phoenix knocked Savita and Coup back to fifth place. Though he remained steady, Kel could imagine the daggers that Coup shot at the rider now ahead of him.

'Dira,' Coup began, 'do you think it'd work if I—'

A sudden, howling wind leeched through the comms. A large blood phoenix ahead suddenly descended as if yanked from the sky, somersaulting through the darkness. The bird screamed with its rider, making the crowd clap even louder as it neared the ground. Other approaching opponents gave the blood phoenix a wide berth, though it corkscrewed through the air so jaggedly Kel was stunned it didn't take out any other competitors.

Distantly, Kel heard the phoenix's collision with the hard track.

Another gale rushed over the Howlers from the impact. The grounded phoenix's flames calmed, paling from crimson to coral. Kel spotted red pools spreading out from the limp bodies; the rider hung awkwardly from their saddle, legs still buckled, as motionless as their mount.

Chapter Twenty-Five

---- ✺ ----

'What the hell was that?' Bekn shouted.

'Coup? You okay?' Kel shot down the comm.

Coup swerved around the empty space where the phoenix had been. There were no hints of what had caused its crash. 'Did anyone see what happened? It wasn't an attack – there are no others near us. The phoenix just fell!'

His voice crackled, but whether with static or fear Kel couldn't tell. Kel and Dira exchanged wide eyes. Coup and Savita continued in a straight line. With the blood phoenix's nosedive, he was back to fourth place.

'There's a rider creeping up on your right,' Dira shouted. 'I don't care if it takes you off-track. Stay above it.'

Kel's head whipped further down the track. The lean firebird was still yards away from Savita, not near enough for Kel to have noticed – but Dira was right. The creature tilted its wings ever so slightly, veering towards Coup's flanks, as if to cut him off.

Coup grunted an acknowledgement, soaring higher. Around him, those strange tiny, sharp colours lit the sky. Kel squinted into the sky, silently begging Coup to stay further away from whatever was lurking up there.

A few seconds later another gust of wind whistled through the comms, and a beige phoenix was ripped from the sky. Kel leaned forwards to see the tumbling creature wreathed in flames as it rocketed to the ground.

The firebird released a high, terrified screech, loud enough that

Kel imagined all of Vohre would hear. The crowd roared, almost as loud, though the roaring turned bitter as the bird managed to straighten. The rider scrambled to regain control. With a handful of slow, laboured wing strokes, the creature caught itself before hitting the track's black tar.

Kel whipped back to find Coup along the track. A cluster of those strange, coloured lights lit the sky directly ahead of him. '*What the hell is going—*'

Kel heard the breath wrenched from Coup's lungs. Sending wild gusts into the crowd, Savita spun in violent, blazing circles through the air. Kel cried out as the crowd cheered. Tiny lights scattered around Savita's hazy outline, and Kel heard the heavy, strained beat of Savita's wings through the comms. Three more phoenixes soared ahead of Savita, sending the Howlers into seventh place.

'*Coup!*' Kel screamed.

Heavy breathing filled the comms. Dizzying seconds passed before Savita's wings slowed, gliding momentarily before climbing higher.

'I'm fine,' Coup stammered. 'I–I don't know what happened. We passed through a cluster of those coloured lights and winds started messing with Savita's wings.'

Coup sucked in a deep breath before adding, 'It was strange – hot and cold. Pulling us in different directions.'

Kel exchanged another helpless look with her teammates.

Bekn leaned towards Kel, speaking into her ear-comm. 'But you're okay?'

'Yeah. Savita is, too. But it's impossible to see the weird lights until you're surrounded by them.'

'Fall back,' Dira commanded. 'I can't guide you if the lights are moving. They're too hard to see from here, but we might have a chance if you slow down.'

'The winds cranked up Sav's flames,' Kel added, peering through the darkness. 'Does she feel hotter than usual?'

Coup's silence was answer enough. Kel pulled out her tele-comm to check Savita's vitals. They were heightened, though barely above what they usually were in a race's peak.

Refusing to slow, Coup managed to swerve around another cluster of floating jewels.

The spinel phoenix placing eighth wasn't so lucky. The pale creature to Coup's right was hurled sideways by an invisible force. Kel winced as the rider's arms bent at unnatural angles, as if their very bones were being tugged in opposite directions. The phoenix spun and spun, red flames glowing brighter. The rider went suddenly limp, falling against the firebird's side as they plummeted towards the ground.

The collision rattled the stands, enough that the Howlers had to grip each other to stay upright. Dazed, Kel scrambled to catch sight of Coup again. Coup and Sav were finally looping back towards them along the enormous track.

Her gaze lifted up, higher, to the nearest cluster of glowing spots. They flared brighter as the blood phoenix placing first raced past, and Kel caught a clear glimpse of their miniscule size.

Familiarity sparked through her. She'd seen these before . . . their coloured lights had been painted on postcards and hovering inside glass columns.

'Coup . . . the lights are moving, right? They're not fixed in place?' Kel asked breathlessly.

Coup inhaled. 'Yeah, they're moving. Not much, but they're floating about a little.'

Coup didn't have time to focus on the lights around him, but if he did, Kel was sure he'd recognize them. 'They're . . . *sprites*?'

The impossibility of it made Kel's words escape as a question.

Rahn gasped and Dira cursed. Bekn remained silent, staring out at Coup, unblinking.

Kel's mind whirled. The sprites had been a pretty sight at the sanctuary, but she knew little about them. They had subspecies, just like phoenixes, that could amplify the rain, the sun, the air itself. But even the dozens of clustered sprites in the sanctuary hadn't been capable of anything more than slowly ambling about. To create winds strong enough to impact phoenixes meant that there were likely thousands scattered throughout the sky.

Another two phoenixes at Coup's sides whirled through the sky. Their wings battled the winds around them. Though they managed to avoid colliding with the ground, they dropped to the back of the race, bumping Coup and Savita to fifth place.

'*Oh, Alchemists!*' Dira gasped. 'CAPR must've arranged them in the sky somehow. The sprites are creating air pockets that mess with the phoenixes' flight patterns! Like turbulence on an airship.'

'Turbulence is created by hot and cold air, right?' Coup panted. 'That's why it's causing the flames.'

Shit. *Shit.*

Some phoenixes glided ahead, speeding up and then tumbling through the air. Others flew slower, more cautiously, avoiding the air pockets.

Kel swallowed a lump in her throat. Coup had two choices. One: slow down to avoid the clustered sprites, and risk not placing. Two: speed ahead, and risk an air pocket sending him and Savita to the ground.

Even before she voiced the choice, Kel knew which option Coup would pick. Even if he hadn't been riding the high off their last victory, even if the heated winds wouldn't risk his life, he'd always choose the second; the more dangerous option.

Bekn's past warnings echoed through her mind.

Coup reached up and adjusted his goggles. He lowered himself against Savita's saddle and instructed her to pin her wings. The movement drove them forward like a tapered rocket. Phoenixes plummeted around them, flaming comets and falling stars. Savita narrowly swerved around a cluster of emerald sprites, close enough that the pocket's heat caused dark flames to encircle Coup's arms.

The faster Coup soared, the higher Savita's flames climbed. Another two phoenixes ahead barrelled into air pockets and plummeted downwards in dizzying spirals. The two collided as they spun, lashing out with confused talons and sending blood whipping through the air.

Coup and Savita quickly claimed third place.

Seconds later, Coup barrelled into another air pocket. Winds screeched and attacked Savita's wings. They narrowly avoided nose-diving to the ground.

Shrouded in darkening flames, Coup and Sav were still ahead of the other cautious riders. Only two phoenixes, through sheer luck, glided ahead of Coup. They soared far enough ahead that it would be near-impossible for Coup to catch up, even if he didn't need to navigate invisible air pockets.

Through the dark sky, the Howlers watched flames lick higher against Savita's feathers, climbing up Coup's back.

Dira pressed a finger to her comm. 'All right, stay steady for another minute and we'll place third. Any faster and you'll risk burning alive. Pull back.'

No response. Then, through the comms, 'I can win this.'

The Howlers exchanged frowns. Coup's words were stiff, said through gritted teeth.

Ice skittered down Kel's spine. How hot were Savita's flames already? Hot enough to melt his leathers?

'Placing third will impress Cristo,' Bekn said, voice unsteady. He turned to Kel. 'Tell him. Make him *stop*.'

Mouth dry, Kel said, 'Ease up. Whatever you're trying to do – it's not worth it.'

There was another long moment before Coup replied, 'I think Savita can sense where the air pockets are. She *wants* to go faster. I need to let her.'

Rahn made a strange, uncertain sound in the back of her throat. 'These leathers are sturdier than your old ones, but they're not infallible. I have no idea how the turbulence will affect Savita's heat.'

Coup was quiet as Savita pulled closer to the leading phoenixes, her flames climbing higher in steady, hungry tendrils. These were no longer anxious, unsettled patches of heat. As Savita avoided air pockets and skirted sprites, her blaze grew until she was more fire than bird.

'What did he say?' Bekn said breathlessly, as if he already knew the answer.

An alarm blared in her jacket. She yanked out her tele-comm. A familiar, red notification lit her device.

With numb fingers, she clicked on the notification. Savita's vitals filled the screen; her pulse temperature, muscle spasm rate. They were all extremely high.

'Coup,' Kel spoke quickly, hoping he could hear her desperation. 'You need to slow down. I've never seen Savita's temperature this out of control. I don't know if it's the air pockets or the rebirth symptoms – but she shouldn't be getting this hot.'

It didn't matter why Savita's temperature was soaring. If Coup didn't calm Savita down, he was going to die.

Oska's screams rang through her skull.

'*Slow. Down*,' she ordered.

Coup ignored her.

Savita pulled forwards, directly beneath the two leading

phoenixes. Kel's veins were ice and her pulse a gale in her ears. Coup had to *stop*.

But she knew he wouldn't. She knew what was racing through his head – because she was the one who had put those thoughts there.

Go on, then. Impress me.

This win is for you.

After their last win, none of them had wanted Coup to hold back. And now that he was letting Savita test her limits, he could feel Savita's joy beneath him. He could feel her excitement, the need to see how high her flames could soar.

One of the phoenixes ahead was yanked from the sky as a cluster of ruby sprites scattered. Savita rose beside the last remaining firebird. Their wings were parallel as both soared directly for the neon finish line.

'Tell him to stop.' Bekn's voice broke. '*He needs to stop.*'

Coup hissed through his teeth, and Kel knew he was in agony. The leathers wouldn't protect him from this kind of heat.

'*Coup!*' she screamed. 'Forget what I said. None of this matters if you die!'

Coup didn't respond.

Savita merely blazed faster. She opened her black beak and released a scream of pure fire – of rage and joy and freedom. Winds battered her wings and sent her spiralling towards the finish line.

Barely a hundred metres from the flags, the blood phoenix ahead collided with another cloud of scarlet sprites. Instead of descending, the larger phoenix jerked to the right – tumbling straight into Savita's side.

Sav managed to swerve, dodging the brunt of the attack. But the blood phoenix's body twisted too far, the side of its head colliding with Coup.

Writhing flames filled the night sky. They smothered Coup. Smothered *everything*.

As Coup crossed the finish line, Kel heard him scream.

Chapter Twenty-Six

---·❀·---

The audience quietened, ever so slightly. Kel didn't know if it was shock or anger keeping them at bay. Newcomer teams never won races of this size, and no team – novice or ranked – ever moved that fast.

Bekn and Kel raced down the benches and elbowed through the dense crowd. Savita was still hovering above the concrete finish line, struggling to lower to the ground. Panicked bodies were running back and forth beneath her.

'Get out of the way!' Kel screamed. 'Clear the space for her to land. He's *injured*!' Her voice broke on the last word.

Bekn turned to the nearest uniformed CAPR officer. 'Get help,' he said, in an eerily calm voice. 'Get a council emergency van here, *now*.'

The officer swallowed, nodded, and ran towards the CAPR booth. Moments later, Dira and Rahn appeared behind Kel. Dira's eyes were dark, focused; searching for options. Rahn's mouth moved in a blur as she spoke into her tele-comm. But no one could help Coup until Savita landed.

Kel tilted her head up and waved into the sky. 'Coup! Bring her down!'

As she waited – hoped – for a response, she realized that the ringing in her ears wasn't white noise, or the ghost of Oska's screams. It was static. Coup's comm was broken.

Kel cupped her hands around her mouth and tried again, '*Savita! Land! Now!*'

Sav screeched in defiance, but her wings slowed. Though Sav obeyed few verbal commands, Kel *knew* Sav understood her tone. The phoenix's flames began to soothe against her feathers. Slowly, with three beats of her sprawled wings, Savita landed on the concrete beside Kel.

Coup was slumped to the side of the saddle. His leathers were tattered and ashen, smoke rising from the fabric in grey waves. His arms hung limply. His buckles – *thank the Alchemists* – were still looped around his legs, holding him in place.

As fast as they could, Kel and Bekn undid the buckles. Kel pushed Sav's head away as her phoenix tried to nuzzle her, unaware of the surrounding chaos. The metal buckles were scalding, even beneath her gloves – but Kel didn't care. She didn't care if her hands caught fire. She didn't care if the entire crowd burst into flames. Coup couldn't *die*.

Memories flared in her mind. Her father, broken and hollow. Oska, torn and mangled. Now Coup. She wouldn't survive it. *Not Coup—*

Camera flashes jolted her back, and she fought the buckles with trembling fingers. When they finally came free, Kel shook Coup's leg. 'Coup? Can you hear me?'

No response.

Coup's limp body tumbled free of the saddle and into her arms. She almost dropped him, but then three pairs of hands helped lift him off the ground. She looked up to see CAPR paramedics. Their expressions were unreadable as they lifted Coup onto a nearby stretcher.

Kel ran to his side, coughing through waves of smoke. Her eyes watered, struggling to make sense of what they saw.

The front of his uniform wasn't ashen or damaged.

It was seared into his flesh.

Where Coup had been pressed directly against Savita's heat, Coup's thick leathers had melted away. The grey shirt he'd worn beneath was gone, too, burnt away to flaking skin, charcoaled tissue and white, fatty muscle across his abdomen.

Coup's right leg – the leg that had been crushed by the blood phoenix – was bent at an angle. The skin around his neck was red and blistering.

Kel couldn't bear to look. But even if she closed her eyes, she could smell the burnt leather, hear the sizzling flesh.

Two CAPR officers covered his stomach with a metallic blanket.

'Is he . . . Is he alive?' Bekn stuttered.

A health officer placed a hand on Bekn's arm. 'We're doing everything we can.'

Kel's vision swam.

Slowly, she looked over to Savita. She felt a broken, exhausted relief to see Dira standing beside Sav's neck, trying to coax the last few flames from her feathers.

Kel felt like she was drowning. Fear sharpened her senses and woke her muscles. There was nowhere to run. Nowhere to hide.

CAPR riders were often injured. Death loomed over every race. Coup knew the risks. Kel did, too. It was why – as team members had come and gone like the seasons – she had never let herself truly care for anyone other than Dira. Savita. She'd felt that kind of loss before, and she'd vowed never to again. Though Oska had crawled beneath her skin, she tried to think of the Asciran girl as little as possible.

But seeing Coup's flayed body beneath her, hearing him heave in deep, rasped breaths, burst a dam inside her. Something new and raw and all-consuming.

The paramedics moved around Coup's stretcher as a van appeared through the commotion, the rear doors swinging open.

'Where are you taking him?' Bekn demanded. His hands were balled at his sides, shaking.

The black-haired woman turned to Bekn. 'There's a council hospital just a few miles away.'

'You're taking him to Cristo Industries,' Rahn cut in, still holding a tele-comm to her ear. 'Canen Cristo will be treating Mr Coupers.'

The paramedic lifted a brow. 'That's not CAPR policy. We can't—'

Rahn held out her tele-comm. Silently, the paramedic accepted the device and pressed it to her ear.

Whoever was on the other end spoke quickly. The paramedic gave a short nod, then glanced back to the rest of her team.

Into the tele-comm, she said, 'Of course, Mr Cristo. I understand. We'll bring the van to your facilities immediately.'

Rahn moved towards the van, but Bekn blocked her path. 'He needs the closest hospital, Rahn. I don't care what Cristo wants, my brother is—'

'Coup has a *much* better chance of recovery in Canen's facilities. Trust me.' Rahn's face contorted. 'Canen has his own private hospital and team of specialists on hand. I've seen patients recover from burns like this in days. Cristo will cover all expenses. Please, let him help.'

Bekn was quiet for a moment. Kel glanced around, trying – failing – to find Cristo in the frantic crowd.

Rahn's face was too calm. Perhaps that was why Bekn finally said, 'Okay. No one's touching him without talking to me first.'

Rahn nodded and moved aside to let Bekn climb into the van with Coup. Kel tried to follow, but another paramedic blocked her path.

'Only one person can ride with us. You'll have to find your own way,' the man said in a clipped tone.

Kel was about to say that she'd climb on the van's roof if she had to, when Savita shrieked behind her. She swallowed down something thick. Sav still needed caring for. As comfortable as she was around Dira, Sav wouldn't let Kel leave, not in a new environment.

Kel let the CAPR paramedics flood into the van. Lights flashed. The siren blared clear a path through the scattered crowd.

Then Coup was gone.

Chapter Twenty-Seven

❖

Cristo's small waiting room was white and clinical; the bare walls occasionally trembled from phoenix screeches.

She'd helped wrangle Sav into a transport engine from the race and had hurried to the hospital with Dira and Rahn. By the time they had piled in, Bekn was sitting in a brown armchair, head between his knees.

He looked up as they approached. 'He's already in surgery.' Bekn's grave eyes met Rahn's. 'You were right to bring him here. Thank you.'

They all reached for Bekn, as if to protect him from what lay beyond the hospital doors. Kel hoped he couldn't feel how hard her heart was pounding.

Kel could still hear the static ringing through her head, and Coup's screams – echoing over and over. As she slumped into the seat next to Bekn, the static grew louder, mingling not just with his screams, but also Oska's, and the voices she'd heard the last time she was in a room like this. Waiting for her father to reappear.

'Canen hires the best specialists across Salta. Coup will be fine,' Rahn whispered. 'He'll be fine.'

Dira squeezed Rahn's hand. They shared a smile, though Rahn's face was chalk-white.

'I knew he'd pull something like this,' Bekn murmured. 'It was only a matter of time.'

Dira nudged Bekn's side. 'It's not your fault. We all got a little cocky after the last win.'

Bekn shook his head. 'No – you don't understand. He's been getting away with reckless stunts like this for so long. He just doesn't care any more.'

Numbness spread through Kel. 'What do you mean?'

Bekn was silent, almost long enough for Kel to apologize for the question. Before she could take it back, Bekn whispered, 'He thinks it's his fault. That I stayed on Cendor after Mum died.'

Dira and Rahn exchanged looks, and the lump in Kel's throat grew thicker.

'I was meant to go to a university in Ascira,' Bekn continued, his head ducked, as if he spoke to himself. 'To study business. But I stayed with Coup after she died. I stayed for *both* of us. Coup . . . he thinks he owes me for that.'

Bekn's words slotted together in Kel's mind. She could see that alternate future, so clearly. Cendor was a home for those comfortable with jagged walls. Ascira, as much as Kel hated the tourism isle, suited Bekn's aspirations much better than Cendor ever would.

She recalled the truths she'd forced from Coup when they'd walked through the conservation centre.

I owe Bekn. And I can repay that debt through CAPR. So, for now, debts overrule self-preservation.

'I used the money I'd saved for school to support us. He thinks earning back the money will make things better. But even if he did, I don't think he'd ever stop.' Bekn's voice broke. 'I don't think he knows how to any more.'

None of them said a word. Kel leaned on his shoulder. She tried to quieten her own breathing, tried to ignore the ringing in her ears. Part of her had already known there was something darker lurking beneath Coup's arrogance. But it hadn't mattered, as long as they won.

'Bekn Coupers?'

They all jolted to their feet as a man in blue scrubs appeared through the door.

'Is Coup all right?' Bekn breathed.

The man's brown eyes looked at the clipboard in his right hand. 'He's going to be okay. He came in with fourth-degree burns across his abdomen. He has a broken tibia-fibula and we had to reset his shoulder.' He looked up. 'But he's out of surgery and should recover in a few days. As far as CAPR injuries go, this is far from the worst I've seen. He's already awake, and asking for all of you.'

Bekn sagged against Kel. Kel tried to focus on the doctor's voice as he continued talking. She was still waiting for the *real* doctor to charge through those doors and tell them that they'd done everything they could, but nothing had worked. Coup was gone. His body was empty, like her father's. His CAPR injuries too deep, like Oska's.

The doctor held open the door at his back. 'Follow me, please.'

Bekn, Dira and Rahn rushed forward in a flurry of limbs. Kel didn't move. She couldn't convince herself that this was real. She *knew* what lay on the other side of those swinging doors.

Coup, broken and bandaged – because of her.

He'd won the race. All because she'd told him to impress her.

The static morphed into fractured screams. Her heart pounded harder than it should have, for a rider she barely knew. For someone she'd *hated*.

Somehow, she had let *Coup*, the swaggering, mocking rider of her nightmares, crawl beneath her skin, far deeper than Oska had, in a way that stole her breath. And now, Kel couldn't do it. She couldn't look at Coup and think about the tangled fear and desperation rushing through her. What it might mean.

So, Kel turned and walked back out of the doors she'd come through.

Chapter Twenty-Eight

※

Kel floated through Cristo's white maze, unsure if she touched the ground. Right now, by her phoenix's side was the only place she wanted to be.

When she reached the entrance to Savita's aviary, she glanced at the door's glass reflection and winced. Her worry for Sav and Coup had declared itself through purple bruises beneath her eyes. But compared to the image of Coup torn open, burns too deep to bleed, she couldn't bring herself to care.

At the sight of her phoenix, the breath she'd been holding finally left her lungs. Savita lay nestled on the ground, picking at the feathers of her wings, oblivious to what lay beyond her glass walls.

Kel quickly checked Sav's vitals on the tablet embedded in the wall. Her stomach curdled, preparing for the worst, no clue how the sprites' magic might have affected Savita's own.

Bitterness filled Kel's mouth at the thought. CAPR had pitted another species against phoenixes for the crowd's entertainment. Coup had been right. Every race was nothing but a pageant.

But Sav's temperature seemed too stable, too calm, to explain the heat that had shrouded Coup at the finish line. Where were the hints of a rebirth? The flames they'd *seen*?

Kel stumbled towards her phoenix, eyes stinging. Cristo was still keeping Savita's vitals from her. He hadn't been able to hide them during the race, when they'd needed a live feed, but now, Kel was back to square one.

She'd barely lifted her gloved hands to Savita's neck when

she heard the aviary's door beep open. Sav lurched to her feet, quickly moving between Kel and the entrance. It might have been endearing, if Savita's tail hadn't collided with Kel and knocked her to the ground.

A moment later, Kel heard a heavy, familiar sigh. 'I knew I'd find you here.'

Kel ducked her head. Guilt rippled through her stomach.

'*Nova Press* has released updates on the riders in today's race. Three died. Four more in critical condition. Coup got off easy,' Dira added, her voice flat.

Kel clenched and unclenched her fists. She kept her mouth closed, unsure if words or bile would come out.

Closing the door, Dira folded her arms over her rumpled uniform. 'Why did you leave?'

'There was nothing I could do there.'

Dira stormed closer. 'Coup asked to see *all* of us. The second we walked into his room, he asked where you were.'

The words battered at Kel's empty lungs. 'He didn't want me there. Trust me.'

'*Bullshit*, Kelyn! They're new to the team, but I would've thought *you* – of all people – would want to be there for him. He's a Howler, and you just—'

'It's *my* fault he's lying in that bed,' Kel exploded.

Dira snorted. '*Alchemists*. Everyone thinks it's their fault. Even Rahn's blaming herself, thinking she could've saved him if she'd spent more time developing sturdier gear. But despite what you all believe, this is no one's fault but Coup's. You heard what Bekn said. Coup doesn't have a cautious bone left in his body. We all told him to slow down, and he refused.' Dira chewed on her bottom lip. 'Coup's ego was always going to end up combusting.'

Kel shook her head. She was too much of a coward to tell Dira the truth: that death stalked her. That it had bound an anchor to her feet.

'I know you, Kel,' Dira grumbled. 'And your self-pity is just as unwanted as Coup's lack of inhibitions.'

Sudden anger sparked at Dira's words, and Kel held tight to it. She let it pull her up, out of the waves and away from the anchor. Part of her knew Dira was right – even if she didn't want to admit it.

Bekn had seen what was going on – the destruction Coup wrought on himself – and now Dira did, too. None of them could let this keep going. If they did, Coup would truly be lost.

Kel swallowed her anger and reached for Dira's arm. 'Do you know how lucky I am that you snuck into that CAPR race five years ago?'

Dira's expression softened. 'About as lucky as I am that you let a random kid demand a bedroom in your cottage. We should both get some rest. We can deal with everything tomorrow.'

Kel forced a weak smile. 'Does this mean you forgive me?'

Dira squeezed Kel's arm. 'I forgave you after our meal in the city. I just decided not to tell you.'

Kel scoffed feebly as Dira shifted forward to embrace her.

'I don't know what's gotten into you lately,' Dira mumbled, head tucked into the crook of Kel's neck. 'Fighting is our love language. But you've been acting off since we got to Vohre.'

'I know.' Kel tightened her hold on Dira. 'I'm sorry. Really. I didn't mean what I said. I'm happy for – whatever is going on between you and Rahn.'

Dira made a contented sound. 'We should head back to our unit.'

Kel stepped back and shook her head, letting brown tendrils fall across her face. 'You go. I'm staying here tonight.'

Dira sighed. She stood there, just for a minute, before shrugging off her black jacket.

Kel frowned. 'What are you doing?'

Dira sat cross-legged on the dirt. 'If you're staying, I am too.'

'That's awful logic.'

'No – you know what's awful? How *you* look. When was the last time you got some rest?'

Kel folded her arms. 'I'm *fine*.'

'I've been watching the bags beneath your eyes grow like mould.' Dira lifted her chin. 'I'm staying.'

Kel didn't object.

Savita huffed and tucked her head beneath her wing as Kel and Dira found a patch of grass to lie on. As they settled into silence, Kel realized just how tired she was. But her mind refused to let her sleep. No matter how many deep breaths she counted, her thoughts kept spiralling back to Coup.

Sleep seemed to evade her friend, too. Through the darkness, Dira whispered, 'We really should tell Rahn about Savita's nearing rebirth. We can trust her, you know. She's not Cristo's minion.'

'I know,' Kel admitted. 'But she worships him.'

Dira huffed. 'She doesn't *worship* him. She just . . . feels like she owes him. He supported her when her parents didn't and helped her get settled in Cendor. He treats her like a daughter.'

Kel snorted. Too many Howlers were letting debts define them. 'What exactly is going on between you and her?'

Dira smiled timidly – such a foreign expression on the winger. 'I really like her, Kel. And I hope she likes me. We've made a chart of rooms to make out in, so I think she likes me. But it's just . . . easy, with her. She's never stepped foot in Dresva, but she gets it.'

'Gets what?'

Dira paused, then said, 'Leaving Dresva was the hardest thing I've ever done. Leaving my parents . . . it was like leaving a piece of myself. But Dresva was their home as much as it wasn't mine.

I knew they'd never come with me – not to a place like Cendor. Bright, dangerous, wild – they'd hate it for all the reasons I love it. And even if she didn't expect to, Rahn's found just as much of a home here as I have. She understands.'

Dira turned on her side, towards Kel. 'I don't talk about my parents because it hurts. Not because I don't trust you. And I just . . . I was worried you'd think I was selfish. For choosing Cendor. Not because I had to, but because I wanted to. I didn't want you to think racing wasn't everything to me, too.'

Kel reached for Dira's hand. 'I don't. I promise.'

A pause, before Dira said, softly, 'As a kid, I'd heard about CAPR races and the money that could come from them. Dresva doesn't offer anything like that. Staying on Cendor and entering CAPR . . . it was all just meant to be one long race. I wanted to get in, get some money for me and my parents, and get out. But now . . .'

Kel gently nudged Dira's shoulder.

Dira huffed. 'Rahn's forced me to stop lying to myself.'

Kel frowned, an unspoken question. After a while, long enough for the heat lamp overhead to wink out completely, Dira confessed, 'My parents have agreed to visit Cendor.'

A shock of warmth flooded Kel. 'Dira, that's—'

'Great, right? That's why I *needed* racing. My plan was to earn as much as I could to get us set up for a life, together. I was going to return to Dresva. And with Cristo's money, I actually can. But . . . I *love* racing, Kel.'

Kel squeezed her friend's hand. She'd always thought that Dira was born for this. 'Then stay. Your parents will understand.'

Dira shook her head. 'Dresva is different to Cendor. It was always my plan to go back. Eventually.' Dira let out a shaky breath. 'Now, I don't know what to do.'

Kel leaned back and rubbed her arms. A venomous fear prickled her skin. Though she'd never said it aloud, Kel had known Dira might return to Dresva. Maybe that was why Kel used to push so hard to learn about Dira's past, her family. If she knew what Dira was missing, she could try to fill that hole. But hearing the pain in her friend's voice . . . maybe she'd never fully understand it, or be able to erase it. And that would have to be enough.

There was a long pause before Dira whispered, 'I know it's early days . . . but it feels right with the three of them, doesn't it? Bekn, Rahn, Coup. They fit.'

A weight settled over Kel. 'Yeah, they do.'

Maybe it was because they all had so much to lose – but their new team *worked*. Months ago, Kel never could have imagined finding anything like it away from her farm.

She didn't want to think about the warmth that followed the confession, and the memory it summoned of her and Coup flying, pressed together, the first of their reluctant truces. She wanted sleep to smother the fear she felt for their rider. So, the two girls lay side by side, with Savita at their feet, and let the darkness consume them, hoping it would consume their fears, too.

Until a sharp noise cut open the quiet.

Chapter Twenty-Nine

---·❋·---

Kel and Dira jerked upright at the sound. They rubbed sleep from their eyes and swapped frowns. Slowly, they tiptoed across the aviary, towards the glass wall that Savita shared with the other phoenixes. Savita didn't seem concerned by the noise – which did concern Kel. Was it nothing to worry about? Or was it just a familiar noise to her phoenix?

Voices echoed around the glass, coming from the larger aviary. The phoenixes' answering noises were somehow wrong – not the usual shriek or squawk, but something stifled.

Nothing could stifle a phoenix.

Nothing but a muzzle.

Kel and Dira hid behind a thick tree trunk. Kel couldn't spot all five phoenixes in the neighbouring enclosure, but the two she could see both wore intricate leather harnesses around their beaks.

Kel clenched her nails into her palms. She'd never seen a muzzled phoenix, never even heard of someone attempting it. The creature would either kill them or the taboo of it would chase them from Cendor.

A muzzle was no better than clipping a phoenix's wings.

Why would Cristo let this happen?

The people in the enclosure wore the white masks and uniforms of Cristo's research division, which rarely had anything to do with the aviaries.

The phoenixes griped and ruffled their wings, but quickly lay on the ground beside the workers. They were clearly used to this treatment.

Kel's breath shallowed as she watched the scientists move around the birds, carrying strange glass instruments. Their words were whispered too quietly to hear, but it was clear what they were doing. A phoenix's collar could only tell a person so much. For whatever reason, these scientists were poking and prodding the creatures for more data.

Kel glanced back at Savita, sleeping peacefully on the ground. Had Savita been experimented on, too?

Dira must have felt Kel begin to shake, because she touched Kel's arm and whispered, 'Not yet.'

Kel quietened her breath and unclenched her fists. She forced her feet to stay planted, even as the scientists bent down to inject the phoenixes and she heard muted whines of pain. They must have sedated the creatures. No grown phoenix would let this happen to them.

Kel knew they had to be cautious. They weren't supposed to be here – seeing this. Storming in there would just get them into trouble. They'd probably be fired for sleeping inside a phoenix's enclosure. They might take Savita from her.

The scientists filled their syringes with blood and placed them carefully in black bags. Then, with gloved hands, they reached for the phoenixes, and yanked.

Their hands came away with feathers.

Kel couldn't stop her gasp. No one *plucked* feathers. Cendor was far from Salta's religious heart, but most Cendorians clung tightly to superstitions about phoenixes and their magic. A firebird's plumage was its last layer of protection. Even if there wasn't a taboo, there was no reason to steal them. Everyone knew that phoenix feathers lost their magic if they were plucked.

So many questions soared through Kel's mind as she watched the scientists stuff their bags, before carefully removing the muzzles and leaving the aviary. They left no trace of their presence.

Both Dira and Kel let out loud, hard breaths when the aviary's door closed. Neither dared to leave Savita's cage that night, and neither dared to feel anything but confusion and fear for what the morning might bring.

Every night that week, Kel and Dira snuck back into Savita's enclosure with pillows, taking shifts to stay awake. They needed proof before going to Bekn or Rahn, who both revered Cristo as if he was an Alchemist himself. Or Coup – who needed to focus on his recovery, and who Kel still hadn't been to see.

The guilt she felt for staying away kept her from eating, and still, she couldn't bring herself to go.

Kel volunteered for most shifts throughout each night. She rarely slept, and when she did, her dreams were filled with dark, brown-speckled irises. They were Cristo's eyes, but something about them was different. Familiar, yet alien, and entirely *wrong*.

When awake, Kel could rarely keep herself from thinking of Coup – *in a bleached room, with no pulse* – and so she tried to let their search for proof consume her. She avoided the world beyond Savita's aviary, which seemed to have very strong opinions about their most recent race. Every broadcasted scene and magazine cover she glimpsed throughout the week seemed to focus back on one shot of Kel at Coup's side. *Heartbroken*, the news had dubbed her. When she'd seen a celebrity psychologist post a video breaking down Kel's red eyes and broken expression, she had shut off her own tele-comm.

Despite the nights spent in the aviary, no one returned. If not for Dira at her side, Kel might have thought she had imagined the whole thing. The pair hid inside Savita's enclosure under the cover of night, and waited, sacrificing mattresses and clean sheets for dirt and smoke.

After a week had passed of their tiring new rhythm, Dira and Kel were almost out of momentum. They were no closer to the truth, but they knew they had to tell their team.

They trudged back towards their apartment the next morning, weary and short-tempered, ready to raid the pre-cooked meals Bekn usually kept on his fridge shelf.

But when they opened the door to their unit, someone blocked their path to the kitchen, hobbling towards them on crutches.

Coup.

Kel's throat thickened. She hadn't seen Coup since the accident, hadn't visited him, despite Dira's pestering. Her worry for Savita had been a wonderful distraction, but now, Kel couldn't swallow the startling relief she felt at the sight of him. Butterflies and guilt tangled in her stomach as he offered a gentle smile.

She should have spent every day at his bedside. She didn't care if he hated her, or didn't want to see her – *she should have been there*. She shouldn't have run from whatever made her stomach flip at the sight of him.

Dira squealed, breaking the tension. She rushed forward as if to throw her arms around Coup but paused an inch away, settling instead for awkwardly ruffling his hair, careful not to put any weight on him.

Coup's shoulders bunched the fabric of his dark grey shirt as he held his arms over the crutches. Other than a lack of riding leathers and faded burns creeping his neck, he looked exactly as he usually did. His chestnut curls crept down his neck in untamed waves, almost reaching his shirt collar. There were no tired lines pinching his face, no fatigue slumping his posture. Even with crutches and red, tender skin ringing his neck, he looked ready to race.

Kel couldn't look away from the remaining burns at his throat. The lump in her own made it hard to breathe. 'They let you out so soon?' she breathed.

Her heart thudded in her ears. *Those* were her first words to him? An accusation instead of an apology? Why couldn't she do at least *this* right?

Coup merely shrugged. 'Cristo's tech is unbelievable. They only kept me so long to monitor my physical therapy. I'm feeling great. Invincible, actually.'

Both Kel and Dira rolled their eyes. The accident might have left him burnt and injured – but he was still *Coup*.

He stepped out of Dira's hold, towards Kel. 'Can we talk?'

Dira looked between them and moved into the kitchen.

Kel tried to clear her throat. 'We all need to. But not here.'

Not where Rahn or any of Cristo's workers could walk in at any moment.

Coup shook his head. 'No, I mean – can just the two of us talk?'

The butterflies in her stomach turned to spiders, knotting webs around her ribs, tightening her chest. 'Ah – sure. But maybe later? Dira and I – we really need to tell you and Bekn what we've found.'

Coup's face was unreadable. He nodded stiffly and walked with her into the kitchen, where Bekn hunched over the stove top, a green apron – his favourite colour – tied around his waist. There were floral initials stitched into the apron's side: *E.C.* Kel's stomach gurgled as the smell of pancakes wafted from the stove.

Bekn gestured to the long dining table. Six plates were set out, two bottles of maple syrup at the centre. She assumed one of the extra plates was for Rahn. She didn't know who the last plate was intended for – maybe Bekn hoped Cristo himself would join them for breakfast. Her pulse raced at the thought.

Kel helped Coup into the nearest chair, trying as hard as she could to avoid touching him.

Kel's stomach growled again as Bekn slid three pancakes onto her plate.

He raised a brow. 'I think I've heard more from your stomach this week than I have from you.'

Heat filled Kel's cheeks as she thanked him. 'Sorry. We've been busy.'

Dira nodded. 'We need to talk – but not here. Not yet. Pancakes are more important.'

Kel agreed, barely cutting her food before shovelling them into her mouth. Bekn filled his and Coup's plates, then took a seat. They all ate in a familiar, comfortable silence, until their plates were clean.

Bekn licked syrup off his thumb and frowned, as if there'd been no break in the conversation. 'Why can't we talk here?'

Dira and Kel exchanged looks. Eventually, Kel said, 'It's . . . about some future simulations that Dira and I have planned. We don't want anyone else to hear and steal our ideas.'

A muscle in Bekn's jaw feathered. 'Coup's just gotten out of hospital. I think training talk can wait.'

'I want to hear about the simulations,' Coup cut in. 'We should go to Bekn's room. I'd bet fifty ceres that his is the cleanest.'

The other three rose to their feet and looked expectantly at Bekn. Their mitigator sighed. 'Follow me.'

They trailed Bekn down the corridor, past the small lounge. The long, leather couch was strewn with blankets and movie cases. The sight sent a strange itch through Kel's bones. But the sensation vanished as soon as it had come, and moments later, they'd filed into Bekn's room.

Scenic posters covered the walls in neat rows. Other than a framed photo of Bekn and Coup and piled documents, his desk was bare. Photographs and *Nova Press* clippings were carefully stacked along his dresser, and his bed sheets were pulled tight.

'*Ashes*, Bekn,' Dira chuckled. She pointed to a nearby corkboard filled with pictures. 'Is that a dream board?'

'Of course not,' Bekn barked, flushing. 'It's just . . . ideas. A plan for the future. *Our* future, if we can win the next race without getting hospitalized.'

Kel traced her fingers over the corkboard, the only cluttered item in the room. It was mostly filled with motivational quotes and Asciran architecture blueprints.

Bekn's life had grown around others' needs, like branches around bamboo. If he was given the freedom to choose, the money they all desperately needed, would he leave Cendor?

Coup settled awkwardly against the headboard and Dira took a seat across the room. Kel perched at the foot of the bed, as far from Coup as possible.

Bekn drummed his fingers against the desk. 'Well? Is this to plan our recovery after the last race?'

From the corner of her eye, Kel saw Coup wince.

Without waiting for a reply, Bekn reached for a pile of papers. 'I've spent the last week working with Cristo, wading through new media partnership offers. Everyone in Cendor is desperate to know how the fallen hero and his heartbroken sweetheart are faring.'

Kel had seen that headline across plenty of race reruns over the past week. She didn't need Bekn reminding her.

Coup cleared his throat. 'Bekn's organized an interview with *Nova Press* for this afternoon. I can do more afterwards, if other newspapers catch word.'

Dira and Kel exchanged stunned looks.

'You're already signing him up for interviews?' Dira asked.

'It was my idea,' Coup retorted. 'Bekn wanted me to rest for another week, but I'm ready. I've been watching the news in the hospital. Every channel is still covering the race, but who knows how long that will last?'

Kel made a noise in the back of her throat. 'You shouldn't be back in the spotlight, yet.'

She couldn't believe that Bekn was encouraging this.

Kel narrowed her eyes at Coup's brother. 'How much say have Cristo's publicists had in all of this?'

Bekn's throat bobbed. 'Cristo's media team thinks this publicity is a good thing. Outlets are still talking about us, but not in a good way. They all think that what happened was . . . Savita's fault. They're saying she's too wild for CAPR.' He turned to Kel. 'That she hasn't been tamed properly.'

'*What?*' Kel rose. 'That's ridiculous!'

'Exactly,' Coup said, voice flat. 'That's why I need to do the interviews. They need to know it was *me*, not Savita, who caused the accident. Otherwise word will keep spreading and it won't be long before the council comes calling.'

Kel stiffened. The council wasted no time if they thought a phoenix – tamed or wild – was uncontrolled. There was only ever one course of action.

Death.

Kel tried to slow her breathing, to remind herself that Savita was *safe*. After a long moment, she said, 'That's not what we needed to talk about. Dira and I – we saw something.'

With a shared glance, Dira and Kel told Bekn and Coup everything about that haunted night in the aviary.

Since that first night, Kel's access to Sav's data had returned. Her phoenix's vitals were perfectly normal; nothing resembling what they should be with Sav nearing a rebirth. The knowledge had kept her muscles strained and awake over the past week. Cristo's team was still lying to her – they'd just gotten better at it.

When neither brother spoke, Dira said, 'We have to tell Rahn. She might know something about what's going on.'

'We can't,' Bekn said quickly. 'Rahn trusts Cristo more than she trusts us. If we go to her with accusations, she'll just go to him.'

Dira's face fell as Coup and Kel voiced their agreement. Kel felt Coup's gaze on her, the hairs on her neck rising. She risked a quick glance at him; he was watching her with a slight frown, a question in his eyes. Kel felt her face redden even more, and kept her focus on Bekn.

'We shouldn't do anything,' Bekn said. When Kel opened her mouth to argue, he added quickly, 'Not yet. You were right to try and find more proof. For all we know, it could have been employees just grabbing samples for research, which is Cristo's right.'

Dira moved to stand beside Kel. 'You're telling me that what we saw *wasn't* super sketchy?'

A muscle in Bekn's jaw quivered. 'No, but as long as Cristo isn't seen actually harming Savita or the other phoenixes, it's not our concern what he does with the rest of his business.'

'But we *did* see them harming phoenixes.' Kel exploded. 'If they weren't hurting the phoenixes, then why would they lock me out of Savita's readings? Why would they pull feathers and *muzzle* them?'

Bekn's face shifted into a look of such sincere pleading that it almost cut through the haze of Kel's fear. Almost.

'You *know* Cristo,' Bekn said softly. 'After everything he's done for us, do you really think he'd try to hurt phoenixes? Until we see him hurt *Savita*, we have no legal way to stop him. So, for now, we just need to do our jobs, and keep an eye out for anything odd.'

Anything odd? Looking around, Kel couldn't believe that Dira was nodding at Bekn's words. But the winger wouldn't meet Kel's gaze.

Kel didn't want to think about Cristo's painted face or sentimental gifts. She wanted to hold on to the rage and fear thrashing inside her. She wanted it to drown her.

How were they just meant to sit back and wait for whatever Cristo was planning? When she could do more to stop it?

Kel knew nothing more could come from this meeting, so when the others left the room to begin the day's work, she stormed off, too.

At least she would have done, had Coup not blocked her path.

Standing crooked with one arm propped over a crutch and the other barring the doorframe, Coup cocked a brow. '*Now* can we talk, tamer?'

Chapter Thirty

---※---

Kel kept her features blank. 'I should really be getting to work.'

'Perfect. I have no duties for at least another week. I'll tag along.'

Kel's jaw clenched. What could she say?

Sorry, Coup, but your presence makes me want to curl into a ball beneath Savita's wing like a frightened hatchling.

'You clearly need my help, anyway,' Coup added, when she didn't reply. 'How is it possible that you look worse than I do? Have you slept at *all* since the race?'

His voice was taunting, trying to bait her into their usual barbed rhythm. But words kept sticking to her throat. She needed more *time*. She needed to figure out what the anxious insects in her stomach meant and why she couldn't meet his eyes.

Kel could tell by the thin press of his lips that Coup wouldn't take no for an answer. Finally, she forced herself to nod. 'Fine. If you're up for it.'

Coup adjusted his crutches. 'A few bruises can't stop me from helping with a chore or two.'

They walked in silence, keeping a slow pace. Kel opened and closed her mouth to speak too many times to count. The quiet between them grew and thickened until a knife could have pierced it.

Kel trudged to her small, square office. She scrambled through the white corridors between aviaries. She updated Cristo's other tamers on her progress observing phoenix behaviour in the different environments of each aviary.

Coup seemed determined not to leave her side.

'I have plenty of recovery ahead of me,' Coup sang, when Kel darted out of another aviary. Coup folded his arms and leaned against a wall. He raised his chin, offering a clear view of the red marks still lingering along his neck. 'I can wait *all* day.'

Kel halted, rubbing her face. 'If it'll stop you lurking, let's talk.'

Kel wrapped a hand around his arm and led him back through the maze. She felt his warmth through the grey shirt, all too aware of how her fingers bunched in the fabric. The pair twisted through the corridors and, too soon, pushed through *The Prism*'s entrance. Kel relished Coup's stunned, slack features as he took in the diamond room.

'Cristo plans to use this place for phoenix rebirths,' Kel explained, as Coup wandered into the centre of the room. 'Theoretically, the diamonds can withstand the heat and stop any damage to the building. When the diamond gets too hot, it'll turn to graphite. But the room hasn't been used, yet.'

Kel drifted towards the nearest corner. Overhead, the only blemish in an otherwise flawless space, a security camera was mounted to a small incision in the roof. There was no light flickering on the camera and there was a film of dust covering the lens; they were truly alone.

She turned back to Coup. 'What did you want to talk—'

'Why didn't you visit me?'

Kel flinched. His eyes were duller than usual, his voice sharper.

'I–I'm sorry.' The words were brittle and forced. The room's light was suddenly too bright. 'I thought you'd want some time to rest.'

The lie drooped in the air between them. Coup hobbled closer. She didn't know how to spark their usual teasing, the frustration of almost every conversation they'd ever had. What had changed?

She tried again: 'I figured you'd appreciate some peace and quiet without me there to lecture you. A gift from the self-righteous sweetheart to the fallen hero.'

'Is that what's wrong?' he asked dryly. 'You're mad because I called you self-righteous? I'm sorry, Varra. I was just . . . I wanted to make you squirm.'

Oh, he'd succeeded. But not in the ways he'd intended.

Kel shook her head, trying and failing to find the right words. 'That's not what I meant.'

'What, then?'

Kel forced her tongue to move, to wrap around words – *any* words. 'If you're going to be sorry for anything, it should be for scaring me to death. You could have gotten yourself killed.'

His brows rose. 'You were worried for *me*?'

'Of course I was! I thought I'd gotten you killed.'

Coup gave a harsh, unamused laugh. 'This isn't your fault, tamer. *I'm* the one who risked our team's future. I almost blew up everything we've worked for over the last months, and I didn't care if I got hurt.'

Coup stood too close, breathing hard. She could almost hear his hammering pulse.

Kel swallowed. 'Just promise you won't do it again, all right?'

The diamonds pressed in sharp peaks at her back and there was nothing but *Coup* in this room. Broken reflections and echoes of his painful words. His eyes darkened to burnt copper, and she couldn't understand the way they darted across her face, searching.

'Promise me you won't do it again, Coup,' she repeated. 'I can't lose – this. The Howlers,' she added, praying he hadn't heard the hitch in her voice.

From the way his gaze flickered to her lips, she knew her prayer had gone unanswered.

Coup stepped closer. He didn't pause until they were just a whisper apart.

She couldn't think about what she'd just said. Not as he leaned towards her and she felt his breath against her lips.

'I can't make that promise, tamer,' he murmured. She was all too aware of him. Every breath, every small movement overwhelmed her. 'Not when we both have too much to lose.'

'I don't *care* about winning.' If he wasn't leaning on crutches, she might have shaken him. 'Just . . . promise me. Before I do something I'll regret.'

Coup's lips twitched with a smirk. 'Like what?'

Kel's lungs emptied. The overhead light stopped buzzing and her pulse silenced and there was only *Coup*, watching her watch him, the scarce space between them threatening to catch aflame.

Kel didn't remember closing the distance between them. She didn't see Coup move, either. Between one breath and the next, their lips collided.

It took everything inside of Kel not to buckle to the floor.

The kiss heated her blood more than his words ever had. They fought for control, stealing air from each other. Kel felt like she was breaking apart, taut and unravelling all at once. Their embrace was unyielding and – she hoped – unending.

Coup shifted closer, crutches clattering to the ground. He kept one hand pressed to the diamond, caging her. His other hand seized her hip in a callused hold. Without thinking, Kel twined her hands in the curls creeping down his neck. Coup pressed tighter against her.

Their teeth clashed as he deepened the kiss. She thought her chest might explode as a low groan escaped his lips.

Her thoughts darted in every direction, desperately searching for the truth. She couldn't want *him* like this. Not Warren Coupers. He was arrogant, and reckless, and . . .

Kel didn't care. The flames racing through her were too consuming. She arched into his touch and breathed everything she was into the kiss. All her anger, her fear, her fire.

His tongue traced her lower lip and she fisted her hands in his hair, tugging him closer. She wanted to feel every part of him. She'd kissed boys before, other CAPR racers, men who frequented The Ferret, but she'd never felt this heat in her belly. She'd never wanted *more*.

Coup dug one hand into Kel's hip and splayed the other across her lower back. He pressed closer, tighter, before shifting to trail warm kisses across her jaw, her neck. There was nothing gentle or tender between them. Just a desperate, aching need. His touch broke her apart and stitched her back together, all sharp edges and brutal warmth.

Kel forced him to spin around so his back was pressed to the diamond for support. Their lips fought and his hands roamed up her back, grazing the skin beneath her breast.

Kel knew it was wrong – now was *not* the time to kiss him, or do the other things that her body screamed for. She needed to unravel more of him, first; to understand his recklessness. *That* was more important than the feel of his lips against hers, his hands tracing rough circles on her hips, his chest pressed against hers . . .

A deeper groan escaped Coup's throat and an ache settled in Kel's core. His hands roamed her back, her sides, as if he couldn't touch enough of her. Kel palmed the back of his neck, trapping his mouth against hers, wanting to feel every inch of him against her—

And then, Kel froze. A chill crept down her spine, replacing the heat from Coup's touch. Her breath came out short and fast and she forced herself back. Her hands lifted from Coup's neck.

Coup's eyes flashed, dark and blazing, like gold beneath moonlight. He kept his hold on her for just a moment, before pulling back. A question filled his features.

But Kel couldn't answer him. She couldn't breathe. She could only stare at her fingers, which had brushed the diamond wall behind Coup's neck.

Ash was smeared across her hand. Though black and grey, it caught the room's refracted light and sparked to life. As if there was still magic inside.

She'd seen plenty of pictures to know what phoenix ash looked like. It was finer than ordinary ash, with small particles of orange and red scattered through it.

This ash contained enough red and orange to look like a tiny galaxy, gleaming on her trembling fingers.

Slowly, Coup bent forwards and lifted a finger to the diamond wall, a miniscule crevasse still coated with ash. 'Is that what I think it is?'

Dread doused every ember of warmth coursing through Kel. 'Phoenix ashes.'

Coup straightened. He reached for his crutches and shifted closer to the wall.

Cristo had said that this room hadn't been used. Had he lied? Or had a phoenix died and rebirthed within the last month?

No matter the reason, these ashes shouldn't *be here*. Every molecule of a phoenix's ashes was swept up in a rebirth; they swarmed into a single pile, as if drawn by a magnet, from which a phoenix was reborn. There was never a single iota left.

If there were ashes remaining, it meant that the phoenix they belonged to had never been reborn. The creature had met a true death.

Kel looked up at the camera attached to the crystalline roof. Cristo would never leave security so lax for a room as priceless as *The Prism*. Yet, the camera was switched off and gathering dust, nothing more than a sleek ornament. The door was always unlocked; locks would draw questions, and no one seemed to know that this room even existed.

Cristo didn't want to draw any attention to the invaluable room. The cameras were switched off on purpose.

So no one would ever know what kind of crimes he committed within.

Chapter Thirty-One

When Kel and Coup gathered Dira and Bekn, déjà vu punched Kel in the gut.

'There's nothing we can do,' Bekn said, his voice like gravel. 'Don't give me that face – you know I'd help if I could.'

Kel wanted to shake Bekn, to wake him up. 'Savita is nearing a rebirth. How can you just stand there when Sav could be next?'

Bekn rubbed his face and paced along the length of the small room. She'd forced the Howlers into her sleeping quarters, not daring to lead them back to *The Prism* and draw attention.

'Of course I care about Savita,' Bekn snapped. 'But I care about *you* more. Neither you nor Coup should be trying to take on a billion-cere business in your spare time. You should be enjoying your work and exploring the city. Maybe even pick up your schooling again, like Dira has.'

Kel swivelled towards Dira, who sat perched on the edge of her bed. The winger shrugged sheepishly.

'Bekn is right, Kel,' Dira said, slowly. 'If Savita is in danger, we need to get her out – but there could be thousands of reasons for those ashes.'

Disbelief sent a chill down Kel's spine. Just this *morning* Dira had been on her side. What could have changed since—

Then she realized. 'You told Rahn.'

Dira folded her arms. 'Only enough to work out if we can trust Cristo. Rahn says that Cristo's doing everything he can to preserve phoenix numbers – both tamed and wild. Why would he spend *billions* on conservation if he just wants to kill them?'

Kel didn't have an answer. All she knew was she had a headache and the thought of Savita far, far away from Vohre was like a soothing balm.

'We have more immediate concerns, anyway,' Bekn said. 'There's another race coming up in a few days. Cristo thinks we need a presence. It's rumoured to be Vohre's biggest race of the year.'

Kel's pulse leapt into her throat.

'What?' she stammered. 'Coup isn't ready to race, and even if we could find a substitute rider, it would take too long for Sav to let them ride her.'

Bekn chewed his lower lip. 'You've raced Sav on occasion, right, Kel?'

Kel blinked, slowly. 'Yes – but Sav's too close to a rebirth. We can't risk taking her out of the compound right now.'

'And Varra hasn't had time to train,' Coup cut in, jaw clenched. 'She needs practice before we throw her into a storm like that.'

'Why would Cristo even risk Sav leaving the compound if she's nearing a rebirth?' Dira added.

Bekn made a pained expression. 'I'm sure he has his reasons. He wouldn't ask this if it wasn't safe. And we don't even need to place. We just need a presence, and it will be good to keep up media attention and prove to the council that Savita isn't a threat.' Bekn turned to Kel. 'Just think on it.'

Kel opened her mouth. No sound came out. She'd assembled her team, hoping they'd help protect Sav. Instead, she discovered that Cristo wanted to strap her to a phoenix nearing a rebirth.

She felt defeated already. Against riders who trained every day, she stood no chance of placing, especially against a race rumoured to be the grandest of the season.

She didn't give Bekn an answer. As he and Dira filed out of her room, Kel wracked her brain for a way to make them stay. She was all too aware of Coup still sitting behind her in an armchair, annoyingly quiet for the first time in his life.

'Don't say I'm overreacting,' she croaked. She didn't think she could take hearing it from him, too.

'For once I think your melodrama is warranted,' Coup said. A tired smile lifted his cheeks. 'I think you're right. The others do, too, even if they don't want to admit it.'

Kel blinked away unexpected tears. 'You'll help me find out what's going on?'

Coup waggled his eyebrows. 'I couldn't deprive you of my investigative skills.'

His words sent her heart falling through her ribs, down to her stomach. She didn't know what had changed between them so suddenly – but as Coup's features widened into their usual easy, teasing grin, something strange warmed her. From calming Savita at races to trusting her suspicions, Coup refused to let her keep him at a safe distance. Even Dira had respected Kel's wariness. But Coup had either ignored Kel's walls, or taken a sledgehammer to them. She'd had no choice but to let him in.

Over the next few days, Kel had to admit that their teamwork off the track was just as frustratingly efficient as it was on the track.

Coup helped her work where he could, and she forced him through his physical therapy every afternoon. Just as Dira had over the past week, Coup stayed by her side in Savita's enclosure each night. She'd demanded that he sleep in his bed, to rest his leg and burns, but unless she physically hauled him from the aviary, she couldn't make him leave.

So they lay together in the muggy dark, Savita curled at their feet like a huge house cat. The phoenix doted on Coup just as she did Kel, and for the first time, Kel watched them with no jealousy.

Side by side, they spoke of everything but their kiss. The memory of it snuck into her dreams and ghosted across her skin, exciting and terrifying, as if she'd been caught in a storm. She didn't know if Coup felt the same charge between them, and she didn't dare to ask. But where their barbed words used to feel easy, familiar, they now felt brittle. Something lingered beneath them, waiting to break.

Still, each night, they stole more bricks from the old, serrated walls between them to build the bones of something new.

Every night they returned to the aviary and saw nothing but empty shadows. Kel even dragged Dira and Bekn to *The Prism* one afternoon – but the room had been cleaned. If Coup hadn't seen the remains too, Kel might have truly convinced herself she'd imagined it.

As they hurried from Sav's aviary four mornings later, Kel whispered, 'Do you think they knew we found the ash?'

Coup looked down the empty hall before replying. 'Maybe. But I doubt Cristo's team cares what two seventeen-year-olds know. If they did, they'd have kicked us out of here by now.'

Kel nodded. 'If the scientists don't show up again, where else can we look for—'

'Look for what?'

The pair spun around. Kel's stomach dropped.

Cristo strolled forward, hands clasped at the front of his blue blazer. His black hair fell in short, unruly waves around his face. The small heels of his brown shoes clicked as he moved closer, making Kel think of Savita's talons hitting stone.

Kel swallowed. She'd lurked outside his empty office a dozen times over the past week, tempted to confront him over what she'd found, and *now* he stumbled upon her? 'We were looking for you, actually. We... We wanted to know when we might be able to take Savita out of the aviary. To an outdoor practice track.'

Cristo cleared his throat. 'Of course, but that might have to wait. I was actually looking for you, Kelyn. To ask something of you.'

Kel blinked. 'What is it?'

'I'm hoping you all have considered participating in the upcoming race. I know nothing of the track details, but a few inside sources have told me it'll be the biggest race of the season. It's crucial that the Howlers are there.'

Kel inched forward. 'I don't know. Coup's still injured, and I haven't raced in almost a year.'

'It's your decision, but it's important that we take quick action to dispel the growing rumours around Savita's... nature.'

Cristo's eyes went to Coup, his crutches, then back to Kel. She felt her face redden.

Kel dug her nails into her palms. She had to protect Savita – by whatever means necessary.

'I'll do it,' Kel muttered.

'What?' Coup cut in.

Kel ignored him.

'Perfect,' Cristo said, a calm smile pursing his lips.

Coup turned to Kel. 'Don't you think—'

'But I'll need full access to Savita's vitals to prepare for the race.'

Cristo's brows rose slightly, and that was all the confirmation she needed. It was no glitch in the system – he'd intentionally cut her out.

'I am sorry for that,' Cristo said after a beat, running a hand through his dark locks. 'Please trust me – it was in your best interest to restrict your access.'

Kel's nostrils flared. 'I'm her tamer. How could it possibly be in my best interest?'

'Your safety is a higher priority to me than your obligations as a tamer,' Cristo said smoothly.

Kel's nails dug deeper into her palms. 'But you're fine with me racing her?'

Cristo's lips thinned. He sighed. 'As I'm sure you've suspected, Kelyn, Savita is nearing a rebirth.'

Kel kept her face blank as icy disbelief filled her. A part of her had still hoped Cristo hadn't lied to her, hadn't known.

Cristo continued, 'I worried that you'd interfere with how we wish to handle her rebirth.'

'And how is that?' Coup demanded.

'Carefully,' Cristo said quickly. 'It's a dangerous process, and it's best if you let my team help her through the transition. I am sorry, Kelyn. I was trying to protect you.'

The sincerity in his voice shocked Kel more than anything he'd said, and for a moment she hesitated. But she had to trust her instincts. She stepped towards Cristo. 'What is your *process*?'

If Cristo wanted to control Savita's rebirth, why would he send Savita into another race?

Cristo gestured behind them, to *The Prism*. 'We'll place Savita in a safe environment, where her rebirth won't hurt anyone. But there's still an unavoidable element of risk. That's why I wished for only the most qualified on my team to have access to Savita's vitals. I was going to tell you – but I didn't want you to worry about Savita, as well as everything else.' His eyes flickered to Coup, then back to Kel. 'I'll make sure that your access is restored, and you can see all past records. You have my word.'

If you race.

She didn't know if Cristo had left the words to hang in the air, or if she'd imagined them. Either way, they rang through her ears like temple bells: inescapable and unending.

'Okay. Count me in.'

Cristo nodded solemnly. Then he disappeared down the empty corridor, leaving Kel and Coup to collect the new truths splattered across the walls.

'What the hell, Varra!' Coup said, his voice uneven, as if trying to find the right words. 'The tamer I knew in Fieror *never* would have agreed to something this reckless.'

'What choice do I have?' she threw back, struggling to keep her voice low. 'Savita's life's on the line. Nothing else matters.'

Coup was right – something fiery and painful had changed her since they'd arrived in Vohre: a renewed desperation to save Savita. But that same fire refused to let her overthink her decision. Cristo was right. If she didn't agree to the race, Savita's dangerous reputation would only grow, and Cristo still had equal ownership of Savita.

'I've got this,' Kel added, warmed by the concern in Coup's eyes. 'I've raced Sav occasionally when we were in between riders.'

'I'm coming with the Howlers,' Coup said, lips pressed into a flat line. 'Even if it's just to fill in your brooding shoes and keep you from doing anything rash.'

'I bet you didn't think *you'd* ever be saying that to *me*,' she said.

'I mean it, tamer,' he said, refusing to return her teasing. 'Stay safe.'

Kel nodded, her lips twitching up. 'I'll try my best, Coupers.'

Part Three

O'er years the rider and knight soared up high
Bound by true valour, legends of the sky
But below the tides, sea monsters dwelled deep
And dragged Ryker down, a trusting soul reaped

Above, Deja glimpsed his course 'neath the waves
She descended for his watery grave
Only fleeting breaths left ere he perished
She vowed to save him, her rider cherished

Verse 5–6, 'The Gilded Lullaby'

Chapter Thirty-Two

---※---

'This can't be the right way, can it?' Kel mused.

She guided Savita across a bed of flattened shrubbery. They'd known nothing about the race prior to Cristo giving them the GPS location. Kel hadn't known what to expect after the two last races; she certainly hadn't expected the GPS to steer them to Vohre's north-east edge, where the forest met the city's border.

To Kel's left, Dira shrugged. 'Other teams have pulled up, and I can hear a crowd up ahead. It must be the right way.'

With other crews guiding their phoenixes ahead and behind them, the Howlers rounded a corner amongst the growing greenery. They wove further from the city's edges, into the outer layers of Vohre Forest. The trees at their sides had been hacked away to create a path wide enough for phoenixes, though a dense forest still guarded against most of the morning light. Nausea swirled in Kel's stomach at the sight of the destruction.

'We don't need to place in this race,' Rahn reminded Kel, her face scrunched. 'Not after winning the last two. We just need to show that Savita isn't a threat to anyone. I'm not thrilled that we're racing without our usual rider, but I trust Cristo.'

The certainty in Rahn's voice made Kel's ears ache. They hadn't spoken much in the past week, mostly because Kel didn't know what to say to the technician. How much had Dira told her? Kel still didn't know how deeply Rahn's loyalty to Cristo ran, and the unknown prickled at her skin.

As they rounded another corner, Kel's mouth fell open. A

massive oval space had been cleared of all trees as a starting line. New, gleaming silver rails illuminated the race's path, straight into Vohre's hungry maw.

'They want us to fly through the forest?' Disbelief soaked her words. 'That's – impossible.'

Crew booths had been haphazardly propped up around the edges of the clearing. Crowd stands had been raised in tall, narrow rows, to make the most of the restricted space. Though spectators couldn't see much of the track beyond the starting line, giant screens had popped up, encircling the clearing. Cameras must have been placed throughout the track to broadcast the race. Kel couldn't imagine how quickly everything had been erected to avoid Vohre's media leaking the details.

Savita could fly through the forest as easily as any racetrack. Perhaps even easier, as she loved to fly in the muggy heat. But Vohre Forest was the last natural habitat of Cendor's wild phoenixes. Groups across the island were already fighting hard to preserve every last acre of the forest. Yet, somehow, CAPR had gained council permission to clear an enormous track through the edges of it.

'We can't compete,' Coup said, shuffling ahead of them. 'This isn't right. Even if it was, CAPR can't keep wild phoenixes off the track if they stumble upon it. Who knows how Savita would react?'

Dira folded her arms. 'And we've never entered a race where we couldn't see the track from our booth. Kel and Sav will be going in completely blind!'

Kel tightened her grip on Savita's reins, palms clammy through her leather gloves. Her phoenix seemed oblivious to the danger, raking her claws along the flattened grass.

'It's better than the alternative.' Kel gritted her teeth. She *refused* to let the council think Sav a threat.

'She's right,' Rahn said softly. 'Canen means well, but . . . he has strict expectations for his CAPR teams. We represent him. If we pull out of the race, I don't know if the Howlers will be participating in future races with his sponsorship.'

Kel's throat tightened. No one said a word as the noise around them grew, excitement and fear mingling in the air.

Kel lifted a gloved hand to stroke Savita's neck. 'We compete, or we lose everything.'

Dira shook her head. 'But you—'

'Wild phoenixes won't venture this close to the edge of the forest,' Kel said, forcing confidence into her voice. 'They won't find the track.'

'And if they do?' Coup placed a gloved hand beside Kel's on Savita's neck. 'Phoenixes – tamed or not – don't take kindly to intruders in their territory.'

Kel had no reply. She knew, without even glancing down the starting line, that CAPR hoped for wild phoenixes to find them. They hoped to provoke the wild creatures with their latest track. Making them living, blazing obstacles.

Kel didn't respond. With the sudden nerves drying her throat, she didn't know if she could. Instead, she tugged Savita towards the burgundy tent stamped with their insignia. She tried to focus on the anger she felt at CAPR instead of the horrors ahead, already prickling her arms with goosebumps. CAPR was willing to clear out Vohre forest, the phoenixes' last remaining habitat, for entertainment. Provoking them for fun. She supposed she shouldn't have been surprised, after the last race. But what else were they capable of?

As her teammates shuffled around her, organizing equipment, she tried to shake free an old echo in her head.

You're no different than the rest of CAPR.

Whether or not Coup still believed those words, she now knew they were true. It didn't matter why she was competing or what she had to lose. He had been right to call her self-righteous, to challenge her. But she didn't know how to right her actions without losing Savita.

Kel placed both hands on the underside of Sav's beak. Her phoenix leaned into the touch, trust keeping her feathers smooth and her tail swishing.

Sirens blared overhead, signalling the looming race. Kel struggled to breathe around a fresh wave of nerves.

Rahn appeared to Kel's right, stumbling beneath the weight of heaving a duffel bag. 'Ready to gear up?'

Her heart jittered. With only a few days to train on Sav, she most definitely *wasn't* ready. Kel quickly tugged the duffel bag from Rahn, easing it onto the ground. She tried to ignore Dira and Coup's heated whispers in the furthest corner of the tent.

Rahn quickly began rummaging through the bag. She nestled an upgraded comms device in Kel's ear, helped Kel adjust Savita's latest saddle, and checked the new full-body airbags threaded into the riding leathers. The last wouldn't protect Kel if Savita heated up like she had during the previous race, but at least she could jump from the saddle and not break every bone in her body.

Rahn's fingers traced Kel's gear with light, precise movements, and she hummed absently as she worked. Kel was surprised to recognize the tune.

'What's got you smiling?' Rahn asked.

Kel hadn't realized she'd been smiling. 'My father used to sing me that lullaby. He was terrible – off-beat and croaky – but I loved the song.'

'The Gilded Lullaby' was one of her favourites. The lyrics snuck into the fissures of her skull, echoing in her father's raspy voice. It sang the legend of Ryker's fatal injury: torn apart by a sea-monster he'd swam too close to, and then reborn through Deja's shared magic.

For two years, Kel had rarely let herself think of such stories. But after seeing Coup so burnt and broken, she wondered if, instead of ignoring the pain, she should let it envelop her. Maybe it would work through her, bit by bit, until she'd drained the pain from her memories like pus from a wound. Until she could think of her father and smile instead of cry.

Rahn's eyes sparked. 'I'd never heard the song until I came to Cendor, but it's oddly comforting.'

Kel watched as Rahn checked the CAPR equipment with hardly a glance. Rahn might not have been born in Cendor – but, like Dira, she was born for it.

'Are you glad you left Ebrait?' Kel asked.

Rahn gave an instant nod. 'I was terrified at first. But Canen helped me make Vohre my home. My mum was . . . she's important in Ebrait. She wanted me to follow in her footsteps. Without someone like Canen vouching for me, I don't think I would have had the courage to leave,' she added, with a soft chuckle. 'He's given me so much.' She shrugged softly. 'And . . . I guess if the Howlers make a name for themselves under Cristo's sponsorship, it'll show my parents that this was the right choice, too.'

'I get it,' Kel said. 'We all have a lot riding on these races.'

Rahn said nothing as she wrapped a thin leather bracelet around Kel's left wrist. One end bore a metal pin that needled through the other end, locking it in place. The Howlers' barbed, flaming insignia had been pressed into the leather.

Kel ran a thumb over the bracelet. 'What's this?'

Rahn had already moved on to her next task. 'Oh. That's just a tracker. There's an emergency button stitched into the underside of the leather, in case you need immediate evacuation mid-race. You have to press down pretty firmly to activate it.' Rahn ducked her head, loose wisps of hair falling over her face. 'I had it made after the last race.'

Kel nodded, understanding. *After Coup nearly incinerated himself.* The memory sent her heart pounding.

'Thank you,' she said.

'Rahn's tech will protect you if anything . . . happens,' Dira cut in, stalking towards them, a tablet in one hand. 'I'll be watching you through your helmet camera. Just stay alive, and we'll do the rest.'

Kel gave a purse-lipped smile.

Dira's gaze trailed over Kel, checking her gear. 'Did you watch the videos I sent you last night? There are a few competing riders I want you to watch out for, but I found some old race recordings flagging their weaknesses.'

Kel grimaced. 'You sent me videos?'

Dira sighed. 'If you don't get some sleep after this race I'm going to start stapling reminders to your forehead.'

Rahn giggled, shifting away – checking a stack of equipment across the tent – and Dira's eyes followed her, returning to Kel only when Rahn's back was turned.

'I keep thinking about what you found in *The Prism*,' Dira mumbled, too soft for anyone but Kel to hear. 'And what we saw in the aviary. I'm sorry for dismissing it. I was just . . .' Her gaze darted back to Rahn. 'If you think something's strange, I'll back you up. We'll figure out what's going on after this race.'

Kel's chest ached. Unsure what to say, she reached out to Dira and squeezed her hand.

The warning siren shot through the air before Kel could respond.

Coup marched over to Kel. 'You don't have to do this, tamer.'

Yes, I do. 'I know.'

Coup waggled three fingers. 'I can give you three pretty sound reasons why you shouldn't. One: *wild phoenixes*. Two: *wild phoenixes*. And three . . . You don't look well.'

Another wave of nerves rattled through her. She fidgeted with her leather sleeves. Kel couldn't think of much worse than crossing paths with wild phoenixes – but what choice did she have?

'He means *terrible*,' Dira amended.

'Thanks,' Kel said dryly, pulling her goggles on.

She didn't bother refuting their insults. She'd been sleeping dreadfully since they'd arrived in Vohre, worrying about Savita and whatever was going on at Cristo Industries. But that same worry filled her with a burning fire that she knew would help her in the race.

Another siren blasted and Kel mounted Savita. Together, she and Coup hurried to guide Savita out of the tent and to the starting line. His crutches were gone, but he still limped slightly, and she knew bandages still cocooned most of his body while his skin stitched back together.

As the other Howlers wished Kel luck and fell back towards their tent, Coup lingered at Savita's side. He reached up a hand to test the buckles around Kel's right ankle. She felt his fingers aound her boot.

'I'll keep an eye on Sav's vitals.' He wrapped a light hand around her ankle. 'Don't get yourself killed, all right? The media loves our star-crossed romance too much.'

His voice had its usual teasing lilt, but the tight lines around his eyes made her stomach lift. '*Hmm*, it's not so fun when your teammate risks their life, is it?'

A muscle in Coup's jaw spasmed. 'Just don't do anything I would do, okay?'

Kel's smile dimmed. She couldn't remember ever seeing Coup so grave, no trace of amusement softening his features. Part of her wanted to reach out and smooth the crease between his brows. To wrap her arms around him in case this race ended as viciously as he seemed to think it might. But despite their kiss, they hadn't voiced what it might have meant – to either of them.

Kel swallowed. 'Okay.'

Chapter Thirty-Three

❈

Kel gripped Savita's reins tight, leather gloves cutting into her palms.

'All right, Sav,' she whispered. 'Let's get through this as quickly as possible.'

Savita shifted between her feet and grumbled. Kel squeezed her thighs around the saddle, still adjusting to the feel of it. It was so much more textured than the worn one she'd owned. She'd trained atop Sav as much as she could over the past few days, readjusting to her racing habits, adjusting to Rahn's improved gear. But nothing could prepare her for what it was like sitting atop Savita at the starting line, surrounded by the phoenix sounds and metallic smells of the starting line.

She was flanked by two blood phoenixes, their riders sitting several metres higher than her. They tossed quick glances her way, expressions guarded behind helmets, goggles and leather masks. The world was tinted from behind her own tempered glass goggles. Though Savita's heated feathers were sharper, her flames didn't make Kel's eyes sting. The sun's glare didn't faze her. The track ahead – a trampled path that veered around a corner too quickly – was muted, its brighter shades of green turned a darker hue.

'How's everything, Kel?' Dira's voice rang through Kel's ear-comm. 'Anything I need to keep an eye on?'

Kel took a deep breath, trying to loosen her throat. She knew her team were standing in their booth behind her. But she couldn't bring herself to look back.

Whatever she might have replied with, she didn't get a chance. From somewhere overhead, behind the towering stands, a sancter rifle fired.

Lightning filled the sky, and the race began.

Savita bent her great legs and spread her wings. Kel barely had to instruct her to fly; Savita knew what the sounds and sights meant – knew she had to shoot forward as fast as possible. She thrust her wings towards the ground and launched into the sky, higher than the larger blood phoenixes at her sides. Kel fell back in the saddle as Savita climbed, the sudden movement winding her. Pain lanced through her hips at the sudden jolt, her back colliding with the saddle seat. Tensing her core as Savita levelled out in the clear sky, Kel swapped her grip on the harness for the saddle pommel, keeping low and steady.

'Tamer,' Coup called through the comm. 'Talk to me. What's happening?'

Savita cried out, a primal sound that made Kel's ears ring. Kel gripped the saddle pommel tighter and forced herself to take a steadier breath as wind whipped against her face.

'We're all right,' Kel managed. 'Just – adjusting.'

Kel traced a line up Sav's neck with two fingers, instructing her to dip as they approached the edge of the clearing, where the forest grew denser. Wild red flames climbed to her right, clouding her peripherals. She remained steady, gaze ahead, knowing that even though they couldn't see the track Dira would be able to guide her through her helmet's camera. She trusted her team.

Another phoenix cried from Savita's left, falling back as they blazed through the first line of trees. The roaring of the crowd dulled, replaced by crackling flames and wild shrieks and branches breaking. Sweat began to bead along Kel's arms, the forest's muggy heat already cocooning her.

Kel thought they were in the first handful of phoenixes to reach the forest's edge, but she couldn't be sure. The cleared track through Vohre Forest was barely wide enough to fit two phoenixes, let alone the twenty in today's race.

She guided Sav around the first bend in the track. Even prepared, she barely held on to the saddle pommel as Sav tilted to the right. Sav's wings brushed loose branches that whacked Kel across the cheek. As the canopy grew thicker, sunlight winked out like a candle flame. Red, orange and yellow foliage surrounded them, like an endless Sheathing Season, the perfect camouflage for wild phoenixes. Thorned leaves the length of Kel's torso brushed against Savita's wings. Instead of withering and retreating from Sav's heat, Kel swore the vines and branches reached closer.

'Why can't she just fly over the forest?' Rahn asked through their comms. 'Avoid the track altogether.'

'We'd have no clue where the finish line is,' Dira's scratchy voice answered.

'Shut it,' Kel grunted, voice muffled through the leather bandana over the bottom half of her face. How did Coup breathe through this thing? It was twice as thick as the last mask she'd raced in.

Mustard flames flashed to Kel's left. She had barely turned her head when talons appeared through the blaze, lashing out towards her. Savita instinctively veered away from the pending attack as Kel yelped. She jerked violently in the saddle.

Kel's forearm cramped as she brushed a slanted line along Sav's neck, instructing her to shift higher amongst the towering foliage so no one could attack from above.

Savita followed Kel's instructions – but not before lashing out in return, swerving to spear her beak at the yellow phoenix. Sav caught a mouthful of yellow feathers in her maw, yanking them back before climbing higher.

The yellow phoenix cried out in pain and fell back.

'What the hell, Sav?' Kel muttered, making a mental note to be firmer in her instructions.

Savita released a deep, triumphant crow. Crimson dripped down her beak. Arms already aching from holding on to the pommel, Kel straightened Sav's path, keeping her phoenix focused on the path ahead instead of any other attackers. She adjusted her legs, shifting forward in the saddle to a more comfortable position.

'Come on, Varra,' Coup barked. 'Just let your phoenix do her thing. Focus on the track ahead.'

'Don't anticipate the phoenixes,' Dira added. 'Let Sav guide you for now.'

Kel held fast to Savita's saddle pommel, wishing she could spare a hand to mute her ear-comm.

She managed the next turn perfectly, though the path soon became less clear. Thin trees dotted the open track. Kel swerved around two before Sav's left wing caught on the third. They hadn't collided hard enough to slow, but two yellow feathers shot into the air, yanked free. Sav continued blazing on, seemingly indifferent to the collision. Kel huffed out a hard breath.

They'd just survived another turn when a phoenix crowed from somewhere nearby. Kel whipped her head around, frantically searching. What if it was a wild phoenix?

The distraction caused them to slow, just a fraction, and another phoenix soared ahead.

'You're faster than that, Kel!' Dira shouted. 'Let Sav enjoy herself at least a little.'

'The gear should do most of the work for you,' Rahn added. 'Just keep Savita along a straight path and she'll know what to do.'

Kel grunted, realizing she owed Coup an apology. She didn't

remember the comms being such a frustrating distraction the last time she'd raced.

'Remember how badly you didn't want me to race, minutes ago?' Kel yelled.

Her teammates fell blissfully silent.

Savita pinned her wings and shot between two trees as thick as her body. Kel heard the rustle of other phoenixes weaving through other ancient trees, leaving smoking trails that drifted above the canopy.

'Stay low beneath the tree line. I know it's dense – but it's better than wild phoenixes spotting you,' Dira called.

Kel bit back an argument. The thick, tangled greenery had barely been thinned for the race. If not for blinking lights along the path's railing, Kel would lose sight of the track in a heartbeat.

A flaxen-yellow phoenix swerved towards Kel, vying for the same narrow path that Savita traced. Sav snapped, flexing her wings.

Kel pressed a hand over the bandana covering the bottom half of her face, wiping away sweat. The forest's heat had already drenched Kel in a heavy sheen and Savita was growing hotter beneath her. She trusted that Coup would alert her if her phoenix grew too hot. But even with riding leathers and a thick saddle between them, Savita's feathers were already near-scalding. Forked, anxious sparks flickered down her back.

They raced deeper into the forest, weaving past blurred groves of carnivorous flowers and onyx shrubs that hissed as they passed. The foliage was too dense to see where they were placing, but Kel didn't waste her breath asking Dira through the comms and risking more unwanted commentary.

The path before them cleared, just a little, and Savita spread her wings to their full width. The other phoenixes blazing around them finally came into view, and Savita nipped at the feathered tail of a coral-red phoenix, who shrieked but didn't have the space to turn back.

Distracted by Savita's open maw, Kel didn't see what lay in front of them until a phoenix ahead collided with the ground.

Savita lifted her wings as Kel yanked on her harness. They barely slowed in time to avoid the phoenix ahead, bellowing and raging, crawling along the dirt. The greenery receded enough that she could see more than a few feet in front of her for the first time since beginning the race.

'Kel . . . what . . . that?'

Muffled voices echoed through Kel's comm. She wasn't surprised that the forest's density messed with the signal. She wondered if her helmet's camera was distorted too, or if they could see what she saw: a blockade of ancient trees across the track. That must have been what the phoenix had collided with.

Kel quickly guided Savita to land in front of the pile of trees. Four other phoenixes and their riders did the same, while the injured phoenix and its rider stayed back. Three riders unbuckled themselves and dismounted to get closer to the strange barrier. The trees hadn't been fully cut down, only enough for them to tilt towards each other, blocking the path while still as tall as the rest of the forest. The silver railing wilted down towards the ground, crushed beneath fallen logs.

Kel swapped a bewildered look with the nearest rider. Had CAPR done this, as an obstacle? There was no way around the great wall of trees. Not unless they flew overhead – but the trees were crowded together tightly enough that it would be near-impossible for Savita to break through the foliage.

They were trapped.

Kel squinted through the shadows around them. The trees had been intentionally hacked; sharp grooves cut into dozens of them.

Were they meant to just turn back, or find a way around?

The other riders posed her questions aloud, swapping frustrated shouts and curses as movement flashed through the forest's darkness. Kel led Sav to the edge of the cleared path, tilting her head towards the movement she'd seen.

Red and orange flashed through the darkness and melted into a strange sunrise. She'd never seen such vivid colours, even when Savita's temperature climbed.

Savita reared back, flailing her wings, and Kel was wrenched back, her tailbone hitting the saddle cantle. The skin on her thighs stretched taut and she bit down on a whimper.

'*Quiet*,' Kel hissed at the other riders.

'What? Did you find something?' a rider asked, nudging their phoenix closer.

Kel raised a trembling hand, silently begging them to stay quiet. They must have understood. A moment later, the clearing fell into a hush.

The only sounds came from around them. Low, grumbling murmurs and claws against stone. The colours moved closer, looming taller.

To the left of the barricade, a dawn of uncollared, wild phoenixes approached the clearing.

Chapter Thirty-Four

※

Kel sucked in a short, silent breath. At least four wild phoenixes moved towards the clearing, clicking their beaks, twitching their heads in agitation.

Slowly, Kel tugged Savita back, into the centre of the clearing. The three riders on the ground stayed frozen, eyes wide and distorted beneath their goggles.

The wild phoenixes prowled through the dense trees easier than they should have. They wove into the clearing and took sharper forms, flames turning to feathers and screeches to thunder.

Fear pounded in Kel's ears, blocking out the static of her broken comms. One flicker of annoyance and these wild phoenixes – uncollared, unfettered – could devastate the entire clearing.

The five riders stayed immobile, helpless, as the wild phoenixes moved towards them. Kel's heart jumped into her throat. Had CAPR planned this? Had she let Cristo sentence her to death in these woods?

Heat surged behind her. Slowly, dread shaking her arms, she twisted in the saddle.

At her back, along the path they'd all raced, another three wild phoenixes loomed closer. They encircled the clearing with easy, graceful steps, their blazes slowly stripping back. Ignoring the hair prickling the back of her neck, Kel pressed a soothing hand to Savita's side, silently begging her phoenix to stay still. Savita was bristling; tiny sparks danced along the edges of her paler feathers.

She could feel her phoenix's legs tensing, feel her heat climbing, ready to pounce forwards.

Sav, please, no.

Kel had never prayed to the Alchemists or the Serpent King before, but now seemed like a good time to start.

Taller flames danced along Sav's back, though she stayed still as the wild phoenixes crept closer.

Rich yellows and reds danced through the darkness, like a bleeding sun. Their flames mirrored their steps, growing when they snapped and shrinking when they stopped. Though terrifying, these beasts were in total control of their own magic.

Ice shivered down Kel's spine. Even if she didn't believe in CAPR rules and collar restrictions, Kel had *never* questioned one thing: that wild phoenixes were dangerous, out of control. Their unregulated power would destroy humans and phoenixes alike. Collaring – to some degree – was for the phoenixes' safety as much as everyone else's.

Alchemists! She'd been *so* wrong. About so many things.

'We don't have long before other racers get here,' Kel murmured. *If other wild phoenixes hadn't already taken them out.* 'We can either hope they let us pass, or try to clear the blockade.'

The other riders muttered at her sides. A moment later, they all reached a silent, fearful agreement: the blockade might be difficult to move, but the wild phoenixes were impossible to survive.

Unbuckling from Savita was possibly the most reckless thing Kel had ever done; she had a much slimmer chance of escape on her own two legs. With shaking, gloved hands, she and the other riders dismounted their phoenixes and crept towards the barrier. They just needed to make a hole large enough for each collared phoenix to squeeze through.

Kel could feel the wild phoenixes' curiosity poking into her back.

As more CAPR phoenixes and riders soared into the clearing and took in the scene, the wild creatures stalked closer.

Soon joined by more dismounted riders, Kel managed to shift one great log an inch to the left. It fell to the ground with a dull *thud*, though none of the phoenixes – tamed or wild – seemed interested in the riders' attempts. The collared and uncollared phoenixes were inching closer to each other, curiosity and confusion sharpening the air between them. With another handful of CAPR competitors pouring in, there were at least fifteen phoenixes closing in on the open space. Silently, Kel begged her phoenix to stay back – but Savita was closest of all to her flaming kin.

Kel heaved, her muscles aching and leathers slick with sweat. The rider to her right – a tall woman with auburn hair creeping from her helmet – helped her dislodge a smaller log. It revealed a narrow gap through the blockade, wide enough for a human to slip through. They just needed one or two more strategic heaves, and they might have a chance at survival.

Kel reached for another log when she heard a sharp cry above. The sound echoed through the trees in a wind that lifted Kel's hair. Savita was silent as she looked up to the foliage overhead. Leaves rustled in the gale, and Kel realized that the rest of the clearing had been swept into a hush, too.

There was another cry, singular and sharp, before fire descended through the trees.

The riders fell back as the largest phoenix Kel had ever seen descended into the clearing. The creature's great wings knocked into the branches of the blockade and sent the structure tumbling down. A blaze erupted along the wood and across the ground, as if soaked in petrol. The heat blinded Kel and she heard human screams echoing around her. When her vision cleared, she saw two figures crumpled to the ground, fire and smoke shrouding their bodies.

Kel lurched away from the blockade, towards Savita, before the structure crashed to the ground.

The clearing erupted into an inferno as the wild phoenix landed, no hint of its true form beneath the sunset flames. Around Kel the shrieks of birds and humans mingled, needling her skin.

She couldn't see much beyond the orange tongues leaping into the sky. Somehow, she had to find Sav through the chaos. The static in her comm had calmed to a defective hum, allowing her own terrified thoughts to fill her head.

'Sav!' she screamed.

She could see the other riders – the ones who were still alive – searching for their phoenixes amidst the blaze. Kel pivoted to avoid a climbing fire to her left and collided with the auburn-haired rider. They shared a horrified glance before the other rider leapt between two snaking flames.

Kel had barely turned from the woman before she heard a deafening *crunch*. Despite the heat, Kel turned back towards the sound, longing to see a crackling fire, a broken log – anything but what she knew had made that noise.

The sunset-coloured phoenix held the auburn-haired rider in its beak. The rider hung limply, like a discarded puppet, her torso flattened in the phoenix's mouth. As fire licked dangerously close to Kel's legs, she stared up at the phoenix helplessly. At the rider who had helped her clear the blockade just moments ago.

The phoenix tossed aside the dead rider and scoured the clearing. Kel forced her legs to move, scrambling over mossy boulders, not daring to so much as breathe. She tripped on a splintered log and caught herself on another rock, jarring her wrist on the impact. Finally at the clearing's edge, she hunched behind the nearest tree. The smoke around her thickened and stole any breath she tried to suck in. Carefully, she rose onto her toes and reached for a higher branch, desperate for a better vantage despite the climbing fumes.

Even metres off the ground, she could barely see through the growing storm.

A wild, familiar screech sounded overhead. Nausea pooled in her stomach as she looked up.

The fallen blockade had cleared a small opening in the trees to the sky. Above the tree line, Kel spotted two flaming dots, dancing together and then separating. Claws lashed out and wings flailed; Kel could just make out a collar gleaming around the neck of the smaller phoenix – *her* phoenix.

Kel hadn't known how Sav would react to untamed phoenixes. Savita was slowly growing more accustomed to the other phoenixes Cristo housed, but those small gains meant nothing here, in a new environment. Did Savita know that this was her true home? Did she know that the wild creatures were her kin?

Kel's numb fingers dug into the tree. She called out to Savita again and again, her voice weakening. If Savita heard Kel above the fire's crackling, the phoenix ignored her. After a few minutes, Kel jumped down from the tree and pulled out her tele-comm with sweaty hands, fumbling for the app connected to Savita's collar. If she could just summon Savita back down through the collar's commands, they could—

Something sharp pressed into her upper back. Kel tried to twist around, and the object was shoved deeper into her back, pressing her against the tree. Slowly, the pressure eased, allowing Kel to turn.

A figure – cloaked in the darkness at their back – held a knife up to Kel's throat.

Chapter Thirty-Five

※

'Don't make a sound,' said the woman holding the knife.

Kel's lungs burnt. The woman's grip tightened around the blade's dark handle.

Slowly, Kel raised her hands.

'Give me your tele-comm,' the woman barked. Kel obeyed.

The woman – dressed in black leathers not dissimilar to Kel's – smiled. Another figure stepped forwards from the unravelling tapestry of smoke and trees. He quickly bound Kel's hands behind her back with thick rope.

Kel risked a glance up. Savita was still fighting the golden phoenix. Blood was dripping from their blinding silhouettes into the hungry flames below.

'Come with me,' the dark-haired woman said. Her skin was weathered and tanned, her navy eyes glimmering in a way that made a shiver run down Kel's spine.

She reached an arm towards Kel and her sleeve hitched up. On the underside of her wrist, Kel spotted a tattooed symbol: two overlain double spirals, red and blue.

Kel met the woman's navy eyes. *The Fume.*

She knew the cult was scattered around Cendor, some hiding in the backs of temple pews, while the more extreme members pulled stunts like the ones she'd witnessed in Fieror, or read about in her mother's postcards; freeing caged sprites or lowering sea-monster nets. But hiding in Vohre Forest, too? Were they so pious that they thought themselves immune to phoenix tempers? To the chaos unfolding in the skies above?

The woman pointed towards a patch of trees untouched by the blaze. Fear lifted the hair on Kel's neck. All she could hear were screams at her back. 'I can't leave—'

The woman pushed the sharp knife harder into Kel's throat. Kel swallowed.

With one last glance at Savita, closing in on the wild phoenix overhead, Kel stepped away from the clearing.

Though she felt the heat at her back, the inferno lit nothing ahead. They were heading somewhere darker. Hungrier.

The two Fume members kept pace behind her. The knife's edge was cold between her shoulder blades.

'Where are we going?' Kel asked.

'Stop talking,' the woman snarled.

The man – barely more than a boy – whispered, 'It's her, isn't it, Bryna? The tamer from Fieror.'

'*Hush*,' the woman – Bryna – ordered.

They walked in silence, the sound of the clashing phoenixes disappearing in the dark. Kel focused on the shadows ahead, searching for escape routes. Were other cultists helping the wild phoenixes? Hurting other riders? How had they found them so quickly in Vohre Forest's wilderness?

The path opened up ahead of them, tall figures appearing through the dim space.

Ashes. There was a whole flock of people hiding out here, all wearing the same dark camouflage.

'Get to the clearing,' Bryna called to the others. 'Those wretched riders will have scattered. Uncollar as many of their phoenixes as you can.'

Kel felt bile rise in her throat. She prayed that Sav remained airborne, free from the Fume's grasp. If nothing else, she was relieved that the Fume only seemed to use knives for weapons. She doubted she could have escaped a sancter rifle.

'What are you going to do to me?' Kel asked, her voice ragged.

Bryna didn't reply. Silently, she led Kel to the centre of the small glade. Kel tripped over a fallen log, stumbling as she adjusted to the darkness. A small lamp hung on a branch overhead, offering just enough light to see that the rest of the glade was shrouded by thick, thorned branches. The path they'd come down was her only escape.

The space was circular, speckled with grey and bright green, and Kel noticed new foliage trying to claw through empty earth.

This must be a rebirth site, Kel thought in awe, despite her fear and numb muscles.

She tried to calm her breathing, steady her thoughts. Bryna had taken her tele-comm. She had no weapons on her and her leathers didn't hide anything useful. The log she'd tripped over, the length of her forearm and lying just to her right, could be useful – if she managed to free herself from her bindings.

She flexed her hands. The ropes were almost tight enough to cut into her wrists. Her leather bracelet slid against the rope.

Kel stilled her movements. She risked a glance back; she could only see so far through the shadows, but she didn't think anyone was behind her. She couldn't move her hands enough to reach for the emergency button sewn into the leather – if it even worked out here – but she *could* grip the bracelet band itself. The sharp metal pin holding the two bands together could be enough to break through the bindings on her wrists.

'If you're not going to kill me, what do you want?' Kel asked, trying to distract Bryna.

Bryna gave a toothy smile. In the dim light, her teeth glistened like a wolf's maw. 'You and any other riders we catch are going to face trial for stealing what does not belong to you. You'll face justice.' Her voice was a low mix of gravel and growl.

'Bryna,' the boy said. 'Stop it. She's not going to help us if you keep scaring her.'

'*Help* you?' Kel scoffed. She wriggled her hands, hoping it looked as if she were easing her discomfort. Pain lanced through her fingers as she tried to rotate the bracelet to feel the sharp metal pin. 'Why the hell would I help you? You've *killed* people. You're not activists – you're monsters.'

Bryna sighed. 'Jaron, go help the others. *Now.*'

Jaron pouted, turning wordlessly back down the faint path they'd come. Bryna stepped towards Kel. 'We've seen your face around Vohre. We know you're the one who helped tame the phoenix released so foolishly in a city centre.' Darkness pooled beneath Bryna's eyes. 'We are not usually so brash. But we will do whatever we must to protect Cendor's true gods.'

'Then we have something in common,' Kel said. 'I don't want to see phoenixes hurt any more than you do.'

As subtly as she could, Kel fumbled for the metal pin. It fell into her fingers a few strained seconds later, cold and sharp enough to cut rope. Kel sent up a silent thanks for Rahn's layers of premeditated protection.

'Then why are you working for a man who would see every one of them in captivity?' Bryna sneered. 'But we don't have time for that argument. We caught wind of this foolish race from some allies and managed to sabotage it overnight.' Bryna laughed. 'Just when I thought CAPR couldn't sink to new lows.'

Kel's stomach dropped. On this, they agreed.

Bryna turned away, just a fraction, and Kel managed to pinch the bracelet bands together, stretching the leather until the metal pin popped free. She felt the emergency button jutting out of the hard fabric and pressed down on it – but her hands were at too awkward an angle to press hard enough. Instead, she pinched the metal pin between her right thumb and middle finger, slowly beginning to saw at the thick rope binding her hands at her back.

Bryna shook her head. 'We decided to use this race to try a first of our own. The Fume should no longer work in the shadows. If CAPR is growing bolder, then we must, too. After setting up the blockade, we lured a dawn of phoenixes here to cause a distraction. The plan was to free your phoenixes and leave any human survivors to find their own way home. But then we saw *you*.' Bryna trailed the knife along Kel's jaw. Kel stilled her sawing, halfway through the rope. 'And we knew that you deserved a choice. Face trial with the Fume's council, or teach us what you know.'

An absurd bubble of laughter rose up Kel's throat. Her chest heaved, hiding how her shoulders rotated as she sawed the rope. She was *so close*. 'What could I teach you? *Why* would I teach you? You'd uncollar every phoenix and let them annihilate the entire island.'

Even as she said it, though, she remembered the uncollared phoenixes, so in control of their own power. But triumph quickly replaced her fleeting uncertainty, as the rope fell to the ground behind her.

Kel flexed her freed hands. The bracelet fell too, before she could catch it, and Kel was glad for the knife on her cheek, because Bryna's gaze was locked on the same spot.

'The media calls you the "phoenix whisperer", you and that *fallen hero* of yours,' Bryna snarled. 'You speak to phoenixes in a way that few can. You've earnt their trust, and you don't try to remould their savagery. You can teach us how to speak with them. We want to protect them – but they don't always let us. You can change that.'

Another short, manic laugh burst through Kel. *This couldn't be happening.* The Fume, who criticized Cendor and CAPR and the media, had bought the ridiculous rumours that had been spread about Kel. They believed what the news outlets had told them. For the first time, Kel was thankful for the ridiculous media coverage.

She had no power. Not over phoenixes or her fate. Cristo was the one pulling her strings now.

'You're trying to protect them, but only how *you* see fit,' Kel spat. 'Everyone believes that *they* know best. That *they* can be the solution. The truth is that phoenixes don't want you to protect them, and yet here you are, going against your gods' wishes under the guise of worship.'

Bryna sneered. 'For all your knowledge, you're still such a naive little thing. You don't think we would leave the phoenixes alone if we could? Phoenixes can't defend themselves against council technology. This is humanity's mess. It's not a phoenix's job to clean it up.'

Kel bit down on her tongue. She hated that she agreed with anything this woman said. It *was* their mess. But beneath the weight of CAPR and council tech, what power did any of them have?

'You can't care that much about phoenix safety if you're out here waving knives around,' Kel taunted, keeping her freed hands clasped at her back. She just needed Bryna to *turn* . . . to give her a chance to flee into the darkness surrounding the glade. The distant screaming would lead her back to Savita.

Bryna raised an eyebrow. She reached into a pocket and retrieved Kel's tele-comm, waggling it in the air. '*You* were armed with a weapon, too. Something that directly controls your phoenix. But you weren't planning to use it, were you?'

Kel opened and closed her mouth. 'I'm not going to help people who threaten me.'

Bryna pursed her lips. Slowly, with a steady grip, she lowered the blade.

Emotion tangled in Kel's stomach. Knots of confusion and

something else – something the same colour as pity, but sharper – tumbled through her.

But Bryna's eyes were averted, and she half-turned as she slotted the knife into a holster at her waist. It was the moment Kel needed. Moving as fast as she possibly could, she grabbed the log to her right and swung it towards Bryna's head.

There was a sickening crunch as wood connected with bone, and Bryna crumpled to the ground with a moan. Kel sprinted towards the path they'd come along.

'Free your phoenix, girl,' Bryna rasped, as Kel fled into the darkness of the forest. 'You know she wants it. She deserves it.'

Kel, swallowing the lump in her throat, refused to look back.

'If you ever change your mind,' Bryna cried, 'you know where to find us.'

Chapter Thirty-Six

❋

Kel leapt over fallen logs and slipped over hot moss as shadows hissed at her sides. She hurtled down the path until the ground opened up like a maw, and smoke and orange gales greeted her.

The clearing's fire had calmed. Or, at least, new flames weren't adding to the bright storm. A few wild phoenixes lazily picked at the ground at the edges of the clearing, though Kel couldn't see a single rider or a collared phoenix. She couldn't see any other Fume members, either. Had the others managed to escape? Kel couldn't even bear to think of the alternative.

A symphony of unholy screeches echoed down the abandoned CAPR path in both directions. Phoenixes. But which ones? Distant trees ignited and flurries of orange streaked the air.

She glanced around the clearing once more, heart pounding in her throat – and sucked in a sharp gasp. Relief almost made her knees buckle. The Alchemists had *finally* thrown her a scrap of luck.

Savita stood at the opposite edge of the clearing, her great head twisted back into the feathers of her wing, no care for the carnage around her. She didn't even glance up as Kel jogged closer.

Kel slowed a few steps from her phoenix. Savita's silver collar still gleamed around her throat.

Nausea rose in her. Never, *not once*, had she thought of Sav as a prisoner. She couldn't start now.

Fire lit the crimson ground encircling Savita like a bloody halo. Around Savita's dark claws, a chain of entrails slithered through the grass. Kel's stomach lurched as she spotted a small mountain of blood, shredded innards and feathers beneath tangled vines.

Kel didn't give herself time to take in the scene. She reached out for her phoenix's neck. 'Ready to get out of here, Sav?'

But just as she was about to pull herself into the saddle, she saw two figures clad in black leathers emerge from the smoke. Fume members. Each carried a small dagger.

Kel lunged to Savita's side.

She ducked her head, again grateful that neither of them carried sancters. Maybe Bryna had been telling the truth. Maybe they'd hold a fair trial before making any kind of fatal decisions? Or perhaps they were worried about frightening the nearby wild phoenixes, picking at their own grim meals?

But as Kel wrapped a hand around Sav's saddle pommel, a scalding pain flared in her right hip.

She stumbled to the ground, a guttural scream escaping her throat. Her knees throbbed at the impact, embers beneath them searing into the leathers. She bit down on her lip too hard and tasted copper blood.

With shaking hands, she reached down and clutched the dagger. Her vision was blurring, burning away at the edges as she pulled the weapon free of her hip. She screamed out as another glint of silver sliced past her. At least the cultists seemed to be aiming at her – not Sav. Kel placed an unsteady hand on her hip. She couldn't feel much beyond the heat, but blood quickly seeped through her fingers.

Savita lifted her head with a low grumble, as if a fly had bothered her. She looked down at Kel, then at the two approaching figures.

As Kel wobbled to her feet, Sav let out a scream the likes of which Kel had never heard.

Kel was surprised her eardrums hadn't burst. The cultists stumbled back from the force of Savita's cry, sharing a wary glance. Even the other wild phoenixes lingering in the clearing skittered back, receding into the skirting trees.

'*Shit,*' Kel mumbled, biting down on the blistering pain burning into her. She tried and failed to lift her left leg into Sav's saddle, more blood pooling into her leathers as she moved.

Biting down on her lip, Kel staggered back to her feet. Savita let out another shriek and lifted her wings. Like a coiled snake, Sav struck her long neck towards the cultists. The two figures scrambled out of the way. Sav's beak came down on the ground where they'd stood, catching a cultist's dark leathers in her maw. She pulled back as the fabric tore and thrust her beak into the sky, towards a small patch of blue above the trees. Perhaps just wide enough for her to fly through.

Sav was ready to leave, whether or not Kel joined her.

Sharp, all-consuming agony speared through Kel's hip as she lifted a foot into Savita's stirrup. She shoved her weight onto the saddle and threw her other leg over Savita's body, an agonized scream tearing from her throat.

Kel pressed a hand to the wound in her side as Savita flapped her wings.

Once, twice . . .

And then they soared into the sky.

Kel glanced down, through the dense foliage. She could see the cultists beneath them already retreating from the now-empty clearing. Kel gritted her teeth as black spots danced across her vision, begging to consume her. She tightened her grip on the pommel and tensed her thighs. She hadn't had time to buckle her legs; if her arms gave out, it would be a quick fall.

She couldn't give in, not *now*. Not until Savita was safe.

Savita screeched as the tips of her wings caught in the branches of trees. Three hard, frustrated beats later, she broke through the foliage. Kel ducked low as Sav pushed, *pushed*, against the last layer of greenery, and then, suddenly, they were above it all.

The sky was a hazy watercolour of blue and grey. A heavy, charcoal cloud rose above the clearing.

Kel bent forwards and lay a palm against Savita's neck. 'We need to get back to the CAPR crowd and find help,' she rasped.

Kel coughed as they ascended through the climbing smoke. Savita swerved towards the forest's edge and loosed another violent scream.

She clung to the saddle pommel as Savita jerked again, and Kel finally saw why.

One of the wild phoenixes – a ruby-coloured creature – barrelled towards them from the heart of the forest. The phoenix's charcoal eyes were locked on Savita, two pinpricks as opaque as the forest beneath them.

The muscles in Kel's arms screamed as she braced herself against the saddle. Sav was flying higher, higher, and Kel's legs were still unbuckled. Then, the smoke thinned and Kel cleared her lungs with dry coughs.

The ruby phoenix – a blood phoenix – was larger than Savita, her wings almost twice the width. But Kel knew that Sav was faster, *smarter*. As the wild phoenix dove and struck out, Sav refused to retaliate. Instead, Sav dashed to the right, then the left, keeping barely a foot from the ruby phoenix's dagger-sharp bill.

Sav dodged another strike, swerving so hard Kel flung a hand back to keep herself from falling.

The wild phoenix released a deep, throaty cry. It struck forward, fast as a viper, yet Sav easily avoided the sharp peak of its beak.

Kel kept one hand pressed to her searing wound and the other clutching the pommel. Sav's movements tossed her around like a puppet and jarred her bleeding hip.

The blood phoenix let out a monstrous *caw* and dove once more.

Savita lurched to the left, almost throwing Kel from the saddle.

The wild phoenix's talons caught a handful of feathers from Sav's right wing. Kel winced as Sav wailed in pain, but the phoenix still didn't attack. She hung in the air, anticipating the blood phoenix's next move.

The wild phoenix was familiar with this terrain, and used to fighting other phoenixes. But Kel had seen the red light gleaming in Savita's eyes when chaos had broken out in the clearing. She'd seen the way Sav had battled the other wild phoenix in the sky, leaving nothing but shredded organs and broken feathers around her.

Slowly, the wild phoenix's attacks grew slower. Its wings heaved faster to stay aloft. The small spurts of fire that had danced across its back were being blown out like candles in a storm.

Only then did Savita attack.

Sav plunged down like an arrow. Kel screamed as Savita speared the wild phoenix's midriff, a great, meaty section that bowed around Sav's beak as she pulled back and struck again.

Again. Again. *Again.*

Kel struggled to keep a grip on the saddle pommel. Savita's movements were too erratic. The wild phoenix was barely conscious, and still Savita launched forward.

Sav pivoted to attack from another angle, and Kel's grip slipped. She flung her hand from her wound to reach for the saddle pommel, but her hand was slick with blood.

Savita tilted to the side, and Kel fell.

Limbs too heavy to flail, Kel dropped through the sky like an anchor. Wind whipped her cheeks and she watched red beads float above her, unable to keep pace. Darkness flared across her vision.

Even as screams and smoke surrounded her, Kel wasn't afraid.

The fall to the forest was short, but not so short that Sav couldn't catch her.

She'll catch me. She'll catch me.
Kel kept falling.
She'll catch me.
As the black dots turned to a blanket, Kel felt the first slivers of doubt.

Chapter Thirty-Seven

---——— ❋ ———---

Harsh lights forced Kel awake. It took a few blinks to clear the sleep. For too long, all she could see was smoke and a red sky.

Eventually, Kel placed her surroundings. The room was long and empty. There was one figure, a thin girl with dark hair, in a hospital bed at the opposite end of the hall – either dead or asleep, Kel couldn't tell. A green blanket with floral stitching cocooned her like a body bag, and the square nightstand to her right was crowded with lilies.

The twenty other beds around them were pristine and empty. Kel tried to prop herself up on her elbows. Her arms wobbled and she gritted her teeth. As sweat began pooling down her back, she surrendered back to the bed.

The only light came from the media screen hovering overhead. The sharp colours sent a pang through her temples and she averted her eyes. They snagged on something to her left, an awkward, unmoving shadow at the foot of her bed.

Coup.

Neck kinked to the right, slouched into the folds of an armchair, Coup's eyes were closed, an open book splayed across his chest.

She squinted back up at the screen. Some news broadcast flashed to a clip of their last CAPR race. Wild flames tore through the video and Kel was back in Vohre Forest, shrouded by smoke and fire and silver weapons.

She remembered the race that had gone astray. The darkness that drowned her.

Savita had let her fall.

Kel shoved down the memory as her lungs seized. She barely felt herself bolt upright, adrenaline numbing the pain.

'*Ashes!* You're awake!'

The book on Coup's lap crashed to the ground and, faster than she could follow, he was by her side. His golden eyes lit the room, chasing away the room's shadows.

'How do you feel? Should I call a nurse?' Coup asked.

Kel tried to suck in lungfuls of the cool night air, but all she managed were thin gasps. 'Sav – is she okay? The other riders . . . are they alive?'

Coup's brow pinched. He searched her face before the crinkles smoothed. 'Four riders died. Three more are in critical care. Two phoenixes vanished. No one knows if they were uncollared or killed. Everyone else got out.'

Kel swallowed. Chills ran down her arms. 'How did we – where am I – when did we – what—'

'You're in Cristo's hospital wing,' Coup said. He shuffled further onto her bed. Not touching her, but close enough to feel his heat. With the strange chill hollowing her bones, it took everything inside her not to curl into his unexpected warmth.

Slowly, she lowered herself back into the bed. 'How did I get here? What happened?'

Coup helped her sink into the pillows. 'One of the riders managed to get a message to the CAPR officials on-site. They found you at the forest's edge, not long after you . . . fell.' Coup's jaw tightened. 'That was almost a week ago. They brought you straight here.'

Kel forced herself not to sit up again. *Alchemists*. Everything *hurts*. 'A whole *week*?'

The red burns at Coup's neck had faded to pink scarring. A year could have passed.

'You were waking up when they brought you in, so they induced a coma and took you straight into surgery.' Coup sucked in a shaky breath. 'The airbags in your leathers cushioned your fall. But the broken bones and internal bleeding . . . you were in surgery for so long, Kel.'

His voice was flat, careful, like a tamer approaching a new phoenix. 'But you're stubborn. I knew you'd never leave Savita.'

Even though Sav had left her.

Kel's chest ached at the thought. 'Where is she?'

'She's safe.'

Kel frowned. The words should have been reassuring, but Coup's tone was all wrong. 'Is she in the aviary? Or – did the Fume get her collar off? Did she rebirth? Is she—'

'She's *fine*. Breathe.' Coup placed a gentle hand on her left arm.

'What aren't you telling me?' she demanded.

Coup made a sound – something between a sigh and a chuckle. 'Savita is in her usual private suite, probably cleaning her feathers and demanding a second dinner. Dira's been by her side every spare second.'

'There's something else, though, isn't there?'

Coup looked back, into the empty shadows. 'Dira would kill me for telling you while you're still healing. But you'll kill me if I don't.'

He leaned to the right, beside her bed. His chestnut curls fell over his forehead. She wanted to brush them away. She wished she could do *anything* but lie here and wait.

Coup sat back up; in his hand, harshly folded, was a newspaper.

'Page six,' he said, grimacing.

He helped Kel flick open the pages and propped the copy of *Nova Press* high enough for her to read. Even in the dim light, her eyes snagged on the giant heading branded across both pages. The image of Savita, more flame than phoenix, took up the top half of the feature article.

Day 70 of the Molten Season, Year 1509 of the Alchemy Republic

HOWLERS' PHOENIX: THE DEBATE IGNITES

The Howlers CAPR team have taken Vohre by storm. Since arriving in Cendor's capital just two months ago, they've already snatched two gold prizes, almost at the cost of their young rider's life.

The most recent race at the edge of Vohre Forest – already dubbed a once-in-a-decade tragedy – seems to have revealed more than cultish sabotage, though. An inside source has claimed that, once more, the Howlers' phoenix is a danger to Vohre's citizens.

The Howlers' tamer – Kelyn Varra, the sweetheart of their dashing rider – was riding the volatile phoenix in the most recent race. Not long into the race, the phoenix, Savita, abandoned Varra to engage in a lethal fight with wild phoenixes. Varra remains in a critical condition at Cristo Private Hospital.

Was this a consequence of the race's unexpected mishaps? Or is their phoenix truly out of control? After beloved rider 'Coup' was injured previously, the latter seems more and more likely. Our source confirms that multiple employees at Cristo Industries are wondering when the Cendorian Council will take matters into their own hands.

Many have speculated on whether tech billionaire Canen Cristo has already spoken with the council, given his close relationship with several councillors. It is suspected that the council will soon assume control of the situation, if they have not done so already.

Rage threatened to explode through Kel. It quickly drowned out the unsettling, knotted emotions she felt when she thought of Sav letting her fall.

She threw the paper to the floor. 'When did *Nova Press* become a gossip magazine? I can't believe this.'

'It's disgusting,' Coup muttered. 'But nothing is going to happen to Sav.'

'Is there any truth to the article? Have councillors contacted Cristo?'

Coup shrugged apologetically. 'If they have, he hasn't told us. He's been locked in his office for the last week. No one has seen him.'

'I need to visit Sav,' Kel said, feeling breathless.

She'd heard the horror stories of council interferences. It was rare. CAPR was a deadly sport, and the council all but endorsed its risks. They only interfered when they decided a phoenix was not just a danger to people, but to their spectacle.

They killed the phoenix and destroyed its remains.

Kel tried to push herself up again, but anger had sapped what little strength she had.

Coup sighed. 'Dira's spent every night with Sav since the race. She's given me updates – with pointless, Kelyn-level detail – every morning. Nothing's changed. No more scientists.' Coup paused. 'We won't let anything happen to Sav.'

Coup had no way to fight the council – and yet his words washed over Kel in cool, reassuring waves. She ached to reach out for his hand, to twine their fingers and thank him for being at her bedside when she hadn't been able to offer him the same. She didn't know how to sculpt the crushing relief she'd felt at the sight of him, slumped in that chair with a book on his lap.

'Thank you for being here,' she forced out, the words stilted and brittle.

Coup smiled, a small hitch of his lips, so different to his usual, all-consuming grins. Kel stilled as he reached out and, gently, traced his thumb across the space between her brows.

'It was so strange watching you sleep for the past week,' he murmured. 'Seeing you without a frown was unsettling.'

He'd stayed by her side the entire week? The thought flushed her cheeks. She hoped she hadn't drooled too much.

'Don't get used to it,' she warned. 'I'll be back to my usual scowling self soon.'

Crescent dimples dug into Coup's cheeks. 'I hope so.'

He leaned his forearms on the side of her bed. Kel tried to swallow her rising pulse. 'Careful, rider. It almost sounds like you missed me.'

Coup's eyes darkened to bronze and a strange laugh escaped him. It was a full-body, disbelieving sound that bathed Kel in the same unusual mix of dread and weightlessness as Savita's screams.

Kel frowned. 'What's so funny?'

Coup shook his head. His smile turned oddly sheepish. 'Can I tell you a secret, tamer?'

Her breath hitched. 'Sure.'

Despite the shadows, Kel swore she spotted the faintest blush creeping up his neck.

'I lied to you, weeks ago,' he admitted.

'What? When?'

'When I told you I'd only met your dad once, in the public aviary I worked at. But that wasn't true. Your dad used to come in all the time to check on the phoenixes. I can't count how many times we talked.'

Confusion buzzed through her. She didn't know what kind of secret she'd expected – or hoped for – but it hadn't involved her father. 'Why is that a secret?'

The blush crept higher, over his stubble, up his cheeks. 'He always asked about me and Bekn – he must've known my mum, or at least known we were distant neighbours – and I asked about him. About his daughter.' Coup's throat bobbed. 'He told me all about you. Your infatuation with phoenixes. Your obsession with Ryker and Deja. Your favourite foods. Your everything. I felt like I'd already met you. I *wanted* to meet you. And then when I finally did on a CAPR track years later, I couldn't merge the idea I had of you with the girl I saw on the sidelines – this worrying, blazing, stunning girl with a temper.' Through thick lashes, Coup lifted his gaze to hers. 'But I wanted to. Very badly.'

Kel fought for breath. The traitorous, beeping machine beside her revealed her shuddering pulse. Disbelief tightened her throat and left her mind blank.

He merely watched her, half-expectantly, amusement flickering across his face. She tried to force her tongue around the right words. *Any* words. This was their rhythm. He mocked, and she teased. He offered a truth, and she peeled one back in turn. He was so much braver than her, always taking the first step, whether it was towards or away from her.

'I think it was easier for me to be angry with you for setting off my nerves,' she breathed, half-hoping he didn't hear. 'In a way that made me question everything. It was easier than admitting why I let you under my skin in the first place.'

Everything inside her screamed to curl up beneath the bed sheets. She felt like a spool of yarn, unravelling. A blister rubbed raw, a book torn from its binding. The monitor beside her bed beeped and beeped and Kel would rather have been anywhere else – back in Vohre Forest, falling in a way that made her less afraid.

She was saved from more spluttering when she felt a warm finger beneath her chin, gently lifting her head. She yielded, raising her eyes to meet the burning, amber ones before her.

Coup reached up and brushed a strand of dark hair behind her ear. His gaze flashed back down to her lips, as if asking permission.

Slowly, so painfully slowly, Coup's face lowered to hers.

His lips stopped, hovering just a hair's breadth away.

'Kelyn,' he breathed, and Kel came undone.

Their lips melted together in a gentle vice. Time slowed to a crawl, the monitor silent, her pulse flattening. His hand against her cheek shifted, tugging her closer to him, and she spread her fingers against the front of his shirt. His palm moved to cup the back of her neck. The gentle touch sent heat rippling down her spine, an aching hunger settled deep inside her. She wanted him to tear every wall down. To burn away her resolve and remake her entirely.

Her lips parted, allowing his tongue past her teeth. Their breath mingled and the air around them heated, at odds with his feather-light touch. Every movement was deliberate, so different to the heated kiss they'd shared in *The Prism*. That had been a coiled spring, teeth and craving leaving no room for what might lie beneath. But now, Kel heard Coup's words echo through her mind, and it only made her tug him closer. She wanted *more*. She needed to test his words. To see if he truly craved her the way she did him. To know if the fire he lit within her would destroy her, or bring her to life.

His lips still grazing hers, he murmured, 'I can't believe it took both of us ending up in hospital for that to happen.' His eyes traced her swollen lips, with a slow hunger that made Kel's stomach coil. 'It should have happened *much* sooner.'

'The Howlers are a stubborn crew.' She laughed softly.

Coup pulled back a fraction more, shaking his head. 'This entire week . . . all I could think of was the sight of you getting shoved into that ambulance.' He rubbed his face. 'And I was so angry. At you. At Savita. At myself – for being so scared, and knowing that *I'm* usually the source of this kind of grief for my brother and the team.'

Although she wanted nothing but to claw her hands through his hair and embrace him until neither had any breath left, his words stirred up old unease and echoes from Bekn. She had thought they were just the overwrought concerns of a big brother until Coup had ended up in a hospital bed of his own.

Now, it was all she could see.

Then Coup shook his head, as if clearing his mind. 'I'm overreacting. *You're* the one in a hospital bed,' he said with a harsh laugh. 'This should be about you, not me.'

Kel moved her hand to his neck and urged him to lift his gaze. She refused to let him break this fragile thing between them, this thing they both needed. 'This isn't about me or you. It's about pain, and what we're doing to stop it. I'm here, getting treated for mine. What are you doing for yours?'

They weren't the gentlest words, but theirs wasn't a bond built from kindness and care. It was forged from barbed confessions and crimson flames.

Coup opened his mouth twice, three times, before words managed to free themselves. 'I'm not in pain, though. That's the problem, Kel. I don't feel *anything*. The only time I feel alive is when I'm around Savita – and you.' Coup's eyes filled with a silver sheen.

Her entire body was screaming to lurch from the bed and take him in her arms.

'Have you ever talked to someone about how you feel?' she asked gently.

Her rider shook his head. 'I've thought about talking to a . . . professional. But I don't want to hurt Bekn, or make him feel like he hasn't done enough. He tries so hard.'

Kel held back a scoff. 'You're only hurting Bekn by hurting yourself. Bekn . . . knows something is wrong. He'll understand.'

When Coup stayed silent, Kel reached up to stroke strands of his hair. 'How long have you felt like this?'

Just weeks ago, this kind of honesty – with *Coup* – would have seemed impossible. Now, she made a silent vow not to let either of them retreat. No matter what happened next, to her, to Savita, to Vohre – she wouldn't lose this. Not when it felt as easy and right as soaring atop her phoenix.

Coup leaned into her touch. 'It's been like this for as long as I can remember, but when Mum died . . .' Coup's voice broke. 'I stopped trying. Everything seemed too unsafe to care for. Except phoenixes.' Coup huffed a soft laugh. 'As much as we might want it, nothing can ever be as infinite as a phoenix. Everything else will be gone as soon as we realize we need it.'

The monitor beeped to life again, fluttering with her pulse. He'd managed to take a feeling she'd felt – for so many years – and mould it into the perfect words. She'd felt the same way for as long as she could remember. Her father's death, her mother's fleeting visits and postcards with no return address, all of it had allowed her to heave more certainty upon herself, protecting her from the world. From warm, wanting, gorgeous creatures like Coup.

As much as Kel wanted to relent, to kiss him and tell him that *they* could be infinite – it would be selfish to take this fragile moment and mould it into what she wanted.

She rubbed her fingers against the back of his hand. 'But that's the point, isn't it? Life is finite. *This* is finite. But neither would exist without pain, so you shouldn't bother trying to avoid any of it.'

The corners of Coup's lips lifted. Seeing that smile was like sun through rain.

Coup removed her hand from his and kissed her palm. 'I think I want to. Talk to someone, I mean. I want to be better. The Howlers deserve better.'

'We deserve you,' Kel whispered.

She hoped he heard the truth beneath the words. What she was still too cowardly to say.

She didn't know if *she* deserved Warren Coupers – but she wanted to. She wanted *him*. Every teasing grin – for the cameras or for her – and every painful truth. She wanted all of him.

She had wanted him for longer than she cared to admit.

Chapter Thirty-Eight

―――――※―――――

Kel gripped the parallel bars tighter. The wood wobbled as she struggled forwards.

Maybe the bars were broken. There had to be *some* reason why she couldn't do this.

She growled through clenched teeth. 'This is impossible.'

'Only if you believe it is,' said the man in green scrubs – Arren. If she could manage to pry up a splinter from the wooden bars, she might jam it into Arren's throat. Anything to stop those infuriatingly positive, cheerful vocal cords from preaching more bullshit.

'I know you can do this! Just a little further, and then you're done for tonight,' Arren added. His nasal voice had haunted her recent nightmares.

Kel was glad for Cristo's medications and machines that had sped up her recovery. She'd been able to spend the last week laughing with friends and carving the Howlers' emblem into their uniforms with her new kit. But right now, she wished for the pain of her old injuries. She would have *preferred* that pain.

Arren stood behind Kel, unmoving, holding the ends of a large, elastic band. The rest of the band was wrapped around Kel's torso, pulling against her as she tried to walk forwards. Pain lanced up and down her hip every time she sucked in a breath, despite the knife wound having mostly healed over.

'I *believe* in you, Kelyn,' he said, urging her forwards. 'But you need to believe in yourself, too!'

Kel bit her tongue. *This is it*, she thought. *I died when I fell, and this is hell.*

Dira, standing to Kel's right, shifted until she stood in front of Kel, just beyond the wooden bars.

'Come on, Kel,' Dira taunted. 'I've seen you move faster when you're cleaning Savita's shit. This is pathetic.'

'Right now, I'd give anything to be cleaning Sav's shit,' Kel mumbled. She managed another step forward.

After tomorrow morning's assessment, she'd be allowed out of the hospital wing. Her team – all crowded around her – had promised her that Sav was safe. But nothing would ease the tension squeezing Kel's lungs other than seeing Sav herself.

Since waking in the hospital, every thought of Sav was drowned beneath flashes of the forest. Her stomach would lift and she'd remember the prickling, half-conscious realization that Sav wouldn't save her. It made her breath catch, every time. But if she could just *see* her phoenix, she knew everything would right itself.

Even Coup had refused to help Kel sneak out of the hospital at night. They were all traitors.

She managed one more step. Another.

'Dira's right,' Coup said, folding his arms. 'I've seen newborn phoenixes wobble around faster than you.'

The four Howlers had come to see her progress; Bekn in an armchair, Dira ahead, Coup to her right, and Rahn rifling through a nearby crate of rehab equipment.

When she'd seen the four of them lined up at the door, she'd wanted to cry. Now, she wanted to throw Dira and Coup from the room.

Bekn stood and rubbed a hand over his face. 'I can't tell if you two are actually trying to help her, but if you are, stop it.'

Dira poked her tongue out. Rahn giggled, encouraging Kel

forwards, before returning to inspect the tools inside the crate.

Rahn had surprised Kel by visiting her in hospital almost as much as Coup had, both with and without Dira. Though it had been a battle of wills to keep Rahn from blaming herself for Kel's fall, Kel felt a newfound ease in Rahn's presence. The technician had brought Kel desserts from her favourite bakery and asked for endless details of her encounter with the Fume, as if preparing to find and battle them herself on Kel's behalf.

After another minute of Kel stumbling forwards, Rahn stood. She moved beside Dira.

'Imagine that I'm Savita. You'd try harder than this to get to *her*.'

Kel ground her teeth as she pushed and pushed until the band around her stomach seemed to loosen, just a little, allowing for two more steps. She was *so close*.

Dira's lips pulled up in a lopsided smirk. 'If you get to the end, Bekn will make enough pancakes to feed every one of Cristo's phoenixes.'

Bekn sighed. 'Only if Kel and Coup promise to stay out of the hospital.'

They all laughed, and that sound – deep and high and gruff and teasing – spurred Kel on. Step by step, with sweat beading down her back, Kel forced herself forwards.

'*I* was moving faster than this on day one of recovery,' Coup taunted. He clutched the ends of the bars ahead of her, drumming his fingers and waggling his brows. 'You really want me to hold that over you?'

'Why is everything a competition to you?' Kel muttered.

Kel grumbled as Coup laughed, and she shoved herself along the last stretch of the bars. The band loosened around her stomach. The shift in pressure sent her tumbling forwards, headfirst towards the hard ground just beyond the matting—

And then Coup was there, catching her before she could hit the floor, arms wrapped tightly around her.

The two hadn't talked more about whatever it was that had so recently blossomed between them. But they *had* agreed to wait until Kel was out of hospital before having that conversation. Still, their agreement hadn't kept Coup from refusing to leave her bedside. It hadn't kept them from stealing kisses when the hospital was empty, and the lights dimmed. They'd fallen asleep together most nights, sharing that cramped hospital mattress. Coup's arms had encircled her and she'd buried her face into the crook of his arm, and it felt as right as if she was curled under Savita's wing.

'Nice work, tamer,' he whispered. She felt his lips faintly brush her.

She heard Arren mutter something before he scuttled out of the room, signalling the end of Kel's session. She hardly noticed, with Coup's arms wrapped around her.

Dira snorted. 'Well done, Kel. You'll recover in record time out of spite.'

Kel straightened, resisting the urge to cling to Coup's warmth. His arms remained on her back, only lightening a fraction.

'Don't you want a reward?' Coup batted his lashes.

Kel's cheeks heated. 'Depends what kind you have in mind.'

His lips twisted into a familiar, wicked smirk. 'The kind that isn't appropriate for a crowd.'

Kel couldn't help it. She laughed, leaning into his embrace, her hands tightening around his arms.

Behind her, the room fell silent.

Eventually, Coup and Kel turned to see the remaining Howlers watching them with slack jaws.

Rahn pointed at Kel and Coup. 'When did this happen?'

Dira pointed between Kel and Coup, as if trying to solve a puzzle.

'No idea. I thought they hated each other. But they're both assholes, so I'm terrified what kind of tyrannical power they'll wield together.'

The winger turned to Bekn. A wild grin was plastered to his face.

'I knew it. I *knew* it!' He laughed, a loud, hearty sound, and threw up his hands. Kel wouldn't have been surprised if he'd broken out into a jig.

'Quit ogling,' Kel said.

'Well, if nauseating PDA is officially sanctioned, Rahn and I will be putting you to shame.' Dira turned to Rahn with a raised brow. After a silent exchange, Rahn nodded, and Dira smirked. 'Last night, I asked Rahn to be my girlfriend. I performed a romantic gesture like none of you will ever come close to achieving.'

Kel beamed. 'Girlfriend, huh?'

Rahn nodded, a slow blush creeping into her cheeks. 'There were rose petals.'

Kel shifted, and Coup slid one hand around her waist. The casualness of his touch made her stomach flip.

'Congratulations?' Bekn said, almost a question. He rubbed his hands together, brow creased in thought. 'Do I need to get HR forms drawn up if multiple Howlers are dating each other?'

Kel's face started blazing. She had no clue if she and Coup were *dating* – and she didn't want Bekn's legal musings to prompt that conversation.

Coup scoffed, seemingly unfazed. 'You don't need to put out a company-wide memo, brother. We're just . . . putting in some overtime, together.'

'And *we're* taking a hands-on approach to team bonding,' Dira drawled, slinging an arm around her newly official girlfriend.

'All right,' Bekn interrupted, raising a hand. 'I'm leaving before I throw up on expensive rehab equipment.'

'Coup,' Dira said, pointing at him. 'You haven't left the hospital wing since Kel was brought in. Go take a shower. You reek.'

Kel mouthed *Thank you* to Dira. Coup placed his hand against his chest in mock hurt before pulling away.

'Go,' Kel laughed. 'Dira's right. You need to rest. You're still recovering, too. Take a shower and sleep in your own bed for a change. I'll be out of the hospital tomorrow, anyway.'

So long as her final medical assessment went well, everything would be back to normal. She could see Savita. She could call the construction team at her farm and check their progress. She could be *free*.

Coup's eyes scanned her. 'Promise you'll try to get some sleep tonight without me there to pin your arms to the bed?'

Kel's stomach tightened at his words, smothering a laugh as Bekn made a gagging sound and hurried towards the exit. Dira and Rahn swapped weary expressions.

'Cross my heart,' she said.

'You better,' Dira interrupted. 'You've been so *cranky* the last few weeks.'

Kel glared at Dira.

Coup inched closer. 'I'll be back in the morning. We can make sure Bekn holds up his end of the bargain and makes enough pancakes to feed the entire building.'

Kel squeezed his arm. 'Sounds perfect.'

Once Dira, Coup and Bekn had left through the main entrance and only Rahn remained, still examining the mechanical rehab tools as if to use them in their next CAPR race, another door slid open. Kel assumed Arren had forgotten something.

Instead, through the side door, marched Cristo.

Rahn frowned, inching closer to Kel.

Ever since Kel had woken up in hospital, Cristo had remained a ghost. She hadn't had a chance to thank him for his facility's treatment, or scream at him for making them enter the last race. Rahn claimed she'd tried to speak with him, and yet even she'd been turned away.

Their boss's blue blazer was unbuttoned, revealing a plain white shirt beneath. His dark hair was slicked back, though stray strands poked out around his ears. When he moved closer, Kel could see the shadows hollowing his cheeks, the red veins ringing his dark irises.

'I'm so glad I caught you, Kelyn. I've been wanting to check on you,' Cristo began. 'I'm sorry I couldn't come sooner. But I've made every arrangement to ensure that you have the best care.'

A strange, unsettled expression clouded his features. Hairs pricked on her neck.

'Is it true what the papers are saying?' she asked. 'That Savita's behaviour might draw council attention?'

After Coup had shown her *Nova Press*'s scathing article, Kel had found several more like it.

Cristo fiddled with his sleeves. 'I'm doing what I can, but yes, it does seem that way.'

'Has the council contacted you?' Rahn asked.

Cristo cleared his throat. 'Like I said, I'm doing everything I can.'

'What the fuck does that mean?' Kel snapped. 'I competed in your damn race and almost died. Just tell us the truth.'

Cristo's mouth thinned. He stepped closer, until only the wooden bars separated them.

He smoothed back his hair, though the few loose waves quickly reappeared. 'Councillor Trystas has contacted me requesting details about the situation. But I've assured him that Cristo Industries is fully equipped to handle any abnormal phoenix behaviour.'

'*Abnormal?* Savita reacted like any collared phoenix would in a race gone wrong. She only fought that other phoenix because *it* attacked *us*.'

Why did the council care? Sav's actions had threatened Kel, not CAPR's spectacle. There had to be another reason for their investigation.

Cristo nodded, unfazed by her outburst. 'I know. But the council will need more than words to be reassured. They'll need records of her temperature fluctuations, interactions with other phoenixes, and film footage from previous CAPR races.'

True fear, like she hadn't felt since she'd seen Coup vanish in an ambulance, engulfed her. It almost sounded as if the council *wanted* to find Savita guilty.

Sav was aggressive on CAPR tracks because that's what spectators demanded. She didn't interact well with other phoenixes because she'd been raised in isolation, like most tamed birds. And her temperature . . . it would be highly irregular, temperamental, because she was approaching a rebirth. What could they do?

What could she do?

Cristo stepped around the wooden bars. Kel broke through the static filling her ears long enough to hear him say, 'I'll do whatever I can to avoid this, Kelyn.'

Cristo didn't wait for a response. He turned to leave and, with one foot through the side door, said, 'I'm sorry.'

Cristo disappeared. Helplessness flooded through Kel in unrelenting waves. She sucked in long, thin breaths, her throat closing around every gasp. Everything she'd done – working for Cristo, racing through Vohre Forest – was to protect Savita. And still, it wasn't *enough*.

A hand touched her arm. 'Canen and Trystas are close friends,' Rahn said. 'Things will work out.'

The words didn't reassure Kel the way they'd probably meant to.

Rahn led Kel to the nearest chair. They both wedged themselves onto the small cushion.

'Are you really sure Cristo would never hurt Sav? He'll protect her?' Kel croaked.

Rahn's eyes lowered. Something clouded her gaze, warring beneath her blank expression. She opened her mouth and closed it, before finally, she said, 'Trust me. There's nothing Canen cares about more than preserving phoenix magic.'

Chapter Thirty-Nine

※

That night, as Kel counted her breaths and stared up at the hospital's dark ceiling, she wanted nothing more than to blink and see the dawn. Though her therapists seemed confident in her recovery, Kel wasn't sure that her doctor would release her in the morning. Progress or not, she'd refused to let anyone take her blood. Her doctor had tried to convince Kel otherwise, but something strange niggled in her veins whenever a nurse loomed with a needle. Her mind filled with the needles that her father had been subjected to, before his spirit flickered out like a candle.

Kel sat up and glanced around the room. The dark-haired girl who'd been lying in a distant bed a week ago was still there, breathing slowly.

The girl appeared asleep, so Kel flicked on the small media screen above her head. Her lips pulled up as the first channel showed a recent interview with Coup. His easy warmth was like a polished dagger, gleaming with confidence, aimed directly at the camera.

She'd once thought his broadcasted charisma was effortless. Now, she saw it for what it really was: a well-rehearsed symphony, each note perfectly tuned. But she couldn't imagine the exhaustion it took to perfect every performance. To command such a presence.

When she'd had her fill of Coup's razor-sharp smile and quips about their team, about *Kel*, she flicked the screen off. With a weary huff, she swung her feet off the bed. The cold tiles sent shivers up her spine.

Between the media coverage, Cristo's hazy promises and her

own knotted feelings around the last time she'd seen Sav, Kel knew she had to find her phoenix.

Finally, there was no one here to stop her.

Her hospital pyjamas rustled as she crept down the hall. She had no clue how to find Savita's aviary from the hospital wing, but she had to try. Tonight – before she was officially freed – might be her only chance to catch Cristo off guard.

Kel paused as she passed the dark-haired girl's bed. Around Kel's age, she was crowded by thrumming machines. Her raven hair fanned her gaunt face like a halo, and her warm, olive skin was pulled taught around her cheekbones. The girl looked strangely familiar – but Kel couldn't think from where.

And she didn't have time to linger.

A nurse hunched behind the hospital's reception desk, but Kel crawled through the shadows without notice. It was hard to tell where the hospital ended and the rest of the facilities began – every room was painted the same pearly shade of white, the night's shadows turning them grey. She'd never ventured down this cluster of corridors and couldn't tell if she was moving further or closer to Sav's aviary.

The wound at Kel's hip ached as she rushed past rooms that looked like research labs. Most windows were tinted, but the few clear panels showed test tubes and microscopes. Down another corridor, she paused before a sliver of startling silver light gleaming from beneath a door. Intrigued, she scrunched one eye and tried to peek through the narrow space between the door and its frame. She couldn't make out much – the hall was cast in darkness – just a huge, long room with silver, jagged walls.

Shock chased the last of her weariness away.

It was another prism. Larger and locked. The diamond room Cristo had shown her was barely big enough to fit a phoenix, but this rebirth chamber seemed to stretch on endlessly, big enough for an entire CAPR track to fit inside. What could Cristo possibly want with a diamond hall so monstrous? She couldn't even fathom how much it might have cost. Why would he lock one prism and leave another open?

Disbelief and dread knotted inside her. She reeled back into the centre of the corridor, just as a door echoed ahead of her.

Voices drifted down the hall.

Kel's heart leapt into her throat. Though the hallways were unguarded and apparently empty of cameras, it was clear that these rooms were restricted. Cristo was already keeping an eye on her and limiting her access. If anyone caught her sneaking around . . .

Kel shook the nearest door handle. It refused to budge. The next and the next – *all locked*.

The voices drifted closer and Kel's pulse rang in her ears. She recognized one of them.

Cristo.

Lights flickered on overhead.

Just as Kel became certain she'd be seen, a door handle budged. Just a small supply closet that she could barely fit inside, but it was better than being a sitting duck in the hallway.

Kel slipped inside as the voices boomed beyond the closet. She couldn't make out the words, but Cristo sounded agitated. Carefully, Kel pressed her ear against the door.

'. . . should occur in the next few days. You were right. That last race sped things up. We moved her yesterday.'

'Good, good,' Kel heard Cristo respond. 'Have you made any headway on the inducement?'

Inducement?

The other man cleared his throat. 'Not yet. It's hard to get close enough to trial anything.'

Cristo made a low, grumbling sound. 'Keep trying. I want it done by tomorrow night.'

When their steps grew further away, Kel let out a hard breath. She moved back from the door. Her foot caught on the handle of a mop bucket and she tripped, flailing her arms for balance. There was a row of lab coats hanging next to her, and Kel put her hand on them to steady herself.

The wall gave way.

Kel toppled over and landed face down on the cold, hard floor. Pain lanced through her back, a hazy reminder of her fall through the forest. Hoping Cristo hadn't heard her, Kel slowly rose onto her elbows.

She looked back at the closet wall – but it wasn't a wall, it was a *door*. The four lab coats had hung along the top of the door, which had been left ajar. The closet she'd hidden in was connected to one of Cristo's labs, hidden away behind tinted windows.

Kel rose to her feet.

She could no longer hear any voices, so she ventured into the centre of the room. A dozen silver benches filled the space, covered with tubes and equipment that she'd seen in Cristo's other labs. At the far end of the room stood a towering glass cabinet.

Kel wrapped her arms around herself, though it did little to protect against the chill. Why did these labs have dark windows?

The closest bench was covered with brown folders. Neat papers lay stacked inside. She flipped one open and could barely read the handwriting scratched across the pages. There were notes, equations, a few hastily sketched diagrams. Nothing incriminating.

Kel moved to the next bench. A microscope crowded the desk. To its right, a pad with more scribbled notes. To its left, a small white box labelled: SAMPLES.

With trembling fingers, Kel lifted the box's lid.

Dozens of preserved sample slides lay in neat rows. As carefully as she could, Kel pulled a few from their slots.

Bile rose in her throat.

Even though the samples were near-invisible, even though the room was ink-black, Kel knew what she was looking at.

Beak trimmings. Clipped talons. Feather barbs. Bone splinters.

Blood.

Chapter Forty

❈

She'd known what Cristo was doing. She'd found ash in *The Prism*. Here, hidden away with only slivered moonlight for company, there was no way to deny the truth. Cristo's team was tearing apart phoenixes to experiment on.

Why?

With numb hands, Kel grabbed at the notepad beside the microscope. Through the darkness, she could only make out a few scattered notes:

. . . historically no way to preserve . . . Trial D-249 offered no new results . . . plucked from a rebirth and preserved amongst ashes . . . when kept at ~2300 degrees Celsius . . . breakthrough . . . Mr Cristo – approved . . .

Those few lines were enough for the bile in Kel's throat to creep higher. A cold sweat broke out along her neck as she moved to the next bench.

More samples, more notes, more sketches of dissected phoenix parts – lungs, gizzards, crops, eyes.

Kel felt lightheaded, but she kept moving. Eventually, she made her way to the back of the room, beside the towering glass cabinet.

A stark white bin stood to the left of the glass case. Pristine and clinical, like everything else in the room.

Kel didn't give herself time to think. She wrenched off the lid and peered inside.

A dry sob wracked her throat.

There were so many – *too* many – bloody tissues and rags. Feather quills and hollow bones. Used syringes and stained vials. Shattered vertebrae and cracked skulls.

Fine, black molecules with miniscule flares of orange.

Ashes.

Kel ran to the nearest sink and heaved up the contents of her stomach.

She wanted to curl up and wake from this nightmare. How many phoenixes had Cristo torn apart?

Against her smarter instincts, she'd let him break through her walls. But she'd kill him for this. She'd take Savita and leave Salta for ever.

Her hands were trembling, violently enough that she could barely lean on them for support. She used her elbows to push herself up from the sink, wiped her mouth, and shuffled over to the glass enclosure. The last remnant of the room to search.

As soon as she focused on the cabinet she realized that it wasn't made of glass. Even in the shadows, she couldn't believe she'd mistaken it.

The tall, chute-like cabinet, gleaming and fractured, was made entirely of diamond. Just like *The Prism*.

Kel couldn't see inside; the front panel was locked. She moved around the thick casing until she found a glass window inlaid into the back.

Even a few steps away, Kel felt the heat emanating from the cabinet. Eyes watering, she shifted closer to peer inside.

The air moved like ripples in a river. Halfway down the chute was a shelf that Kel assumed was also made of diamond, though it was blackened and cracked.

A pile of ashes sat at the centre. Red and orange grains flashed amidst the black heap, like burning stars. A circle of feathers was carefully arranged around the ashes. Each feather was a different hue, with a different pattern. Each from a different subspecies of phoenix.

Kel pressed closer to the small window. She didn't care about the heat. She didn't care about the vomit in her throat or the lead in her bones. Nothing existed beyond the confines of that little, lonely window.

Dancing above the ashes, writhing above each feather, were flames.

Phoenix flames.

It was . . . *impossible*. Every Cendorian knew that all traces of phoenix magic died with the phoenix. Despite superstition, despite what underground markets claimed, there was no way to preserve their magic for human use.

There was no way for the flames above the ashes and feathers to exist.

The fire meant that the objects inside were still *alive*. No matter how small, no matter the detachment from the phoenix, Cristo had preserved phoenix magic.

How was this possible?

Kel edged away. She bumped into the nearest desk and sent a stack of papers flying across the floor. Her trembling fingers made it impossible to pick them up.

She needed to get out of here. She needed to get *Savita* out.

Savita . . . who was nearing a rebirth. Whose ashes Cristo could harvest.

Kel turned and stumbled for the exit. The closet's darkness quickly enveloped her and she skidded into a bucket, sending a mop clattering to the ground.

Heart drumming in her ears, Kel fled the lab. She didn't know what Cristo planned to do with the magic, but she didn't care. All that mattered was Savita.

Kel sprinted down the hall, limbs heavy and aching, every movement jarring her hip. She raced through a maze of corridors before finally, *finally*, spotting a familiar hall.

The halls near the aviary were empty; the one scrap of luck she'd had tonight. She didn't know where Cristo had disappeared to, but he'd been wandering through the far eastern end of the building. He was nowhere near Savita's aviary.

And, Kel realized, as she tore towards the glass dome, neither was Savita.

Kel didn't have her security pass to let her in, but she didn't need it. She moved around the dome's walls, squinting up into the trees. There was no sign of Sav. No flash of red amongst the green, no rustling in the leaves.

Kel's mind raced back to what she'd overheard.

We moved her yesterday.

Had they been talking about Savita?

She flitted through the other scraps of conversation she'd heard. Cristo had mentioned an *inducement*. They must have been talking about Sav's rebirth. The fear coursing through Kel begged her to slow, to *think*. Instead, she ran, her hip screaming in protest. She knew exactly where Cristo would be keeping Savita.

As she sprinted, Kel told herself that Savita – for better or worse – was drawing too much publicity. She was on the council's radar. If she suddenly vanished, Cristo would have to answer to all of Cendor.

That was what Kel told herself, even as she stumbled towards Sav's aviary. Even as a shadow pooled along the ground around the next corner and she couldn't stop fast enough.

Someone with rough hands knocked the wind from her lungs and shoved something coarse over her head.

'I'm so sorry, Kelyn,' a voice – *Cristo*'s – said.

Darkness consumed her.

Chapter Forty-One

✻

Kel fought against the cold hands urging her forwards. She tried to kick, to fight, but the electricity in her veins had fizzled out. All she had left was fear, ringing through her ears like a distant phoenix scream.

'Let me go!' Kel screamed.

No response. She tried to keep count of their steps and turns, but there were too many. Where were they taking her?

Eventually, she was forced to a jarring halt.

'I won't keep you here long, Kelyn.'

Cristo. His words were gentle and kind, just like every other lie he'd told her.

'You deserve the truth,' he added.

Then the cold hands were shoving her forward, and the bag over her head was ripped away.

Kel squinted through an unexpected brightness. She'd half-expected her surroundings to be filled with mad scientists, weapons and uniformed soldiers. A skeletal shrine to the Alchemists themselves.

Instead, there was only Cristo, sitting on a tall stool on an empty podium.

The rest of the room – a lecture hall, she realized – was unnervingly quiet. Overhead lamps were lit, but they weren't quite strong enough to banish the night. Cristo's hands were clasped in his lap. There was a small desk in front of him, jumbled with a tablet, a keyboard, pens and tangled cords. Behind him, mounted to the wall, was a smart screen the size of a phoenix.

Cristo gave her a pursed smile. Gone were his usual blazer and slicked hair. Instead, the man who sat in his place, with glasses perched low on his nose, was the same dishevelled man who had reassured her after Coup's injuries.

Cristo waved towards the stool beside him. Reluctantly, Kel trudged forwards.

'It's not like you gave me much of a choice,' she mumbled.

He laughed weakly. 'I know you probably don't believe me, but I am sorry about how all of this turned out. I thought I'd have more time.' He lifted his chin. 'I have a very busy day ahead, and I imagine that you're quite cold. I won't waste either of our time with small talk.'

Kel folded her arms. 'Why tell me anything?'

Cristo grimaced. 'Though I think it will cause more heartbreak than is necessary, I made a promise to explain Savita's fate to you. She felt I owed you that.'

Confusion battered at Kel's anger. Who was he talking about?

Slowly, Cristo stood and moved towards the screen behind her. The wall blared to life, projecting a row of tablet files.

Kel raised a brow. 'Did you really bring me to a lecture hall to *lecture* me?'

Cristo ignored her. A remote in hand, he opened one file, then another, each a seemingly random mixture of numbers and letters. Finally, he clicked on a folder labelled, 'Council Presentation'.

'I wouldn't do any of this if I had a choice, Kelyn,' he croaked. The red veining his eyes seemed even starker than earlier today, like cracked porcelain. 'And I think that would be easier for you to understand if I just show you what I've prepared for the council next week. I have a meeting to discuss further funding.'

Inside that folder were two more, labelled, 'Trial One' and 'Trial Two'.

He clicked on Trial One and turned back to Kel. 'What do you wish to know?'

Kel lurched to her feet, her bandaged torso screaming in protest. 'I want you to tell me why you're killing phoenixes. Why you think that stealing their magic is worth destroying Cendor!'

Cristo simply nodded. The movement was jerky, almost manic. He clicked on an image that Kel immediately recognized. It was a classical painting used in temples and textbooks, depicting Landon Ryker and Deja. The image, bordered by fire, showed one very specific moment from their mythos: Deja's rebirth, and the resurrection of Ryker.

Cristo ran his hand over the enlarged image, as if to brush his fingers along Deja's flaming wings. 'Deja called forth her own rebirth to save her rider. She shared her ashes with him, and when she was reborn, Landon Ryker was by her side. Healed.'

Cristo raised his arms and gestured around the empty room. 'My research is the closest anyone has ever come to making that myth a reality. No phoenix can biologically call forth their own rebirth, but if I could preserve the magic of their ashes, I could share it with the people who need it. I can cure AB before it destroys everything.'

His voice broke over the last words, and understanding washed through Kel. She thought back to what he'd said when she'd first arrived in Vohre – thanking her for stopping the train for the dead mother and son. Claiming that curing AB was his purpose.

She drank in Cristo's haggard features and mottled skin. He looked battered and feverish, like a man teetering at a cliff's edge, a trapped animal desperate for a door.

He didn't want a phoenix's magic for their fire, or flight, or even strength. He wanted their regeneration powers.

Her hatred was still there, sharp and consuming. But the pity in her gut fought a little harder for control.

'You . . . are you sick?'

Cristo startled her with a sharp, barked laugh. It was anything but warm. 'I wish it was me.'

Kel frowned. Who would he risk so much for?

Cristo jerked towards the screen, and Kel used the distraction to scour the room. The exits were probably guarded, and with her half-healed injuries, she wouldn't get far – but maybe she didn't need to.

Kel glanced down to the small, cluttered desk on the podium. Amongst the cables lay a black-and-gold fountain pen. It wouldn't be a useful weapon from a distance – she'd have to get right beside Cristo . . .

'This might have started in desperation, but I'm so *close*, Kelyn,' Cristo muttered. 'Close enough that I'm willing to rely on some ancient myth.'

Cristo slid a finger across the remote. Another document appeared, full of formulas and chemical symbols. Kel didn't understand much of it, but she could recognize phoenix temperatures.

Her fingers itched to grab the sharp, expensive-looking pen on the desk. But she needed to keep him talking. She needed him distracted.

'In the story, Deja *willingly* shared her ashes with Landon Ryker. Deja didn't die,' she said.

The veins in Cristo's eyes seemed to darken. 'Phoenixes are not the affectionate creatures of legend. You of all people should know this. Your beloved phoenix let you fall to your death in the forest.'

Kel winced. She'd tried not to think about it, about that moment – but Cristo was right. Kel had always loved Savita's ruthlessness. Her power and savagery. And despite everything she'd learnt, everything her father had taught her, a part of her had always thought that *she* was the exception to Savita's nature. She thought that Savita would protect her.

She'd been wrong. Her time in the hospital was proof of that.

But that didn't mean Sav deserved to die. It just meant that Kel had let her hopes pervert reality.

'Savita did what *any* phoenix would do. She doesn't deserve to die just because her nature doesn't suit yours.'

Pain flashed across Cristo's face. 'Maybe you're right. But either way – one thing is clear from my research. A phoenix needs every single molecule of their ashes for a rebirth. We can't save our own unless they die.'

Unless Savita dies.

Kel inched forward. Just a mere breath from the pen.

'You can't get away with killing her,' Kel barked, as Cristo turned to face her. 'Everyone in CAPR knows Savita's name. If she disappears, there will be questions.'

Kel's stomach dropped as Cristo's lips twitched. 'What makes you think I didn't plan that?'

Kel tried to calm the shaking in her hands. 'You're lying.'

She *hated* this. The back-and-forth – the game of cat and mouse. Cristo might claim he was sorry, but no one with regret would make a fucking *slideshow* of their victory.

Cristo's smile deepened, the first truly menacing expression she'd ever seen cross his face.

'Despite what you probably think, I didn't recruit you for this purpose. At least, not at first. When I initially asked my recruiters to keep an eye on the Howlers, I had no idea Savita was nearing a rebirth. But I have very intuitive people working for me, Kelyn. One of my best scouts – he used to be a tamer, you see – was convinced that Savita was nearing a rebirth. We have technology monitoring every race across Cendor, tracking every phoenix using Cristo tech in their collars. Even before you arrived in Vohre, Savita's vitals were fluctuating in ways I'd been carefully searching for. So when I heard that you'd refused my offer, I . . . *nudged* you in my direction. Your farm was already so deep in disrepair. It just needed a little spark to catch alight.'

Ice trickled down Kel's spine. 'You . . . *you* destroyed my home.'

She'd thought that *everything* had been her fault. But Cristo had burnt down her aviary. Cristo had been pulling her strings towards him all along. Was that why he'd helped her start the farm's rebuild? Out of guilt?

The regret twisting Cristo's features confirmed Kel's suspicions. 'I had the emergency team on-site paid off to report it as an accident. I never wanted you hurt. I was simply running out of time.' He ran a hand through his hair. 'Once you'd accepted my offer, I began fanning the flames of the Howlers' publicity. Savita needed to seem wild, untamed, so the council would step in. Then I would have a councillor deem Savita dangerous and unfit, and they'd allow me the courtesy of killing Savita myself. It would be a tragedy, but a legal one.'

Kel's nails dug into her palms. She refused to process his words, refused to let him distract her. She just needed him to turn away – just once . . .

'You couldn't have known what would happen in Vohre Forest that day,' Kel snarled. 'You can't take credit for any of this.'

Again, Cristo merely smiled, his face unshifting. 'I funded the latest race through Vohre Forest to see how Savita responded to different environment stimuli. I wanted to see if reintroducing Savita to her ancestral home might speed up her rebirth.'

Kel's eyes bulged. 'You can't have known the Fume would show up.'

Cristo shook his head. 'No, that was a tragic error. But I needed to conduct more research on Savita, and the only time she's comfortable enough to allow her vitals to shift is when she's racing.

Your first race in Vohre went too well and didn't give me the results I hoped for, so I . . . *engineered* two more anarchic environments with competing species to test her reactions. The sprites gave us some headway, but it still wasn't enough.'

'Coup almost *dying* on the track wasn't *enough* for you?' she snapped. Disbelief sharpened her words.

'Coup is a wild card, and largely did my work for me.'

'But why would you risk Savita rebirthing outside of your compound? Somewhere you couldn't control?' The questions sputtered out of Kel like a dying engine.

He wasn't making sense. But then again, Kel recognized the desperation on his face, that of someone willing to go to the ends of the earth for a loved one. He was lost to fear.

Cristo frowned, as if the thought had never crossed his mind. 'I have people tracking Savita's vitals every hour, every second. There was no chance of her rebirthing away from my compound. I simply hoped it would speed up the process. And since I own the majority of Vohre's news outlets, I've always controlled the narrative.'

Dread shivered down Kel's spine. She'd never thought of how Cristo's power would seep beyond his compounds. How could the world let *one man* have so much control?

Cristo's eyes shined. Kel couldn't see the person who had given her a new carving kit, who had promised her safety.

Kel wanted to spit at him – to scream, to cry.

But she refused to waste her anger – or the opening. When Cristo turned back towards the screen, Kel made her move.

She lurched for the pen and jumped towards Cristo. Shoving her elbow into his back, Cristo cried out, stumbling forward. With the weight she'd thrown at him, Kel lost her balance and toppled down on top of him.

They fell to the ground in a heap. Pain speared her hip, but she managed to climb onto Cristo as he began to crawl away. Pen in hand, she let him rise onto his knees. She manoeuvred behind him and though he was strong, the second he felt the cool, sharp metal against his throat, he froze.

Kel half-expected a dozen armed soldiers to burst into the room. But nothing changed, nothing shifted, other than the pen as Kel tried to keep her hand steady.

'We're going to walk out of here,' Kel spat. 'And you're going to take me to Savita.'

Kel jammed the pen deep enough into his throat that red beads flashed against the metal. 'Do you understand?'

Chapter Forty-Two

※

Cristo raised his hands, as if in surrender.

Then, he sighed.

'I'm a dreamer, Kelyn. Not a fool.'

Faster than a phoenix strike, Cristo ducked his head, latched on to her arms and thrust her forward. The pen flew to the floor as Kel tumbled through the air, over Cristo. She landed in front of him with a hard *thud*. Her hip spasmed, sharp and hot. Black spots danced across her vision.

Kel sucked in thin, agonized gasps. Splayed on her back, she felt like someone had rammed her lungs with a hammer.

Cristo reached out a hand to her. 'If we had more time, I believe I could convince you of my cause.'

She had no breath and no defence – and still, Kel fought. She flipped onto her hands and knees and crawled towards the pen, reaching it before Cristo.

She wanted to jump up, to stab Cristo wherever she could, to make him feel her pain, until he promised to free her family.

But Kel couldn't grasp the pen.

She tried and tried, but her hands kept shaking. No matter how hard she focused, she couldn't steady them enough to tighten around the pen. She flexed her knuckles and curled her fingers, the pen was *right there*—

And then a boot kicked the pen from beneath her trembling fingers, and hands seized her, pulling her to her feet.

Two men stood behind her, restraining her arms. The lack of

sleep, the fear, the rage – it was all catching up with her. The familiar static was in her head and the room spun around Cristo.

As he moved towards her, she spat, 'You're evil.'

Cristo shook his head. 'The kindest people in this world think they're the cruellest, and the cruellest think they're the Alchemists themselves.' His jaw clenched. 'I am neither cruel nor a god. I simply have the stomach for hard choices and the resources to find a cure.'

'At what cost?' Kel spat.

'For her, I'd bleed Salta dry.'

'*Who?*' Kel sneered, though the word turned to a yelp as one guard tightened his grip on her arms.

Cristo turned back to the screen and exited the file. With the guards holding her upright, Kel was forced to watch. The screen switched to a strange map of Cendor, annotated with red and black dots. A large cluster of red hovered over Fieror, and a cluster of black just north of Vohre, in the forest. The red seemed to crowd Cendor and Ascira, while Ebrait and Dresva held most of the black.

The map was gone before Kel could decipher the annotations, the guards jostling her back towards the exit.

'*Alchemists!* Why tell me any of this if you're just going to lock me up!' Kel screamed.

A muscle in Cristo's jaw feathered. 'Rahn convinced me that you and the other Howlers could be trusted. She wanted me to tell you all when you first signed your contracts. *Contracts* . . .' Cristo paused, '. . . that clearly state that if you reveal any of this to people outside Cristo Industries, you'll be serving a prison sentence long enough that many phoenixes will live and die without your guidance.'

'Rahn . . . Rahn *knew?*'

She'd suspected it, but the confirmation still knocked the air from her lungs. For all the times Kel had doubted the girl, all the nights she'd spent worrying over whether Dira could trust her, she'd let herself believe that Rahn was a friend. A Howler.

She'd been wrong, about Cristo and Rahn. She'd been so wrong about *everything*.

Cristo drummed his fingers against his folded arms. 'Of course she did. Now, if you'll excuse me, this has taken up more of my morning than I planned for. Estra has only days left. I have to resort to my last measure. Savita *will* rebirth by tomorrow evening.'

Something echoed in the back of Kel's mind. *Estra*. Was that who was sick?

'You can't know that,' she spat, her anger simmering, threatening to melt her from within. 'There's no way to control her rebirth.'

Cristo's silence made it clear he disagreed. She wanted to keep screaming, demanding more answers – but the fire was eating her alive. As the guards tried to tug her away, she fought with every ounce of strength she had left. 'Wait! Stop! You can't do this! Don't you *dare* touch Savita! If I ever meet this *Estra*, I'm going to do to her what you're going to do to—'

'Stop,' Cristo said, short and clipped. The guards paused. Kel dangled from their grips.

Silently, Cristo marched towards Kel. He paused just an inch away, lifting her chin with a single finger. 'What did you say?'

Kel sneered. 'I said, if I ever meet Estra, I'm going to—'

'What do you mean, *if?*'

His tone wasn't threatening. His features sharpened with a cold, calculating curiosity.

Kel merely frowned. 'What are you getting at?'

The name conjured a fleeting sense of familiarity but nothing else.

Cristo's mouth parted. He stepped back and looked over her, slowly.

'I see,' he breathed, throat bobbing. 'I am so sorry to hear that, Kelyn. I truly am.'

Before Kel could demand an explanation, Cristo instructed the guards, 'Take her to the cell. As soon as her phoenix is dead, move her to the hospital wing. Make sure she's as comfortable as possible.'

Kel's heart pounded. Was he going to experiment on her, too? Chain her to a bed? 'What—'

Cristo turned towards the other end of the hall. The guards dragged her from the room and down the hall. No matter how loud she screamed or how hard she kicked, no matter how much her body ached to lay down and *rest*, the guards didn't stop.

As they dragged Kel back to the cell, they passed a small window. Through it, Kel saw the soft rays of the early sun.

Savita didn't have long.

Chapter Forty-Three

❈

Kel barely caught herself before tripping to the ground.

She landed on her injured hip and hissed in pain. Knotted clumps of hair fell over her face as another set of hands clutched her arms.

'Get off me!' she screamed. 'I'll kill you, you—'

'*Kel?*'

She froze. Her gaze lifted from the still-spinning floor. This had to be a dream. That couldn't be the voice she thought it was. *He* couldn't be trapped, too.

She almost didn't want to lift her gaze. But the hands grasping her arms softened.

She met a pair of blazing amber eyes.

Dread skittered through her stomach.

'What are you doing here?' she asked Coup.

He wore gloves and unzipped riding leathers over a grey shirt, as if they'd been thrown on in haste. His dark hair was a tangled nest and his eyes were puffy.

Coup's hands roamed her arms. 'You're not hurt?'

Kel shook her head, ignoring the aches shooting through her. 'No – what happened?'

Coup rubbed his neck. 'I couldn't sleep, so I threw on my gear to check on Savita. But she wasn't in her aviary. I was worried they'd done something to her – then I came to check on *you* – but the fucking hospital receptionist wouldn't let me inside. Even in the middle of the night, he'd never stopped me from visiting before. I *knew* something was wrong. So, I shoved past him and saw your empty bed. The receptionist called security, and I ran.'

Coup wrung his hands and glanced behind Kel to the white door. 'I was on my way to wake up the rest of the team when two of Cristo's goons grabbed me and threw me in here.'

'Did they hurt you?' Kel demanded.

She was caught in a flurry – thoughts scattered, taking one step forward for every two back. If they hurt Coup . . .

Coup reached forward and tucked a strand of matted hair behind her ear. 'I'm all right, tamer. Are you?' He gestured around the pearly, windowless cell. 'Why the hell are we locked in here?'

Kel looked back at the door; there was no sound from the other side.

She let out a shaky breath. 'You might want to sit down.'

Huddled together in Cristo's prison, Kel told Coup everything she'd discovered. About Cristo trying to induce Savita's rebirth, about his failed – and successful – experiments, and what he was planning on doing to Savita . . .

Coup frowned. 'What could he possibly want with a phoenix's magic? Immortality, rebirths, fire – that kind of power doesn't belong to us. What could be worth . . .'

Coup shook his head. Kel knew what he hadn't been able to voice.

There was *nothing* worth killing phoenixes for. No one knew how Saltan creatures tended the land, but if the Alchemists' teachings had made one thing clear, it was that the creatures and islands shared a skeleton. You couldn't destroy one without destroying the other.

Kel wanted to move, to break things, to *blaze*. She couldn't lose Savita. She *couldn't*.

Coup huffed. 'How long are they going to keep us here?'

Kel wrapped her arms around her knees. 'Cristo made it clear that he didn't want to risk me interfering with Savita's rebirth. He won't let us out until she's . . .'

Coup removed his gloves and placed a hand on Kel's jittering knee. 'We need a distraction,' he said, because he couldn't offer any reassurances.

She needed to think of something – *anything* – but Savita. 'Like what?'

Coup shifted to trace the valleys of her knuckles, the scars across her hands. Identical to his own. 'How do I convince Bekn to leave this damn island?'

Kel's brows rose. '*That's* your distraction? You want to trade one unsolvable task for another?'

Coup slid his other arm around Kel, and she leaned into his warmth. 'Well, I doubt that guessing about the weather will provide much of a distraction.'

His hand traced circles on her knee. It did little to soothe the vibrating in her bones, begging to *move*. She tried to focus on the heat building beneath his touch. 'Why do you want Bekn to leave?'

Coup gave her a pointed look. 'You know as well as I do that Bekn isn't built for Cendor. He could thrive somewhere like Ascira. I know he still wants to leave, too. Buy him three shots of blood gin at The Ferret and it's all he talks about. It's the reason none of his relationships ever last longer than a few months. But he's too stubborn.'

Kel placed her shaking hand over his. 'He's not going anywhere, Coup. Whether he's on Cendor, or the furthest reaches of Salta – he's going to be okay.'

She couldn't tell him that he was overreacting – not when AB had stolen his mother away. Nobody was safe from AB – not Coup, or Bekn, or any of the Howlers. Loss didn't follow any maps; it wove through joy and pain and years as easily as lightning through a storm.

No one knew where it was going to strike – only that it would.

'If – when – Bekn leaves,' Kel continued, 'I'm not going anywhere. You're stuck with me.'

Coup twined their fingers together. 'That's a funny coincidence, because you're stuck with me, too.'

Despite everything, despite *Savita*, Kel's lips hitched up. 'Even if we're trapped in here for the next fifty years?'

Coup huffed a short laugh. 'In here, in Vohre, in your dusty little cottage in Fieror. Anywhere.'

Warmth unfurled through Kel, dulling the pain in her hip. She imagined Sav in her old aviary, or chasing rabbits through a paddock. 'The aviary's construction is only a month away from completion. I think the Howlers are due a trip back home.'

If Savita survives that long.

The unbidden thought made Kel choke back a sob. She tried to force her attention on Coup – on anything but her phoenix.

Coup pressed his lips to the side of her head. The warmth made her shiver. 'Say we get out of all of this. We free Sav. We stop Cristo. We could go back to your farm and finish rebuilding. We probably have enough money by now to take a break from racing, at least for a month or two. We could just . . .' Coup leaned closer to her. 'Be this. Us. For a little while.'

Kel leaned her head against Coup's shoulder. The parts of her body touching his burnt feverishly hot.

'I should have told you how I felt when you were injured,' she whispered.

Coup chuckled. His thumb swept lightly over her thigh. 'We're both fools who spent far too long fighting instead of doing . . . other things.'

He said the words as if they'd caught him by surprise. Kel's stomach tensed.

She focused on the growing heat in her blood, helping her forget why she was here. Where she was. Why it was a bad idea to want Coup to burn, too.

Coup's gaze lowered, just below her eyes. His brow wrinkled. '*Ashes*, Kel. When was the last time you slept? The bags under your eyes look like bruises.'

Kel frowned. She wanted so many things from him – but none involved him pointing out how awful she looked. She needed him to distract her from sleepless nights and Savita's future and the wrong kinds of fires.

Kel's lips were pressed to Coup's before she realized she'd moved. Words weren't enough. She needed something stronger, headier, to block out the fear and the pain seizing her hip.

Coup met her kisses with his own swift hunger. In one breathless moment, they were a tangle of limbs on the floor. The fire in Kel cooled, overcome by a different kind of heat.

Coup hovered over Kel, one hand against her uninjured hip and the other propped against the ground. She pressed his weight closer to her. With one hand bunched in his hair, trapping his mouth against hers, she let her other hand trail down his back. His muscles rippled and tensed beneath her fingers, and Kel liked how she could make him shiver. Could make his breath hitch with the lightest touch.

His lips moved down to her neck. A soft moan slipped past her lips. Coup's grip tightened at the sound. She slipped a hand beneath his unzipped leathers, to the hem of his shirt and then under it. He mimicked her touch, forcing her to arch into his embrace.

Memories flashed through her mind. His warmth on the top of a hill as her aviary burnt. His hands against her hips as they rode over Fieror on Savita. Her bones aching to protect him from the sight of the dead mother and child. The feel of him wrapped around her in the hospital bed.

Lightning burnt through her – sweet and blessedly distracting – as she danced her fingers across his back, around to his stomach. She relished his groan against her neck as she splayed her palms against his muscles.

Her entire body tightened at the sound. She wanted more. She wanted *him*.

Kel moved her hand lower and wiggled her fingers across the waist of his trousers. Just an inch lower and she could feel—

'*Shit* – Kel, we can't,' Coup panted.

He jerked away and ran a hand through his rumpled hair. His breath came out in short, ragged breaths.

Kel propped herself up on her elbows, wincing as she was forced back into her body. 'What's wrong?'

Coup's eyes darkened as they ran across her. His throat bobbed and he shook his head.

'This is *not* how I want to do this. Not here, of all places.'

Kel sighed. Sure – a fluorescently lit prison cell wasn't where she'd imagined having sex with Coup for the first time. But she didn't know what awaited them on the other side of that door. If this was her only chance to feel close to him in this way, she didn't want to waste it.

When Kel opened her mouth to object, Coup pointed to the roof. She turned her head to follow his finger.

Oh, right. She'd forgotten about the damn cameras.

Coup chuckled. 'You really want our first time to be watched by Cristo and his goons?'

Kel bit her lip. She didn't particularly care. But she could see that Coup did.

She sat up and raised her hands in surrender, trying to swallow down the resurfacing aches in her muscles. Savita – *burning, alone* – flashed through her mind. She needed a diversion from the pain –

from everything.

'Fine,' she relented. 'But we need a new distraction.'

'Your mother,' Coup sputtered, still short of breath. 'You write to each other, right? When did you last hear from her?'

Kel bit the inside of her cheek. Yes, her *mother* was just as good as an ice-cold shower. 'I thought she'd be calling every day once she heard I was here, living with *the* Canen Cristo. But she hasn't tried to contact me since we came to Vohre.'

Kel had thought for sure that Madilyn would call and ask for a place to sleep, money, perhaps an introduction to Cristo. Instead, there had been total silence.

Coup frowned. He pulled away slightly, turning to face Kel. 'That's not true.'

Kel mirrored his posture. 'What do you mean?'

Coup's brow deepened. 'I've seen postcards from your mother on the kitchen table. I've seen you reading them. I heard you talking to Dira about whether or not you should reply.'

Kel scrunched her nose. 'I think this cell is getting to you. I haven't heard a single word from Madilyn Chambers since we left Fieror. I wouldn't forget that.'

Coup's frown knotted into something uncertain. A muddled silence filled the room, and Kel could see the tired cogs in his brain struggling to turn.

Finally, Coup opened his mouth and—

'I'm going to toss you into a cage with starved phoenixes!' a deep voice rang out. A moment later the door behind them slivered open.

Kel heard another throaty, familiar voice speak, 'I'll lock you in a cage with *myself*. Trust me, you'd fare better against the phoenixes—'

The cell door yawned wide open.

Chapter Forty-Four

※

Kel rushed back to avoid the swinging door. The guard in front of them rubbed his face. 'Ten minutes,' he said wearily. 'Then you need to leave.'

From behind the guard, a voice said, softly, 'Thanks, Lucian. I'll be quick.'

Kel rose to her feet as Dira barrelled into the room, launching herself at Kel. She coughed from the force, but quickly wrapped her arms around her friend.

Behind Dira, Kel spotted Bekn locking Coup in a similar, vice-like embrace. Another figure moved slowly through the door, around the guard.

Rahn.

The guard exited the room and slammed the door shut. Rahn stayed by the door, her head ducked and dark hair hiding her face.

'What's going on?' Kel asked, voice muffled through Dira's hair. 'How did you get here?'

'These guards grabbed us from our rooms this morning. Rahn was there and told us everything. I'm sorry, Kel,' Dira mumbled, burrowing herself deeper into Kel's arms. 'I screwed up. I trusted her.'

Kel tightened her hold on Dira and shifted to face Rahn. Slowly, the technician lifted her head, eyes filled with a silver sheen.

'You knew this whole time,' Coup spat at Rahn. He moved closer, though Rahn didn't back away.

'I'm sorry,' Rahn whispered. 'I just can't let anything go wrong.

I don't expect you to forgive me – but I never wanted to hurt any of you.' Her gaze darted to Dira. A tear trickled down her left cheek. 'You deserve to know the truth. Canen is just trying to save everyone.'

Kel moved past Dira. 'Everyone but Savita.'

Rahn's jaw clenched. 'You're asking me to choose between a phoenix and a human. If it was us or Savita, which would you choose?'

Kel's throat went dry. She couldn't – *wouldn't* – even imagine that.

'That's what I thought,' Rahn muttered. She shook her head and held something out towards Kel.

'Here,' she mumbled, eyes on the floor. 'That gown can't be very warm.'

Kel snatched the clothes – a sweater and brown trousers – and folded them against her chest, silent. She didn't want anything from Rahn and she certainly wasn't cold. But whatever came next, she didn't want to face it in an open-backed hospital gown.

When no one spoke, Rahn sighed. 'I didn't know Savita was nearing a rebirth until the CAPR race with the sprites. Phoenix rebirths don't come around often, and Cristo thinks that he's finally found a cure. This is . . . this is his only chance. I am sorry – but not for refusing to choose.'

'You *are* choosing,' Dira cut in, nostrils flared. 'This is not nature running its course. Cristo is *murdering* the creatures that created this island. What happens when there are no more phoenixes to bleed dry for his experiments? They're gone, and a handful of people – chosen by Cristo – are allowed to escape their fates. You're not helping people, or Salta, or Estra. You're only helping Cristo.'

Kel frowned. She hadn't mentioned Estra's name. She hadn't even thought about it since Cristo had spoken it. It was as if the name was too fragile to grasp.

Dira spoke it as if she knew the girl. But Kel had never even heard of her before Cristo mentioned her name. Kel felt like she was trying to jam the wrong puzzle pieces together.

Rahn's throat bobbed. 'Before I joined your team, I'd never spent much time with phoenixes. I helped developed tech, but this was my first time on a real CAPR team.' Rahn hung her head. 'Ebrait made us worship phoenixes. They force us to worship *all* magic. I had no control over any of it. Tech gave me some control. And Canen . . . he didn't just bring me here to work on tech.'

Rahn's voice broke. Dira drifted a step closer to her, almost instinctively, before stopping herself.

Rahn went on, 'Like I said, my mum's an important figure in Ebrait. She has a lot of power in our temples. She . . . she's worked with Fume delegates before. Trying to find a compromise. Trying to understand the best way to preserve Salta's magical populations.'

Shock flooded through Kel, even as Dira spat, 'You've told me all of this. What does it have to do with you locking us in a cell?'

Another tear trailed down Rahn's cheek. 'Canen knew my mum wanted me to take her place, eventually. I think he knew she'd passed on what she knew about Salta's magic, the research Ebrait had done on its own. After a while, I trusted him enough to share what she'd taught me. About how AB flares up the most in places cleared of magic. It made him think to look to phoenixes for a cure.'

Kel froze. She thought back to the annotated map she'd seen in Cristo's files. The red dots clustered over Fieror – where most of Cendor's AB cases stemmed from – and the black dots hovering over Vohre Forest – where Cendor's remaining wild phoenixes thrived. There had been hardly any overlap of the two, hardly any red dots appearing in Vohre, particularly the border near the forest.

A startling laugh bubbled up Kel's throat. 'He thinks phoenixes can cure AB because there's no cases near where they live. AB is thriving where wildlife populations have become extinct!'

Rahn merely nodded. 'There are hundreds more cases in Fieror than Vohre, because Vohre backs onto the forest. And there are thousands more cases in Cendor and Ascira, because Ebrait and Dresva protect their animals. They don't exploit them.'

Ebrait worshipped its sea monsters through religion. Dresva protected its serpents because magic bonds between snakes and humans helped their agriculture industries. But Ascira had no qualms about clearing sprites for new attractions. Cendor didn't hesitate to kill phoenixes for entertainment or city expansions.

Could it really be so simple? Could AB really be the product of extinction? Of Salta's magic withering away?

Answers slammed together in Kel's mind. Cristo hadn't just recruited Rahn for her tech aspirations. He'd known she might have knowledge of Salta's magic that he wouldn't otherwise have access to. Vaguely, Kel wondered if that was why Rahn had asked Kel so many questions about the Fume while she recovered in hospital. She was already connected to them, in some small way.

Bekn stepped forward, in front of Dira, Coup and Kel. 'That can't be right. Someone would have figured it out.'

'Not if he's paid off anyone who realizes,' Dira muttered.

Adrenaline chased away the edges of Kel's fatigue. 'But this means there's another way – no one needs to die.' *Not Savita, or any other phoenix.* 'Salta is *telling* you how to fix this. Cristo doesn't need to do any of this. He can just—'

'He can't just wait for Salta's creatures to repopulate the islands,' Rahn said, her voice hardening. 'It would take a century. Estra barely has days left.'

'We know you see Estra like a sister,' Bekn said. 'But killing *phoenixes*? Cendor won't survive it.'

Confusion coiled tight in Kel. If Rahn saw this girl as a sister, wouldn't Kel have heard of her before?

Bekn cursed under his breath. 'Let me speak to Cristo. He can still stop all of this.'

'I'm sorry,' Rahn croaked. 'You deserve answers – but I can't let you out.'

'Estra can talk to him,' Dira pleaded. 'She'll help us.'

Kel's frown deepened. She went to speak – but Coup beat her to it.

'I spoke to Estra a few days ago,' he said. 'She still has enough strength to give us a chance. We just need to try and convince *her* to talk to her father.'

'*What?*' Kel burst out. 'Cristo has a *daughter?*'

Too many emotions – confusion, anger, shock – whirled through her. If Cristo had a daughter living in the compound surely Kel would have met her.

Yet . . . it made sense. The way he'd spoken about grief, how he'd understood what it was to love the dead and dying. But why would he have kept Estra a secret?

Slowly, the four other Howlers turned to Kel. Each of their expressions mirrored the next, brows raised, lips parted.

Eventually Dira broke the silence. 'Kel, what are you talking about?'

'Me?' Kel threw back. 'How do you all know this girl?'

'This *girl?*' Bekn repeated. 'Kel, you know Estra. You've told me that you like her more than me.'

Kel's stomach dropped. 'I've never met Estra, and a few minutes ago I thought none of you had either.'

The room, flooded with white light, seemed to flicker.

Kel met Coup's eyes; she saw nothing but fear.

'Kel,' Dira said. 'You remember Estra, right?'

Dira's words were slow, enunciated. As if she was speaking to a child. Kel didn't know what was going on, but they didn't have the time to play games.

'Of course I remember her,' Kel lied, clutching the clothes tighter as dread pooled in her gut. 'But that doesn't change what we—'

'She's lying,' Coup muttered. He stared at Kel. 'You don't remember her, do you?'

Kel struggled to breathe. Why were they all staring at her like that? They didn't have *time* for this.

Coup exchanged a sharp look with his brother.

Slowly, Bekn said, 'We met Estra in the dining hall, the first day we arrived. Though we didn't know she was ill, then. She told us after a few weeks.'

Kel inched back. Something barbed fluttered in her stomach.

What was going on?

'She's watched us practise on the training track,' Dira continued, her voice uncharacteristically shaky. 'She fought with her dad to stop you from competing in the last race. She likes the same weird, old music that you do. She's come to our weekly movie nights for the last month.'

They had *weekly movie nights*? Kel flicked through the dusty tabs in her memory. Some words sent a soft wave of déjà vu through her, but most were alien, spoken in a language they'd created behind her back.

'You're lying,' Kel spat. The trembling in her hands spread up her arms, wracking her body. 'This is some cruel joke and you all—'

'She doesn't remember her mother's postcards, either,' Coup said in a low voice. 'She thinks her mother hasn't contacted her since she left Fieror.'

Dira let out a dry, humourless chuckle. 'Kel, you complained about your mum every night that we spent in Savita's aviary. Come on, you must remember.'

Kel backed away. The walls of the cell were so much smaller than they'd been minutes ago.

'Stop,' Kel barked. 'Just *stop*.'

She wanted to hurt them. She wanted to cry. She hated how her friends – her family – were staring at her. Like she was a ghost brought to life.

'Kel,' Coup whispered.

She never thought her own name could break her heart.

'Short-term memory loss,' Coup went on, eyes glazed. 'Tremors. Insomnia. Confusion. Paranoia. A short temper.'

All at once, Kel understood. She'd heard those words a thousand times. On the news, in hospital ads.

They weren't just words.

They were symptoms.

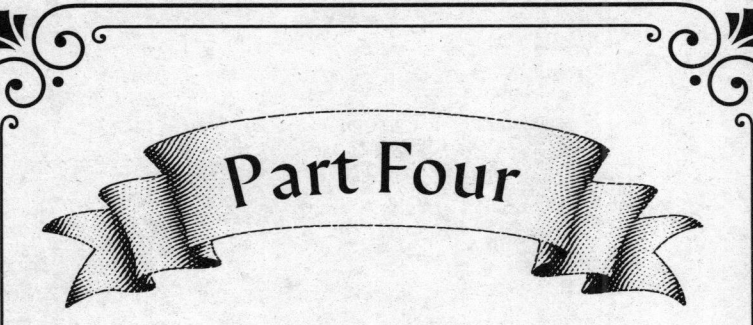

Part Four

With talons so fierce, Deja clutched him tight
Spurning Ryker's end by a kraken's bite
She called a rebirth, sharing her god fire
And so became ash, reborn from the pyre

A harrowing end for any but lore
Deja chose to save the bravest of Four
With magic she swore, Ryker would live on
Their tale immortalized here in this song

Verse 7–8, 'The Gilded Lullaby'

Chapter Forty-Five

---※---

A wild, painful laugh burst through Kel. 'You think I have AB? That's ridiculous.'

'You've barely slept since we left Fieror,' Dira said quietly. 'You've always had a temper – but the past weeks have been different. There's this rage in you that I've never seen before.'

Kel's mouth dried. It was true – over the last two months, a new kind of fire had entered Kel's veins. Though it had sparked at strange times, she'd welcomed it. It had helped her learn what she needed to try and save Savita.

'AB patients' symptoms flare up around each other,' Dira pressed. 'That would explain why you don't remember Estra.'

Kel's memory whirled back to the mother and son they'd seen on the train, struck down by AB. Although AB wasn't contagious, it was strange to see two sick people near one another. Symptoms flared up when victims were in close proximity, like adding petrol to a flame.

'This isn't real,' Kel said, desperately trying to stop the shaking in her hands. 'This has to be a dream. None of you would ever be this cruel.' She choked back a sob.

'Kel,' Dira merely said, voice trembling.

In that moment, when Kel saw a gleaming wetness in her friend's brown eyes, Dira's words hit her. Kel had *never* seen her best friend cry.

Kel looked down to her shaking hands. She scoured her mind, searching for any grains, any moments, that proved that they were lying.

Kel could only think of how little she'd slept since leaving Fieror. The strange, itching paranoia that blazed through her and flared without warning. The sudden anger. Even the trembling that had stopped her from grabbing Cristo's fountain pen.

The memories that escaped her.

Kel was flung back to the lecture hall, beside Cristo. Back to the last words he'd said to her.

Move her to the hospital wing. Make sure she's as comfortable as possible.

Even he'd known.

Kel resisted the urge to look at Coup. She thought of what she and Coup had said to each other, just minutes ago. Plans of returning to Fieror. Plans for a future.

Kel forced a deep breath. 'Okay, so I have . . . AB. This doesn't change anything.'

Anger and fear tried to swell in her chest, tried to drown her. She shoved it all down. She buried it all alongside her father and Oska and her mother's postcards. She focused instead on Savita, flaming and everlasting, and her chest eased, ever so slightly. She didn't have the energy – or the time – to worry about herself *and* Savita.

Dira made an incredulous sound. Seconds later, the guard peeked his head through the door. 'Time's up. Rahn, Canen needs you.'

The other Howlers turned to look at their technician. Rahn had been silent, frozen, for too long. Shadows fell across her pale face, deep lines carving into her forehead.

'I didn't know,' she breathed, almost too softly to hear. 'I didn't – *Ashes!* Not you, too. None of this was meant to happen.'

More tears streamed down Rahn's face. The guard called again for her to leave, but she didn't move.

'None of this was meant to happen,' Rahn repeated. Her jaw set in a hard line. 'I'm sorry.'

She turned and fled the room. The guard slammed the door behind her, the sound of a lock jamming in place.

'We still need to save Savita,' Kel pressed.

Her friends looked at her disbelievingly, and Kel raised a hand. 'Look – Cristo's not going to let me out of here until Sav rebirths. I don't know what he's planning, but he thinks he can make it happen by tonight. Once she rebirths, he wants to move me to a hospital. So, no matter what happens when Savita rebirths, my fate is sealed.' She still couldn't bring herself to look at Coup. 'But hers doesn't have to be.'

Dira was still looking at her hopelessly, silent tears streaming down her cheeks.

Coup's eyes were hollow.

Kel pressed on. 'I don't care if phoenixes can cure AB. If any of you let Sav die, I'll come back and haunt you all until Salta burns.'

None of her friends seemed to find her words funny.

Eventually, Bekn managed, 'We're not letting *anyone* die. You hear me?'

He held Kel's stare until she forced a nod. Bekn knew as well as anyone that there was no true cure for AB – but at least with Cristo's facilities, she wouldn't be in pain.

'I'm going to kill them all,' Dira breathed, her voice too frail to give any weight to the threat. 'They'll wish they'd never heard of the Howlers.'

Kel tried to force a smile, though as she turned to Coup, it vanished. He stood statue-still, his face slack.

She placed a hand on his shoulder. 'Look at me.'

There was nothing but smoke and ash in Coup's eyes. 'I knew,' he breathed. 'I *knew* something was wrong. I'm so sorry, Kelyn.'

Kel cupped his face. 'This isn't your fault. It isn't anyone's.'

Coup shook his head. 'I should've seen it sooner. I thought . . . I thought we had time.'

Kel wished she could reach out and steal the pain from his features. She wrapped her arms around him, and a moment later, his hands were clutching her back.

'We still have time,' Kel lied. 'We just need a plan.'

They held onto each other as Dira cursed and pounded on the cell door with weak fists.

Kel didn't know how to untangle the wrongness coursing through her. Fear, anger, absurd amusement – it was all too much.

She didn't have time to make peace with AB. Though guilt rippled through her at the thought of Coup and Bekn losing *another* person to this barbaric blight, Kel only had the time – the energy – to focus on one thing.

Savita.

If AB refused to rear its head until near-death, then Kel refused to surrender. She refused to die, until death forced her hand.

Because now she was made of fire too, and she'd fight like hell to make sure Savita's didn't go out with hers.

Chapter Forty-Six

---※---

Hours seeped by as they pounded on the door, searching and shouting and holding back tears. Kel had no idea if it was day, night, or if perhaps she'd already died. Being locked in a cell with her team was a strange mix of purgatory and paradise.

Is Savita still alive? Has Cristo already succeeded?

Questions tumbled through her mind in dizzying circles.

'You should rest, Kel,' Bekn said gently.

Kel ignored him, pacing the square room, her knees cracking as she walked. She felt a strange, warm trickle above her lips. When she wiped her nose, her fingers came away with dark blood.

Shit.

Kel quickly ducked her head and wiped away the rest of the nosebleed, thanking the Alchemists that the others hadn't seen. She took another step, and the pain in her injured hip flared, forcing her to stumble against the wall. Coup was at her side in an instant.

'You okay?' he breathed.

Kel paused.

Without the sudden pain, the idea might not have come to her. It wasn't the most foolproof plan, but it was the only one she had.

Kel shifted so her back was to the door. Then, she whispered her plan into her team's ears.

A minute later, Dira, Coup and Bekn nodded.

Kel didn't know if anyone was watching through the cell's camera. But if they were, Kel was about to see just how sincere Cristo's pity was.

She shuffled around the room for several minutes, letting her steps grow heavy. Her shoulders sagged and she ran a hand across her forehead, as if wiping sweat. One more step – and she let herself tumble to the ground.

Kel landed on her knees. She bit her lip to hide a groan of pain and squeezed her eyes shut. Flopping gracelessly to the floor, her legs were crooked and her arms propped at awkward angles.

Bekn screamed, the raw sound echoing around the room. Coup hurried to her side, and Dira shouted, 'Help! Someone, help!'

Seconds later – sooner than she'd expected – the door creaked open. Kel held her breath as footsteps – more than one person – hurried closer.

'What's happened?' a voice demanded.

Coup's breath came out in ragged pants. She felt his weight hovering over her. 'I don't know – she just collapsed! She needs to see a doctor!'

A pause, and then another voice said, 'We're not to move Ms Varra until Mr Cristo gives us further instructions.'

Dira swore, though she somehow made the filthy word sound like a plea. 'You're meant to take her to the hospital, right? Move her now! She has AB. Do you really think Cristo would want you to let her *die in here?*'

'If Cristo thinks any part of what he's doing is legal, that's going to end if he denies a child medical care,' Bekn spat.

Another long, heavy pause. Kel tried to slow her breath, to soften the rise and fall of her chest. Splayed hair covered her face; she dared to peek through one eye. Two pairs of black boots were planted in Coup's long shadow.

'*Please*,' Coup begged. 'Just take her to a hospital. Any doctor. Just – help her.'

Eventually, one of the guards mumbled, 'Cristo did tell us she has

AB. He wouldn't want a kid's death on his conscience.'

'Lucian, grab her feet,' the first guard said, sighing.

Footsteps echoed around the room. She heard Coup shift further away. Kel opened both eyes.

Just as hands wrapped around her ankles, the Howlers lurched into motion.

Hair still blurring her vision, Kel launched at the guard bent at her feet. He looked up at her with bright, wide eyes that Kel gouged her fingernails into.

Lucian screeched, the kind of sound she'd only heard from phoenixes. Blood streamed down her fingers as she dug deeper. When Lucian tried to shove her away, Kel danced back.

The man covered his face with his hands, stumbling back – right where Coup stood. He wrapped his arms around Lucian's sides, pinning his arms. The guard flailed, kicking wildly, and Kel hurried forward, landing a kick to his midsection, as high as she could manage in her snug trousers. The lead in her bones kept the blow from landing evenly, but it still winded him.

Kel risked a glance across the cell. Bekn had straddled the other guard, while Dira crouched around his head, shoving his face into the hard ground.

Lucian screamed. Though he had a strong, stocky build, he wasn't able to break free of Coup's steady grip.

Kel took a heavy step towards the cell's open door. 'Come on! Let them go – we just need to lock the cell behind—'

A tall shadow glided through the door before she could reach it. A muscled woman with dark eyes locked Kel in place, arms raised. A sleek, silver rifle aimed high.

A sancter rifle.

The weapon that practically shot lightning, far too lethal to point at anything but a phoenix or the sky.

Kel's stomach filled with dread. They were so close. *No no no—*

'Kelyn,' Coup panted. 'What's wrong—'

'Hands up,' the guard grunted, aiming her weapon straight at Kel's head. 'All of you. Now.'

The room quietened. Slowly, Bekn and Dira rose, their arms raised.

The guard shifted her sancter to face Coup, who was still grappling with Lucian. 'You too. Let him go.'

Slowly, reluctantly, Coup released Lucian. The seven of them stood motionless, watching each other.

Kel's entire body tensed. Cold shivers wracking her spine.

The guard with the sancter tilted her head, indicating back out the door. 'Lucian, Pike, get out of here. Cristo wants—'

She never finished her sentence. Instead, a loud *clang* rang through the room, and the guard stumbled forward to her knees. The sancter rifle clattered along the ground and Kel winced, half-expecting lightning to fill the room. Coup dashed forward a moment before Lucian did, grabbing the dropped weapon.

The woman fell motionless to the floor, and someone stepped around her. Coup raised the sancter as a lean figure entered the cell.

Chest heaving, Rahn lowered the wooden bat clutched in her hands.

'Come on,' she said. 'We don't have much time.'

Chapter Forty-Seven

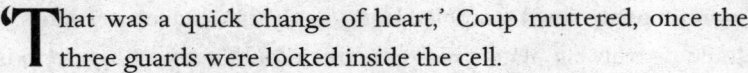

'That was a quick change of heart,' Coup muttered, once the three guards were locked inside the cell.

Kel stuttered an agreement. But they didn't have time to question motives – not when Savita was caught so keenly in Cristo's grip.

Rahn glanced between Kel, Coup and Bekn, before looking at Dira. There was an unfamiliar hardness to her features.

'We need to move,' she urged.

Kel glanced down the pearly hall, wary of taking her eyes off Rahn. The corridor was empty, but she imagined others might soon stumble across the unguarded cell.

Dira shifted forward. 'Tell us why, first.'

Rahn swallowed. 'I thought I was doing the right thing. But seeing you locked down here . . .' Her gaze flickered to Dira, then Kel. 'I couldn't just leave you.'

Rahn shook her head. 'I don't know what's right – killing phoenixes or letting people die. I trust you, and I trust Cristo. But I've made a decision, and that's the end of it.'

She stared at them. Willing them to challenge her.

No one said a word.

Rahn flipped the bat in her hand. 'I know how Cristo plans to induce Savita's rebirth. If you want to stop it, we don't have much time.'

'How?' Kel demanded.

Rahn glanced back down the hall. 'Savita is one heat fluctuation away from a rebirth. The only thing that gets her excited enough to heat up is racing.'

Bekn frowned. 'That makes no sense. Cristo's going to put her in another race? He won't be able to control the environment.'

Rahn's throat bobbed again. 'He can if she stays in the compound. In a prism.'

An image flashed in Kel's mind, so lucid it felt like a dream. The gigantic prism she'd stumbled upon in Cristo's hidden corridors – could he truly simulate a race in there? Would it be enough to fool Savita into causing an inferno?

Dira ran her hands over her face. She reached out, snatching the bat from Rahn, clearly not trusting the technician with a weapon.

Rahn bit her lip. 'Cristo changed my future. He gave me everything. He made it seem like phoenixes were these pests that needed to be controlled. I didn't question him. Not until I started competing with the Howlers.'

Kel rubbed her arms, goosebumps pricking her skin. Savita flashed through her mind. Flaming, shrieking, collared. Was Kel really any better?

'You don't have to trust me,' Rahn blustered. 'But if you want to save Savita, we have to move. Now. I have a plan.'

Kel didn't trust Rahn. She doubted any of her friends did, now. But Kel didn't have the luxury of time to hold grudges.

Silently, Rahn turned and began jogging down the white, labyrinthine hall. One by one, the other Howlers started trailing her.

They ran through a set of doors and down another empty corridor. Kel focused on the sound of her breathing, refusing to voice her pain. Savita was all that mattered.

After a few minutes, Rahn skidded to a halt.

They all tried to silence their heavy breathing as footsteps pounded ahead. They huddled in a small corridor alcove as two figures marched past, their hushed whispers echoing through the silence. Once they moved out of sight, Rahn tugged the Howlers back into the hall. They passed a window, looking out into an open sky. Evening shadows streamed through the corridor windows. Kel couldn't believe that she'd lost an entire day in that damn cell. *Savita* had lost so much time.

Was Sav already dead?

Kel shook her head, refusing to let the thought linger. Instead, she watched Rahn ahead of her.

'Where are we going?' Coup asked, after they'd hidden once more from stray workers.

Rahn urged them to the left. 'Cristo has his makeshift track guarded by about half his staff. We can't get to Savita unless we can move those workers somewhere else.'

'How do you plan to do that?' Kel panted. *Alchemists*, she was tired.

'With a distraction,' Rahn said, smiling wryly.

With fatigue blurring her vision, Kel hadn't realized where Rahn had led them. They'd taken a much longer, more intricate route to avoid other workers, but even still, Kel should have recognized their surroundings. She'd walked here hundreds of times over the past months.

Behind a panel of glass, Kel could see familiar rhythms of red, orange and yellow. Four phoenixes were shifting about inside. She recognized each of them.

'Where's the other phoenix – Lynx?' Kel asked. 'There's usually another in this enclosure.' She'd worked closely with two in particular – Gaia and Lynx, both carnel phoenixes. She'd spent countless mornings earning their trust and testing their behaviours and patterns. All for Cristo.

Rahn's lips pursed. 'Cristo's taken about half a dozen phoenixes to the track to help simulate the race. Just enough to convince Savita it's real.'

Kel's stomach dropped through the ground.

As Rahn went to swipe her security pass through the gate, Kel reached out to stop her. 'Cristo will know we're here.'

Rahn paused. She glanced down at her watch, then shook her head. 'I disabled the security cameras.'

The other four Howlers exchanged frowns.

'What's going on?' Kel demanded. She took in the surrounding halls. 'Where is everyone?'

There were always bodies milling about in this section of the building. Yet, aside from the scant workers they'd passed, this section of Cristo's anthill was empty.

Rahn ignored her. 'We need to free as many phoenixes as possible to cause a large enough distraction. Hopefully, the others can help the phoenixes ultimately escape the building, but we need to try to open as many aviaries as we can.'

Coup raised a brow. 'The *others*?'

'I believe she means us,' a voice called.

Kel spun around. The familiarity of the woman behind her – navy eyes, weathered skin and dark hair – was quickly buried beneath the memory of flames licking at Kel's sides, a phantom knife stabbing into her hip.

Bryna's lips quirked up. 'It's good to see you again. I'm glad you changed your mind.'

Chapter Forty-Eight

'What the hell is going on?' Kel barked.

Bryna lifted her arms in a seemingly peaceful gesture, though she held a sancter rifle in one hand.

'Who's this?' Coup asked, frowning. 'And why does she have a *sancter rifle?*'

'I met this one' – Bryna pointed to Kel – 'during her jaunt in Vohre Forest. I made her a proposition, and I'm so pleased that someone else on her team was smart enough to take me up on it.'

Confusion barrelled through Kel. How did Rahn know Bryna? Behind Bryna, figures stirred in the shadows. People were patrolling the hall, dressed in black leathers that were almost identical to Cristo uniforms.

'She's a leader in the Fume. She almost killed me,' Kel sneered.

Bryna *tsked* and waggled a finger. 'I did no such thing. I just offered you the chance to prove your intentions, and your friend here has done just that.'

Bryna looked to Rahn, who was fidgeting, her face white. 'We only have three more aviaries to secure. Cristo's other guards are tied up out of sight. The keys you gave us let us into the security offices. We waited until their scheduled breaks and overpowered them easily enough. Just like you said.'

Rahn nodded. 'Someone will discover the breach by the next change-of-shift in half an hour. If you have a way to communicate that to your team, make sure they know. Though hopefully we'll be out of here by then.'

Kel threw her hands up. 'What the *hell*, Rahn?'

Rahn swallowed, the confidence draining from her face. 'I–I'd never heard of Bryna before. I didn't know there was a group of them hiding in Vohre Forest. But I knew enough about the Fume to convince them to get here. Because of my mum – they've been trying to convince me to spy on Canen for them for years.'

The venom in Rahn's voice was so alien. Even Dira's eyes widened in shock.

Rahn turned to Kel. 'The leather bracelet I gave you for the last race didn't just record your location – it recorded all audio. The signal was weak and the data didn't come through for a few days, but . . . I listened to everything that happened in the forest. So I snuck out to retrieve the device. And have a word with the Fume.'

The Howlers gaped at her.

'I knew they'd listen to me if I gave them my surname,' Rahn continued. 'So, I took one of Cristo's fastest armoured bikes and found some of the Fume near where Kel dropped the bracelet.'

She said the words so simply, as if venturing into Vohre Forest, alone, was as simple as a stroll through the city.

After a pause, Rahn added, 'I went to speak with Estra in the hospital this morning. But . . . she's unconscious. She's alive – but I couldn't wake her. I – I think it's too late for her. So I did the only other thing I could.'

Guilt fluttered in Kel's stomach. None of them had time to waste on indecision – but Rahn's entire world had been forced upside down. Even Dira's eyes softened.

Coup, on the other hand, folded his arms. 'You've got to be kidding. You invited a Fume leader into Cristo Industries?'

Bryna *tsked* again. 'Not just a Fume leader, boy. As much of the Fume as I could gather at such short notice.'

'It still might not be enough. He'll have an army protecting the race hall and plenty more sancter rifles than I could steal for you. But this was the only way I could get us back-up in time,' Rahn said, glancing down at her watch again. 'We're out of options.'

Bryna sighed. 'I don't trust you and you don't trust me, but for now, the enemy of my enemy is better than trust. We're here to take down Cristo Industries. Whatever comes next – well, we'll figure that out once these phoenixes are safe.'

Reluctantly, Kel nodded. On that, at least, they could agree.

Bryna paused. Then, in one jerky motion, she extended her sancter to Kel. 'You look as if you're about to collapse. You need this more than I do.'

Adrenaline sparked as Kel wrapped her hand around the cold grip of the sancter. She could feel a gentle crackle of electricity beneath the metal.

Bryna nodded, then glanced back. 'The aviaries are open, but Cristo has his phoenixes well trained. If we want a distraction, we're going to have to force them from their cages.'

'Get a water bottle and spray them a couple times,' Kel said, pointing the sancter to the ground in as loose a grip as possible. 'They'll flee their cages faster than if you'd shown them a rare steak.'

'I'll grab us some water guns and divide up the aviaries with Bryna,' Rahn cut in. She turned to Kel. 'You need to get to Sav.'

Kel's pulse quickened. 'Where are you going to find water guns?'

Rahn eyed her carefully. 'The top floor, with the pool. We used them a month ago, when we went for a midnight swim. With Estra.'

Kel's response lodged in her throat.

As Bryna fled down an empty hall, the Howlers divided into two groups. Kel forced Dira to accompany Rahn to the remaining aviaries. Whatever tension was brewing in Dira, the winger and technician still worked the best together.

Bekn, Coup and Kel started towards the diamond hall imprisoning

Sav. They snuck through shadows and huddled in dark corners when guards strode past. Other figures in black leathers loped down nearby halls, and Kel hated the confidence with which the Fume moved, as if relishing the growing chaos.

It became clear when Dira and Rahn had succeeded in their own mission. The screeching of freed phoenixes began thundering across the building. Kel heard wood splintering and metal crashing, sending vibrations through the floor.

A smile curved her lips – and quickly vanished, as they tiptoed around the corner to the hospital wing.

They were heading towards the eastern end of Cristo's buildings – she should have known they'd pass the hospital. There was no receptionist in sight; the room was empty of all but the distant cries of phoenixes stalking the halls.

Bekn stopped. When Kel and Coup looked back, his eyes darted to the hospital doors, behind the receptionist's desk.

'You could wait in there,' Bekn whispered, pleading. He turned to Kel. 'You could help us by staying safe.'

Coup reached for Kel's hand and shook his head. 'She can't – not here. Estra's in there. Kel's spent the last week in the same infirmary as another AB patient. It's probably why her symptoms are so obvious.'

Though Coup's tone was gentle, his words ground at her like sandpaper. No one had known Kel had AB, and so they hadn't questioned placing her in the same infirmary as Estra.

Despite the number of heartbeats she had left, despite her desperation to free Savita, Kel couldn't stop her feet. She glided towards the hospital doors in a trance. Neither Bekn nor Coup stopped her as she pushed open the doors and took in the empty rows of beds.

Empty – except one.

At the far end of the hall, shrouded by shadows and machinery, lay the girl Kel had passed the last time she'd been here, with black hair and an aura of familiarity as palpable as the sweat coating her skin. The green, hand-stitched blanket still swathed her, with the same flowery initials Kel had seen sewn into Bekn's apron: *E.C.*

Though her eyes were closed, Kel knew that if she opened them, her irises would be near-black and speckled with brown. The same ones – so like Cristo's – that had haunted her dreams.

'Estra,' Kel whispered.

The girl – *Estra* – was little more than a thin layer of skin stretched over jutting bones. Her breathing was a low rasp, her fingers twitching against her blanket. From the inner corner of her right eye, a drop of dark blood trailed down her cheek.

Kel leaned forwards. Gently, she reached down and wiped away the blood. The scent of lilies flooded her nostrils.

Memories flashed through Kel's mind. The dark-haired girl who had eaten with them their first day here. The extra plate Bekn had laid out for pancakes. The movies she'd seen scattered across their couch – for a *movie night*. The child's drawing in Cristo's office. Rahn calling Cristo a dorky dad. The figure she hadn't recognized during their first day training in Cristo's compound. The girl Cristo had been chatting with at the race with sprites.

This was Cristo's daughter. But Kel still had no memories of Estra's face, no threads she could tug on to reveal the missing fragments of her memories.

There was nothing. Just the knowledge that her friends had diagnosed her correctly.

Estra and Kel both had AB, and both would die.

'Do you recognize her?' Coup asked, moving forward to squeeze her hand.

Kel swallowed. Her breathing slowed to match the slow *beep, beep* of the machine monitoring Estra's pulse.

'No.'

Another inhuman shriek echoed across the walls, rattling Estra's bed.

Before Coup could respond, Bekn urged, 'If you're not staying, then we need to move.'

Slowly, Kel turned back to her friends and nodded. 'Let's go.'

Kel lingered, letting Coup and Bekn move ahead as they left the hospital. She wiped more blood from her nose.

A moment later, an alarm screamed.

The world flashed red, stealing the shadows they clung to. Kel tried not to wince at the jarring noise as they sprinted towards the diamond hall. Squawks and distant screams smothered her short breath. Kel struggled to keep pace with Coup and Bekn, gritting her teeth through pain and panting directions. The lead in her bones had returned, anchored to something below the ground. Her body begged to lie down against the cool floor.

It was only the thought of Savita – flames shrouding her as she neared death – that kept her moving.

The alarm began battling other echoes: phoenix screeches, shattering glass, stampeding feet – likely Cristo's guards investigating the noise. Kel's knees almost buckled with every near-encounter, relieved she didn't have to attempt to aim the sancter. She tried to focus on that relief – on anything but the brittle fear making her flinch with every new sound.

Where was Cristo? Had Bryna brought enough people to defeat Cristo's numbers? Was the race already over? Was Savita . . . ?

Kel couldn't bring herself to finish the thought.

Ahead of her, Bekn and Coup skidded to a halt as the door to the diamond hall came into view. Or, at least, where it should have come into view. Kel couldn't see the white door, or even the walls beside it.

Kel yanked Coup and Bekn around a corner, out of sight.

The sound of freed phoenixes and the compound's alarm had hidden what lay ahead. Chaos consumed the entire hall. Cristo's guards tangled with the Fume in a web so intricate that Kel couldn't tell black uniforms from black leathers. White lightning shot from sancter rifles, ricocheting around the hall and striking people through with electrical burns that made Coup's CAPR injuries look mild. She didn't dare fire her own rifle for fear of hitting the wrong person.

'*Ashes*,' Bekn cursed.

Kel's brain was whirling in a hundred directions, trying to spark the smallest flint of an idea, when a hand touched her arm.

She spun around and lifted the sancter, expecting to see one of Cristo's guards. Instead, Dira and Rahn stared at her.

'Put that thing away before I hit you over the head with it,' Dira whispered, the smallest smile on her lips.

Kel lowered the sancter. 'Did you have any trouble?'

'There was one guard hiding in the aviary, but we managed to tie him up,' Rahn replied.

Dira glanced around the corner. 'How are we meant to get through that?'

There must have been hundreds of people streaming past; Kel couldn't believe that so many cultists had managed to congregate in Vohre in mere hours, all by Rahn's command. There was no way to tell which team would have the most people left standing.

The thought made Kel queasy.

She took a deep breath, and turned to Rahn. 'Do you think he's started the race yet?'

'I'm sorry, Kel,' Rahn answered, fidgeting. 'I don't know.'

Kel didn't have time to stew on the unknown. She peeked below

Bekn's arms. The screams and lightning shots had shifted, ever so slightly, towards the other end of the hall. They still blocked the door – but there was as clear a path as they'd get.

'The fight's shifted. We can get to Sav,' Kel urged, voice weak as she pointed down the hall. 'If she just *sees* me, she'll know something's wrong.'

Coup squeezed Kel's hand. 'You're not getting yourself killed.'

Dira nodded. 'It's safer if we wait until the fight's finished.'

Rahn, surprisingly, shook her head. 'No – Kel's right. The Fume might have the numbers, but they're not trained. Cristo's guards might still win. If his people are distracted, this might be our only chance to get to Savita before . . . the race is over.'

Coup's lips tightened. 'And how are we going to open the door? It's locked – and I can't imagine one of his guards will let us in.'

Rahn reached into her trouser pocket. She pulled out a small, white card. 'We don't need him. I have a copy of his skeleton key.'

Coup let out a breathless laugh. 'How did you manage that?'

'He gave it to me ages ago. He trusts me.'

Guilt clawed in Kel's stomach. She half-turned to her teammates. 'You don't – I can try to sneak in on my own and get Savita. None of you have to—'

'Oh, shut up,' Dira snorted. The others quickly echoed her words.

Kel smiled weakly. No matter how slim, she refused to waste this chance.

Staying low, the Howlers dashed towards the lightning.

Kel had been right – Cristo's security was moving down another corridor, their backs facing her. Bodies littered the floor, a barrier between the live soldiers and the Howlers. Red blossomed across battered corpses. Kel would have armed their allies with enough sancters to light up the sky, if it meant saving Savita – but she still felt heavy, seeing so many broken people strewn across the floor.

Staying low, Rahn and Kel stepped over bodies and picked their way towards the hall's door. Sensing Coup at their backs, Kel spun around.

Offering him the sancter, she said, 'I can't hold it steady.'

Coup took the rifle without a word. He moved to her right as the three of them edged forward, Dira and Bekn watching their backs. The walls were too thick to hear anything from within the hall – but Kel could imagine Sav shrieking, calling to her.

One of Cristo's guards turned around, and the five Howlers skidded to a stop. Coup fired the sancter, sending waves of brilliant, charged air towards the uniformed woman. Her rifle fired at the roof as she stumbled back.

They were mere breaths from the diamond hall's entrance when two more guards happened to turn their way. Coup fired off quick rounds of blinding electricity at one of the guards, but the other already had their sancter raised.

Straight at Rahn.

With Coup distracted, the Howlers had no weapon to fire with. The narrow-eyed guard cocked his rifle, and Kel bent down, ready to push Rahn to the ground—

Just as Dira leapt through the air and struck the man across the head with her bat.

The guard fell into another of his comrades, and Dira made quick work of them, too. She then moved back to her position behind the group. As if nothing had happened. As if she still couldn't bear the sight of Rahn.

Kel had always known her best friend was bred for Cendor, and now she knew she didn't need to worry about the Howlers' future. From an army or each other, they could protect themselves.

As they reached the entrance, Rahn scrambled for the security card in her pocket.

Kel half-expected nothing to happen. Cristo was too smart. He couldn't possibly trust Rahn enough to—

A light flashed green overhead, and the door clicked open.

Chapter Forty-Nine

❋

The Howlers stumbled forwards and slammed the door behind them, dulling the screams and rifle fire behind them. Whatever chaos continued to brew in the hall was nothing compared to what lay ahead.

Fire of every hue spiralled around the great room. Light reflected off the clear, fractured walls, blinding Kel from a thousand directions. Heat shook the air.

Sweat pooled down Kel's back as she inched forward. She peered through the pulsing heat, resisting the urge to clamp her hands over her ears to block the deafening screeches bouncing off the diamond. Her sweater was too thin, her feet bare against the uneven ground. Even if she reached Savita, without her gloves or leathers, what could she do?

Phoenixes raced around the hall in clustered infernos. Their fiery wings transformed the room into a flaming cathedral, the diamond turning to a glass mural of reds, oranges, yellows, browns. To Kel's left, a panel of tinted glass resembling a mirror shimmered with the growing heat. The darkened panel rose to half the ceiling's height, the only piece of the room not coated in twinkling diamond.

Kel edged further into the hall as phoenixes soared in narrow circles above her. Every step forward made her skin prick, reawakening the pain in her hip. She tried to peer through the heat, desperately searching for Savita, but it was near-impossible to make out one ball of flames from another. She could tell that none wore saddles, though bands of silver collars glinted through each flaming cloud.

There was something strange about the rhythmic pattern. Even when they'd been trained to race, phoenixes were difficult to control. In such a contained environment, these phoenixes should have been lashing at one another, flying in all directions. Not racing along the faint, melting lines along the ground. Was Cristo controlling how they moved? Had he made the phoenixes train in this hall, for this moment? How many times had he stolen Savita from her aviary to teach her how to die?

Coup placed a warning hand on Kel's arm, but she kept moving. Sweat poured down her forehead, evaporating almost as fast. Wind battered her skin, drying her mouth. She blinked, trying to see through the growing smoke and shimmering heat and – *there!*

There she was.

Copper talons glinting, feathers and flames as deep as blood in some places and pale as sunrise in others. Two onyx eyes locked straight ahead, as hungry and determined as any god.

Kel cupped her hands around her mouth and screamed, '*Savita!*'

If the phoenix heard Kel, she ignored the scream. Savita was too busy fighting for space amidst two other flaming beasts, her feathers turning more molten with every second.

'Which one is Sav?' Coup asked, moving to Kel's side.

Kel pointed, trying to follow Sav's path beneath the ceiling. 'She's in between those other two,' she shouted hoarsely.

Rahn shifted to Kel's other side. 'Even if she heard us calling her, I'm sure Cristo has a new collar on her to keep her racing. He'll be guiding her wings. She won't be able to stop.'

'We need to get out before the heat gets too much,' Bekn barked, nearest to the door. 'Maybe we can find Cristo and force him to stop this. But we can't do anything from in here.'

Kel followed Rahn's hazel gaze to the tinted window. It looked like the same tinted, thickened glass that she'd found in Cristo's lab, preserving the flaming phoenix ashes.

'He's there,' Rahn breathed, almost too faint to hear over the roaring blaze. 'Behind the window. Controlling the phoenix collars from where he can watch. I know it.'

'What?' Dira shouted. 'He's on the other side of the window?'

Rahn nodded, slowly, distractedly. 'There's an adjoining room behind the window, but the door to it is across the other side of the building. It'll take us too long to get in.'

Before any of them could question the strange pain cutting through Rahn's words, Rahn pivoted to her right, towards Dira. The winger frowned, though her brow quickly smoothed as Rahn pulled her into a swift kiss.

Dira froze, dropping her bat. For just one, short moment, the winger and the technician clutched each other in a knotted embrace, straining their arms, until Rahn forced them apart.

She glanced at each of them, her eyes dark, pleading.

And then the newest Howler lunged towards the track's fracturing flames, into the path of six burning phoenixes.

Dira screamed, a wordless, gut-wrenching wail, as the firebirds barrelled towards Rahn. Horror and confusion collided inside Kel. She would never reach her in time—

Flames. Kel was the only Howler meant to die.

Chapter Fifty

---※---

As if colliding with an invisible wall, the phoenixes froze, mere feet from Rahn. Their heat should have caused her to shrink back, but she stood still, a fragile statue beneath six blazing gods.

The phoenixes twitched, hovering in mid-air momentarily before their wings relaxed and they lowered to the rough floor. The birds let out confused grumbles. Kel spotted Savita at the centre of the small horde, onyx eyes bloodthirsty, ready to win this race. Whether it was because of Cristo's new collar or her nearing rebirth, Sav blazed wilder than Kel had ever seen.

Slowly, Rahn turned to face the tinted window. The phoenixes' screams calmed, and their heat cooled to blurred feathers. Only Rahn's voice echoed around the hall, commanding the silence. 'Estra wouldn't want this. It's *too late*, Canen.'

Understanding finally rushed through Kel, and she almost sagged to the broken floor. Whatever she and the others thought of Cristo, it was clear that Rahn believed he'd never hurt her. And she was right; he'd paused the entire race to save her life.

A sharp, static noise blared through the hall. Through a speaker that Kel couldn't see, a low voice commanded, 'Move, Rahn.'

'No,' Rahn shouted. 'So, either let them kill me, or give up.'

Kel moved across the floor, the other Howlers at her side. The phoenixes tried to snap and claw at them, though their collars seemed to hold them taut. Even Savita, with anxious, confused flames shrouding her, watched them hungrily. Kel couldn't see the invisible, electric restraints curbing their movements, but she could almost hear them. It was a steady murmur in the air, like insect wings or a distant crowd.

'Estra means something to all of us,' Bekn called, stepping forward. 'But this isn't the way to save her.'

The speaker crackled before Cristo replied, *'Move.'*

The phoenixes fought harder against their collars. Flames thrashed about and Lynx lashed out at the smaller phoenix to his left. Cristo allowed them to fan out across the painted track line, just enough for Savita to spread her wings without colliding into other feathers.

Kel moved without thinking. Though her legs felt heavy, she sprinted towards Sav, weaving between open beaks and wincing at the overbearing heat. She heard someone shout at her back, but she couldn't make out the words through the growing, crackling flames.

Pressed between writhing flames and nipping beaks, Kel stopped, ignoring the heat biting her skin. A sob slipped from her throat.

Savita.

She could still hear Rahn and Cristo arguing, both voices growing frenzied, but she ignored them. Savita's head craned towards Kel. The phoenix's neck was circled by a darker, thicker collar than usual. The flames around Savita's head had pulled back, ever so slightly, though heat still bit into the air, hotter than Kel had ever felt.

Kel didn't care if she turned to ash. With no leathers, for the first time ever, Kel reached a hand forward.

As she neared Savita, the heat turned to pain. Searing needles stabbed into her palm, as if peeling back her skin and branding her bones. Grinding her teeth, she pressed forward another step.

Then, the pain shifted to a sharp numbness, the kind of scalding heat that felt like ice. Kel bit down on a whimper. She leaned forward as the heat turned to something more tangible, pressing back against her hand as firmly as any brick wall. She kept moving forward towards Savita. Black stars danced across her vision.

Just as the heat turned unbearable, just as she thought it might consume her, Savita closed the remaining distance between them.

Tears carved trails down Kel's cheeks. Her fingers pressed against the yellow feathers above Sav's beak. They felt exactly as she thought they would – like velvet sunlight. The heat remained, but the pain ebbed, a shadow beneath the sun. Kel's skin reddened, but it didn't burn away. She wondered if the diseased fire in her veins now matched Savita's.

'I said I'd get you out,' Kel murmured to her firebird. 'I keep my promises.'

Savita blinked and pushed against Kel's hand. The heat soothed her like a balm.

She didn't know why Sav had let her fall. She didn't know what *she* meant to the phoenix. But she knew Savita deserved better than Cristo – or even Kel – deciding her fate.

This close, Kel could make out more of Sav's shape. Ash-black feathers were scattered beneath outstretched wings. The feathers along her wings' edges were darker, too, as if dipped in ink.

She hadn't seen her phoenix since her fall in Vohre Forest. Since Sav had *let* her fall. But Savita's heat consumed the pain of the memory. As Kel touched Savita's feathers for the first time, she felt invincible. Just for a moment, she felt as immortal as Savita herself.

She took a closer look at Sav's new collar. Though sturdier-looking than her old collar, the edges were soft, uneven. She stared, just for a moment, unsure what she was seeing – until she spotted two red wires poking out of the top of the collar, frayed and melting.

Her breath hitched. Blue sparks flared beneath the collar, almost hidden by Savita's own fire. Her phoenix was *so close* to a rebirth – Sav's very heat had begun to melt Cristo's controls.

Was this normal? Or was it because Cristo's collar hadn't

been tested? Kel didn't know – she thought she'd have more time to research rebirths. But the dark veins along Sav's wings were spreading before Kel's eyes. Savita barely had minutes before she'd combust.

Coup appeared at Kel's right, and Savita swivelled towards him. He raised a gloved hand, as if to touch her, though kept a few feet away.

'How are you so close to her?' Coup asked Kel. 'I've never felt this kind of heat.'

'I don't know,' Kel whispered.

She glanced over at the others. Rahn was still shouting, trying to reason with the tinted mirror. Cristo spoke back, though Kel couldn't make out his words as Savita grumbled above her head. The other phoenixes were growing more agitated, wings spreading and necks craning. As if preparing to take flight again.

Kel whipped around. Rahn was still firmly planted at the centre of the diamond track. If Cristo resumed the race – if Estra's life was worth more to him than Rahn's – none of them would survive much longer.

Kel tried to lure Sav off the painted track.

'Come on,' Kel pleaded, when Sav resisted. 'For Alchemists' sake. It's not a real race. We need to get you out of here.'

'We can't take her through the door,' Coup whispered in Kel's ear, daring a step closer, as if Cristo might hear them breathe. 'The sancters will take her out in a heartbeat.'

Sweat dripped down Kel's arms. 'We need to do *something*,' she hissed. 'Look at the other phoenixes – they're preparing to get airborne.'

Coup glanced over at the other phoenixes. Some were bending their legs, others ruffling their wings. Ready to begin racing anew.

There were no other doors, no other windows. But they hadn't come this far just to let the flames devour them.

Kel managed to encourage Sav a few steps from the other phoenixes as she heard Cristo bellow, 'Enough, Rahn! I won't kill my own daughter.'

Hairs pricked along Kel's neck. Cristo's voice rose with clear, rabid desperation.

She saw Dira and Bekn exchange looks, Rahn firmly planted between them. Unmoving.

They couldn't wait in here forever. Even if the race was stopped, Savita *would* rebirth, soon. Kel could feel it in the heat rolling off Savita in erratic waves, like tiny fireworks seeping into the air. Cristo had already half-succeeded.

She and Coup tried to lure Sav further from the other phoenixes with little success. Bekn and Dira shifted towards them, as if to help, and Cristo's voice rang out again through the overhead speakers.

'*Move*, or I'll make you,' he roared.

Rahn remained motionless.

Kel's knees wobbled. The phoenixes behind Sav grew more agitated, gaining more momentum. A larger phoenix lashed out at the smaller spinel phoenix to its left. Its beak came away dripping with crimson.

'Rahn!' Kel called, her throat cracking.

Rahn either didn't hear or didn't acknowledge Kel. Kel didn't know what she would have said, anyway. Rahn was the only thing keeping Cristo from restarting the race. But the fear making Cristo's words sharp and clipped hitched Kel's breath.

From her position, Rahn couldn't see the phoenixes beginning to stir.

Blue sparks leapt from Sav's collar. The phoenix's head jerked up. Sav shook her head, as if fighting some invisible force.

'I'm sorry, Rahn,' Cristo cried.

Dira turned back to Rahn, arm outstretched, gaze darting between Sav and the technician. 'Rahn, I think you should—'

A symphony of unholy, agonized shrieks filled the air.

Five phoenixes – all but Savita – were yanked off the ground, wings thrust up in stiff, controlled movements. They catapulted forwards, down the hall, along the track.

Towards Rahn.

Dira screamed and lunged for the technician. Rahn lurched to the right, towards Dira. But neither was fast enough.

A hurricane of claws and stiff wings collided with Rahn; the phoenix furthest to the right caught her with a sharp slice.

The familiar, acrid smell of burnt flesh filled the hall. The world began spinning too fast. Rahn fell to the ground as the five phoenixes shot past. Her skin bubbled and bled as Dira bolted to her side. Savita screamed and more sparks flew from her collar, melting and charring around her neck. Kel's phoenix thrashed her head, fighting Cristo's burnt circuitry.

Bekn, Coup and Kel helped Dira lift Rahn further from the track, as gently as possible. Dira threw off her jacket and covered Rahn's slashed shoulder, thick, open marks torn through flesh and muscle. The technician was lucky only her shoulder had been caught – but the right side of her face, neck and torso had been burnt away, reminding Kel so clearly of Coup's burns in his last race. Too much blood pooled around her head.

Rahn whimpered as Dira cradled her. Kel felt hot tears trail down her cheeks.

'We need to get her out of here,' Dira sobbed. 'Maybe the Fume hasn't hit Cristo's medical wing yet?'

'They hadn't when we ran past,' Bekn managed, voice low. 'I don't know if there's anyone still there – but it's her best chance.'

Rahn whimpered again. Phoenixes raced along the other side

of the hall, their combined heat still not as overwhelming as Sav's. The smell of burnt electrics grew stronger. Savita spread her wings and craned her head towards the other phoenixes. Her eyes glowed, ready to claim a victory, whether or not Cristo forced her to.

If they didn't figure out a solution soon, Sav's rebirth would beat the blight to Kel's heart. It would kill them all.

Dira winced as she tried to lift Rahn from the ground. Kel glanced down to Dira's hands. They were almost as burnt and charred as the right side of Rahn's body. Dira had been too close to the phoenixes when they'd blazed past; she was lucky that only her hands had caught aflame.

'Let me,' Bekn said gently, and lifted Rahn from the ground, cradling her close. 'We'll get her out of here and regroup.'

'Savita won't have that long,' Kel whispered, doubting anyone heard her.

Bekn shifted closer, towards the door. Rahn jerked in his grip, groaning as she lashed out a hand to Kel.

She gripped Kel's sleeve with her left arm and fluttered her lashes. 'Canen wasn't meant to build a window to watch,' she croaked. 'It was . . . he didn't trust everything to go right unless he could *see it*.'

Adrenaline seeped back into Kel's bones. She glanced down at the glint of silver at Coup's hip – the rifle she'd given him. The same weapon that was used to signal the start of CAPR races.

Kel turned towards Cristo's window, and embers of an idea collided with her adrenaline. She didn't know how large the room was on the other side of the window – but it was near the edge of the building. Perhaps with another window, facing the outdoors.

She glanced between her teammates. 'Go – but I'm staying. I can get Sav out.'

'Kel,' Dira breathed.

'No,' Bekn barked, stepping towards the door. 'Whatever you're planning – you're not strong enough to fly Sav on your own. And Coup's the only one who can fly Sav if you . . .'

Bekn's cracked words broke Kel's heart. In the months she'd known the mitigator, she'd only seen glimpses of what lay beneath the stoic surface. But the glimpses she had seen were of a boy who grieved and screamed and wanted as much as the rest of them. He might not be filled with Dira's steel or Coup's wildness – but he could protect himself as well as any of the Howlers.

Instead of replying, Kel turned to her best friend. Dira folded her arms and clenched her fists, loose curls around her face, climbing flames at her back and sweat wetting her lashes. The picture-perfect Cendorian.

'The farm is yours, if you want it,' Kel said.

Dira swallowed. 'It's *ours*. I'll convince my parents to live there, with us. The four of us can take care of each other.' Dira's eyes darted to Rahn's broken body. 'Or maybe five.'

Kel nodded with a shaky smile. 'I can't wait.'

It was the most heartfelt lie Kel could muster.

Kel turned back towards Sav, placing both hands on her phoenix's side, above her wing. Raw heat bit into her palms, and she welcomed it.

'Wait – what are you doing, Varra?' Coup asked, latching on to her elbow. His voice was high, pleading, as if afraid of the answer.

'I have to get on Sav,' Kel said flatly. Every word felt heavier than the last. 'Go with the others.'

Bekn was calling to Coup, Rahn in his arms, hurrying towards the door. Yet Coup remained unmoving.

'There's no saddle – what are you meant to hold on to?' Coup shifted closer to Kel. Kel saw him grit his teeth at the heat at his back.

Savita twitched her head around the diamond prison, too many lights demanding her attention. She barely noticed – or cared – when

Kel ran her palms under her thicker layer of feathers, trying – failing – to find a hold. She bit down, straining her lead muscles.

'I'll figure it out,' Kel groaned, moving forward and failing to boost herself onto Sav's back. Savita grumbled in frustration, tail swatting at Kel's scrambling form.

Before she could stop him, Coup gripped her around the knees and lifted her up, climbing up the phoenix's wing behind her. He was careful not to grip her injured hip, but pain still lanced through her side. Her breath hitched, but she refused to make a sound.

'What are you doing?' she seethed. 'If this goes wrong – no one else needs to get hurt.'

Though Coup wore his riding leathers, she doubted they'd give him much protection.

She didn't have the strength to shove him off. If she even closed her eyes, she mightn't be able to open them again. Even blinking was becoming a gamble with fate. But she couldn't risk Coup's life as well.

'You'll fall off on your own,' he threw back, wrapping his arms around her waist. 'I can handle the heat long enough for us to get out. Just hurry up and tell me your plan.'

Cristo shouted something through the comms, but over the crackling of Savita's flames, Kel couldn't make out the words. Sweat streamed down her neck and the other phoenixes bellowed across the hall.

Beneath Kel, Savita was a growing furnace. Waves of fiery heat rose up into Kel's face. She struggled to swallow down the steaming air. The collar around Sav's neck was now barely a thin, crumbling chain.

They were out of time.

Kel swore. Then she twisted towards Coup and whispered her plan.

Coup clutched the sancter in one hand and she clenched her shaking thighs tighter around Sav. She bit down on the pain and leaned forward. With trembling fingers, she palmed the yellow feathers at the top of Sav's neck and guided the phoenix forwards, back towards the black track streaking the diamond.

Kel coaxed Savita into a crouch. She risked a glance towards the hall's door – just in time to see Bekn, Rahn and Dira sprinting through. She exhaled.

Kel forced down a deep, hot, smoky breath, and screamed, 'You wanted a race? Fine! You'll get one.'

Kel guided Savita into the air in two easy, quick feather strokes. It took almost no convincing for Savita to spread her wings and launch into the air, finally allowed to compete.

Coup tightened his hands around Kel's waist, holding her steady as she directed Sav forwards, *faster*. She gained speed quicker than Kel could have expected in a contained space. Three other phoenixes shrieked as Sav shot past, two more following seconds later.

Fire danced and swirled around the hall, crackling and filling Kel's ears. Savita pivoted, soaring along its fractured length. Flames licked the reflective walls, cascading across the diamond in a reddened waterfall. Lynx nipped at Savita's tail and another phoenix pulled to Sav's left. But whether it was because of her nearing rebirth or the ruthlessness she'd been born with, no phoenix managed to outpace Savita. She flew along the hall faster than Kel had ever seen her move, hotter than she'd ever felt. Soon enough, she'd burn Kel and Coup alive.

They lapped the hall. Despite the furnace climbing over her, despite the pain she knew Coup felt at her back, Kel spurred Savita faster. *Hotter.*

Another lap, and fire singed the damp hairs pressed against her cheeks. Another, and Kel felt as though she sat on a bed of burning coals, seeping into her blood and demanding she scream. Another lap, and Savita became too hot to touch. She felt her legs blistering and her weight tipping.

One more lap, and when Savita swooped around the hall's edge, furthest from Cristo's viewing window, Kel screamed, *'Now!'*

The sancter rang out at Kel's back. The sound needled at her ears. Lightning fractured the hall and crackled through the air. Phoenix screams mingled together, crashing against the diamond in a tangled, deafening web. Halfway down the length of the hall, towards the tinted window, Savita's wings beat a chaotic, frightened rhythm.

Coup had timed the shot well. The phoenixes were moving too fast to stop, even if Cristo tampered with their collar controls. Each of these phoenixes had participated in enough CAPR races to know what a sancter shot meant: for the next few hundred metres, their track was clear, straight.

Savita's confusion slowed her, and two larger phoenixes shifted ahead of them. Each of the six firebirds battled their own instincts. They'd been conditioned to fly straight after that sound, to use a burst of strength to climb ahead on a track. But had they been conditioned enough to collide with a window?

Even if they'd wanted to stop – the phoenixes were moving too fast. Through scorching winds, Kel risked a glance up, ahead of them, and spotted her own wide-eyed, blistering reflection. She saw their future as it collided with the glass panel, flexing beneath the heat.

Kel leaned as far forward as she could, hiding her face. Before she scrunched her eyes closed, before the world shattered around them, Kel noticed that two other phoenixes were still ahead of Savita – just a few inches.

As they collided with the wide window, Kel had never been happier to place third.

Chapter Fifty-One

❋

Hot fragments of glass glistened around them like sprites. The broken window cut a jagged river through the air and sliced thin cuts into Kel's arms. Kel gripped clumps of thicker feathers through the pain, relieved that Savita didn't seem to bear any deep cuts. The two phoenixes who had broken through first flailed in the air, confusion and rage clear in their cries. Ruptured glass rained to the ground, an electric, tinkling sound filling Kel's ears.

Kel drank in the new room, so much darker than the diamond hall. Three figures cowered on the ground, as far from the shattered window panel as possible. Kel spotted Cristo limping out of the adjoining room, blood trailing after him as he vanished into another layer of his labyrinth.

He must have been injured by the shattered glass. But Kel didn't care where he'd gone. She squeezed Coup's hands around her waist and he squeezed back. Relief shuddered down her spine as she glanced upwards – spotting a skylight. Moonlight guided their path.

Kel directed Savita towards the glass panel. With two other blazing phoenixes also in the small room, the standard glass had already half-melted by the time they reached it. There was no hesitation, no doubt in Savita's movements as she soared towards the ceiling.

Into the night sky.

As they crashed through the window, Kel refused to look back. She guided Savita into the clouds with numb fingers, staring straight ahead. She wouldn't say goodbye.

Kel would see them again. All of them.

Coup's hands tightened around Kel's waist, his chest pressed tightly to her back to keep her steady. They had no buckles to secure their legs or saddle pommel to grip on to, but Savita's feathers were sturdy enough for Kel to bunch them for grip. Kel sent Sav a silent plea, hoping that her heat wasn't as painful for Coup as it had been during his last race. The firebird rose higher and higher into the dark sky, until they floated above the facilities. Above Vohre and Cendor.

Almost automatically, Kel guided Savita south, towards Fieror, though the farm would be the first place Cristo would look for them.

Vohre Forest, Kel thought sluggishly. *We can hide out with the Fume until it's safe.*

Kel guided Sav through the stars and to the right, where—

'Look out!' Coup bellowed.

Savita screamed, almost loud enough to bury the sound of a sancter at their backs.

The phoenix jerked to the left as lightning flew past Kel's hip. Kel almost lost her grip on Sav's feathers, burning beneath her white knuckles. Sav zig-zagged through the clear sky as more electricity shot past.

Kel's anger climbed until it matched Savita's raging inferno.

Leaning into Coup's steady grip, she twisted around and squinted through the darkness, just as more lightning soared past her.

Nestled between a pair of great red-and-copper wings sat Cristo.

Chapter Fifty-Two

❈

'We have to land!' Coup screamed.

Two more sancter shots raced past them. Coup tried to shoot back at Cristo with his rifle – but without a saddle, it was too hard to balance. His shots were wild and nowhere near Cristo or his phoenix.

'If we land, he'll take Savita,' Kel shouted, gripping Sav's feathers tighter.

Desperately, Kel tried to spur Savita faster. Cristo must have had a saddled phoenix waiting for him, in case something went wrong.

'He'll shoot us if we don't!'

When more electricity raced past, Coup added in a low, pained voice, 'She's growing too hot, Kel – I can't hold on much longer.'

Nausea flooded Kel.

Cristo would rather shoot Sav – shoot *them* – than let them escape. Kel knew Sav could outpace Cristo's phoenix if she wanted to. Her rebirth was helping her to soar faster than ever before. Faster than a *god*; she'd almost entirely burnt through Cristo's collar. Kel doubted it had any controls left in it. Sav likely had no clue the collar was useless any more. But Kel could smell Coup's burning leathers and could hear the pained groans he tried to swallow.

She felt her heart break as she pressed her fingers against Savita's neck, guiding her firebird towards the ground. Towards her death.

Kel wasn't sure where they were. Perhaps somewhere just beyond Vohre's southern outskirts. She could see the distant, shadowed outline of the forest connecting Vohre to Fieror. A few miles east, she could just make out the train tracks that ran between the cities. But there was no familiarity to their surroundings. Just brown grass and cracked dirt and the kind of scorched earth that likely meant a phoenix had rebirthed here, decades – perhaps centuries – ago.

Cristo landed just a few yards away. Kel gritted her teeth against the gales beneath his phoenix's wings as she and Coup climbed off Savita, who tilted her head in confusion. Sav wanted to return to the air, probably to find somewhere safe to rebirth.

Kel placed a shaky hand against Sav's flaming wings.

'I'm sorry,' she whispered. Kel prayed that Savita understood.

In the sky, Kel hadn't been able to see more than Cristo's bobbing head. Now, she watched him limp towards them in black riding leathers. His phoenix – a large, mahogany-red creature – stayed still, tamed far beyond what phoenixes ought to be.

Cristo approached, pointing his sancter at Kel as Coup aimed his own rifle at Cristo.

'It's too late for Estra,' Kel breathed, leaning into Coup for support. 'Just let Savita go.'

There was a wild gleam in Cristo's eye. His gaze darted between Savita's charred collar and Kel. 'I wish I could. But it's not too late; if I let your phoenix go, I'm sentencing my own daughter to the grave. You can't make me do that, Kelyn.'

Cristo's voice shook. Kel caught a glimpse of the man he might have been when he began this crusade. Before he chose to slaughter phoenixes. Before his only thought was of his daughter.

'You can't even force her back to the track. She's burnt through your controls,' Kel spat.

'You don't know that Savita can heal Estra,' Coup added. 'None of your experiments have been successful.'

'You're wrong,' Cristo shouted, raising his sancter higher. 'The last phoenix that rebirthed – we managed to contain the magic of their ashes. We've kept it alive. But the longer the phoenix stays dead, the weaker the magic grows. We didn't stabilize those ashes in time to have enough magic to heal my Estra. But with Savita...' he said, as panic winked in his eyes like fading stars, '... I know it will work.'

'Warren – you won't be able to shoot me before I take down one of you. Are you willing to risk it?' He gave a slow, maniacal smile. 'I am.'

Coup's arms shook. He shifted in front of Kel, and, slowly, lowered his rifle.

'Toss it,' Cristo sneered.

Coup obeyed, cursing under his breath.

Smiling, Cristo walked forward. He picked up Coup's rifle and threw it towards his statue-like phoenix. 'I was just like you when I was young. Ambitious. Zealous. And I would have given my life for my phoenix.' He ducked his head, though something about the movement felt staged. Scripted. 'Their magic lures us in, and we hope that if they simply trust us, they might offer us a taste. But in the end, they're nothing but wild, heartless monsters.' He glanced at Savita, then Kel. 'Savita is not tame, Kelyn. Take her collar off, and she will leave you here to die.'

Kel's fingers itched at the challenge. She wanted to defy his truth, to prove that his words were nothing more than lies manufactured to suit his needs. Savita was hardly even collared any more, and she was still here, wasn't she?

But then she thought of her failed race through Vohre Forest. When she'd fallen from Savita's back, and she'd been so *sure* that Sav would catch her. She'd trusted her phoenix down to the fiery depths of her soul, and Savita had chosen to abandon her. Would Sav do the same now, if Kel removed the familiar weight of a collar?

The itching in Kel's fingers crept up her arm. Cristo's words echoed through her bones.

'You're wrong,' she breathed.

Kel didn't believe that Savita could save her. But Sav's worth didn't come from what she could offer humans. Somewhere, in the buried crevasses of her heart, Kel *knew* that Savita was a wild beast. She'd known it from the first time she'd seen the phoenix. Savita deserved to roam freely, unhindered by a collar or Kel's whims.

Savita owed Kel nothing beyond what she chose to bestow. She was the rightful god of this island, and Kel considered herself lucky that she'd known Sav at all. She'd felt a god's touch, and as long as her fiery, immortal beast was safe, she didn't care if AB took her. Her family was safe.

She might not have a phoenix's power – but she had her own. She had her father's name, and the ruthless fire that all Cendorians possessed.

Kel lifted her hand. Cristo's eyes sharpened, tracking her movements. She only had a second to act.

As fast as her leaden muscles would allow, Kel pitched towards Savita. She grappled with what remained of the collar, shrouded by blistering heat. The thinned metal fell away like clumps of charcoal.

'*No!*' she heard Cristo shout, maybe Coup too, as a sancter shot filled the air once more.

Lightning burnt through Kel's shoulder just as she heard the sharp *click* of Savita's collar. The metal fell to the ground.

A moment later, Kel did too.

'Kelyn!' Coup screamed, and then there were hands on her. Coup's face floated to the centre of her vision, surrounded by black spots. She couldn't *feel* the wound – but she could feel a strange, hot numbness spreading over her. It made her blood flare hotter.

Beside her, Kel felt Savita's heat flaring, too. Without the collar, her magic was no longer tempered. Savita's flames flickered from honey to orange to scarlet. Squinting, Kel watched Savita shine brighter than she'd ever seen. Brighter than the stars above them. *Brighter than the sun.*

Savita's light chased away the shadows that tried to pull Kel under. With Coup's hands pressed against her wound, she tried to turn her head towards her phoenix. Her beautiful, immortal, merciless phoenix.

Two more sancter shots echoed through the sky, but Savita was faster. If Cristo wanted her dead rather than free, he'd lost his chance. Faster than she'd ever seen Savita move, the firebird launched into the sky. She was no longer a bird, but a trail of fire and rage.

More lightning followed Savita's path, but she'd climbed too high. Though the injury to Kel's shoulder might not kill her, she couldn't find the energy to stand. She wanted desperately to see the patterns that Savita carved through the sky, to watch the red and orange and yellow smother the black. But by the time Kel managed to turn towards Savita, towards the great screeching that claimed the sky, she saw only smoke.

Savita was gone.

Chapter Fifty-Three

※

Savita was a wild thing that couldn't be tamed. She was a god destined to live forever – and Kel was nothing but a mere speck of dust that fluttered across her centuries. Kel should have freed her months – maybe even years – ago, when inklings of guilt had first crept beneath her skin.

Kel had loved Sav with every fractured piece of her heart, and had tried to want nothing in return.

And yet, still, it *hurt*.

Slowly, Kel managed to sit up. Coup held her to him, muttering words she couldn't make out in a low, soothing voice.

Cristo lowered his rifle from the sky. His arms shook, barely containing his rage. 'Well done, Kelyn. You've just sentenced yourself to death.'

Kel held back a whimper; she knew she didn't have long left, but hearing it aloud hit her like a wave. 'You'd rather I help you kill phoenixes?'

His eyes welled, something warring in their stormy depths. 'You'd rather *I* kill my *daughter*?'

Kel tried to shake her head. Coup clung to her tighter, as she said, 'No. But if you believe that the story of Landon Ryker is true, then what of the other myths we hear as children? What about the story that tells us a star will fall if a phoenix dies, and the sun will explode if they're extinct? Where are we to draw a line between fact and myth?'

Cristo's eyes turned black, and his nostrils flared. Though his sancter rifle was lowered, Kel noticed his grip stiffen. The rage inside him shook his entire body, desperately trying to claw to the surface.

Weeks ago, Kel knew she'd seen a kind man buried beneath the desperation. But she wasn't foolish enough to think that man would reappear.

Slowly, Cristo pointed the sancter at Kel.

She could see down the barrel, to the glint of metal waiting inside, like Death looking at her with one eye.

Coup released Kel and took a step towards Cristo. 'Get away from her,' he snarled.

Kel tried to shove Coup away, to keep the sancter trained on *her* – but her strength was gone. The weakness in her limbs contradicted the fire in her veins; her body was a blazing cage.

A single, glistening tear trailed down Cristo's cheek. 'You can't imagine the pain coming for her, Mr Coupers. This is a much gentler death. Trust me.'

'Coup – move,' Kel managed, though Coup didn't seem to hear her.

She tried to shove him, push him out of the way. But Coup refused to budge. He said to Cristo, 'You'll have to shoot me first.'

Cristo's fingers, clamped around the rifle, shook. 'I don't have time for this. I need to get back to my Estra.'

The muscles in his face tightened and moved again, and Kel thought he might unhinge his jaw and swallow them whole.

Instead, his hand around the sancter steadied, and he aimed the weapon at Coup.

Shivers wracked Kel's body. She wanted to shout, *No! Coup, you idiot – move!*

But she couldn't form the words. Not loud enough for him to hear. She could only shake and stare at Cristo, silently begging him to lower his rifle.

'You won't believe me, but this is kinder. It is,' Cristo added under his breath, like a prayer.

Kel tried as hard as she could to keep her eyes open – but she couldn't. She couldn't watch Coup die.

She heard Cristo cock his rifle.

'Coup,' she breathed, as a scream tore open the sky.

The sound – so familiar and yet so alien – filled Kel with electricity. Summoning every ounce of strength she had, she glanced up.

And then there was Savita, nothing but flame and fury as she barrelled straight towards Kel.

Chapter Fifty-Four

❈

Savita blazed across the night sky, no more bird than a bonfire was. Cristo raised his head to the stars as she soared closer. His jaw fell slack and his fingers loosened around the sancter.

Kel felt Coup move from her side, but she couldn't look away from the fierce mass of red that vaulted across the sky. Savita was almost too bright to look at.

She was here, a growing shape that tore towards them like a comet. Her firebird. Her *Savita*.

The phoenix released another long, ear-splitting screech, and it broke Cristo from his trance. His gaze darted to Kel.

He lifted the sancter, pulled back the hammer with a sharp *click*, and fired.

Kel wasn't sure whether the sound that came next was lightning or a phoenix scream.

She didn't realize she'd closed her eyes until red flared through the darkness. She waited for the familiar, electric pain to replace the lead in her bones.

A tiny, petty part of her hated that Cristo had beaten her before AB could.

But no lightning came.

When Kel finally opened her eyes, there was no rifle pointed at her. No weapon or even Cristo. Just a pink pile of shredded muscle and skin.

Splattered blood covered her trousers. Small, splintered bones stuck out at angles from the torn skin and oozing red, but Cristo's skeleton had been obliterated to white ash that glowed against the night.

Settled behind the mess, picking at scattered remnants of Cristo's carcass, was Savita, burning hot enough to evaporate the blood seeping towards her.

Kel didn't have the strength to process what she was seeing. She forced every scrap of adrenaline in her body to help her stand up. As she wobbled to her feet, Savita looked up. Those ink-black eyes pinned Kel in place. Kept her standing.

Coup was at her side a moment later. He lifted a palm to her cheek. 'Are you okay?'

Kel nodded, slowly, though the question almost made her laugh. 'Are you?' she croaked.

Coup only offered a shaky smile.

Then, Kel did laugh. A desperate, hoarse sound that tore through her throat, though there was nothing funny about what lay ahead of her. Cristo was gone. Savita had left him as little more than a few scraps of pink.

As though she'd heard Kel's thoughts, Savita snapped her beak. Ducking her head to Kel's height, Savita crept towards her tamer. Kel felt the phoenix's temperature lower, and her presence was like rain against her skin. Painful, but bearable.

Kel couldn't make out any of Savita's body. No feathers or wings or beak. Just two eyes staring at Kel.

Then, through wisps of fire, Kel could make out one feather. Two more, then three. A trail of feathers was cleared of flames along Savita's side, and then her back.

Where Savita's saddle would have sat.

Kel couldn't breathe.

Sav couldn't be offering what Kel thought she was. She couldn't be . . .

The phoenix merely stared at her, motionless.

Kel risked a hand against Savita's wing; the narrow stretch that was now free of flames. The feathers were still silky soft, and not nearly as hot as they should have been.

Coup stepped closer to Savita. As Kel held out her hand to Coup, Savita clicked her beak – or at least, the darker flames that Kel assumed were a beak – and released another roar.

The pair winced. Coup stepped back, and Savita calmed.

His features were taut as he said, 'She's too hot, Kel. I can't get any closer. How can you stand it?'

Kel frowned. She turned back to Savita's wing, spreading her fingers across the darkened feathers.

Maybe it was a numbness from AB. Maybe she was delirious from the sancter's shot. Or maybe – just this once – Kel would let herself believe in the lullabies her father had sung to her. Maybe she'd pretend that Savita trusted – *needed* – Kel, too. Maybe the raging fire in Kel's veins had never been AB, but a gift from Savita. To prepare her for this. For now.

Kel bunched her hand in Savita's feathers. Savita grumbled, as if to say, *Hurry up*.

Kel laughed again, softly this time. The electricity was already fading from her veins. If she was going to do this, she needed to do it *now*. 'I have to go, Coup.'

If she stayed, she'd die. She'd fade away in comfort, surrounded by family. It was more than most people got. Maybe that should have been enough for her.

But Savita was offering her a chance. Not a promise; a chance at another future. Even if there was more pain ahead of her, more fire and blood, it was worth it. If it meant she could stay with her family, it would always be worth it.

Even though Cristo was gone, Savita was still in danger. Kel would die and Cristo's allies or sponsors would want Savita. Maybe even the Cendorian Council. Neither of them was safe. Not yet.

But maybe . . . maybe Savita's rebirth could save them both.

Coup's throat bobbed. Despite Savita's grumbling, Kel stepped away from her firebird. Instead, she stepped into Coup's outstretched arms.

And then they were both crying. Not soft tears or glistening eyes, but harsh sobs and wails coughed into each other's necks. Pleas and promises and words they hadn't spoken yet, but had known.

Sobs turned to breathless kisses and those turned to a deeper embrace. Kel tried to memorize everything about him; the salty taste of his lips, the feel of his callused hands, the way she felt his brow furrow when he deepened their kisses. She wanted to learn everything about him – every dream he'd ever had and the future that he'd weave them into. But if this was all that fate would allow, she'd take it greedily. It would never be enough, but it was more than she'd ever hoped for.

When Savita's grumbling turned to thunder and too long had passed, Coup pulled away. He nodded towards Savita. 'You better come back in one piece, or you'll have hell to answer to.'

Kel managed a grin. 'That's the best pep talk I've ever heard.'

With a shaking hand he tucked a strand of knotted hair behind her ear and said, 'I'll make sure that Cristo Industries stops their experiments. If there's a cure to AB – we'll find it another way.'

Kel thought of Dira, as much her family as her father had been. She thought of Rahn, who'd lost Cristo and Estra. They'd all lost so much to AB. Kel didn't doubt that Coup's words were true.

Kel kissed him one last time, a soft, lingering touch that she seared into her mind.

Then Coup helped her onto Savita's back.

He could barely stand close enough to boost her up. Kel could feel Savita's heat, but it was nothing compared to the heavy lead in her bones and the comforting fire in her veins. She laid low against Savita's back and gripped fistfuls of feathers. Whatever happened next, she was ready.

Savita screamed again and wasted no time before launching into the sky. Kel let out a scream alongside Savita, wondering if anyone below could see her amidst Savita's blazing glory. If they could see the girl riding the sun across the starry sky.

It took all of Kel's strength to hold on. She didn't know where Savita was heading – somewhere safe, or perhaps to Kel's death. She could feel the phoenix heating up around her, the flames expanding and shifting colour.

Preparing to rebirth.

Savita flew higher. Clouds soared alongside them. Below, Kel could see not just the red, dry dust and speckled forests of Cendor – but all of Salta. Ebrait, swathed in water and blue temples. The emerald isle of Dresva. Pale buildings and shimmering sprites across Ascira. All she'd ever known.

Would Savita coat Kel in her ashes? Or would she leave Salta to find a new freedom, and kill Kel with her rebirth? Kel didn't have an answer. But she had hope – and a family to return to.

And now, soaring over sapphire oceans and fiery gales, Kel would be damned if this was the last time she'd fly.

She didn't believe in myths and legends. But Cristo, despite his brutal flaws, *had* proven the science of his dream. If Savita permitted it, maybe rebirth was possible for her, too.

Savita rose higher into the sky. Kel bit down on her lip to keep from screaming. The fire around her was starting to eat at her fingers, her hands, ghostly beneath the softening moonlight. Soon, the blaze would envelop her entirely. But it wasn't painful.

The fire felt like bottled sunlight. Like a fast breeze or a sharp melody. Harsh and unstoppable – and something Kel wanted to bask in for ever.

When Savita rose above the grey clouds, the first rays of dawn glimmering along the distant horizon, her screams changed. They were no longer pitchy and shrill, but piercingly clear. Notes that rose and fell carefully, in a familiar rhythm that Kel could sing in her sleep.

It was her song. *Savita's song*.

The tune that Kel had sung to the uncollared phoenix in Fieror. The lullaby her father had always sung to her at night. She felt Savita's voice swell around her, coaxing the flames higher, like obedient serpents. The song was made of windchimes and lightning and barren heat. It was Cendor, in all its sharp, wild, breathtaking beauty.

Kel twined her voice with Savita's, though not in song, but in a hope.

A promise.

Epilogue

※

Warren Coupers crept through the Varra Farm's empty paddocks.

Crickets serenaded the encroaching dusk. The knee-high grass shivered as rabbits darted between fields. The critters had grown arrogant without Savita to chase them.

Coup inhaled the scent of pollen, weeds and wildflowers. He felt like he'd been between breaths all month. Ever since . . .

Feet heavy, he stalked towards the reason he'd returned to Fieror.

Even if Cristo had lied about everything else, in this, he'd stayed true to his word; Kel's new aviary was an architectural wonder, all gleaming panels and sleek silver bones. The dome soared twice as high as its predecessor, a crystal cathedral stark against the horizon. Coup peered through the glass. Cristo's contractors had already filled the aviary with heat lights and native greenery, ready if Savita returned home.

It was a wonder. Coup could imagine Kel's grin – rare and just as wondrous – at the sight of it.

He wanted to burn the damn thing to the ground.

Five weeks. How had it only been that long? A lifetime had passed since Kel vanished into the dawn. He knew the other Howlers felt it, too. Time bent at odd angles around them, swift and slow, never quite reaching the empty space at his side. Leaving the memory of her pain-stricken face untouched.

Coup's eyes traced the aviary's steel skeleton, forcing his mind to empty. Despite his best attempts, every thought led back to Kel.

He'd hoped checking on her farm would be enough to pacify the fear shrouding her name, even in his mind. More than anything, he feared never having another chance to speak her name while looking into those storm-grey eyes. He'd never again call her *tamer* or *Varra*, and relish how her nose scrunched in response. His heart would never race the way it did when she said his name.

Footsteps crunched behind him. Then, a whistle of approval. 'This puts Cristo's aviaries to shame.'

His brother's shadow loomed along the earth, meeting Coup's. Bekn's hand landed on his shoulder. 'She'll love it.'

Coup flinched. Bekn remained certain that Kel would return, or, at least, he pretended to. But that false certainty kept ripping away any scab that tried to heal over Coup's heart.

'You didn't have to come,' Coup said softly.

'I wanted to. I needed a solid excuse to spend a few days off camera.'

Bekn came to Coup's side, head tilted towards the dome. Dark stubble traced his jaw and his jacket hung awkwardly off his shoulders, as if he'd lost weight. This was the stillest Coup had seen him since Kel vanished into the sky. Bekn had been busy these past five weeks, making sure to tell their story before anyone else could; it had stopped Cristo's loyalists from forcing the Howlers into infamy or intercepting their tale.

While Bekn was preoccupied, Coup had learnt as much as he could about phoenix rebirths. It usually only took a week or two for the ash to reform into a chick. Some reports suggested longer, over a month. Every new scrap of hope tore at the pit in his gut; a bird flitting about in the corner of his eye, a flash of Kel's face on the news. But what if Savita had abandoned Kel to rebirth, leaving her alone, whimpering in pain as AB consumed her?

Or what if the legends were true, and Savita had healed Kel just as Deja had saved Ryker?

He'd read that when phoenixes rebirthed, they usually reformed much larger than when hatched from an egg. About the size of a small horse. Strong enough to be ridden, if the rider and mount wished to return home.

Bekn's tele-comm chirped. They both glanced down as Bekn pulled the device from his pocket.

Bekn scanned the new notification and laughed, a short, sharp sound. 'It's from Dira. Rahn – she's awake.'

Relief slumped Coup's shoulders.

Death had circled Rahn's hospital bed for the last month. They'd stabilized her quickly enough, but no one had seemed sure when she would wake. Dira had refused to leave her side, with one exception: when Estra's pulse had faded, and they'd buried her beside Cristo's meagre remains.

Coup's throat tightened.

Though Kel hadn't remembered her, Estra had been one of their own.

The Howlers had lost too much.

'How's Rahn feeling?' Coup asked.

Bekn shook his head. 'Not sure – I'll call Dira and ask. Are you . . . ?'

'Go call her. I'm fine. I'll meet you up at the cottage.'

Bekn stared at Coup, before turning back towards Kel's small house, head bent over his tele-comm screen.

Coup didn't know how his older brother managed it. Hundreds of notifications had littered Bekn's tele-comm over the past few weeks. Everyone was desperate to know how Canen Cristo, Salta's richest tech mogul, had perished. And Bekn was the only one who could satisfy their hunger.

After Cristo fell, his grip on the isles was impossible to deny. The four councils were crippled. Once the Howlers had laid the truth bare, Bekn was flooded with demands, pleas to travel to each island and recount their tale. The requests hadn't just come from reporters but scientists too, once Bekn had revealed what they'd learnt of AB's origins. Saltans seemed equally ravenous and riled to hear the part they'd played in spreading the disease. Somehow, Bekn managed to appease both.

For years, Coup had prayed to the Alchemists to find Bekn a way off Cendor. He hadn't expected a response in the form of a dead billionaire.

Or a dead tamer. *His* tamer.

Coup shook the thought loose. *No.* She wasn't dead. He didn't care if that made him a superstitious fool. Kelyn Varra would come home to him.

That was the other reason why he'd stolen onto a train back to Fieror. He and a group of council tamers had searched what they could of Vohre Forest. If Savita hadn't taken Kel there, it made sense they'd fly somewhere they both felt safe.

He pressed a hand to the aviary's cool glass. A sigh rattled through him. He'd lingered here long enough.

He turned from the aviary and began tracing Bekn's steps towards the cottage. Even if it broke him to leave – to admit any kind of defeat – he refused to let Bekn clean up Cristo's mess alone. They had to return to Vohre before nightfall.

Still, he paused. Visiting the Varra Farm had been the last thread – the last hope – keeping him upright. If Kel wasn't *here*, where was she?

Dark spots swam across his vision. The mere question made him want to empty his guts across the grass. He couldn't bear to leave. Not yet, not now – because what if there was nowhere else to look? What if Kel was just . . . gone?

He'd rather try to rewind time than believe that. But the world was moving on, stealing that choice from him.

Coup allowed himself one moment to close his eyes, to indulge the hollow pit inside him, before he pressed on.

Halfway to the cottage, a great shadow darkened the ground.

Coup froze. The vast silhouette crept along the grass, liquid darkness against dry earth. Distant thunder – or something too similar – boomed overhead. His nose filled with smoke, blotting out the wildflowers' sweetness.

The thunder grew louder.

Coup's heart pounded, trying to stitch itself back together even as he begged it to stay tattered. If he was imagining this . . .

A familiar laugh trailed through the sky, echoing around him.

He heard Bekn launch from the cottage, flinging the old door open.

Wild laughter and beating wings roared overhead.

Finally, Coup looked up, into the hazy, coral sky.

Kelyn.

Acknowledgements

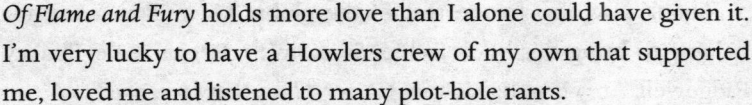

Of Flame and Fury holds more love than I alone could have given it. I'm very lucky to have a Howlers crew of my own that supported me, loved me and listened to many plot-hole rants.

Before all else, I'd like to acknowledge the Traditional Owners of the unceded land on which I live and work, the Wurundjeri people of the Kulin nation, and pay tribute to Elders past and present.

To my literary agent, John Baker, the small god of hype, the best agent a writer could ask for. You plucked me from the query trenches and it's been a wild ride ever since. Thank you for always being in my corner, for choosing to be 'the phoenix guy', and for taking this book places I never could have imagined. To Julie, and the rest of the team at Bell Lomax Moreton.

A collective thanks to my three amazing editors. Across time zones, drafts and email threads, you've made this journey a dream. Thank you for welcoming me to Macmillan with such an incredible, global effort. Your insights and ideas have made this book what it was always meant to be.

To Cate Augustin, my UK editor, for seeing the heart of this book so quickly. Your editorial guidance and suggestions are as fun as they are brilliant, and your endless enthusiasm means I now have a digital folder of comments to revel in any time I want to happy-cry.

To Asia Harden, my US editor – from our very first call, far before anything was official, I was desperate to work with you. It was so clear that you cared for these characters more than I thought possible. Thank you for championing this book.

To Claire Craig, my Australian editor, thank you for bringing your expert eye for detail and helping *OFAF* truly shine. From drinks in a dim Melbourne cafe to bringing this book to an Australian audience – thank you for all of it.

To my copy editor, Ross Jamieson. Without you, Kel would've been ten-feet-tall within two chapters.

Thank you also to the rest of the global Macmillan team, for helping to bring this book to life: Sam Smith, Rachel Vale, Tracey Ridgewell, Amy Boxshall, Grace Carter, Gaby Salpeter, Namra Amir, Kimberlea Smith, Louisa Sheridan, and Tatiana Merced-Zarou.

To Virginia Allyn, the artist responsible for the breathtaking map of Salta. You've captured the four isles so perfectly. I'll never truly be able to express what it means to have your work in my debut.

To Ellyse Moir – for the memes, the gifs, for being the person I pitched this book idea to and who called it a 'Dragon Booster AU'. You're always the first to see my words and the first to tell me how terrible they are (lovingly). Sister, critique partner, friend, No. 1 Bekn stan, tech consultant, reluctant Canva tutor, unhinged meme generator. Thank you for the countless Rosie pictures when I need a mood-boost, for never sugar-coating, for always hyping, for the best and worst of everything.

To my writing friends who've been here from day one. Sophie Clark, my oldest writing friend and one of my oldest friends, for endless hours of back and forth, for being there for every frustration and every celebration. I still can't quite believe we're debuting together. Bori Cser, for always being willing to brainstorm, for being such an incredibly talented friend, for giving me yet another reason to be thankful I'm on Team JJ. Ande Pliego, for your early thoughts and late thoughts. Poppy Rose Solomon, for supporting *OFAF* in its infancy. Kaela Tai, for your early read and perfectly gory medical insights.

To Nat, for being my number one fan from the moment you learnt I write. To Lauren, for celebrating every step. To Bec, for being my Italian mum and offering me meals on deadline.

To Chernie, for always shouting your excitement for this book. I'm sorry for missing the City to Surf (again) to meet deadlines. It'll happen one year! To my dad, for having no clue what the YA Fantasy genre is, but never failing to be excited anyway.

To Hannah and Susanna, for never letting me be humble.

To Jack. Just for being you. Thank you for teaching me about turbulence, for listening to me ramble about giant combustible birds, and for making it so hard to write romantic drama and angst. You've made it so I have no experience to draw upon.

And finally, thank you, dearest reader. You deserve the best of the real world and the fictional ones. Whether you enjoyed this book or not, you've stuck around for the acknowledgements, and so I feel obliged to say: let's set more (figurative) shit on fire.

About the Author

Mikayla Bridge is a fantasy author living in Melbourne, Australia. She can often be found playing board games, drinking too much coffee, and lovingly tormenting her characters. She grew up on a small-town farm and completed a BA with Honours in Political Science and International Relations. Raised on horror movies and musical theatre, her writing is often a frankensteined love letter to both. *Of Flame and Fury* is her debut novel.